*Ben Jones*

# The Rope Eater

Ben Jones majored in English at Yale University and was awarded a grant from the National Endowment for the Humanities. He was an editor for the Adventure Library, where he edited classic tales of exploration. Jones lives with his family outside of Boston.

ANCHOR BOOKS

*A Division of Random House, Inc.*

*New York*

# The Rope Eater

*A Novel*

BEN JONES

FIRST ANCHOR BOOKS EDITION, FEBRUARY 2005

The Library of Congress has cataloged the Doubleday edition as follows:
Jones, Ben, 1968–
The rope eater: a novel / Ben Jones.—1st ed.
p. cm.
1. United States—History—Civil War, 1861–1865—Fiction. 2. Survival after
airplane accidents, shipwrecks, etc.—Fiction. 3. Military deserters—Fiction.
4. Whaling ships—Fiction. 5. New England—Fiction.
6. Whaling—Fiction. I. Title.
PS3610.O616R67 2003
813'.6—dc21 2002041484

Anchor ISBN 1-4000-3368-3

*Book design by Nicola Ferguson*

www.anchorbooks.com

Printed in the United States of America
10  9  8  7  6  5  4  3  2  1

For my three:

Alisa, Olivia, and Sophie

So stand

And overcome your panting—with the soul,

Which wins all battles if it does not despond

Under its heavy body's weight.

—*Inferno,* Canto XXIV

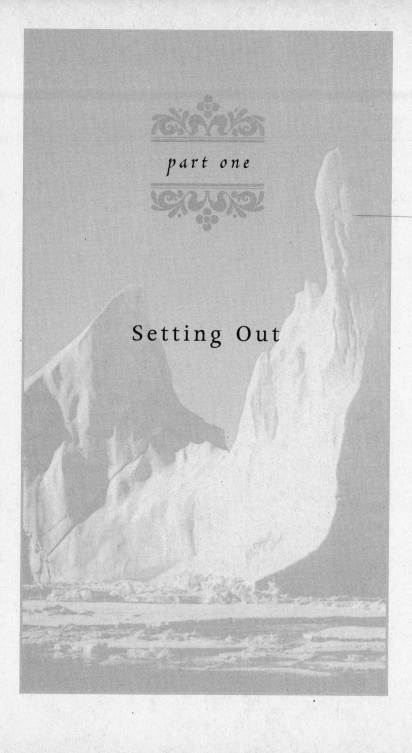

*part one*

Setting Out

*o n e*

There was a day my heart did not beat. Sometimes I wonder what day it was exactly that it began, a day when there was peace, when peace was possible, the day that peace ended. It is, of course, a day I cannot remember—a faint cleaving in the red darkness, when my heart welled up and drove me squalling into the world.

My heart has troubled me ever since, shuddering me through my days, too strong for its casing. It is not the seat of passionate loves and great despairs—I wish it were. It is simply too strong, a brute muscle whose pounding has kept me awake nights, shaking my bed and rattling the glass on my nightstand.

I grew up in a small town, in a small house with a church on a rise next door. In the evening, the long shadow of its spire fell over our house. My parents were hardworking and unremarkable people who seemed to live baffled by their lives. My father stood on the porch every year as the first snow fell, as amazed as if he were see-ing it for the first time. My mother would lift up her eyes from the table for a moment, then duck her head again quickly as if she'd be singed for looking too long. She was not meek, but rigidly contained, and she lashed out at impertinent variety—the weather, pass of days, other people. I was delivered in a stream of obscenities so thick that the midwife scolded her for it during the labor. They named me Brendan for my mother's father and Kane for my father, and neither name bespoke anything but a lack of imagination down through several generations. They had no other children, and even their intermittent attentions were smothering to me.

I took refuge for a time in a mossy library down the road from our house. It was all but abandoned, with shelves of moldering books that promised hints of life different from my own, but unmoored to it, as if under glass, with no means to reach its expanse from my own cramped days. As my heart grew stronger, those pages grayed and crumbled; the library musted and shrank until I too abandoned it.

When I was seventeen, the pound of my heart drove me out on a wet, fragrant spring day. There was still snow in the shadows of the hillsides, but the air was warm and sweet; the land was quickening and I knew if I stayed long, it would catch me and hold me for another summer, another fall, another year. I paused at the roadside, waiting for the tug of a restraint that did not come. South I drifted, blind to the land I moved through, south down fog-shrouded valleys, along a river, until I found myself at the edge of the ocean.

There I found work in a small tavern, where I passed an empty fall and a cold and empty winter. The tavern was grimy, and it stank; the tables were chipped and broken and graven with names on names. Business was good—sailors mostly, who kept me from seeing the sameness of that world, from feeling the sourness in me, the rise of bile, the staling air as the world pressed in.

Their bulbous mouths smiled wary smiles, flecks of grease trailing onto stained shirts as they enthusiastically wrestled bits of gristle from their teeth. I moved among them with loathing for myself and disdain for them, provoked by the heart that pummeled my chest. I boozed it quiet with beer and sweet West Indian rum, and I would sleep for a night, but it would rouse me again to spoiling meat still clutched in drunken hands—old men incontinent from their pleasures and clouds of regurgitation floating in warm beer. I might have sunk into this life, waited as the fluid world cooled and congealed, thinking the days were changeable, were not mounted in lockstep one dusk to that same day's dawn, until I found myself, like the sailors, on the other side of my possibilities, shiftless and baffled. I suppose I should be grateful.

That day I had awakened sour and tired, and but for the bobbing of his tall black hat over the crowd, I might have passed the day inside, and so on in the string of days that held me. But I did see it, first a stovepipe in the fashion of a decade ago and greasy, and then his face, broad and flat, cut from rough lumps but with his eyes alight within it. He approached with a jostling and barking crowd of retainers, did not beckon, and moved past. I felt the weight of his gaze rest on me for a moment, then lift, and felt myself pulled into the crowd and down onto the docks.

He clambered onto a barrel, leaning on the shoulder of one of his lieutenants to steady himself, and turned to regard us. He raised his hands gravely and the crowd subsided into silence.

"Gentlemen," he began, "I greet you this day in joy and in sorrow. From beyond our borders, men look to us with eyes ablaze with hope, their spirits vexed by chains of law, of tradition, of religion, of economy. They feel themselves in dim prisons growing feeble. They see us free, and each imagines himself free, imagines loosing his chains and passing through the world as a man among men. In their hearts, their tyrants fear us—not our generals, nor our leaders, but most our men, for they know in each lies a force that they detest and struggle to extinguish in their own people.

"Now we find that liberty carries responsibility and the spirit of justice calls us to arms. If we are to preserve what is most precious to us, we must look within our borders, at our neighbors, our brothers, at ourselves. We must seek out that which has decayed within us, whether it dwells in a distant community or in our own; whether it is called just or unjust; we must see that there is a truth beyond the truth of today and we must tear this half-truth from us, carve it from the living flesh of our nation before our healthy eyes fill with jaundice, our spirits with lead, our hearts with stone. And so, my countrymen, I call you to battle and to arms; I call not for words nor ideas, but for guns and knives, for cannon, sword, and bayonet. And it is for that that I sorrow today.

"Mothers, I am calling for your children; fathers, for your sons; wives, your husbands. I harbor no illusions that any may be spared; our streets will wash with blood. And for what? No lifetime of ease for the living, no marble tombs for the dead. But you will have preserved, if only for one moment, the spirit that is essential to man; you will have shown the world, and the generations that will follow you, that difficult justice is possible, and that man can give his life in service to man. Fearful mortals! Archangels are not the champions of liberty—we are.

"Yours will be the stories that good men teach their sons, each a witness to what you have borne, each a reminder of what it means to live, to shine in use; your remembered feats will offer hope for the despairing, regeneration for the ailing, strength for the downtrodden. Those lost and weak spirits will join with yours, and those before you, into a great and mighty host, the host of just and righteous men. There is no nobler company."

I stood on the dock and felt his words fill me, felt my troublesome heart fall into step with their rhythm. The dock swelled with applause; men set their faces and squared their shoulders. He knelt first, stiff and awkward, and then stepped delicately down. The crowd fell in step behind him as he returned up the narrow street, following him to join up in that moment. I marched with them, my bile rinsed away and my heart pounding joyfully. Two days later I found myself boarding a train to take my place in this new world, to fight and die for it. In the space of that half hour, my world had been transformed; the old had dropped away and seemed already dim and distant, and the new sprang up in rich and vibrant colors, as if I had always been living this life.

At first, life in the army was good; we were issued a uniform and a rifle and taught to march and fight, taught to bear ourselves as soldiers. At night we filled the barracks with our projected exploits and their bawdy rewards. I kept quiet, and held on to the words that I had heard on the docks as the flags snapped in the wind and the horizon sped away.

From training, we marched west, and south and west again. At first people cheered for us, and handed us cakes and bottles of beer as we passed. Then there were few, then none; cows munched dully in barnyards in front of darkened houses, and meadows fell to seed. Feral children ran chattering past in the underbrush, and harried us from trees like monkeys.

The battles were smoky affairs, with men rising up from nowhere and fading again, and a stream of shouting and cursing, screaming, of trumpets blaring and the crack of rifles and the crump of the cannon; later, when the guns subsided, the groans of the dying would swell. In the falling darkness, men called for water, and for whiskey, for their wives, for blankets to ward off the cold. Men sought their friends, and found them, and could do nothing. One and then another man was appointed to lead us, each younger and less certain than the last.

I marched through the heat unscathed. I was not brave, but I tried to do as I had been ordered and was not shot, not stabbed, not clubbed. I did not succumb to the fevers that descended in waves, nor to sunstroke. My blisters did not infect, my scratches did not become gangrenous. Instead, I remained free to watch my companions die, free to feel helpless at bedside after bedside, free to watch their bodies rot while they walked, to watch red fingers of infection creep up their legs, across their chests, to watch red turn black and black turn green. I had the luck to hear the dying words of man after man until I could not remember whose children or wife were to be told what, or where they might be found. Day seeped into day across the empty fields, fever into fever, blood into dust.

There were some ghouls, as there will always be, who sought to make what profits they could from looting. They disguised their thievery as care, laying a man gently to rest, then relieving him of his few coins. They descended at the end of every battle, flitting from body to body. I began to follow them, gathering not rings and coins, but the letters that seemed to peek from every soldier's pocket.

I stuffed them into my pockets and lined my jacket with them. As we marched south, I gradually emptied the gear from my bag and replaced it with yellowing packets of letters. I did not read them—they were not for me to read, for my edification or my ghoulish curiosity, but their gathering was a duty and a means of insulation, of holding back something from the rough pox of bodies, of connecting, somehow, these dead men with a dim and distant land of living.

Once in a great while, as I lay waiting for sleep, I felt the dim echoes of the words that had drawn me here; I tried to follow my trajectory from the dock out, and down, tried to discover the moment when I had been carried by my momentum into this other, this alien world.

Balaam's Hill was the worst. I found myself stumbling among

bodies swelling in the gentle sun, my eyes watering from the stench as I gathered the letters to me. I moved back from the dead to the living and saw things I should not have seen. Arms and legs stacked like cordwood outside the medical tent. Blind men shuffling forward and tripping over the dead and dying. Men staring in amazement at the gaping interiors of their own bodies. Men cried for their lives and cursed the world; they told stories of home, of the faces and hearts of women and children, and died in shame and anger. I moved among them trying to avoid their faces and glassy eyes, looking only for scraps of paper. One man seized me by the collar and pulled my face close to his. A stained deck of cards spilled from his vest into a pool of blood draining from his belly. His eyes were flat, yellow to red to black; his mouth gaped around flecks of spittle, but no words came. He glared at me, bellowing, grinding his teeth, then pushed me away.

That night I huddled close to the fire. Winter was leaking down from the north and the night was clear and cold. The stars stood distant in the sky, neither warming nor illuminating. Outside the circle of the campfire, I could hear the snuffling of dogs as they fed. I looked around at my companions and I tried to imagine their thoughts, tried to think to speak, but could find nothing, imagine nothing. I felt within myself a great severing—it was as if I were suddenly surrounded by giant insects, staring at their impenetrable compound eyes, the clacking of their mandibles, and the jerky flicking of their forelegs. I found myself alone amid them, shivering in the cold and darkness.

I sneaked out of camp that night, walking north. I carried only the letters with me, stuffed inside my shirt and jacket, under my cap, bundled with straps over my shoulders and straining against the seams of my bag. I woke to blue and black and white skies, clouds moving quickly, the sunlight flashing, bright but not warm, the wind bristling through the trees, driving the clouds, pulling warmth from the sun, leaves from the trees, life from the land, a scouring wind, making ready for winter. The moon rose early, the silver light, unlike the sun, transforming the land beneath it—changing shapes and forms, obscuring what it revealed, a magician, a deceiver.

The fierce orange of sunrise gave way to a bright white gold, and the deep blue of a clear sky promised a beautiful day. But the sun cut off its climb and started to slink across the horizon. The white gold of the morning faded to a weak yellow by ten o'clock. The wind was strong, shaking shutters and flinging trees, but the day seemed weak and ineffectual, a day where little of worth could be accomplished, a day to be tolerated, to be endured in hopes of better days to come. But each one was like this, over as it began, passing swiftly from birth into age, hastened by strong, chill winds.

I hid out in the daytime, sleeping in barns, and crept along the edges of roads at night, crashing into the bushes at the faintest sound or light. I stole my food from gardens and henhouses; I learned to fear dogs. I stumbled on other deserters in the woods; we regarded each other with shame and anger, and slunk away to hide alone. The hills caught fire as I made my way north, yellowing and bursting red, then smoldering. Cold rain stripped the trees bare. Snow fell.

I made my way to the coast again, not seeking the sea as much as trying to escape from the land. I took the ferry over to New York, dragging through the polluted water as it passed sluggishly into the sea. From the landing, the muddy, narrow streets were filled with the detritus of a city day: an open sewer leaking toward the prone form of a man; gaunt, shrill children fighting over a mound of rotting cabbage, their faces chapped and red with cold; dark shapes huddled around a pile of smoldering garbage, wreathed in foul smoke; the wail of cats and discordant, implor-

ing voices. The people I passed had the haunted look of conspira-
tors awaiting secret signals. Some doors shut and locked, shades
were hastily but incompletely drawn; other doors opened and sal-
low light spilled out. Cunning, furtive boys raced past on errands;
women hurried, fearful, or paused with lascivious arrogance.
Grates exhaled a pestilent fog that settled over the street. I kept
my head low and strode on. A man hailed me from a stoop with a
stranger's name, and cursed me as I continued past.

The street I was on narrowed and began to twist, and its squat
houses gave way to larger buildings. Alleys branched off into the
garbage that spilled from sagging buildings into banks of gray
snow. I strode now down the center of the rutted street, skittering
clear of the patches of black ice. Overhead the buildings arched,
hiding all but a strip of sky. I became aware that there were other
men walking in the same direction. At first there were only a few,
but more appeared from the alleys or jumped from low windows,
more and more, all silent and purposeful, hats pulled low, walking briskly, trotting.

I rushed with them, into a small square already crowded with
men, and streams of others came in behind us. At the far end a
bonfire blazed and in its light two men exhorted the crowd from
a platform. Their faces in the firelight were grotesque masks and
their language was brutish and unintelligible.

As if by some prearranged signal, the speakers ceased and I
could hear the lick and crackle of the fire. In that sudden silence,
the mob drew in a breath that ran through the square and up into
the branching streets. Then glass shattered somewhere, and the
mob erupted with a roar. Men began rushing in all directions, lit
brands from the bonfires and fired buildings. They cursed and I
recognized the sickening sound of clubbed flesh. A man staggered
past me, his face blurry with blood. A pack of fierce, calm men
looted a store with cold precision. Torches flew and windows

shattered. Shouts of gleeful anger, moans, terrible, joyous shrieks rose: a man on his knees fell beneath a hail of blows, and all around me I felt the pulse of men in the dark rush of chaos. The mob's energy rose in me, intoxicating me.

Beware, you who crave release from the work of making order, for you see chaos truly only when fires are burning and blood running, and you will find your hope is a weak thing; I stooped and closed my hand around the coolness of a stone. I ran with the horde, hurled rocks into the darkness, flowed down the shuttered streets.

Some ran terrified before us, searching frantically for sanctuary; some joined us, exhilarated and ravenous. A streetcar halted, we charged; it leaned, and toppled, its windows shattering onto the cobbles; we beat it with axe handles and iron bars. More men seemed to pour from every street, and mob joined to mob. Trapped in the clogged streets, the crowd set upon itself in senseless frenzies, group turning on group and man on man. I was wedged against a wall by the crush of sweating bodies; I could feel the mass of men writhing against me like a river in flood. I struggled for the breath to cry out. I lost my footing and was pinned up to the wall, my feet kicking vainly as the mass of heads and the flames began to waver before me.

The wall behind me sagged and gave way. I tumbled back, bricks clattering on top of me. I was buried, trampled, struck at; faces loomed over me. I lost consciousness, and when I opened my eyes, I found myself lying on my back alone inside a large warehouse. Through a jagged opening in the wall I could see the mob rushing past. I slid back into the shadows. Retreating deeper into the warehouse, I found a set of stairs that led down into a tunnel strung with lanterns. I hurried down, listening for the swell of the mob behind me.

As I went down, however, the noise of the riot subsided in the distance. The gentle light of the lanterns and the cool smell of dirt soothed me; my panic faded. The tunnel led to a network of others and I sped through them. I emerged deep underground in a much larger tunnel that was crisscrossed with railroad tracks. It curved away in the distance and its roof arched into darkness. I sat on the tracks and wiped my head with the sleeve of my shirt. It came away damp with blood, still slightly warm in the cool of the tunnel.

I unstrapped my bag and pulled out a packet of letters, spread them on the ground before me. In the dim light, I could not decipher their scrawls—some small and cramped, some large and expansive, barely fitting onto the envelopes at all. Each scrap of paper seemed to be part of a pattern that should resolve or reveal itself as I stared. I moved them about, scrutinized them, put them into piles, and laid them out again. Nothing. I selected one and opened it, as if it somehow held an answer, the answer, as if this particular man, by dying, had come to know something and that I would receive it, deserved to receive it because I had rescued his letter. I saw before me the man with the scatter of cards who had grabbed me. His face had in it no peace, no wisdom; he had found no answer, had merely died.

I was roused by a low sound in the distance, the sound of panting breath. I peered down the tunnel, looking for the flickering torches of the mob. A train appeared, clouds of steam billowing from its stack. It moved toward me and as it drew abreast I ran alongside and threw myself into an open door. I made my way among stacked crates and collapsed gratefully onto the bare floor. For once my heart ceased to riot and released me into a gentle sleep.

*two*

The train pulled into New Bedford in the early morning. The chaos of the previous night had drained away and I was left tired but uncleansed. The rail yard, scattered with lumps of sooty snow, and the gray, indeterminate sky both seemed unreal, as if they were a stage set behind which the riot continued unabated. My arms ached as I struggled with my bag; my head throbbed and itched where the blood had dried. Men like ants in the distance moved to unload other trains. I rubbed my face, shouldered my bag, and started the walk into town.

The air was cold, but with remnants of warmth; winter was hovering, reluctant. I made my way to the post office. The letters felt dead to me now, mere weight, and I wanted to be rid of them.

The New Bedford post office had an elaborate marble facade with high windows, a large, elegantly lettered sign, and broad steps that led to a massive door. Inside, the postmaster swept the floor of his office and adjusted the papers on his desk. I went to the counter and leaned on it, watching him with no particular interest. After a few minutes he saw me, and made his way over. I hefted my bag onto the counter and let it spill out.

"Been robbing the postman?"

I reached into my pockets and brought out other letters, shook them from the lining of my coat, pulled them from the sides of my boots, from the inside of my hat. He whistled a low, tuneless whistle.

"They're soldier's letters," I said, "and I don't suppose there's much rush to get them delivered."

He shook his head slowly and began to run his hands through the stacks.

"How'd you come by them?"

"I just . . . I never . . . they were everywhere."

There was a long pause as he put his spectacles on and started to read the addresses; I watched in silence as he sorted them. He kept his head tucked low and turned his face to the side.

"There's still a charge to send them," he said quickly. "I don't suppose that you . . ." I stared dully at the top of his head for a moment, waiting for a flash of anger, but it never came. I dropped my threadbare pouch onto the counter and left.

I don't know what I expected to feel—angry, relieved, cleansed, free?—but I didn't feel it. The air outside had turned bright and razor clear. Before me the streets were rawly waking; men straggled from sleep, brows furrowed in pale yellow sunlight, the young with faces of worry or ignorance or false cheer, the older with faces of resignation or bewilderment. I sat on the steps, waiting for nothing, only a dull pounding in my chest to remind me that there was no rest in this finishing.

At first I did not notice the man standing staring at me, but he persisted until I did. Then he dropped his head as if he were deep in thought, and rushed into the post office. I watched him go in, then turned blankly to the road, to the sidewalk, to the patch of step between my dusty boots.

I don't know how long I had been staring, nor, by extension, how long he had been standing in front of me again, waiting for me to take him in.

"You're the man with the letters." Not a question.

"Without the letters," I said, trying to summon a laugh.

He leaned forward, squinting behind thick glasses, until his face was just a few inches from mine, poring over my face with a fierce glare. He had a hat pulled low over small, thick glasses; a gray nose protruded over a wiry, sparse, colorless beard. One of his eyes had a milky spot on it, from which a delicate webbing spread over the whole of his eye. I found myself staring at it, leaning even closer with curiosity. He straightened up abruptly— which changed little, as he was very short.

"Hmm. Yes. Well." He seemed to be in conversation with someone else, someone who was doing most of the talking.

"So," he said at last, apparently satisfied with the appraisal of his invisible companion, "what now?" I must have looked lost, because he added, with a hint of exasperation, "Now, now that you've delivered the letters. You haven't got a job, have you?"

I shook my head.

"Family?"

Again.

"What sort of—I mean, have you much—are you—you have things? Possessions?"

I spread my arms to show my thin coat.

"Hm. Yes, well, good. Not good. I mean, well, yes, in its own way, quite good indeed." And so he sank back into silent conversation, turning his head slightly to the side to study me further. I expected him to prod around in my mouth or poke my shoulder with a stick. At length he pulled his hands from his pockets and rubbed them, preparing to speak, as if he were starting to get impatient with his silent companion. Resolved, there was no stutter in his voice.

"I have a job, if you'd like it, on a boat. Two years of work, steady wages, but the work's hard. Extreme cold, months of darkness and isolation. It is quite an opportunity," he said entirely without irony.

Again he leaned forward, as if to press this thought into my brain. I waited for him to elaborate, but it was clear that he was through. I suppose in other circumstances I would have laughed at this peculiar man squinting behind his glasses, his webbed eye, this bizarre interview. But I could see that I would be told little else, and in my blankness I realized that it made no difference. I could not see the afternoon take any shape before me, much less a month, a year, two. It was a relief not to have to find my own way.

"Yes," I said, "fine, I'll take it."

"Excellent," he replied, not at all surprised. "We leave tomorrow morning. Be at the dock by seven to catch the tide." He scribbled an address on a piece of paper, handed it to me, and left with a low, gliding shuffle.

I roused myself and made my way down to the shore beneath the docks to rinse my face. Feeling the sting of salt in my gashes, I shuddered; I tried to summon the feeling of the night before, the maniacal energy the mob had ignited in me, but in the bright, bland light of day, I could find no hint of it. I sat back from the water's edge, watching the lap of waves over the rocky beach. Overhead, I heard the clump of feet on the wood, the crash of crates, and the creak of ropes. Above them I could hear the faint squalling of the gulls. I rested my head against a pier and, lifting my face to the sun, drifted again to sleep.

I awoke to find that the tide had shifted and the wavelets were now lapping at my feet. Birds with wet wings fought to escape the gray grasp of the sea. The sun had moved over the pier and I shivered. I rose and stretched and climbed back up to the streets.

Aimless rather than curious, I wandered along the docks to watch the whalers set out. New Bedford was a whaling town and its every industry and service was tied back to the massive whaling ships that arrived and departed in constant streams. Men were singing as they loaded barrels and tied off lines, and calling out in loud voices. In their quick hands and eager faces, one could see all the promises of the ocean—of the action of the hunt, the endless novelty, and the assurance of wealth; it was the promise of tests through which each man imagines that he will be proven worthy. I remembered those faces from the marches; boys put them on in the days before we fought, when they knew we would be fighting and that men would die, but before they realized it could be them. For each in his heart refuses to connect that death to himself—it remains as scenery for the great stage of his heroism, the consecration of his success through the blood of less important men. The excitement and the fear are the anticipation of being measured and revealed— or unmasked. And after the battles, as they lie bleeding, they are shocked to discover that death includes them, that the glorious story they told to themselves the night before was wrong, that the nameless, faceless death that had decorated their stage was their own.

The Marlinspike was a tavern down by the water, its timbers gray with salt and saggy, listing toward the sea. I entered, stooping beneath the massive lintel. The ceiling was low and heavy with beams, and the floor canted unevenly. Two small windows, oddly high in the walls, let in a greasy, diluted light. The thick, familiar scent of tobacco and rum seeped into me like molasses. Men took their supper at the bar, and a few set out to drink in earnest. As the evening wore on, the latter displaced the former and the bar was filled with beery laughing. Around me, men talked without listening and listened without hearing; some tried smiles and abandoned them. They guzzled their glasses to avoid speaking, looked away in their swallowing pauses, then filled them because they were empty. They looked over each other's shoulders for other distractions, for other, better entertainments. The same few men told endless stories, boring even themselves in the middle, but forging ahead until they had launched into another. Mouths moved and heads nodded and shook; men gestured and prodded their listeners, each unintelligible to the others, each pretending to understand as he waited his turn to speak. They seemed to be crabs, nestled in their clumsy shells, protected and isolated from their companions, shuffling and clacking their claws noisily.

Tired but not sleepy, I passed my last coins to a silent bartender and retreated up the narrow staircase to the bunk room. I pulled myself up into a free bunk and gathered a mothy blanket around me. Beneath the steady chorus of snoring, men whimpered and cried out, a word or name emerging from soft, insistent mumbling, a short curse or bark of laughter. I lay awake for a long time listening to their unconscious discontent until I slipped away into my own dreamless discontents.

In the morning, bolstered by a bowl of gluey oatmeal, I headed out to find the dock. The day was cold but clear, the sun just dawning. It took me several inquiries to find the address, a private dock some way out of town, and I rushed to get there before seven. Finally I headed out a side road that opened onto a bracken-filled field leading down to the water. A low dock stacked with crates sat at the head of a narrow cove. Out on the mooring was a small and squat ship, its hull rounded like a salad bowl. The wood was jet black, with copper sheathing the lower sections, and the sails were a dark reddish brown. On the side, in red script against the black, it read: *Narthex*. It had none of the ornamentation of the whalers, just bare wood with grim lines. There were two masts, a main and a foremast, which were placed far forward.

In place of a mizzenmast, there was a small smokestack rising from behind the deckhouse. In the low light of morning it was a gloomy and dismal introduction to my new home.

On the dock, a group of men huddled around a stack of bags and boxes. I could see others ferrying a load out to the ship in a small bark. The men on the dock sat silent as I approached, so I sat. Finally, one spoke:

"So, what do you think, eh?" This question was addressed to me by a beefy, red-haired giant of a man who sat opposite me. "She's a beauty, isn't she?" He nodded toward the water.

"Well, she's . . . I've . . . I've never seen one like her."

He roared with laughter.

"That's an honest one, that one," he said, to no one in particular. "She's a beast, if ever I've seen one." He rose and walked with elaborate solemnity to the end of the dock. "I christen thee *Toad*," he said, "and may your voyages add to your warty splendor." He cast a last few drops from a flask toward the boat and turned back, chuckling.

"Well, not the queen, boys, but I'll have to do." A few of the men laughed. He returned and sat next to me.

"I've spent my life at sea, and I've never seen a monstrosity like her, not even close. I'm just as glad we're leaving from up here. The jeering we'd take at the town docks'd sink her for shame." He shook his head and spat. "Still, boat's a boat as long as she stays business side of the water, I suppose. You been out before?"

"Just along the coast, some trading, before the war," I lied.

He grunted. "Reinhold," he said, not coldly, and offered up a giant hand. He had a meaty face, not fat, but cut in rough, crude strokes below a thick crop of red hair. His face was scarred heavily, especially around the eyes, so much so that he seemed barely able to see out of them.

"Brendan Kane," I said as he crushed my hand. "A pleasure."

The other men sat and smoked; one slept with his head against a stack of crates.

"Pulvis Creely," said a white-haired sailor.

"Philip Pago," said another, with dark skin and dark hair and eyes that he did not bring to meet mine.

"Will Adney," said a fair-haired young man from atop a set of crates.

"Preston," Reinhold told me, pointing to a small, pale man sleeping in a pile of bags; the man started to cough, gently at first, but then more violently, eventually shaking himself awake. He wiped his hand across his mouth, blinked at us, and resettled himself.

"What's this all about exactly?" I asked, trying to sound casual. "I just signed on and didn't get the whole story."

"Not much to get," said Reinhold, shaking his head. "Two years of work, maybe more, low wages, but a shot at some real money if it goes well."

"Whaling?"

"It'd be mighty small whales we'd be hunting in that boat," Creely said. "One good-sized right and we'd have to tow her back in just to cut her up."

"It's a mine," said Adney, with a shine in his eyes. "Up in Canada. Gold, and West knows where it is. He won't say anything because he doesn't want anyone to follow us up. He figured out where a river of gold comes gushing out into the air." He whirled his hands to demonstrate, his face held gravely. Then he burst out laughing. "And besides, I saw a load of picks and shovels being loaded last night."

"It's not mining," said Pago, "it's whaling, sure enough. There's a fjord on the western coast of Greenland where the whales get trapped every year. It's long and deep enough to draw the whales up into it; but there's a huge glacier at the mouth, so when the wind shifts, it blows a load of icebergs down and blocks off the mouth. You can just walk out on the ice and spear them when they come up for air. We don't need a big ship, because we're building a camp up there to clean them and try them out. Once we're established, West'll send back for a fleet of cargo ships to haul it all back. He's already got a gang of Eskimos scouting it out. They won't hunt there—they think it's cursed. West figures he's damned already, so he might as well turn a profit on it."

This was greeted with a sprinkling of laughter. We fell silent as men rolled these ideas around in their heads.

"Who is West?" I asked.

"Your boss," replied Reinhold. "It's his ship, his trip. Plenty of money, no matter how he came by it."

"What does that—"

Pago cut me off sharply.

"That'll do," he said.

"What does that mean?"

"It means that today and tomorrow are more than enough to preoccupy smart young men, and no need to dwell on yesterday."

"I was just—"

"You were just nothing," he said evenly. "Minding your own business is plenty."

The bark returned and landed at the dock. We roused ourselves. After a moment the head of the man from the post office appeared over the edge of the dock. He scrambled up and regarded us with that sharp gaze I had seen on the steps.

"Right then, boys," he said, "this is the last one. Let's load up and be off. Tide's already turned, so snap to it."

We formed a line and loaded the last set of boxes and bags. The ship, which looked strange from a distance, became increasingly bizarre as we approached. The wood seemed to grow darker, as if it swallowed the light; when we drew alongside, it sat lower and heavier in the water. The rigging was very simple, almost crude. Two sets of sails on two masts, with a scarcity of shrouds and stays to bind them; there was a short bowsprit with a thin jib attached. It looked like a child's drawing of a boat writ large.

The bow was dominated by a huge windlass wound round with a massive chain. The anchor that hung over the bow was not proportionately gigantic, but it had a single long, curved tine like a fishhook. In addition to two whaleboats of familiar size and proportion, I noticed two boats of odd but not inelegant design hanging from stern davits; they seemed very small, and were curved sharply upward at both ends, with high sides.

The deck was covered with crates and piles of bags and stray pieces of machinery. Most of the boxes were stowed rapidly and the rest were lashed to the deck. As we worked, the man from the post office conferred quietly with another man.

"Which one's West?" I asked Reinhold.

"Neither. The little man's the captain, Captain Griffin, and the other's Dr. Architeuthis. West's already below. Keeps to himself mostly. You'll know him when you see him."

The doctor was tall and blond; his face was chiseled and flawless, his eyes bright blue; his teeth flashed as he talked. His whole figure radiated energy as he stood over us. It seemed impossible not to admire him.

After everything was stowed and lashed to the satisfaction of the captain, he gave the order for us to be under way. A second, smaller anchor was hauled up and we pulled out toward the bay.

The boat moved clumsily as she came around, but quickened with the wind behind us, and we soon moved before a crisp breeze. Despite the odd boat and odd company, it was impossible not to feel my spirits lift as we pulled out into the bay. The sun was bright over high white clouds, and the air was clean and cold. The land began to fall away; the empty horizon beckoned.

# three

Griffin summoned us to the front of the deckhouse as soon as we had cleared the bay. With no ceremony, he broke us into shifts and set us to work: Reinhold, the butcher, marled meat on the foredeck with Pago. They knelt amid a pile of raw beef; Reinhold hacked free great hunks that Pago salted and spiced, then coiled into a tight bundle and bound with rope. Both Reinhold and Pago were stripped to the waist, despite the chill breeze, and they were drenched with beef juice, both of them massive and powerful with broad shoulders and thick necks. Pago was smaller than Reinhold, but filled with corded muscles, his shoulders thinning to slim hips; he was Portuguese, with ink black hair and coffee-colored skin with a tinge of copper in it. They looked like golems, lumbering monsters formed from the flesh they cut and bound. Reinhold's huge hands tore effortlessly through the meat, and he kept up a stream of bawdy shanties as he worked. His voice boomed over the deck, infusing all of us with his easy, crude, good cheer.

Over them flitted Adney, disappearing into the rigging with

the bound meat to hang for curing in the sail north. He was the youngest after me, fine boned and fair, his eyes always flickering happily. He had come from a good family and was the only one of us who had gone to college.

Hume, the mate, and Creely were set the task of cataloguing the stores, calculating the needs of the crew, and repacking the hold accordingly. Hume was a vile little toad of a man—small eyed with pinched features that gathered around thin, pursed lips, his cap wedged tightly onto his bald head. Even his pleasures had the stench of smallness to them. He preferred to work with Creely because he knew he could safely bully the older man.

Creely had white hair and a straggly white beard that framed a face lined by the accumulation of frustration and doubt—the product of a lifetime of work that had brought neither wealth nor wisdom nor peace. His chest and arms were covered by the oxidized copper green of mariner's tattoos that the sag of skin had left vague and illegible. He was still strong under that sagging skin, his muscles knotty from years of rough work. He was a man who had worked all his life, not because he loved it, as some men do, nor because he was driven to it by that relentless energy that possesses some men, but because he could not find the means of avoiding it.

Behind the deckhouse was the carpenter's shop. The carpenter, Ash, was assisted by Preston, and they made a good pair. Both were silent, aloof men, so the only sound that emerged from that cramped shop was the chuff of the saw and the crump of hammers. Ash was a tall, slope-shouldered man, deep red from the sun, with a bland, cunning face. He found that Preston worked quietly and well, and that suited him. He swiftly disregarded the rest of us, and did not indulge us with politeness or respect. He did his work, and he expected to be disappointed with ours.

He treated Preston with indifference rather than respect, but Preston raised no objection. In fact, Preston objected to little except gregariousness. He was slight and milk pale, with deep-set eyes edged in red. His hair was black and hung in loose clumps over his forehead. He smiled little, spoke little, demanded nothing, and gave nothing in return except what was demanded from him. He was the only one of all of us who did not speculate about our fortunes.

Each of us prodded and pried in our small ways, gathered in our clues, measured them against our private hopes. All open facts were dissected, arranged, examined, torn down, and rearranged endlessly. One group, headed by Pago, held fast to the well of whales. Adney held to a gold mine, and I was inclined to believe him. With each retelling, certain ideas carried through and others were lost; ideas fragmented and facts became distorted and open to interpretation; each teller added weight to his particular fancies and so obscured what few facts we had; desire-bred and fancy-fed, great shapes rose over us, at first airy, then suddenly palpable, possible. Every meal, every watch was filled with dreamt shapes, every sleep deferred for the hushed sharing of schemes.

Preston would watch us from his bunk—not interested but not wholly dismissive either—brooding, silent, his eyes lurking and darting like small fish. But for their activity, he might have joined that legion of faceless men that crowd our acquaintance unmemorably.

I was a monkey boy—doing whatever mindless work I could be trusted with; I trimmed sails, adjusted rigging, making whatever of the thousand changes the captain felt would help us to move along, and at the same time received my first instructions in the operating of the ship.

The captain was, above all, a man of process. There were precise steps to be followed in the accomplishment of any task. To skip a step, or to perform it out of its proper order, was to fail, and what's more, to be directly insubordinate to him. He would lean out of the deckhouse, scowling and shouting, until he could no longer contain himself and had to charge out to be sure that something was being done correctly. Any idle moment was instantly filled with deck cleaning or rope coiling. His eye saw chaos in the least disorder, and sloth in every slowing. Despite our regular work and excellent weather, he seemed ill at ease and irascible.

Much of his wrath fell, appropriately, on my shoulders. I spent most of the first week retying knots and readjusting rigs. I jumped regularly at the sound of his voice and immediately began to redo whatever it was I was doing. Gradually I learned to tie my knots and run my rigs even, to reef the sails in the wind and coil the ropes. The only area I did not enter was the aft cabins, where the officers and the doctor lived. None of the men went below there except Hunt, to deliver meals. None of us were called to work the boiler, and the smokestack remained dormant as we sailed north.

Adney remained aloft virtually all the time—ferrying meat, mending stays and sails, and helping to adjust the lines. He moved fearlessly, singing gaily as he worked, and told an endless stream of jokes and stories whenever anyone was in earshot.

Hunt, the cook, worked below on the stores; he was a small, plump, worried man who appeared not to enjoy the company of sailors. Reinhold would not let a meal pass without bellowing, "Hunt the cook! Roast him over a fire! This meal's not fit for pigs to eat!" He'd roar as Hunt reddened and scurried back to the galley.

The first week, we had strong, gusty winds and a few scudding clouds in a swelling springtime sea. We passed from the bay and the traffic of fishermen and traders to the roll of the open ocean.

As we cleared the coast, my duties shifted. I became the doctor's assistant, helping him to record data from his many instruments and to execute his experiments. My first task involved measuring and recording wave height and frequency using a set of marks built into the hull of the *Narthex,* and deducting from them a set of variables for our own speed, the wind speed and direction. After I had been faithfully recording for a week, the doctor explained what he was after:

"The size of the waves is driven by so many variables that we cannot hope to identify them all: the depth and shape of the bottom, wind, distant storms and earthquakes, and their echoes across the open ocean and around intervening landmasses, and so forth. And yet, by getting information about the base patterns of waves themselves—for they obey common physical laws—it is possible to identify anomalies that may be helpful to us. For example, in a perfect, mathematical world, waves will naturally combine to form larger waves in predictable ways: one in four will be twice the size of the base wave; one in seven, three times; one in two hundred and fifty, four times, and so on. This is why there are single huge waves on calm seas—rogue waves—simply the accumulated energy of many small waves in the correct progression. So we gather the data and map it against our models, and perhaps we will find interesting deviations. It is our baseline that you are establishing."

This was both fascinating and terrifying information. I tried to track the progressions in my head, and kept my eyes out for huge waves rising up from the calm seas.

In addition to the wave work, I helped him rig all manner of spinning gauges and tubes of colored oil, governors, scales, and valves. I scurried to check them in regular rounds so that the doctor could add them to his book. Several times a day, he brought out elaborate instruments from belowdecks, long strings of silver balloons filled with different gadgets that he trailed up behind us like kites, or nets of vials that he lowered into the sea at precise intervals, shouting to me when it was time to retrieve them. Regardless of what numbers I reported, he nodded, recorded them, snapped his book shut, and sped off again. His intensity and rigor drew me, and I felt proud to be the one to support him, believing that the success of our trip depended on the accuracy of those endless strings

of numbers. I volunteered whenever I could to take on extra duties—staying up through the night to monitor the nets, or rerigging
an anemometer farther out on a spar to get more accurate measures
of the wind. He regarded me with an amused suspicion, and though
he did not reveal more about his purposes nor allow me into his laboratory, he was pleased that I had taken such an interest.

The captain took pains to steer us away from other ships. When
we did pass close by, he dismissed them with a brusque wave, or if
imposed upon by an insistent captain, he offered a few curt words
of the barest civility. We outpaced the spring as we sailed, awakening to colder mornings and the sparkle of frost in the rigging.

As we approached Newfoundland, we were summoned to the
deck by the captain. We gathered expectantly, our eagerness
spilling over into scuffling and nervous laughter. I shivered in the
frosty air while Griffin eyed us imperiously.

"Right," he said, "we'll be landing at St. John's to take on
dogs and a final load of supplies. Mr. West, Dr. Architeuthis, and
myself will go ashore. For the rest, you'll stow the meat and load
the crates. You will wait aboard for our return. In the meantime,
no idle chatter and no foot ashore. We'll not be long."

Adney, from a perch in the rigging, burst out: "And then,
sir?" We all waited.

Griffin glared at us.

"You'll know what you need and when. You have your orders." He turned and moved to the door of the deckhouse. "We
are headed north and, for the execution of that end, have acquired
clothing for those that lack." He pointed to a pile of sacks by the
deckhouse. "Hume will distribute it once the meat has been
stowed. That is all." We dispersed quickly, a little disappointed.
Still, we had some new information: dogs, which meant we were
headed far to the north, and overland. For me, this all but con-
firmed our goal: it must be a mine.

We cut down the meat from the rigging and were forced to stow it anywhere we could find belowdecks—under our bunks, between the bulkheads, into every open crack and crevice we could find. Hume made interminable rounds of inspections and then finally begrudged us the sacks of clothing.

Inside were all manner of ragged coats and sweaters, woolen underwear, pants, socks, odd hats, and unmatched gloves of all descriptions. Mine fit, mostly, but some, Reinhold in particular, were not so lucky. He grumbled as he squeezed into a jacket, then laughed heartily as he split the back open. Hume shot him a look, and challenged the rest of us to mock our new clothes. I got woolens, a hat and peacoat, a set of thick pants, and a huge sweater. My prize was a set of lined boots—scuffed and scarred, but still sound. They were several sizes too big, and I had to stuff the liners with sawdust to get them to fit snugly. It did not occur to me to find it odd that none of the crew except Adney had proper clothes of their own.

Our ship, clumsy and sluggish as she had been in the swells, was snug and stout, and we were bundled in our mismatched warm clothing. We felt ourselves fired with the secrecy of our mission; there was a fierce playfulness in our work, a brimming over of our energies. Each of us was eager to grapple with whatever the ice brought, each of us eager to measure himself against it, each hungry for his dream-rich rewards.

We landed at St. John's after a gray and drizzly day. The town looked as if it were huddling on the shore for warmth. The last of the fishing boats had come in and the docks were covered with the silver gleam of cod. Above the docks, tiny flickers flashed from tiny windows, and the smoke of chimneys rose weakly into the gray sky. We sailed to the south end of the harbor, away from the fishing piers. The dock looked deserted as we approached; we spoke in furtive whispers. Even Griffin held his voice low. On the dock, dark shapes coalesced and came forward to take our lines. Faceless and silent, they moored us and raised a gangplank. As we landed, the doctor and Mr. West emerged from the deckhouse.

West was a broad, not immensely fat man, round at all the edges as if he were a heap of melting pats of butter. His face was mounted on a foundation of chins that drooped away in all directions, lapping over his collar in the back as well as in front. The face itself was small and shrewd; he had full lips that he held closed beneath a bulbous nose. He paused as he emerged from the deckhouse to survey us for the first time. His eyes, languid behind small spectacles, looked on us as if we were tools that he was appraising for use in some repellent duty. He wore a dark jacket and suit, finely made but not ostentatious. His gloves were lined but not trimmed, utilitarian; he held his arms stiffly at his side, fists clenched. West, the doctor, and Griffin descended; the gangplank was pulled away; they disappeared.

As we waited by the docks, I sat with Creely, watching the last of the fishermen unload in the dusk, their nets slapping onto the decks.

"Fishing's no work for a man," he said softly.

"How do you mean?" I asked.

"I mean it grinds you down—good on the good days, when the sun is shining and the fish are running, but the rest is a trial. Freezing cold days, nothing in the nets, or sharks tearing them up. You got to go out every day, and every day has got to be good for you to get ahead. But they're not all good, are they?" He smiled ruefully.

"That's what you did? Fished?"

"Fished, traded, whaled. Broken my back one way and another."

"How'd you sign up for this?"

He eyed me for a moment through the smoke of his pipe, then back at the deserted docks.

"I've been working for the captain right along now. I was working a slaver before the war, and they mutinied off of Haiti. Cut up most of us and left the others in a lifeboat in the Sargasso with nothing. Turned the ship back for Africa. I was the last, when the captain picked me up. He's a good man."

We sat in silence for a long time. The wind dropped to nothing.

"And the captain's been working for West?"

He snorted, then sighed.

"Captain got himself stuck. We lost a ship—could've happened to anyone—and he couldn't get another commission. We had quite a dry spell and the captain couldn't seem to pull out of it. Some men just get the stink on them and nobody wants to risk a boat in their hands. He tried a bit of gambling to raise a stake— imagine the captain trying to do that!—just for his wife and children, who were coming into some trouble. Lost to a man who owed West, and here we are."

"You and the others were a part of his crew?"

"I was," said Creely proudly. "The other men I don't know. I heard some of them were in prison. West's brother is a warden. Set up some tests for the men, and those that won got free to come with us."

"Which ones?"

"Reinhold, Ash, and Pago for sure. Maybe Preston. They'll only sail as far as they have to—soon as they get off the boat, they're free, so mind your step." He paused, puffing his pipe. "And whoever's manning the boiler. He must have come with West. The captain's a sailor—he wouldn't use a boiler if he could help it."

"Who's manning the boiler? You mean there's someone else aboard?"

"Of course there is," said Creely irritably. "None of us work on it, do we? Someone's down there making sure it's ready to go when we need it."

"But we haven't had to use it yet. Maybe Ash has just made it ready and we'll be sent down when we get to the ice."

"Ash wouldn't dirty his hands with it. Besides, I heard someone moving around down there when we were repacking the hold. Everyone else was on deck."

"So why haven't we ever seen him? It must be awful to stay down there all the time."

"It's unnatural is what it is. Make a man crazy to stay below by himself all this time." He glanced into the bowl of his pipe, which had gone out. He grunted, waved it vaguely at me, and went below for more tobacco. I moved into the deckhouse and stared at the brass speaking tube next to the wheel, and then at the aft hatch. I had seen both of them every day since we sailed, but they had seemed inert, just a part of the floor. Now they seemed to hold a sinister ripeness. I moved up to the tube and thought about calling down, but Hume came scowling into the deckhouse and I moved back on deck.

The doctor, West, and Griffin reappeared an hour later with a yelping, yowling sea of dogs. They dropped a plank and drove them up. The dogs flowed aboard, a torrent of scraggly fur, flickering teeth, and alien eyes. They enveloped the deck, swarmed around the mast, rooted in the piles of rope. They pissed everywhere, snarled and whined, rolled and roiled over one another; fights broke out and subsided, like waves breaking over rocks. They bumped and brushed my legs as I stood on deck, surging with savage energy, flashing a hundred sinister yellow eyes, and red tongues amid broken white teeth. My gorge began to rise as I felt them press in; I imagined them shifting their energies as a mass, bristling and swelling over me, the burning tear of their teeth in my flesh, my ineffectual efforts to rise against them, and the contentment at their full bellies and their swaggering ease.

From among them Reinhold arose, one wave above the rest. He

waded through them swinging a club viciously and they parted before him, howling with pain when he struck. They cowered away and gradually the dog sea subsided. The sickening crack of wood on bone faded to the thump of boot to ribs, and finally the dogs were quiet. As I moved among them cautiously, the metallic taste in my mouth and the sickening weakness of my legs lingered on. Once the clamor subsided, the captain, West, and Dr. Architeuthis came aboard.

West and the doctor retreated quickly to their cabins. Griffin barked out the order to cast off. We moved to our places, scattering the dogs, and put out again to sea. There was little light in the harbor now except the flashing of the lighthouse on the headland.

With our preparations largely complete, we had little to do besides sail the ship and clean up after the dogs. They filled us all with an urgent energy, now excited, now snappish. I found it hard to sleep that night, and the next. With the smell of meat seeping from beneath my bunk and the snuffling respiration of the dogs, I felt as if I were in the belly of a huge, rank beast.

The land, when we sighted it, was still draped in snow. A few drab bushes poked through in places, and dark rocks were laid bare by the battering of waves. The first small floes drifted past us, dirty gray and deeply pitted. West showed himself on the deck more frequently now, though he did not speak to any of the crew. He followed the doctor to analyze the numbers brought in from the instruments and to scan the horizon with his telescope.

The presence of ice meant a furious new round of measurements and experiments—hauling small blocks up onto the decks, launching fleets of tiny bottles and recording which floated and which sank and at what intervals, with Dr. Architeuthis shouting down the seconds from the deck and noting the results in his blue-bound log. I watched him hanging from the spars, scarf flying out behind, building numbers into currents and patterns, and patterns into paths. It seemed suddenly clear to me that fate is merely possible, that there is one destiny for each of us, but no certainty that we might reach it or be equal to it at the moment we happen to intersect it. But there are a few blazing men who find their destiny right before them—the world rippling back in waves as the days march into focus—and they find themselves equal to it in will and capability and strength. The doctor seemed to be one such man, ascending to a precipice with the world spread submissively below him. I was glad to be near to him, to tag along. As for me, it seemed that my own destiny remained distant—in some other time, or in a far-off city I would never have the fortune to visit—that my own potential would pass in some subsidiary function, some mere utility that I could make of what I would, and I felt lucky to be able to offer it up for Dr. Architeuthis.

I was put on a shift with Preston, Reinhold, and Hume. Hume stayed at the helm mostly, steering and calling out only when he needed something. His constant presence in the deckhouse gave me no opportunity to find out more about our mysterious fireman. Preston kept to himself. Reinhold and I speculated about the disposal of his certain fortune; I resisted for a time, feeling that my rigidity somehow bolstered the doctor's rigor and that I was helping by not revealing the secret nothing that I knew. But Reinhold's easy cheer wore me down, and I joined him in thinking about what was to come. Never are we so inclined to sympathy, to indulgence, to confidences about the odd shapes of our desires as in the low hours before night turns. We become free to dream ourselves into shapes preposterous in the daylight and hidden in more rational hours even from ourselves.

"Say, Kane," began Reinhold on one such night as we sat draped with dogs on the foredeck, "I'm thinking about Nebraska when we get back."

"What about Nebraska?"

"You know, a farm, settle in. Find a hearty farming wife to keep me topped up with pies and roasts. Raise rabbits, wheat maybe."

"Rabbits?"

"Sure, can't miss. Start out with a pair and you'd have more than you could sell in a year. Easier than driving cattle. Don't need to worry about them stampeding." He laughed.

"You'd quit the sea?"

"Damn the sea," he said, "and damn the salt. I'd quit it today if I could. I will, once we find the mine." He fell silent.

"You scrape along for so many years," he said, "you just get sick of it. Smell of salt makes me sick. And the damp. Just think of golden wheat and blue sky and the wind soothing you like a cool drink.

"What about you, Kane? Got a sweetheart to keep in dresses? Or will you be buying up the railroad? Lots of money in the railroads, you know. Use money to make money—that's how the lazy brains can get so fat. You just need enough to get you started."

"I don't know what I'll do . . . travel around some, I guess." I became embarrassed as I paused to think. My own dreams were meager and faint—of the world casting up mysteries and me conquering them; the speech that had sent me down to the war had moldered away and left me, and aside from the bright hope of the doctor's scientific work, I had little. I could not see a way to explain what I felt only dimly myself—about how doing the work I was given might shape my own ambitions, and that I held no vision of my own for how my life might turn out. I fell silent.

"Have you ever beaten a man to death with your hands?" asked Reinhold, in the same drifty, almost dreamy tone.

"I—no—never . . ."

"It's the oddest feeling," he continued. "At first you're just struggling to survive, to keep off the panic. And then something changes—you get a surge of energy and you feel invulnerable, as if there's nothing he can do to hurt you. You can see him weaken and fade until, *pop*—he's just gone, and it's an empty sack of meat under your hands. Takes a long time—longer than you'd think—but you don't feel it. And there's a lot of blood."

"When did—"

"Oh, he was a monster," said Reinhold, with a wave of his hand. "Deserved it, and worse. There's a lot of men not even worth dirtying your shirt for."

He paused, then turned laughing to me.

"Not to worry, Saint Brendan. I'm a mouse. That was a long time ago."

When our watch was over, I felt an air of menace around Reinhold. But he was relentlessly cheery, and easily the strongest man on the ship, with a ready hand for unpleasant work; it was hard not to be happy to see him.

The glow of the sun lingered near the horizon until nearly midnight, but the hours were colder and the weather worse. A few nights, when it had begun to sleet, I swallowed my fear and burrowed down among the dogs for warmth. They seemed then not so fierce, but most companionable, happy for the added warmth and not bothered about the rest.

On one of these nights, I had just gotten settled when Hume roused me with a kick to relash the boats. Reinhold moved up next to me in the drizzling darkness and leaned over the railing to watch the water slip past. He had a tiny black hat perched on the back of his head. He began a shanty under his breath and I joined in softly. We moved about the deck as we worked, and the shanty caught, like candles lit from candles, from man to man, each singing softly, a susurration that joined the lap of the waves and the whistle of the wind as we moved into the darkness.

*four*

Four nights later, under the waning moon, Hume sent Reinhold aloft to watch for icebergs. It was the first time I had been alone with Preston, and I felt uneasy. We stood, stiff and slightly formal; I longed to sink down amid the dogs. I watched his restless eyes moving over the water.

"Say, Preston, so what do you think we're about? A mine?"

He turned to me, scanning my face, then shifted back to the water. "That's what you think, is it, Kane?"

"Well," I said, "I don't know. I wouldn't raise any objections if it were." I smiled lamely.

"To fill your pockets?" he said, sneering slightly. "And then what? Stuff your gut with candy and wine? Smoke cigars?" He laughed bitterly.

"Say now, Preston, there's no cause for scorn. What's wrong with a full belly? And full pockets, for that matter?"

He replied sharply: "The others are the same—full pockets, full belly, full house—very admirable. You want to sit and rot out your years in an easy chair, peering over your swollen belly; wander, limping from gout, to your bath, then to your bed with its fancy bedclothes and your fat and stupid wife?"

I was stung and did not reply; we sat in silence in the cold. I was relieved when Reinhold descended and Preston went aloft.

The morning following our conversation I was woken up early by the sounds of shouts on the deck. I rolled from my bunk, pulled on my boots, and trailing sawdust, made my way to the deck. We were in a thick white fog and it chilled me. The sea appeared in black patches over the rail and was lost. The sailors were crowded around the foredeck winch. They were gathered around Adney, who knelt over a sodden trunk of the kind that most sailors have: long and low and black, designed to stow beneath a bunk or under a bar stool as the need be. On one end was neat lettering: SEAMAN BROMMER, H.M.S. UNDAUNTED. The chest was badly scraped and soggy, but sound.

Adney looked at Griffin.

"Yes, go on then."

Adney took a bar and twisted the hasp free from the case. Slowly he opened it. Inside was a neat pile of clothes, carefully folded and packed. Two shirts, a set of fraying woolens, a raincoat, wool socks, a set of polished boots, and the oddments of a sailor's life—a razor, a mirror, a knife, a tiny book of Psalms, a steel flask. On the inside of the lid was the sepia photograph of a square-faced older couple, their faces set grimly against the onslaught of the photographer. They looked out at us suspiciously from the front of a small cottage, with a line of fencing in the blurred background. A pall fell over us as Adney removed the objects one by one. But for the name on the end, that was my plain and poor store of goods; I didn't even have a photograph. A wave of sadness coursed through me at this mean memorial, and a shudder at the meagerness of my own. There was, in those neat folds, the tracery of a man's care and effort, the work of a man's life, now swallowed by the sea or, more likely, crushed in the ice in that same *Undaunted*.

Adney repacked the trunk and we dispersed in silence. I returned to my bunk and stared sleepless at the bunk above. Trailing my hand over the side, I traced the edges of my chest—not even mine, but given to me by the captain—with its anonymous and threadbare clothes, inherited from strangers, its pictureless lid.

I struggled to think of mines and gold, of my pockets bulging, my stomach bulging, of my boots polished enough to shine. I shuddered and drew myself deeper into my blankets, trying to work myself from melancholy to pity and from there into sleep at last, where I could forget my life of borrowed clothes. The work of the doctor lost some luster in the damp, the columns of numbers trailing off into nothing. The ship slid and slapped through the waves. Close to sleep, I listened to the tramp of feet on the deck and the muffled singing of Pago and Adney in the rigging. My heart thudded dully, keeping me from rest, refusing to release me or warm me, and so I huddled until Hunt called me to my meal and my watch.

I pulled myself into the galley and sat opposite Reinhold and Creely. Reinhold was deep into his bowl, already eyeing mine as he gulped. Creely said nothing; Reinhold nodded and guzzled.

On deck, the wind had risen and there was a perceptible swell. The gray of the morning had turned decidedly darker and the fog had thickened into a spitting rain.

"Looks like a blow, boys," said Adney cheerfully as he headed below. "Enjoy yourselves! And don't call me when I'm sleeping."

We reported to the deckhouse and were waved off by the captain with barely a word. We moved onto the deck—Reinhold took the first watch aloft, and Creely and I relashed the stores. The dogs huddled glumly in the rain, not even bothering to try to extort something edible from us. My hands chilled rapidly from the spray and I had to stop frequently to warm them inside my coat. After we finished, I returned to the deckhouse to check in with the captain.

"Looks like a bit of a blow, sir," I said. "Do you think it'll be bad?"

The captain stood silent. I waited, and tried again, a little louder.

"The wind's picking up out there, sir. Shall we start reefing?"

"Blow, blow, all right, look at the swell. This one's been brewing for a while. Probably come all the way down off the pole." He paused and strained into the deepening dusk, as if reaching out to the pole to see for himself.

"Shall we start reefing then, sir?"

"Reef them, all but the foresail, and keep that in tight." He turned and shouted into the brass speaking tube that was mounted next to the wheel: "Keep her boiling for now, but low. Hopefully we won't have to steam at all, but we'll have to be ready if we do."

I looked at it for a moment, startled. Here was our man at the boilers, suddenly made real. The stack had been dormant for so long, and I so busy, that I had forgotten to figure out who he was.

"*And that, Kane, is quite enough!*" Griffin was shouting at me and I started. I moved out quickly to the sails, but still puzzled over the engine and its mysterious operator. Creely and I reefed the sails and then he replaced Reinhold aloft.

"Freezing up there," said Reinhold. "It'll be a nasty night. I don't imagine Adney and them will be getting much rest. I just hope that this storm isn't driving the ice down on us. I'd hate to hit an iceberg in this mess." I nodded and peered over the rail.

"Who's running the engine?" I asked, pointing to the smoke dissipating into the flat gray sky.

"I don't know," replied Reinhold. "The captain's got someone below."

"Someone who has never come up on deck?"

"There's a lot going on down there that we never see up on the deck, and none of it good. It's probably some poor half-wit West dragged off the streets. Chained him to the boiler and gives him a candle every other day. That way West doesn't share more than he has to. I'm sure he'd have monkeys sailing us if he could."

"We're not exactly the royal marines, are we?"

He looked at me sharply for a moment, then burst out laughing. "You know, I might rather have some monkeys than these stiffs," he said.

The *Narthex* rode the swells heavily, ducking under the lip of each wave and sending water cascading over the deck. Despite her bowl-like shape, she did not stay well up in the water, and seemed to be straining, though the sea was not yet very high. The swell was still long, with the waves only starting to steepen.

The gray deepened to black and the waves rose. The rain began to fly directly in our faces, as if the ocean and sky were being compressed into a narrower and narrower corridor and the force of the storm were pushed horizontally at us. The rain was pelting us now and thunder was rolling in the distance.

As the swell steepened and quickened, the wash over the deck became thicker. Each wave split into eddies that licked out into each corner of the deck before dissipating. With each wave, a bundle of dogs would be dislodged and sent skittering across the deck. Reinhold seemed very amused by the prospect of the storm, and not at all discomfited by the wet or cold. He stood in the middle of the deck and let himself tumble, childlike, with the dogs in the water. He delighted in the flickering lightning and roared with the roar of thunder.

"He's a nutter to be sure, that one," shouted Creely in my ear.

I nodded, grimacing. The ship had begun to lurch heavily as it swung down the face of the waves. It sped down and plowed into the bottom of the next, before bobbing resolutely to the surface and climbing up the face of it. It was sickening to stop so completely at the base of a wave and see it loom over us. I could feel each pausing before it began to crash; I felt sure we would swamp—the wave holding us just long enough to dump its full weight on us, or, pulling us upward steeply, upend us into the storm-tossed sea. I thought stupidly about the wave progressions, and wondered if the same patterning were true for storms, that they arrived in sequences of predictable variance, and that one in four might be twice as severe, one in 250, one in 5,000, tried to work out the oblique mathematics of catastrophe, and tried not to imagine where we might be in the sequence. I clung to the brass door handle of the deckhouse and tried not to think of icebergs.

In the midst of the tossing sea, I saw, by a flash of lightning, the fore hatch spring open; then the deck was black again.

"The fore hatch is sprung," I shouted to Creely.

He looked emptily at me.

"Well, you'd better go close it before we're flooded."

I glared back, and stomped out onto the deck. I had my head down and both hands on a shroud when I felt a heavy hand clap me on the shoulder.

"Hi there, Grandma! Is the ladies' auxiliary meeting in the hennery?" Reinhold roared with laughter. He was bareheaded, and squeezed into an old black raincoat.

"She's a beauty, eh?" he said. "Looks like we'll have a night of it tonight!"

He seemed gleeful and bursting with energy, even leaning forward as we sped down the wave, as if willing the boat to go faster and faster, then throwing his head back as we crashed into it. He began a shanty, building it as we rose up a wave, rushing as we rushed down the face, and shouting it out as we buried ourselves beneath the next one. His fierce playfulness cheered me and I began to sing along. He made it seem like an excellent game that we were playing, and that I was brave and reckless for playing it with him. I still felt afraid as the face of a wave loomed over us, still felt my breath leave me as we struck, but it returned as we mounted again, and my spirits began to rise.

The lightning cracked sharply above us, and I winced for a moment, fearing that our mast had split; but it rode straight and proud, pressing through cascade after cascade. The rain had turned to hail, and sleet that pounded into us on fierce gusts of wind. Reinhold looked down at me at the end of his song, still grinning, and looked back at the ship. Gasping, he pointed and shouted down.

"Good God, the dogs!"

The dogs were in a bad state, washing freely about the deck and scrambling to hold themselves in loose bunches against the assault of the waves. Several had caught themselves in the water-ways and were kicking desperately to stay aboard. Others were tangled in loose rigging and being battered against the bulwarks. In the middle sat Creely, disconsolate, clutching three dogs and the mast.

Reinhold scrambled back to the bulwarks. Pulling out his knife, he cut free the tangled dogs and coiled the rope over his shoulder. He grabbed two of the dogs and staggered up to the mainmast with them. He looped one end of the rope around the mast, then around each of the dogs, and tied it off. Making his way to the waterways, he pulled out the dogs and heaved them over toward the mast. Grabbing another long coil of rope, he fastened one end to the bulwark and began to tie off the dogs one by one in a line, wrapping them over their shoulders and cinching the rope firmly. I followed, dragging or shoving the dogs as best I could;

they sat limply and whimpered. Reinhold strode over the deck with two tucked under his arms, standing as a wave broke over him and then making his way forward again. As often as not, I would be sent sprawling just as I reached the mast and was washed to the far end of the deck. The waterways were too small to admit a man and, I would have thought, too small for our hearty dogs. But under the force of the crashing waves, I saw one stuffed in, held for a long minute as we climbed a wave and shot down, then buried in water and gone when the water was gone. They were bedraggled and pathetic now, no longer fierce; they looked impossibly scrawny and naked with their fur plastered to them.

We were joined by Adney, Pago, and the doctor, and we formed a rough chain—each ferrying a dog between waves from one firm hold to the next. Behind us I could see Creely and Ash working to secure the whaleboats. Hume stood in the deckhouse beside the captain, his arms crossed beneath a scowl. Working slowly, we gathered most of the dogs and fixed them in a web that ran along the windward side, out to the mainmast, across, up the lee side, and then out to the foremast.

With the dogs secure, I felt all the energy run out of me. Each wave seemed heavier than the last, and each blast of wind more fierce. I had swallowed so much water that I began to feel that it was pointless to keep battling when it was so simple to succumb. I imagined myself bobbing gently in the waves as the *Narthex* battered her way into the distance; I imagined the stiff clutch of my heart slowing to a gentler cadence, my sickening weakness fading into a feeling of weightlessness.

As if in answer, the storm increased its fury, causing the masts to creak and sway fearfully. The jib came loose and shredded in the wind; it took long minutes with our stiff fingers to rig another. The water piled up with such force that it buoyed the dogs up to the edge of the railing and threatened to pull them over.

"Let's move aft before this gets worse," Reinhold shouted in my ear. His face was still glowing and had lost none of its fierceness. In fact, he seemed pleased that the storm had worsened. He was no longer playing; his face had in it the light of passion, as if the storm had charged him with a supernatural energy and he was struggling to contain it.

Creely stood, bedraggled, but surprisingly solid beside Griffin. Griffin stood ramrod straight, his eyes shifting relentlessly from the compass to the deck. From behind the glass we could see the dogs in flashes of lightning, jerking helplessly on their lines.

"Poor devils," shouted Reinhold. "I hope we don't lose many. It's a poor night for swimming." He smiled grimly. Griffin leaned over to the speaking tube, screwing his face up in an attempt to hear.

"Fine, fine," he shouted, "I'll send a man down immediately." He turned and, looking past Pago and Preston, shouted to me: "Kane, get below to help with the boiler. Down the aft hatch, to the back of the cabin, is the ladder down." I climbed down the aft hatch and into a narrow passage. Despite the rush of the storm, I was excited to be venturing below, to see what might be happening there that we had not known about. To the left were the doctor's cabin and the captain's cabin. Behind me was the black wood of the king post, filling the entire passage. To my right was the door to West's cabin.

I heard a murmuring from beneath the roar of the storm. At first I was not sure if I heard it at all, but as I moved toward West's door, I heard the faint moaning of a pianola. Like Reinhold's shanty, it seemed to match the tempo of the crashing of the ship, rising slowly, then crashing down into silence, then beginning again slowly but building, in rage and fury, as if goading the storm to greater heights. As I listened, the music took on an air of challenge, a trumpeting of victory in battle though the storm continued unabated—as if West were claiming victory in the heat of the fighting, holding himself up in the teeth of the storm.

I retreated backward from West's door and continued my descent. At the back of the narrow passage I found a large hatch, which I pulled back. Below me was a small, neat cabin lined with bookcases, and lit by a lantern that swung crazily. The floor was built on a raised platform, but even this was covered with water. At the far end of it was a doorway from which there was a deep red glow, and the ferocious clanging of metal.

I rushed in and found myself standing before the open mouth of a large boiler, being stoked frantically by a dark-skinned man who was stripped to the waist and pouring sweat. The water was over my ankles, and hissed mightily where it struck the underside of the boiler.

"The pumps have jammed," he shouted. "We need to keep the boiler on full to keep it from being flooded. You stoke and I'll clear the pump." I tore off my jacket and shirt, already starting to sweat from the heat of the open boiler. He passed me his shovel, and as he did so, I noticed that he had an extra hand, perfectly formed, that protruded from beneath his right wrist and grasped the handle of the shovel along with his regular hand. Shocked, I recoiled, and the shovel clattered into the water between us. As he stooped to retrieve the shovel, I struggled to say something.

"I'm sorry . . . I was just . . . I didn't expect to . . ."

"Think nothing of it," he said easily. "Happens all the time." He did not have an accent, but his speech had a singsongy cadence to it. He presented the shovel to me again, and waited until I had hold of it.

"Aziz," he said, and flashed a bright smile from the depths of his sooty face.

"Brendan Kane," I replied, trying not to stare at his hand. He splashed past me and edged behind the boiler, and I began to shovel. The coal was piled loosely in a huge bin next to the boiler. The bottom of the bin, like the floor of the room, was full of water, so the coal slid on its uncertain footing, and around the floor. The footing was so treacherous that I dared not lift my feet. I found that I got a good deal of water as well as coal as I shoveled. When I dumped this on the fire, steam blasted out, scalding my face. I braced myself against the edge of the cabin and struggled to shovel as the ship pitched. The boiler creaked with each pitch, straining against its fastenings.

In those interminable hours, faced with the ghastly glow of the boilers and choked by the sullen heaps of smoke, with my feet numb in the waters and aching from trying to keep my balance, and my body roasting in the blasts of steam, I, exhausted and hammered by the pitching cabin and the pound and shriek of the wind above me, became lost to the balance of the day. I became convinced that the ship had deserted the face of the ocean and was, in fact, plunging downward with each wave; I saw the ship, tipped over the edge of a vast maelstrom, pounding her way deeper and deeper into the black depths of the sea. As I worked, and watched the waters rise to my shin and press up to the very lip of the boiler mouth, I struggled to grip the shovel, which twisted in my sweaty hands, struggled to keep my feet as the floor pitched and warped, struggled to hold to the flicker of reason that told me that I must keep to my task. The world of the deck was gone now, and gone my companions; I saw only the yawn of the boiler and the sway of the boiler room. The storm mounted, and the beams of the ship creaked and shook.

My body did not retreat into numb work, but instead strained with each load; my arms felt pitifully weak, until I seemed to be shifting only tiny lumps with each shovelful. Countless times I mustered myself, gritted my teeth, and resolved to work with renewed effort, but each time my energy faded quickly, and I found myself dragging the half-full shovel across the water. I worked to the point where I became convinced that my body must break, must tear into pieces, and still my arms lifted, still my back plunged. The imagination is a poor instrument for measuring the terrible power of our bodies to endure. We beat on and on, mind failing, will failed, and still the body moves, and finds the boundary of pain is a greater pain and a greater still, and so we trace out the recesses of our own power carved by suffering invisible to our imaginations and lost to us in days of ease.

The fire seemed to be losing some of its fierceness, its white glow subsiding to orange and red and flickering blue, threatening to extinguish with each roll of the ship.

Finally, from behind the boiler, Aziz reappeared. His body was striped with soot and grime, and burned white in many places. His face was totally black, but for his eyes, which glowed out of their sockets with an unnatural brightness. Without a word, he took his place beside me and shoveled, flinging the coal into the boiler furiously.

His quiet industry spurred me on, and my delirium began to subside. I was grateful for the company of my peculiar companion; in his presence, the boiler room lost its air of unnatural hellishness. Gradually, the fire resumed its white glow. My shovel lightened, and the boiler blazed merrily. He must have cleared the pumps, for the water subsided quickly. The rolling of the ship faded also; we resumed the long roll of the afternoon, and the sickening crashing had stopped. I heard the faint lament of the Pianola above me, the final strains of West's playing dropping into silence.

Aziz and I slumped back against the walls of the boiler room, our arms limp at our sides. After a time, Aziz roused himself and disappeared into his cabin. He returned in a few moments with steaming tea in cups made from an intricate silver filigree. He shut the door of the boiler and we sat sipping our tea. He had brought a cloth with him, and began to wipe himself off. I could not help but stare at his hand, which was very delicate and graceful. He held it off from the scrubbing, touching it only now and then to his face. From beneath the layer of grime emerged a bright, quick face, with deep-set eyes. His skin was coppery beneath the soot, and it shone as if polished.

I believe I slept now, though I was so exhausted it is impossible to be sure. I thought that I was watching him quietly, but there seemed to be illogical skips and gaps in what I saw. I felt a wave of gratitude to him; but for the exhaustion of my limbs, I am sure that I would have leaped to my feet and embraced him on the spot. There passed between us a silent recognition of the strength of each, in our simple persistence. Such a moment, unspoken, is a treasure, for it lets you believe for a moment in the possibilities of your own strength, of your own courage, and lets you deny the weakness and meanness that filled you through your struggling and disavow the boundaries you felt but surpassed, lets you believe for a moment that you have vanquished them rather than merely chanced to keep them at bay.

I thanked him quietly for the tea, and ascended the ladder once more. The passageway outside of West's cabin was silent now, as was the deck. I found Griffin still stiffly at the helm; his knuckles were white on the wheel, and his red eyes still scanned the horizon. We nodded silently to each other and I stepped out onto the deck.

The wind was blowing briskly and cold, and the sun was burning through a weak gray mist. The deck was scattered with debris—ends of lines, pieces of sail or rigging, shards of wood. Two spars on the foremast dangled in a knot of lines like crippled limbs, knocking against the mast in the wind. Behind the deckhouse, Ash worked on the two smaller boats, which looked badly mangled. On the foredeck, Preston moved slowly through the dogs, untying them carefully, rubbing their coats with his gloves. They moved stiffly over the deck, like foals finding their legs. Several had patches of fur missing where the rope had been tied. A number refused to get up despite his coaxing, and lay miserably on the deck.

I walked around, checking the lashings of the whaleboats; both had had some thwarts smashed but were otherwise intact. I untangled some of the loose lines and recoiled some ropes. Gradually the others emerged from the main hatch, blinking in the light. The doctor ascended to the roof of the deckhouse and began checking his instruments. Everyone did his work in silence, still not believing that the storm had passed, that the world was again the world that we knew.

Griffin called hoarsely for me to run up the sails, and I found Adney and Creely joining me at the mast to help. I climbed aloft to disentangle some of the shrouds and was joined by Adney. From my perch on high, with a view of the gray-green water stretching out before me, I swelled with pride for the victory of our ragtag crew and our awkward, plucky ship. We had been bloodied, but were slogging ahead. That we had borne up under the weight of water and wind could not but bode well for the tests that were to come. Surveying the deck, I watched the steady work of Ash and Preston as they hauled one of the damaged boats onto the deck. At the very peak of the bow, I spotted Reinhold, asleep in a coil of rope like a big unruly boy.

In the distance, the sun had burned through the last of the fog and burnished the water to a golden emerald green; I was dazzled by the flash of sparks of blazing whiteness that danced in the waves. It was the ice—I raised a shout and the entire crew crowded to the deck. Even West emerged and peered out through his glass. We whooped and shouted and clapped each other on the back—the ice, the ice, at last the ice.

*five*

Reinhold rose, stretched, and went below for a great stack of marled meat, and even the most forlorn of the dogs scrambled to eat. As they ate, more and more of the dogs swarmed up from odd hiding places—under coils of rope, beneath stowed sails, out from piles of debris—until the deck was crawling with them again, and the steady cacophony of the yipping and snarling resumed. We had lost, it turned out, only about four dogs—though several were badly wounded by their buffeting; we were left with around forty-five. They resumed their scornful proprietorship of the deck, though with an added edge of affection and even the barest hints of respect.

I was the object of intense interest for my sojourn below. Adney, Reinhold, and Pago gathered around me on the deck and interrogated me.

"Did you see anything outside or around the cabins?" asked Adney.

"No, the doors were all shut. West was playing a Pianola."

Reinhold laughed.

"Perched up on his merry-go-round, no doubt, riding out the storm."

"And the fireman?" asked Pago.

"His name is Aziz." I was going to mention his hand, but something in the belligerence of their tone made me hesitate.

"Is he a half-wit? Or mad?" asked Adney. "Why is he held below?"

"He seemed perfectly intelligent to me," I said. "And he doesn't seem to be restrained—there were no locks or chains or anything."

"What do you mean?" asked Reinhold. "You mean he's choosing to stay in the boiler room all of the time?"

"It was actually quite nice—he had some books, and had built a raised platform to keep out of the water a bit."

"What kind of man stays alone in the darkness?" said Adney. "It can't be healthy for him."

"Too good for the crew quarters, I'd say, and too good to help with the work," said Pago. "West's pet freak in his little cave. What's he up to?"

"We were just working the boilers. I didn't see anything else going on."

"It's the first time we've run the boilers since we started. What's he been doing down there?"

We lapsed into silence as Hume emerged from the deckhouse, and moved off to work.

By nightfall we were moving through small floes and dark slushy islands of brash ice that made the boat hiss. We were forced to remain more alert on our watches—no more sleeping with the dogs—and we kept a man aloft always to watch for icebergs. Most of the ice was what they called growlers, pieces a few feet in diameter and low in the water; it was gray and dirty looking, and bobbed away wearily as we moved past it.

We gathered on deck and tucked into a feast prepared by Hunt—a stew of dumplings and salt pork and a cup of rum from the captain, and for dessert, sailor's duff—a paste of flour and water sweetened by molasses. Aziz emerged from below, to the stunned silence of the crew. As Griffin introduced him, he stood back, most likely to avoid shaking hands—not that anyone offered. He had wrapped himself in a long, loose jacket. When it fell away, the crew caught sight of his extra hand.

"What the hell is that?" said Pago, pointing.

"Lovely," said Adney. "Tell me, Doctor, did you build him yourself? I'd have a closer look at the plans next time."

Aziz slid the hand back into his sleeve and regarded them with quiet equanimity. The others said nothing to him and they moved up to the bow singing songs and telling stories. He greeted me quietly but warmly, and settled beside me with his bowl of stew and dumplings, and his cup of rum.

"Never mind about them," I said.

"If that's the worst they've got to say, then they'll be the kindest crew I've ever met. Any introduction that comes without a beating is a good one as far as I'm concerned." He laughed with surprising lightness.

After we had eaten and rested, Griffin gathered us around the mast and read a psalm with humility and solemnity. His voice was low and tremulous. He rumbled into silence, and so we all stood, after our amens, our heads bowed, listening to the hissing-past of the brash.

In the morning, Ash pressed Reinhold and Adney into service in order to repair the boats and the spar, and to prepare the ship for the ice. Hume and Creely were once again rooting through the hold to be sure that nothing vital was damaged or ruined. They brought out boxes of powder and blasting caps, long poles, and a wickedly sharp saw blade fifteen feet long. These were stowed on the deck and lashed down.

Aziz's appearance started a new round of speculations about the nature of our expedition, and he was perceived at first as a focus (with his special treatment), then as a necessity (that he held some key piece of information), and eventually as an obstacle—reducing the shares of the men and intruding in some unknown but surely unfavorable way. As the conversations turned, the reflections about Aziz himself turned darker—what else did he have hidden under his robes? What was his relationship with West, with the doctor? Why would a man choose to stay alone in the darkness?

We spent two days sailing through small chunks of ice, diverting our course only occasionally for a larger floe. We spotted several icebergs, behemoths in the distance, moving sedately along the horizon. Most of the ice was low-lying and gray. As the days passed, it increased in size and frequency, until it bumped against our hull often, thudding dully and scraping past. At night we reduced our speed and kept a careful watch. The sea slowly turned white to match the lengthening of the light.

On the morning of our third day, we arrived at the great blank face of the ice edge itself. The long bay at the edge was already dotted with several ships, slim and graceful whalers. Beyond them, the ice edge stretched unbroken, white to the horizon. The sky above it glowed with reflected light, promising ice on ice beyond the edge of our sight.

The whalers had moored to the ice edge; they ran races on the ice, but the appearance of some walrus caused the game into break down and turn to slaughter. They scrambled for their rifles and the air filled with the sharp crack of bullets and the smell of gunpowder. The whalers hauled some of the corpses out onto the ice to hack their tusks free, but most they let sink, or left floating where they had been shot, their ocher bodies hanging in the water as the screeching gulls descended.

The surface of the ice itself was quite varied; though most was low and level, some pressure ridges ran ragged into the distance, like the tunnels of giant moles beneath the surface. We ventured into a number of small cracks, but each dead-ended quickly, either filled with thick new ice or still joined by older, still-firm ice. We dropped our sails and steamed back to the bay. The pack was unsettlingly flat and calm after the steady roll of the open sea. Waves were swallowed at the edge and my eye could not even see the tremors of the current farther in. It should have been soothing, to see the ocean quiet and calm, but it was not; it was menacing and unnatural—it was not just a simple boundary that marked the edge of the frozen north and the more temperate south, but a barrier where laws as well as customs were unreliable and strange.

All of us strained for the work of breaking through the ice to begin. Unlike the whalers, who seemed to regard the waiting as an excuse to joke and make merry, we chafed under the enforced idleness. Our tempers became short—especially Griffin's—and we paced past each other without speaking. Griffin paused before the dynamite many times, but he forbore to use it.

The rest of the crew was no more usefully occupied than I. Creely sat on the deck with a length of rope, nervously tying and untying knots. Preston, Pago, and some others pulled oakum and stuffed seams, while Dr. Architeuthis released a kite tied to an ink pen that scrawled a map of the patterns of the wind. Adney and Ash worked to repair damaged spars, while Reinhold patched sails.

We were washing down the decks once more—it was the only steady work that we had—chipping the ice from the lines and scraping and swabbing the deck. I was scraping the frozen excre-

ment from the foredeck. Adney and Reinhold moved behind me
with mops and buckets of warm sand. It was not unpleasant work,
actually—the process of freezing did much to contain the stench,
and the activity kept us warm. Adney was, as usual, chattering
away, joking about the smell recalling the stew of the night before,
celebrating the work as the zenith of his ambitions. He launched
into a congratulatory speech about how lucky he was to have the
opportunity.

"It is indeed an honor, gentlemen, an undreamt-of honor, to
have the chance to work with material of such a rare and distinguished quality, borne of specially bred Arctic dogs, fed exclusively on a diet of fine beef and rare Oriental spices. It is not any
dog that can produce such a savory, such a succulent bouquet—
and such a marvelous consistency! I think you'll agree, gentlemen,
that it equals if not surpasses the pearl of the Alps, Lemerde de
Berthillion thirty-eight, long held as the gold standard of rare
excrements, possessing as it does the same reticence, the same
subtle, savvy front masking a deep and passionate robustness. I
believe I am within my rights, am I not?" He surveyed us for con-
firmation before continuing.

I nodded gravely.

Reinhold regarded him scowling, and said, his voice rising,
"Will you please shut up!"

Adney turned on him. "And on my left, you will recognize
that triumph of modern science Mandrake Reinhold. An evo-
lutionary dead end from the early Pleistocene, he was frozen
in glacial ice aeons ago; the dedicated scientists of the Mittel-
schmerzhausen Clinic of Vienna managed to revive him using
magnetoelectric oscillometers of great power. Having been raised
on raw meat in a culture that lacked even the most basic tools, and
just learning to walk upright, he can now, after years of rigorous
training, affect the nearly flawless, though slightly primitive,

imitation of a modern man—albeit one of extremely low intelligence and crude manners. Still, even this must be considered a triumph when we consider the baseness of his origins."

Reinhold's face reddened as we burst into laughter. "Shut up, blast you!"

"As you can see, he has even mastered the rudiments of language, though his savage brain takes most naturally to curses and invective. He does understand nearly half of what is said to him, especially when concerning women or food, and has the reasoning capacity of an uncultivated but precocious five-year-old child."

Reinhold dropped his mop to the deck and advanced a few steps toward Adney, who continued brazenly: "Being unused to tools, and possessing a brain of frightfully limited capacity, he often forgets himself, and returns to the use of his hands, abandoning his tools, and with them, his carefully constructed veneer of civility."

The entire crew was laughing now, and had gathered around the two of them as Reinhold growled and Adney danced behind the mast.

"Remark, if you will, gentlemen, how quickly the instincts of the savage hunter return to him, even in this civilized setting. You will recall his disastrous meeting with Her Highness Queen Pompula of Bratavia, when he strangled her prize peacock, Prince Zebulon, and proceeded to eat his head on the floor of the ballroom. She was absolutely inconsolable."

We were howling by this time, as Adney had turned to us to demonstrate the queen's distress, when Reinhold sprang on him. His huge fists crashed into Adney's face with astonishing speed, peppering his face with blows. Blood gushed onto Adney's shirt and spattered the deck. By the time we managed to pull Reinhold back, Adney was swaying on his feet, his face a pulpy mess of red and purple. Reinhold pulled free and struck Adney again in the face, and he crumpled to the deck.

"How do you like that, you prize peacock?" spat Reinhold, standing over him, his shoulders quaking. Pago backed Reinhold away, and Preston and I moved to help Adney. His face was mashed; blood flowed freely from his nose and from a cut under his chin. Both eyes were swelling rapidly and his breathing was shallow and ragged. The doctor and West arrived, and we backed away from him, ashamed of ourselves. Dr. Architeuthis bent over Adney and pressed at the bones of his face; West regarded us all contemptuously.

"Like children, the lot of you. Like pathetic, beastly little children." He clipped his words, as if to avoid wasting more breath on us than was absolutely necessary.

"Nothing broken," said the doctor, "but that eye will take some stitches and he'll have quite a headache when he comes around. Let's get him below."

Adney remained unconscious overnight. The second watch was eating a glum breakfast when we heard him call out weakly: "Hunt! Hunt! I believe you have neglected my crumpets!"

I ran into his bunk, laughing with relief. His face was very discolored and his right eye was swollen shut. He gave me a wan smile and struggled to sit up. I managed to get him to drink some broth, and he fell back asleep. Reinhold took his dinner on the deck and remained glowering there through the evening watch. I was in the galley helping Hunt when Reinhold finally lowered himself down and made his way to Adney's berth. I peered in with trepidation; Pago moved protectively to Adney's side, but stepped back as Reinhold drew close.

Adney sat up and looked Reinhold defiantly in the eye. Both were silent, until Reinhold dropped his head. Adney spoke first.

"Prince Zebulon raised quite a racket, didn't he?"

Reinhold shifted on his feet. "Sorry about your face," he said.

"Sorry about yours," replied Adney.

In the days that followed, Griffin doubled our work shifts: scraping the anchor chain, greasing fittings, repairing and adjusting rigs. Every piece of metal on the ship shone, every plank was clean enough to eat off, every coil tight, every seam stuffed, and still he kept us at it.

On the evening of our seventh day, the wind finally shifted around to the north, and we could hear the ice start to rumble and creak. By midnight the wind had increased, and we could hear cracks like gunshots where the ice was starting to splinter. I awoke to the clank of the anchor being raised, and the slow thud of ice against the copper sheeting of the hull. When I emerged in the morning, slim black leads threaded into the interior, a vast labyrinth of crisscrossing lines, all in sluggish motion. Adney was bounding through the shrouds, singing out. Captain Griffin sat in the crow's nest peering through his glass, trying to plot our route. Finally, at eight, we nosed into a lead barely wider than our hull, and commenced the next stage of our journey.

At first we made good progress, moving several miles due north through a lead that seemed to open as we advanced. It spread to almost a mile in width before narrowing again to two hundred yards or so. It ended abruptly in an iceberg that had, no doubt, carved the lead itself, in the grip of a submarine current. Thus I learned one of the first essential lessons of ice navigation: that the pack is driven by the whim of the wind, shifting as the wind shifts, but the mighty bergs, extending into the deeper and more secret depths, move through the pack like great souls through the world—obedient to their own deep currents, which are invisible to those of us who battle and fracture our way on the surface. And so these seeming allies are often in deadly clash, and it is the bergs that wend their steady way, shattering the shallow pack as they move, making visible, for a moment, the deep patterns of the ocean. Eventually, worn by wind and waves and the grinding erosion of the pack, some icebergs lose their deep hold, fracture, and skitter over the surface, wind-driven and lost. Others move placidly south, dwindling at last into the great vastness of the sea.

This iceberg was made up of layers of pitted gray curves building to a rounded peak perhaps a hundred feet above the water. The floes had piled against it as they moved past, creating a zone of densely packed ice fragments that shifted occasionally with a squeal, like tearing metal. The clashing of the iceberg in the pack had created a soup of slushy pieces that was not solid enough to support the weight of a man, nor would it permit the passage of the ship. So moored, we resumed our waiting; but the wind rose, and with it the temperature, and we were away again.

Griffin remained in the crow's nest without respite, straining his eyes. He did not seem to sleep, and ordered endless cups of coffee brought.

Pools of bright blue meltwater formed on the grayish ice. The ice seemed softer and we moved more swiftly, covering perhaps ten miles by noon. The sky was cloudy but the wind fresh, as if the spring were finally catching us from behind. By midnight we were moving due north again, deviating only occasionally for a large floe or iceberg. I turned in, expecting the sea to be wholly open by the morning.

I was not entirely wrong, as it had stayed open, but with the heat had come a deep white fog, and we had been forced to slow again to a crawl. The fog was extremely dense, enshrouding sections of the deck so thickly that the rest of the ship would disappear, and I had only my feet beneath me to assure me that I had not floated free.

Griffin ordered the boilers fired, and we picked our way ahead with great caution. The low, dense pack had given way to a loose conglomeration of larger floes and more frequent bergs. The crashing and squealing of the pack was gone now, and the fog swallowed the clank of our boilers. It wracked my nerves, after the bright clashing of the days before, to creep ahead thus; monstrous shapes loomed up out of the fog and disappeared. Griffin ordered soundings every hour. In our blindness, I suppose any measure was a comfort. The white fog grayed, and night fell. Griffin was anxious to take advantage of the open water but was fearful of moving in fog and darkness, and ordered us moored to a floe.

In the morning the nature of the fog had changed; it was no longer deep white, but a jaundiced yellow-gray. We could see sunless corridors open before us of a desolate sea; icebergs drifted past, no longer white but sickly yellow. The effect was as if we had sailed into a land dissipated by pestilence, a land where the last quiver of life had rotted into emptiness and not the stench but the gloom of death remained, and the silence that follows the demise of the final mourners. We found ourselves talking in whispers. Even Adney could not pull himself into good cheer. There was nothing to mark progress or movement; the floes slipped past us or we past them; the exhalation of our wake was soon swallowed by the obscurity that trailed us. We picked our way among floes as among bodies, and slunk to our beds at the end of an interminable day.

In the morning the gloom had lifted, and we could see the ocean once more. Light flitted on the water like a swallow, and the wind played in the sails. We had two days of fine sailing and made excellent progress. The days were getting longer as we moved north with the seasons; the sun rested above the horizon until past midnight, and had bobbed up again before we arose at five. We began to see walrus on the floes and once, in the distance, the sleek deep blue of a whale. Birds rested in our rigging and circled in our wake, igniting frenzies among the dogs. Adney shot four fat geese one afternoon and we feasted. Hunt, for all his worrying, was a magnificent cook, and we toasted him with our tea deep into the Arctic twilight.

We were treated to a steady diet of Arctic atmospherics—rainbows and pillars of light and sundogs—the phenomena where glimmering hints of other suns and soft arcs of light surround our one sun. It is not the vulgar dazzle that some sailors recount, but the insistent, wavering suggestion that the world you knew is not so firmly rooted as you believed, and that other possible worlds hover nearby.

Two days of steady progress were as much as we could expect at that time of year. On June 1, the winds shifted back to the south and the temperature dropped. The ice ceased to be an obstacle course and became a vast and shifting labyrinth. We stopped battering through the floes and were often forced to pick our way through leads, or wait interminable hours for them to open, or to backtrack and backtrack again.

Despite the clumsiness of her handling, I began to see the merits of the *Narthex*'s peculiar design. The bowl-shaped edge let us slide easily up onto the floes, where the weight of the hull could crack them. The hull took a terrific battering but did not spring the smallest leak. Other methods of passage, we quickly discovered, were more difficult.

In narrow leads where new ice had formed but was not thick, we sent a boat forward with our ice anchor aboard. Once the anchor was placed, four men would gather around the massive windlass and warp the ship forward, pulling her onto the new ice and splitting it open. This was Sisyphean work for those on deck, as the anchor frequently broke free and the ship slid back, or seemed only to drag the floe toward us. I took my turn at the winch as we all did, straining my shoulders and back against the dull weight of the ice.

We awoke to a cold and drizzling day, and the dogs huddled on the deck eyed us evilly. Hume called out that the barometer was falling steadily, and we looked at each other despondently. By five there was a low but perceptible swell moving through the pack, and the rumbling of the ice had increased to a steady crashing and crackling. The wind swelled, driving the rain through our thin coats, and the sky closed in over us.

Griffin began pounding us through the low pack, throwing us recklessly into tiny leads and using the full force of the boilers to batter at the floes. We made little progress, and most discouraging, we found no iceberg to which we might moor.

The barometer continued to fall, and the captain called Dr. Architeuthis to the deckhouse for a hurried conference. Griffin emerged and rushed aloft. He spent long moments peering into the storm with his glass while we waited anxiously below. We were in a narrow lead running north-northwest between two enormous floes. The lead was formed by a slight convex curve in the western floe. Without the momentum of the engines, the wind quickly drove us against the eastern floe, its gusts banging us against it like the loose shutter on a house. Griffin descended from the mast and ordered us into the whaleboats.

We dropped into the water and threw ourselves on the oars. The waves were not considerable, as they were much stifled by the pack, but the wind was strong and right in our faces. The spray froze quickly on the oars and on our seats, so we slid off, or lost our grips, smashing into each other. Add to this the saw blade, which, because of its length, had to be laid on the thwarts in the center of the boat. Still, we managed to forge our way across the lead, arriving at last at the broad floe. It had a lip that extended some twenty-five feet into the lead; we were able to row about halfway, then were forced to drop into the ankle-deep water and drag the boat up. The floe was several hundred yards long and looked to be around two hundred in width.

Ash ordered us to pull the boat a long way onto the floe, and when we returned, he was drilling swiftly with an auger into a narrow gash of new ice where two floes had come together. He set a charge in the hole, and we retreated to the whaleboat. The charge exploded with a flash of red and a shower of ice. Over the wind we could hear a ragged cheer from the ship.

We returned from the crater and set up the saw, crossing two poles at about eight feet over our heads and hanging the saw vertically with a rope so that the saw hung down between the poles into the gaps created by the blasting. Then, as we pulled the rope back and forth, the saw rose and fell, its own weight drawing it rapidly through the ice. Reinhold and Pago worked at the edges of the crater with picks, clearing openings for the saw to begin new cuts. Preston and I hauled the saw up and down. We moved toward the center of the floe while Pago and Reinhold moved out into the water, hacking and splashing. We soon had a long groove cut. Ash called out and we dragged the rig to the other edge of the crater and began to cut. Reinhold and Pago moved to the top of our cut and began to hack across. Glancing over my shoulder, I could see the *Narthex* turning to face us across the lead, fighting to keep herself headed.

Ash wrenched the saw free and ordered us back to the whaleboat. He stood calculating for a moment, then laid another set of charges in the cut at the top. He had not even reached us when this one went up, showering us again.

We peered from behind the whaleboat and saw that our hole was open. The wind was mounting and the lead was bound to close soon. The hole seemed impossibly small, but it would have to do. Ash signaled the ship from the edge of the floe and we stood off anxiously as she gathered steam for the charge. She moved off sluggishly, the waves threatening to turn her to the north. Halfway across the lead she seemed to be barely moving at all. We huddled in a small group, bouncing with excitement, chanting under our breath like gamblers at the track. Twenty-five yards away, she still seemed to be dragging, as if hauling herself through gravel. Just as she reached the ice lip, she charged forward, grinding her way over it easily. At the edge of the floe she rose slightly, then slid into her harbor as gently as a lady into her slipper. We broke into rousing cheers on the ice, and stumped our way back to her arm in arm, singing in triumph. The hole was just large enough to keep her afloat; she knocked against the sides with the swell, but was well protected from the intrusion of other ice.

From the deck we received a hearty cheer, and the dogs added in their baleful voices—even West stood with a smile on his face. Griffin produced a small bottle of rum and added this to Hunt's pot of tea and raised a glass to us all: "Fine work, boys, that's fine work. Stout ship, hard work, and good luck, that's all you can hope for."

"Lusty women!" called Reinhold.

"Full pockets!" added Pago.

"Well now," said Griffin, coloring slightly, "fill your bellies, and first shift turn in, though I recommend you sleep in your clothes."

Griffin remained stiffly at wheel, though the ship was moored. I could see that his hands were trembling.

"Why don't you head below yourself, sir?" I said. "You've been up here longer than the rest of us combined."

He turned to me distractedly; his face was haggard and his beard was stained with tobacco.

"Really, sir, we'll wake you if need be, but we're quite safe."

"Yes, I suppose you're right," he muttered finally. "Not much

I can do here, is there?" He stared out into the storm for a moment more, and then headed below.

"Poor bastard's dead on his feet," said Reinhold as he disappeared. I got the urge to go below and see how Aziz had fared. He had been left to stoke by himself the entire time. But I was drowsy, and leaned against the wall of the deckhouse; I was sure, as I nodded off, that he was doing the same.

I awoke to the yipping of the dogs. The storm was still blowing fiercely and the deckhouse was dark and freezing. Despite the cold, the others were sleeping as I had been—Reinhold stretched on the floor with several of the dogs draped over him, Pago and Creely slumped on crates. On deck, the dogs were very disturbed, whining with excitement and turning in small circles. I peered out at the deck and onto the floes, straining to see what the trouble was. The swell was slow and regular and the ship seemed silent. Then I felt a slight tremor. I spun and looked into the lead behind us. At first I could see nothing, but then, to the south, I could see the lead had started to close. The tips of the long bay had already met, and the edge of our floe was beginning to ride up on the floe opposite. A grinding roar started, like a thousand engines revving and a thousand guns firing. The sliding stopped abruptly and a ridge began to form, both sides pressing in and up. The entire lead was narrowing. To the north, the edges met also, and a ridge exploded upward. Like a gigantic vise, the floes pressed together, causing our ship to shudder in its tiny harbor.

With a shout I woke my watch; Griffin's head appeared from the hatch before I had a chance to open it.

"What is it? What's happening?"

"It's the lead, sir, it's closing from both ends."

He rushed to the deck. The whole floe was shaking now, blocking out even the motion of the swell.

"Get the men on deck now!" he shouted, and turned back to the lead.

Pago ran to the fore hatch and yelled. The pressure ridges were not far now—about two hundred yards to the north and perhaps 150 to the south. The grinding roar had drowned out the sound of the storm completely.

*"Everyone to the ice!"* he shouted, and we scrambled for the ropes. Hume and Creely put West in a harness and lowered him; the rest of us dropped rapidly. Aziz appeared and slid down a rope.

"What about the dogs, sir?" asked Reinhold.

"They'll have to fend for themselves now," he replied. "There's no time to unload them."

And indeed there was not: the lead was barely fifty yards wide now, and the pressure ridges continued to close. They were seven or eight feet high to the south, and a hundred yards away. To the north they were farther—perhaps 150—but still closing. Chunks of ice the size of small houses rose up and toppled. At seventy-five yards to the south, the ridges slowed suddenly and stopped. I held my breath, suddenly aware of the whining of the dogs.

With a roar, the southern ridge started again, jerking forward at first, then sliding again with that same awful slowness. We retreated farther and watched helplessly as the ridge closed in to fifty yards, forty, thirty, twenty. The noise was utterly deafening now, shocking through our ears like lightning. The ice of our hole cracked and the ship rose up. The ridge plowed into the hull like a freight train, picking her up out of the water and spinning her sideways. She listed way over to the port side and shot across the ice, her copper sheeting peeling away like the skin of an orange. The pressure ridge formed behind her, closing out the last of the lead. The floe shuddered for a moment, and was still. The *Narthex* lay on her side like a wounded animal, the fresh dark wood showing like stripped flesh under the sheeting.

Griffin and Ash toured the ship to assess the damage. The screw had been badly bent and the rudder was damaged. We began dragging parts from the hold and helping Ash repair the screw. Hume and Creely had pulled the sheeting back toward the hull and tacked it on. Ash and Preston patched the rudder, which had been somewhat protected by the hull underneath but had had no protection against the ice intruding from behind. At last, Griffin ordered us to our bunks, where diligent, beloved Hunt met us with a pot of tea and we collapsed.

I believe I have never had such an awful sleep as that night. Shivering in my soggy clothes, I was too tired to fall asleep, my nerves still jangling from the closing of the lead. Each slight tremor of the ship brought me to full wakefulness, sick with terror that the ship was being crushed again. I imagined us on the ice as the ship split like a nut in a nutcracker and slid below, leaving us in the midst of the jostling pack with no food, no shelter, and the wind shrieking around us. I slept in short fits, shivering myself awake in fear and cold. The stove in our cabin glowed steadily, but it could not seem to reach the deep cold I had inside me. I could not remember how it felt to be warm.

We were not awakened for the first watch, nor the second, and with the exception of myself, I believe we slept well and soundly. By morning even I began to drowse and drift off.

The captain raised us at noon, and we shuffled wearily onto the deck, leaning to keep our balance. The wind had died and the air felt warmer, but the sky was still dark gray.

"Quite a pinch, gentlemen, quite a pinch. We'll do a full shift this afternoon to pack an emergency supply kit in the deckhouse in case we get pinched like that and need to abandon quickly. Should have been done a long time ago. After that's finished, we'll go half shifts to repair the hull and screw until the morning, unless the ice opens before then."

Hume was put in charge of the emergency kit, and we spent an hour ferrying out various supplies and bits of equipment: pemmican and biscuits, a lamp, tins of kerosene, a barrel of potatoes, one four-man tent, spare sleeping sacks, matches, a pot, two rifles and five hundred rounds of ammunition, fishing line and a hook, a knife and saw, a tarp, and some other odds and ends that he crammed into the back of the deckhouse as we finished. Hunt had cooked up some of the marled meat in a thick and savory stew, and we returned to our bunks warm and full, and slept like dead men.

Adney roused me for my watch at two in the morning. I emerged onto the deck into a soft gray twilight. The wind had disappeared and the air felt positively tropical. The ice was finally silent and still. The moon had settled, like a feather, in the eastern sky. Around the ship, broken ice lay in pieces, and the pressure ridges extended away like ancient battlements fallen into ruin. I felt as if I were an archaeologist, surveying the remains of an ancient, alien city. What temples these, with what altars raised? What truculent gods descended? In the gray light, their walls lay shattered, script indecipherable and lost, fragments now dispersed and buried in a thousand graves.

The sun slid over the horizon and washed the ice in soft shades of red and lavender and changed its shadows from razored black to velvet blue. Around me the ice creaked with the last of the swell, and the ship rested unstirring. I was loath to wake the captain and rouse the crew, and so I sat until my stomach began to protest and I rose to pull them into the day.

The ice showed no signs of yielding that day, though the temperature had risen higher and streams and pools of meltwater appeared on the floes. Reinhold took the dogs down to the ice and let them run freely. They took to it slowly at first, but were soon scampering like puppies, tumbling over each other, and racing playfully around the ship. We gathered on deck and took quick baths in sun-warmed water; some rinsed their filthy clothes and hung them in the rigging to dry. There was no sign of West, but Dr. Architeuthis emerged from his cabin to scrub himself off and rinse his clothes.

"Remarkable, isn't it," said Pago, who stretched beside him, "that the temperature can change so quickly and so completely?"

"Yes," said the doctor, "remarkable."

"It's a miracle," I said happily.

"A matter of pressure," he said sternly. "The cold air sweeps through and the warm comes in behind it."

"A miracle," I persisted.

"Now, now," said the doctor, shaking his finger at me like a schoolmaster. "You, of all, should know there are no miracles."

I could not tell whether he was joking or not.

"It is only a matter of time and effort before man will have marched into every dark and dusty corner of nature and set it in order."

"Oh I see," said Adney with mock gravity, "so you're a sort of intellectual washerwoman for the world."

"Exactly," said Dr. Architeuthis, smiling with our laughter. "Once fully understood and set in order, its various forces can be turned to our advantage—powering our cities and feeding our people. At every edge of the planet are dumb generators that are waiting to be subdued to the useful and the good. As soon as we can comprehend them and learn to direct them, our power over the world increases exponentially. Even here in this forbidding wasteland are great engines, waiting for us to ignite them.

"Imagine the power of the ice pack turned to the generation of electricity—all the miners in the world could retire immediately and devote themselves to more useful ends."

Reinhold snorted. "You'll never hook up the ice to a—a turbine. It's ridiculous."

"That is merely a matter of a turbine of sufficient design to use the force it would generate. I imagine that within a hundred years, these waters will be crowded with men making their livings off the power of the ice. It'll be tamed and settled in a generation or two."

"Men'll never come up here, besides the Eskimo. They'd never survive," Adney said.

The doctor snorted.

"Man needs only two things to survive here or anywhere: meat and heat. With fuel to drive his body and warmth enough to keep his extremities working, man can live as easily here as he can in the tropics. It's only our ignorance and weakness that keeps our own capacities hidden from us. I imagine that we will learn much that is useful in the course of this trip." He glanced, smiling, at Reinhold, who scowled in return.

"Allow me to demonstrate." He rose, took an axe, and descended to the ice. He chopped a hole about two feet across. Then, to our amazement, he stripped off his clothes and dove in. He bobbed to the surface, gasping, but with a look of steady concentration, his breathing returned to normal, and he continued his lecture:

"So you see, my body can quickly adapt itself even to this cold. Given the right fuel, I could remain here indefinitely, heated by my own internal combustion. The Eskimos have merely discovered the balance of fuel they need to remain warm. So it is with the whole of the world—it remains only for our reason to dispel our own feeble perceptions that keep us huddled in the dark." He remained treading water for a moment, then pulled himself onto the ice and dressed slowly. His body was a clear, empty white, as if bloodless.

It seemed astonishing to me—as if he had with that one act conquered the whole of the ice we had been battling against.

"Quite a trick, Doctor," said Pago when he had returned to the deck. "Where'd you learn it?"

"In Holland as a boy," said the doctor, laughing. "It was the first of my experiments. I was testing the body's reaction to extreme temperatures." His face turned serious again. "I have come, in part, to help us prepare for the coming ice."

"What ice is that?" asked Pago.

"We are enjoying a brief respite, in geological terms, but ours is in fact an ice age. It shall not be so many generations of men before the glaciers will sweep down again, and man must be prepared to overmaster the ice. It is the focus of many scientists."

Dr. Architeuthis droned on, and I climbed the shrouds to see if the ice had opened. In the crow's nest I found Captain Griffin, scanning the horizon with his glass.

"Had enough of the good doctor?" he asked without lowering it.

"Yes sir," I replied, laughing. "Enough school for today. How does it look? Any signs of a breakup?"

"We'll be under way tomorrow—with luck through the leads. The trouble is that we're drifting south with this pack. We've lost more than fifteen miles already, and it'll cost us in time and coal to make it up."

I had had no sensation of drifting. The world of the pack seemed totally immobile, and it was a cruel trick that it was carrying us away from our goal.

"Are you sure?" I found myself asking.

"Of course I'm sure," he snapped, closing the glass impatiently. He frowned at me and clambered down to the deck.

I glared out at the ice, wishing that I could batter my head against it until it gave way before me. This feeling stayed with me through the day, and I found myself churning in my bunk that night, still furious.

The following morning the ice showed clear signs of breakup; dark leads were opening in the distance, and I could see the curling tendrils of frost smoke rising in the distance. By noon we were all aching to be away, aching for the work. Griffin had us pull out the ice anchor and try to warp our way over the floe, but even with all of us on the windlass, it would not go. At five, after a day of staring out at the unmoving ice, Griffin finally gave the order for us to blow it.

Ash and Preston descended to the ice, and Ash had Preston drill a staggered set of holes every ten yards to the far end of the floe along the line of the newer ice. He set the charges, returned to the ship, and handed the detonator to Griffin. Griffin glared at the ice for a moment, then set off the charges. They blew in sequence, starting closest to the ship and moving away quickly. At first the charges seemed to have made only a series of holes, but as the smoke cleared I saw narrow cracks between several of them.

We set the anchor closer to the ship this time, figuring that we needed only to tilt it to starboard and it would slide into the water by itself. The anchor set, we moved to the winch and crowded onto the beams, locking shoulders like rugby players in a scrum. We strained, grunted, bellowed, rocking on our heels. The ship shuddered, leaned, and the floe split with a deafening crack. The ship dropped into the water, throwing us all to the deck. We rushed to dislodge the ice anchor and move the ship into the channel. Griffin ordered us ahead, and the ship hummed with the turning of the screw. We nudged our way, scraping the sides as we went. After interminable minutes, we shook ourselves free of the floe entirely and moved out into open water. We danced and shouted as we moved to raise the sails, and we started a rowdy shanty. The sails shook and filled, and we were under way again at last. Though it was past midnight, the sun sat gaily on the horizon, as if to watch over us as we sped along. It proved to be a most maddening spectator.

We moved quickly for about five miles before the lead narrowed again, and we were forced to pick our way, by stealth and by force. We commenced a section of the trip that can only be described as a battle. It was to last for ten days in all, and its parts blur mercifully in my memory.

The most difficult and most maddening part of this battle was not the unceasing labor, or the frustration at our lack of progress, but the deafening uproar of the ice as it ground against itself and against our ship. There was, first, a constant rumble, like the grinding of giant teeth; then there was the crack, like shots, of the ice splitting, and a whine and squeal like tearing metal. Occasionally, the entire pack shook with deep booms, the echoes of distant catastrophes. The effect of the whole was as if we were trapped inside a gigantic machine that was being forced to work far beyond its capacity and was straining and dragging its way to a final collapse.

These torments were exacerbated by the unsetting sun. It wobbled along over the horizon, circling drunkenly but never disappearing. Thus, the ceaselessness of the work was mirrored by the endlessness of the day. After three days of light and noise, how I craved darkness and silence! I grew to hate the staring Arctic day and its deafening racket. We, being deprived of our normal measure of rest and peace, grew bleary-eyed and irritable.

The deeper we went into the ice, the more we relied on the boilers to drive us. I was ordered to help Aziz stoke and manage the boilers, and so was relieved from the sun and the crashing ice. Stoking was rough work, but it was warm, and the darkness and silence were a wonderful respite from the world outside.

Aziz was an excellent companion—hardworking, uncomplaining, and thoughtful. He rigged a kettle over the boiler and made pots of a smoky, spicy tea. He had an amazing range of books crammed onto his small shelves—philosophy, poetry, accounts of the great explorers. He told me their stories as we worked, of Ibn Battutah in the middle of the Sahara discovering people who lived in houses made of salt, and of the eunuch Zheng He sailing from China in twenty-seven thousand ships. He told me about Ubar, a spice traders' city made of red silver that was swallowed by the Sea of Sands in Arabia.

He asked with great interest about my own travels—the war and my desertion, the riot, how I came to be aboard. He asked the questions in such a way that my own actions seemed to take shape as I answered—that there was beneath my meandering a shape and force, a searching, though with its object still not clear.

"How did you come to be aboard?" I asked cautiously.

"That," he said, laughing, "is a story for another time." And instead he described for me the Kyrgyz tribesmen training hunting falcons in the Alai mountains of central Asia.

On the fifteenth of June, we were fighting our way through a region of low pressure ridges and small, crumbling floes. Griffin sent me below to help Aziz as usual. We kept the boilers on full, and battered, retreated, and battered again.

The rest of the crew sat on the deck, waiting to be called to action, and I believe this long period of inactivity more than anything led to their decision. We became aware that something had changed after a long silence from the deckhouse. The engine was not engaged, though the boilers were fully stoked, but we were given no new orders. We collapsed on the coal, happy for the rest, and Aziz brought me some water. For a time we rested, but as we recovered, we began to get uneasy.

"Do you think we're frozen in?" said Aziz.

"I doubt it," I replied, "because if we were, then Griffin would have ordered us to turn down the steam."

We sat awhile, then Aziz rose and called up the tube. There was no response.

"What do you think?"

"I'll go up and see what the trouble is," I said, and made my way to the deck. The crew was massed around the deckhouse, scowling and silent.

"What's happening up here, boys? Why've we stopped?"

"We've had enough, is why we've stopped," said Reinhold angrily. "We're working like dogs out here and we decided that we'd at least like the dignity of knowing why. Captain tried to tell us that we'd know soon enough, but we've heard too much of that. We need to know, and to agree, or else we told him that we can just drift south until we're free of the ice. He can put me off if he wants, but I'll be damned if I'm going to keep working myself to death."

Several of the others seconded Reinhold's view vociferously. Some others—notably Preston—had not joined this group but were still at their places, not opposing, but not joining either. Hume was pretending to be busy on the foredeck. Griffin was nowhere to be seen.

"The captain's gone below to talk it over with West and the doctor," said Reinhold. "You might as well stay for the fireworks."

I moved out of the deckhouse and sat on a coil of rope, displacing a sleepy dog. A few moments later, the hatch swung open and Griffin and West emerged, both of them grim-faced. The crew gathered around. Griffin spoke first.

"Gentlemen," he said, his voice shaking, "let me first say that I am extremely disappointed in your conduct. You have violated the terms of our contract, which specify your wages and duties, and give you no right to refuse your work." He glared at us each in turn.

"If it were left to me, you would be dumped unceremoniously

on the ice and left to make your own way. I warn you that if there is even a whisper of this behavior again, you will be prosecuted for mutiny on our return. The ship is Mr. West's and it goes where he commands it; if you will not go farther, we will put you in a whaleboat with food and supplies, and you can go where you wish. Are there any of you who wish to leave? If you stay, I expect, under the penalty of death, that you will follow your orders from here forward. Who will leave?"

We were all silent; I hung my head with shame. For all his faults, Griffin was unfailingly decent, and he worked harder than any of us. I felt very selfish and petty before him.

Griffin stepped back and West stepped forward.

"I understand, gentlemen, that you are curious as to the object of our search." He smiled broadly but without warmth. "I am afraid that I cannot offer you a definitive answer at this point, but perhaps I can help you understand my reluctance to say more. We are headed out to the north of Lancaster Sound—above the North Water of the whalers. We will be moving into territory that has never been explored fully, but I have strong reason to believe that we will find something there so extraordinary that if anyone were to catch wind of it before we had seized it for our own, we would never be able to keep it."

The men shifted on their feet. Pago put his hands into his pockets.

"That sounds like damn lies to me," said Reinhold. "Just tell us what it is, and let us keep the secret for ourselves. Once we know and agree, we'll work that much harder—knowing what we're working for. Besides, we're on a ship—there's no one to tell."

West turned to him, his smile turning harder.

"Think of it as a vault which hides your money, and myself your banker—would you have me give each man a set of keys and let him come and go as he pleases? I thought not. I am protecting it for you from the loose tongues of your fellows, and you can trust me when I assure you that not one of you will be disappointed. We may still meet with whalers in the sound, and so we must continue our discretion. I, for one, have staked my life and considerable fortune upon the object of our quest. You will be made aware of all of the details as soon as we have passed beyond Lancaster Sound and left our final letters. Is that satisfactory?" There was some grumbling, but the group had lost its force and no one dared to speak further.

"Then, gentlemen, to your work and to your fortunes." West turned from them and returned below. Griffin ascended the mast in silence, and began giving orders. I lingered on the deck for a moment watching the men disperse; West, to his credit, had turned their anger from him to mistrust for their companions. Men glared and glowered at each other, and worked with angry carelessness, thrashing the ropes around and letting the sails jerk to the end of their halyards before restraining them. The general discontent had fragmented into tiny furies, each man harboring and breeding his own. I hoped we would not be in the pack much longer.

*six*

As we moved north, the pack began to change in character. Where there had been large, low floes with pressure ridges between them, there were smaller floes and broader leads. There were also more icebergs, carving their own, often contradictory paths through the pack. They created many lanes for us to follow, and enabled us to make excellent progress. The icebergs, too, changed as we sailed north: their edges became sharper, their summits higher. Farther south, they had had smooth, sweeping lines and were mostly gray-white in color; here they showed angles of fracture, like gemstones, fresh from the glaciers that had spawned them, and tended toward a dazzling blue-white, but with a full range of greens, pinks, and yellows.

At noon on the third of July, the coast of Greenland appeared on the horizon and we made directly for it. The coastline consisted of sheer rocky cliffs carved out by low glacial valleys. The water was thick with bergs along the coast and we had to pick our way carefully. Some lanes appeared to be wide open, but were blocked by ridges of submarine ice; others closed quickly as icebergs collided with great momentum. In the pack, we could rely on the low ice to keep us somewhat safe—if we got badly pinched, we would simply rise up on the ice edge. Here, sheer walls rose higher than the tops of the mast. If we were to get pinched, there would be no escape, no blasting free. I kept a nervous eye on the barometer. The icebergs moved with a silent majesty; it seemed impossible that they could glide so noiselessly past, and yet there they went. Gone was the crash and battle of the pack, replaced by the cascade of winds through these corridors of ice. There were still explosions occasionally, to be sure, when the icebergs collided, unearthly shudderings as submarine ridges ground at each other, and great splashes as chunks of ice melted free and fell into the water, or shot up from the bottom as if fired by submarine cannons.

We tried to skirt them by hugging the coast. Most of the larger icebergs ran aground while the *Narthex,* with her shallow draft, was able to slip past. As the coastline steepened, however, they drifted right up to the face of the cliffs, and we were forced to dodge out to sea. Finally we ran into a huge iceberg that was aground in the deep water and had trapped a shelf of ice behind it. We were forced to turn south and then west to skirt the edge of the pack that had accumulated behind it. We moved out of sight of the coast again before we were able to continue north into a dense field of icebergs.

Griffin was very animated in the crow's nest, muttering to himself, debating his invisible companion, swinging his glass fretfully from side to side, snapping it shut, and jerking it open. He stood with his hands on the rail and strained forward, willing a way to open. He threw down curt words to the silent Creely.

At times Griffin would bob up and down, like a mating bird, entreating the icebergs to shift, for lanes to open. His voice, when I could hear it, shifted from pleading to commanding, soliciting, tempting, begging, challenging, cursing. He cast down his head in despair as a lead narrowed, then swung it forward again, his eyes hopeful, his body tensed. He shouted at us in a frenzy, then subsided into murmuring. The wind was almost undetectable and the engines still, yet we glided steadily through the water. The sun was low in the northwest, the sky a golden gray over us, and we were lost amid the velvety shadows of the icy peaks.

As the night wore on, Griffin's soliloquy spun itself into an incantation, wove us into the ice like fog into mountains. He battled no longer, no longer tried to tempt or bully, to challenge; instead he supplicated quietly and earnestly, his voice even and soft, a gentle paean over us. Under the low sun's light, the ridges of the icebergs were extraordinary reds and yellows, shot through with brass and copper, the shadows hyacinthine, blue-black. Rays caught and reflected by the tips of the icebergs refracted through facets, pearled, coruscated on the water, cast light where there should have been shadow. There was no white and no black, only rich and vivid colors, a world lit wholly, colored wholly. Through this pageant, the ship moved darkly, a void in this world of light, driven by the chanting hymn of the captain.

We approached a gap between two massive faces, their tops towering over our mast, their bulk blocking suddenly even faint hints of the distant sun. They rose like ramparts in the darkness, with flying buttresses spreading off to the sides. We nosed into a gap about forty feet wide. No glint of light showed in the distance. The soaring walls pulled my breath from me, impelled my eyes upward. I watched the last edge of the light disappear as the passage curved and a luminous darkness fell. We sailed thus in silence and darkness for long moments until, from the crow's nest, the light of a single lantern flared. Griffin stood rigidly upright as the walls closed in; the passage became scarcely twenty feet wide, the spars nearly scraping on either side. I could see the edges of the fractured ice, just beyond the end of the davits, and still we did not slow and still we did not turn. The murmur of Griffin's voice held us transfixed, joined the lapping-past of the water.

High above the mast, a strip of golden red appeared. Its glow spread down the upper reaches of the walls, suffusing them with crimson and saffron. It was as if we were submerged, as if we had spent our lives in the muck of the ocean depths and for a moment had caught sight of the world of air and light, the dazzling, distant, alien world of the surface, and could see it, unreachable, over us.

As quickly as the glow had built, it subsided. The iceberg's effulgence gave way to the glare of the morning as the passage opened and we sailed out into the ordinary yellow of an Arctic day.

Release came finally on the twelfth of July. A lead widened and then simply dropped away, and the icebergs faded behind us. A few small floes straggled behind, and a few stately bergs sailed on the horizon, but otherwise there was only beautiful blue-black water as far as the eye could see. The day was clear and bright, as if the sky went on forever, and a steady wind pushed up from the south. It was exhilarating to stand on deck and hear only the whip of the sails in the wind and the breaking of waves beneath the bows. Freed from the backbreaking frustrations of the ice and the quiet menace of the icebergs, men were themselves again—enthusiastic, hopeful, cheerful. Shanties burst out in gushing streams and men sped happily to their tasks. Like that, the world had righted itself and ran as it should, responding to our demands of it and rewarding our labor with progress. The promise of knowing what we sought hung out over the horizon, and we strained to meet it.

The waters we sailed into were teeming with life. Gulls descended on us in squadrons, squawking at our dogs and drawing frenzies of barking in return. Kittiwakes and guillemots dove sharply after fish, and sleek flashes of silver passed in the water as seals did the same. Arctic geese and eiders passed overhead in massive flocks, darkening the sky for miles and taking hours and hours to pass. Ghostly clouds of plankton and tiny shrimp hung in the translucent water. Adney spent the days with the rifle on his shoulder, procuring ducks and dovekies to liven our steady diet of salt pork stew and biscuits. The tops of the cliffs were still snowy, but sheltered stretches showed brown and green in gently sloping valleys. The icebergs when they passed now seemed like companions, fellows, throwing off cascades of blue-white meltwater like gentle hurrahs. Great herds of walrus crowded the rocky shore, lolling in the sun, their bellows and grunts echoing over the water. Once, in the distance, we saw the blue strength of whales pulse beneath the surface.

We sailed along the coast for a day, skirting the mouths of two deep fjords; the waterfalls off their cliffs looked like gateways to faery kingdoms, impossibly sparkling in the sun. The cliffs bristled with birds and the water exploded with fish.

In the evening—though there was none; the sun remained the same throughout, only nodding to the horizon in the west—we moored in the bay of a small island. Adney, Pago, Griffin, Dr. Architeuthis, and Reinhold went ashore first. Adney and Pago were dispatched to hunt walrus and seal for the dogs, while the others hunted for rock samples. Those who felt we were seeking a mine—Hume in particular—walked the deck with a pronounced smugness. The officers returned with bags of rocks, while the men returned draped in meat that they threw in a heap for the dogs.

After their frenzy, the dogs lounged, their bellies distended. The crew sat on deck, waiting for Dr. Architeuthis, who was analyzing the samples he had collected. Soon, Griffin came up from the officers' quarters.

"Hume, take four men ashore with picks and shovels. The rest of you will go in the other boat with the doctor."

"Gold, sir?" called out Adney.

Griffin snorted.

"Coal, gentlemen. Just coal."

Pago sagged, as did Hume. We went ashore and tromped through the snow to a ravine where dark veins of coal ran diagonally upward, like the shadow of flames. We set into mining and had half filled the empty sacks when we heard the welcome sound of Hunt's bell. Rather than keep us from our work, the captain had Hunt bring the dinner ashore. Two watches filled the scuttles and we were away.

It was a low, gray morning as we moved north, the sky mimicking a range of low, gray-brown hills, the wind from the southwest carrying a hint of rain. I ached from the mining and longed for my berth. The boat moved sluggishly, and the sails, heavy and stiff with frost, opened reluctantly. At least there was no ice.

In the afternoon we rounded a long cape and saw a remarkable range of cliffs to the north. They were still covered with snow, but the snow was tinged with long, broad streaks of red, like the upwelling of faint rivers of blood beneath the surface. Griffin had moved up to the rail beside me and he spoke softly, almost under his breath: "And the land cannot be cleansed of the blood that is shed therein but by the blood of him that shed it."

He stood gazing for long moments, his jaw clenched tightly, then turned and returned to the deckhouse. We moved slowly past the red cliffs. They seemed clearly to be a sign, but whether it was a crying out of past wrong, or an augury of the future, I could not tell. I was happy when they disappeared to the south, though I remained troubled by them that evening in my berth.

As we moved through Lancaster Sound under a quick breeze and flashes of sun, I was ordered to leave Aziz and assist the doctor again. Architeuthis ran endless strings of tiny red bottles out behind the boat, and sent me out to sound, or up the mast to read gauges. He lit fires of different materials on the platforms of small balloons and we mapped the dispersion of the smoke at different altitudes. I dropped brightly colored fleets of wood in the water and mapped them as they were borne away. The crew's only work was shifting the ship as he caught some new breeze or current. First we sailed north, then east, then west and south again. We doubled, and circled, and anchored in the middle of nowhere, then left again abruptly. The doctor seemed not to sleep at all but to be constantly prowling; I did my best to keep up, but was soon stumbling, my eyes red-rimmed. Dr. Architeuthis dismissed me and continued to work.

We sighted land to the north on the eighteenth—low, unremarkable gravel islands. This part of the sound was more barren— we saw only a few birds and no seals. The islands were identical heaps of brown and black rocks and dirty gray ice. After passing several of them, we turned into a small bay and dropped anchor. Dr. Architeuthis and West went ashore, rowing the boat themselves, as we sat and smoked and stomped to stay warm. I perched beside Creely, whose fingers ceaselessly knotted and unknotted a length of rope. After several long hours, they returned without a word. We weighed anchor and continued along the coast. This went on for several days—nosing into bays and going ashore, then moving on again. Once we sailed into a bay or strait for two days, before retreating again. The most remarkable feature of the landscape throughout was its drab sameness; Adney joked that it was a gravel mine we were starting.

On the afternoon of the twenty-third, after a day of circling and testing, we were gathered on the deck as usual. We moored in a channel perhaps four miles across. Dr. Architeuthis had been running his tests all day, but now he stood calmly behind West, the traces of a smile clinging to his lips. West looked out over us imperiously for a moment, then spoke:

"Gentlemen, we have come to our point of turning. We move now into unexplored and uninhabited territory, where we will remain, with luck, until the end of our voyage. Tomorrow we will build a cairn on that headland"—he pointed to the east—"and there deposit a record of our plans and any such letters and notices that you would like to leave behind. You may occupy yourselves tonight in that endeavor. Tomorrow night I will reveal to you the purpose and nature of our voyage and detail to you your stake in it. You are entering the arena of your trials. If there are any of you who do not wish to go, we will put you ashore here with such supplies as you need to survive. In a week, these waters will be teeming with whalers and you will have no problem being picked up and returned to New Bedford. None of you will be compelled to come, but neither can you turn back after tomorrow. From here we go only forward." He looked over us, smiled his cold, officious smile, and returned to his cabin.

Dinner that evening was surprisingly somber. There was little speculation about our fortunes, about mines or whales. Men sat and ate in silence. Even Adney was subdued; he volunteered to write a letter for those who could not.

I retired to my bunk early with a scrap of paper and a pen and set out to compose a leter. I began several times and crossed out my words. I had no one to write to—my baffled parents, I supposed, because they were obligated to care whether I lived or died, because they should care how I met my end, if end I was to meet. I had no substantial friends from the tavern, from the war. I had passed away from them now; I had begun a new life on board the *Narthex,* one only faintly connected to my previous one.

Writing to no one, I struggled to find something to say—was I writing a will? A testament? A philosophy? I had none; I understood nothing. There was nothing I could venture that did not seem at once ludicrous or trite, that was not the vague and false regurgitation of some other, better mind, the reflection, no doubt, of some other, better life.

For a moment I wondered where that life was being led and who led it, wondered if the air might taste different, or the light of the morning pass brighter through those eyes. I looked out at the crew in their berths and back among the men in my battalion—dusty, sunburned faces—back to the sailors in the tavern, to my poor bewildered parents. I thought of all of them stumbling into their days, and wondered who might see differently—if the doctor, with his instruments, or Aziz in the darkness—if the world shaped itself around them. I had the vague hope that whatever West had promised was true—that it could be worth his health and fortunes, that it could make mine. I tried to ask what it was I wanted, what I might hope for.

Perhaps I should suck rocks. Then at least I would have something to crack my teeth on, and feel the bits of teeth in my mouth, feel the unnatural jaggedness of broken teeth, taste the salt of real blood. Then at least I should taste something real, the weight of a real answer to no question, but an answer nonetheless, and the accompanying taste of salt and tooth and stone.

You hold back in your heart the secret hope that there is actually glory to be had, that there will be a day when a choice is presented to you and in that choice the hope for a new world that this one so badly needs. If you seek madly, if you flee and ask and blunder, batter your way against the world, the days pass the same, each with its pain, its build and crest, each with its slide into darkness, and you amid them are revealed the same: you stand naked, compromised, barren.

And thus I lay there for long minutes as that blank face accused and indicted me, blank page for my blank mind, blank my history. I thought for a moment of Seaman Brommer, of his chest with its neat, careful folds, and his grim-faced parents. Surely it was not love that made him keep their picture; surely it was habit or guilt; surely it was fear of being exposed as alone, a last insulation. Surely love is not such a weak thing, such a twisted and lost, such a distorted, compromised thing, surely that is not love. I knew not. I had none. I crumpled my paper and I slept.

The deck was cold and the light weak; it did not feel like a day to be seeking fortunes, but a day for hiding out, for licking wounds, for waiting again, and perhaps tomorrow would be brighter, fresher, would open to work more readily. West stood on the deck and looked out at the headland. He heard my footsteps and dropped his head to one side.

"Kane, morning. Are you ready?"

"For what, sir?"

"To meet your fate, son."

"I don't know, sir. Hard to say. I need some sleep."

He chuckled.

"Some sleep indeed." We stood awhile in silence and looked out at the barren headland. Other men made their way to the deck and we all stood in silence. Griffin emerged and stood in respectful silence, then Dr. Architeuthis, then Aziz. It was as if West were waiting for some signal, some clarion call to blast out from the headlands to send us charging into battle. The wind whipped at the sails and the gravelly headland stood dumb. He turned to me at last.

"Well, Kane? Let's go."

We lowered the boats and made our way to the beach. West charged up the scree slope while we plodded behind. He had already begun to gather a circle of stones when we reached him. He stopped as we arrived and let us take over, brushing his hands on his coat to restore some of his dignity. His eyes glowed behind his glasses.

Once we had gathered a substantial pile of stones, he motioned for us to stop. With great care, he placed a small silver cylinder in the center of the circle he had made. Griffin produced a clean meat tin and offered it around for letters. Men added their scraps and ends to the tin and Griffin sealed it with a wax stopper. Then, still silent, he motioned us forward and we buried them beneath the rocks. We built a tower about seven feet high and filled the gaps between the rocks with sand. Over this we poured water and let the whole thing freeze solid. We stood a moment with out heads hung, and so buried our last records, so marked the boundary between known and unknown. I trembled a little to see our pitiful assertion when what we needed was a shriek of terror. We made our way down to the boats without looking back and began to launch them when Adney took a spare oar from beneath the thwarts and rushed back up the hill. He jammed the oar in the top of the cairn and, stripping to the waist, tied his red undershirt to the top. He gave a wild yell of defiance and joy and raced back down to us.

As we pulled away I was glad to see the shirt snapping smartly in the wind. It was the one spot of color in the whole of the dreary horizon, the one spot of man in that whole world of rock and ice.

part two

Brute Province

*seven*

We dropped anchor in the twilight, unremarkable miles stretching behind us. We had dragged along the dreary gray-brown gravel coast all day. Black water rippled lifelessly under a northerly breeze. I was even relieved to see the return of bobbing floes flashing in the distance. Color was draining out of the land, leaching into the black sea; there were no seals and a few stray, desolate birds.

After dinner, we were summoned to the doctor's cabin for a meeting—*the* meeting—and yet, for our months of talk, we were oddly subdued. Aziz, I noticed, was not among us. We shuffled in and arrayed ourselves on crates that had been placed in a semicircle around the low white laboratory table. The table was made of unblemished white marble, with a small groove cut around the edge that ran into a hole in one corner. The laboratory was large, filling nearly all of the aft quarter starboard, and had no bed or any sign of personal effects; I suppose the doctor slept on the slab. Arrayed around the crates was his careful architecture of instrumentation—globes and beakers brimming with colored oils, spinning governors, glass tubes running into heated copper coils and out again into balloons that aspirated like living creatures. Crystals slowly formed in delicate glass cages and slowly dissolved in others; heavy drops fell from suspended tanks into tiny vials; hidden generators clicked, and the steam hissed, and there was the sharp, acrid smell of chemicals eating through metal. A row of glass terrariums held large balls of vine along the windows, each the size of a man. The lower part of the walls was covered by racks of bottles and beakers; each was labeled by his tiny, precise hand. They were organized by both color—all in shades of red, from a light, whitish pink to a dark, black red in order—and size, ranked like tiny soldiers ready to head off to the slaughter.

The area above the bottles held a single chart that stretched the length of the cabin. It was covered with marks—astronomical, navigational, geographic, geological, hydrographical. There were notations of time, temperature, current strengths and water temperature at various depths, salinity, wind strength and air temperature at ascending heights, cloud shapes and colors, rock formations, elevations, depths, light strengths and angles of refraction, measures of humidity, rates of ice formation and dissolution, strengths, thicknesses, and, of course, wave heights and frequency—each in the same tiny hand as the bottles. I could see at last the fruit of my long labors—my own small observations translated into the doctor's hand. The notations were cut through with a webwork of lines of dense complexity—arcs intersected over measured angles marked out on overlapping grids of the same reds that distinguished the bottles. Peering closely, I discerned that the arcs were not smooth curves but in fact themselves composed of a smaller webbing of rigidly straight lines, each angled slightly beyond the last; beneath these lines were others, fainter, infinitesimally small, with their own sets of notations and shadowy calculations. As I stared, the surface of the map receded before me, each set of lines giving way to another and another beneath, cut into grids upon grids and hinting at grids beyond, each spot of clarity shattering silently into its component trajectories and their tangents and sub-tangents. The effect on the color of the overlapping lines was painfully refined up close, but at a distance resolved into dark crimson gashes butchering the wall into blocks.

The door shut and I sat quickly on my crate as West and the doctor took their places at the slab. West waited until we were silent, then pulled out a small tattered notebook. He placed it with elaborate ceremony in the center of the table and paused.

"Here, gentlemen," he said finally, "is our mine, our well of whales." He looked around at us and smiled his heatless smile. We leaned in. His thumbs were pressed white against the edges of the drab cover, as if it threatened to explode and he was struggling to contain it.

"This is the journal of a man—a Dr. Felix Strabo—a scientific dabbler and eccentric who happens to have been my great-uncle. A peculiar man from birth, according to my grandfather—obsessed with insects. He dedicated his life to the study of the frost-resistant genitalia of beetles. Apparently he was always compiling a master study of his investigations, the magnum opus that would reveal to the rest of us what these genitalia had told him. Unfortunately that will remain lost to us, as his work was cut short by his disappearance some fifty-seven years ago. This notebook drifted up in a cod net and was sent to my grandfather four years later; the water destroyed much of it, but what remains is intriguing.

"The journal itself was nearly thrown out by my grandfather, its markings indecipherable and assumed to have been ruined by the immersion. But a colleague of my great-uncle's was struck by the uniformity of the degradation to the text and worked to find some patterns in it. What he found was the remarkable first mystery of the journal.

"My great-uncle had spent many years in the Amazon as a part of his studies, owing to the great profusion of beetles and to the deep knowledge of their variety, habits, and characteristics possessed by the savages there.

"He spent many years with one tribe in particular, the Nemoami. They were a sort of beetle-worshiping group; a great part of their medicine and the bulk of their cuisine was based on beetles. They had their own language, which fascinated my great-uncle nearly as much as the teeming masses of beetles. It drew from them a whole vocalization based on the clicking and skittering of the beetles. They had no written language, of course, being savage—in fact they were very angry when old Strabo proposed to help them create one, and resisted it mightily.

"Their language was remarkably unstable—it had few words that ever remained the same. Most of their communications consisted of entirely new words, made up by the speaker in the process of communicating. Even when relating the speech of another person, these confused people used different words, or made up their own, or changed them around entirely. Part of the problem lay in the structure of the language itself; it had few nouns; thus they had no way to fix things, to hold them steady and define them in order to communicate clearly. Instead, they relied on a string of verbs, of descriptions of states and transitions between states. They had a great terror of time, you see, and refused to attempt to override it by fixing definitions onto things. Their world was a fluid outpouring of constant newness, where a tree in one minute was no longer a tree in the next, though it may return to being a tree, or at least treelike, in the future. Their role as speakers and observers was one of reporting, not of establishing, and their notion of identity was not one of definition, but one of revelation.

"As you can imagine, this made them nearly incomprehensible

to each other and an utter mystery to strangers—even if you managed to effectively translate a word or thought once, it had already changed once you had repeated it. In order to keep up with the stream of new words, it was necessary to be in conversation without interruption so that you could carry along the meaning to the new words as they emerged. This was not a problem for them— they were a small and gregarious tribe, and were used to understanding this endless flow of new meanings."

"What do we care?" said Reinhold. "Are we needing to talk to the beetles?" West regarded him evenly, then continued as if no question had been raised.

"Dr. Strabo believed that he could help them by teaching them English—just the mental energy saved from trying to understand each other would free them up tremendously for other things. At first they were amused by him—they thought he was simpleminded and were entertained greatly by the simplicity of his speech. Being used to a constant stream of new words, they learned the words of English very rapidly.

"But as he patiently repeated them over and over and over, they became alarmed; they were afraid he would become stuck in time somehow if he did not continue to move along—that his thoughts would become fixed and his bodily functions would slow and eventually he would turn into stone.

"They mocked him at first, but gradually grew afraid for themselves, that he would spread this thickening to their own thoughts, like a disease—would moor them in the forest and turn them into stones. He thought they were terrified of learning, that their heads would fill and burst, but the simpler he tried to make the lessons, the more upset they became—and they, in turn, believed that he was starting to turn to stone in front of them, speaking fewer and fewer words, then simply single words over and over. They packed up and retreated into the rain forest, pushing him away violently and threatening him when he attempted to follow them.

"After a week or so they returned to him—to see what he looked like made of stone, no doubt. They were astonished to see him walking around, but shrank back again when he repeated the same set of words he had when they saw him last. Puzzled, he tried to speak to them in French, and they came forward again, translating it effortlessly into their own tongue—until he began to repeat himself again and they became wary. Then he switched to German and then Latin, and the little Italian that he knew, and a few words of Russian. They were delighted, and began to chatter freely again, leaping enthusiastically into whatever tongue he offered—supposing that his fever had passed and his thoughts were beginning to unlock again. Perhaps he wouldn't turn to stone after all. As they spoke, he took notes on the sounds and sound patterns and began to understand the dynamics of their language—for there were no stable structures. The sounds formed and re-formed in cascades of new meanings, and there were patterns to the cycles that he could follow if he listened without interruption.

"He began to understand at last how their language worked, if not comprehend its meaning, and he was surprised to hear in their own speech echoes of English and French—constructions and patterns that were familiar to his ear, though broken and re-formed. At first he assumed they were parroting badly what he had tried to teach them, or were mocking him again to themselves, but as they cycled back again and again in different forms, he began to see how the invention built on itself, taking pieces of recent speech and blending them with new pieces and then blowing them apart again and rebuilding new words with the pieces.

"Here is a passage where he describes it:

It is like a dance of the mind, their speaking, and each of them speaks a kind of private language that only mingles with the others at the edges—it seems profuse, exploding like the rain forest—it suits what they see—when new varieties of the *alto-canus nemoamus* emerge in the space of seven or eight generations—within a single week—it seems foolish to attempt to shackle its identity to a single word.

"And so he ceased trying to teach them English and worked to learn their speech—he felt it was the best way to gather their understanding of the coleoptera, and eventually became convinced it was the only way to understand beetles at all.

"He devised his own written notations for it, and the remainder of his journal is composed entirely in that notation. As you can imagine, it was therefore fiendishly difficult to translate, as it requires one to understand the leaps and gaps of his own mind as it creates new words for the same objects or ideas. It has been a painstaking process to reconstruct, and even then we cannot be sure we have accurately tracked the progression of his thoughts. But as I came to understand some bare hints of what it contained, I became increasingly interested in its contents."

"Get on with it," grumbled Reinhold.

"I was able to fill in many of the gaps in Happy Strabo's life, and unveil for us a discovery most remarkable—the second mystery of the journal. My family had thought Strabo was safely ensconced in the research faculty of a small university, hunched over his bugs—didn't keep a close eye. He was no sailor—hated to travel—and yet according to this journal, he had sailed out of Boston on a twelfth of June in the sloop *Blythe,* outfitted for a two-year solo voyage through the Canadian Arctic in search of the fossilized remains of prehistoric beetles.

"Clearly mad, he sailed north into the pack alone, but—fools and children—somehow made his way north into Lancaster Sound and began exploring the inlets along the northwestern coast, digging into the frozen gravel for traces of his precious genitalia even as his little sloop fell apart.

"As he passed north out of Lancaster Sound, he encountered a number of unusual phenomena: rapidly developing storm systems with far heavier snow than is generally found in this region; sudden, powerful currents that pulled his ship from side to side and once drove it backwards through the water despite full sails; and air and water temperatures that diverged greatly from anywhere else in the Arctic.

"Unfortunately he had little chance to explore these at any length. The storms damaged his ship badly, and he was forced to remain in the hold, pumping and patching as he drifted further and further to the north. He found himself in a bay free of pack ice but ringed by two great glaciers that calved masses of icebergs, and between them was a vast high wall of ice he called the Barrier. The bay itself was filled with dense fog and chaotic turbulence from the constant flipping of the icebergs.

"With his ship leaking steadily, his rudder and mast gone, he limped forward, looking for a stable shelf of ice so he could safely abandon. As he moved north, however, the entire Barrier disappeared—it was an epic mirage, created by a current of extremely warm water that passed down between the glaciers. Once past the mirage, his ship ran aground, and he waded through the now-temperate waters to the shore.

"He made his way along the channel, the air and water temperatures rising steadily. At the end, he found a temperate archipelago covered by trees of fantastic colors that grew from the heat of the earth rather than the sun—a lush Garden of Eden in the heart of the Arctic—and the rest, coleopterists, is unfortunately lost.

"Imagine: a temperate archipelago in the heart of the Arctic! It will be our triumph: Westland! It will be our fortunes."

"But sir," said Adney, hesitantly, "how so? Is there gold there?"

The doctor laughed.

"Trade in your beads—here is the new world," he said.

West leaned over the table.

"There will be more than enough shiny trinkets for you mockingbirds—the rotation of the earth acts as a centrifuge, separating the heavier metals from the lighter, and concentrating them near the openings on the surface, where they may work their way out. But that is the least and smallest of our rewards—trust me, it will seem like nothing. Perhaps we will find something beyond gold—something unique from the hidden core of the planet, and so rarer and a thousand times more valuable. Whatever treasures we find—and there are sure to be many—we will divide between us, in proportion to our role. We shall each have lands named for us, and plants and unknown animals. Whose name will grace the gateway to these Elysian fields? Adney Strait? Or Mount Reinhold? I will give the honor to the first man who finds it. We are Columbus, Balboa, Cook—we shall be legends." He sat back decisively.

"But how is such a thing possible?" asked Pago.

"My family naturally believed, like you, that these were hallucinations or lies, but with my great-uncle lost and the journal being found in the nets, my grandfather contracted an investigator to examine discreetly what had really happened. He found little—Strabo left nothing in his quarters at the university, except for diagram books of beetle genitalia with notes in his peculiar notation. They gave no clue to his whereabouts. He was toasted on New Year's and forgotten. I had put him from my mind until a conversation with Dr. Architeuthis resurrected my interest. I'll allow him to explain the rest." West sat back as the doctor unrolled a chart onto the slab.

"I was involved in volcanic research in Iceland when I met Mr. West. Over the course of the evening I was intrigued to hear the story of his strange relative, and we began some exploratory research. This is, in fact, our second expedition, as Mr. Preston can attest." I turned to Preston in surprise, but he kept his eyes resolutely forward.

"First I will share with you some of my own geologic theories. My research has led me to believe that the surface of the planet, both land and sea, is made up of a thin crust of solid rock that is fractured into pieces that grind over each other with some regularity. These pieces float on a sea of molten rock thousands of miles thick, and this molten rock carries them here and there, just as ocean currents carry boats. Yes?" He looked up for a moment before continuing.

"This molten rock performs much like water, except at a much slower pace—it flows into the shape of its container, the globe, extending itself where the opportunity presents, and receding when enough pressure is placed upon it. We discovered in Scandinavia that the weight of ice, in sufficient quantities, can depress the land surface greatly. In Sweden even now, the land is springing back from the weight of ancient glaciers; families with land on the coast see their holdings improve with each generation as the surface springs up from the sea.

"On Greenland, the ice cap is, we estimate, several miles thick and weighs many millions of tons. The center of Greenland is therefore many hundreds of feet below sea level in the center. It is a huge bowl, with the coastal mountains forming the upper rim, and the rest beneath, filled with ice.

"So the landmass pushes down into the molten layer and forces it up on either side"—he pushed his palms down and out to demonstrate. "This has two effects. First, it places tremendous strain on the crust, which is not at all elastic and so must fracture. Second, it forces the molten rock nearer to the surface around the bowl's edges. On one side you have Iceland—a volcanic land filled with hot springs and lava flows that are continually creating more land. However, according to my analysis of the mass of Greenland's ice, the greatest pressure is not to the southeast, but to the northwest, because it is there that the ice is the thickest, hence there is the most pressure." He paused expectantly.

"Thus it is very likely that there is a region to the northwest where this geothermal rift erupts, an area of considerable size. It seems certain that this rift would naturally create a long, steep valley, similar to the rift valley of Palestine, between the spreading ridges of the surface plate. If that valley were properly shaped, and wind conditions permitted, the hot air that emerged from the molten layer would remain trapped beneath the colder, heavier Arctic air. Thus trapped, it would form a temperate valley in the heart of the Arctic. Given the shift of the portions of the crust, it seems likely that the valley would spread, and the islands Dr. Strabo saw be created, as the center of the rift moved. It is possible, therefore, that a temperate archipelago could form—which Dr. Strabo seems to have stumbled upon.

"Many puzzling aspects of his account are thus explained— the intense storms, created by the divergence in temperatures between the rift valley and the surrounding area; the size and speed of the two glaciers, formed by moisture evaporated from the valley and powered by melting from the land beneath; the swift currents and the flipping icebergs, also melted from below; the peculiar plant life, powered by geothermal energy below rather than the light of the sun; the bank of sulfurous fog, released by the volcanic vents; even the mirage, formed by the bend of light from warm air to cold, a remarkable feat of disguise!

"Now if you examine this chart—vastly simplified—you see the developing heat indexes in air and water rising steadily as we near the area just beyond Jones Sound. Estimated ice masses increasing here, and the estimated iceberg volume here"—he indicated the northeastern edge of Lancaster Sound—"are beyond the amount a simple landmass could generate. Hence there must be something that is attracting sufficient moisture to generate the icebergs and sufficient heat to force them south. Our archipelago." He circled an area on the map around the seventy-eighth parallel, between eighty-five and ninety degrees west.

"The influence of the currents of warm water and rapid glaciation and melting is of a distinctive channel marked by variation in temperature, salinity, ice structure, et cetera. We need only to find this channel and follow it up to the Barrier." He pointed to a jagged red gash extended up the side of the map.

The men rumbled and shifted. West rose up from his chair.

"Your lack of imagination is disappointing," he said, "but not unexpected. If we find the islands and if they are as we anticipate, I will fill any man's locker with money if he is not satisfied with his share. Will that do? A number of you have already gotten the treasure of your freedom, and should count yourselves lucky for that." He glared at Reinhold, who glared in return but said nothing. We sat a moment in silence, expectant. Then West again:

"That will be all."

We shuffled out in silence and returned to the deck. We cast off and moved into the thickening ice, each man mulling his fortunes. My watch divided into cells—Reinhold and Adney rode in the rigging, Pago sat in the deckhouse with Creely. I went below to find Aziz, edging past West and the doctor in the hallway, who dropped their voices and waited for me to disappear below before continuing their conference.

"Well?" said Aziz, pouring me a cup of tea. "What do you think of their marvelous fairy tale?"

"It sounds incredible," I said. "Do you think it's true?"

"I think it is well worth the chance that it might be true."

"Why didn't you come to the meeting? Were you on the previous expedition?"

"Yes," replied Aziz. "And it was I who translated Strabo's journal."

"You did? What else does it say? Anything about what we will find on the islands?"

"Some remarkable beetles," he said, laughing. "It is very difficult to say with certainty what it says at all. There is nothing in the journal about gold or precious metals of any kind, if that is what you are asking."

"Then why is West promising us fortunes? What is he hoping to find?"

"West and Architeuthis have their own ideas about what we will find there."

"What are you hoping to find?"

"I don't know," he admitted. "I am hoping to discover something unique in the world—to see something no one has ever seen before. I think we may find extraordinary things." I had a thousand other questions, but I was summoned to the deck by the captain to help reef as the wind came up.

With Reinhold and Adney above me, the reefing went quickly, and we moved to lash down loose items on the deck. The evening grew steadily colder, and with the help of low clouds, a soft twilight settled. I thrilled at the prospect of finding this new land, of taking one unique step where no other human foot had stepped, where I was not stepping onto generations of death and rot and decay. Reinhold clambered down to meet me.

"What do you think?" I asked.

"Another guzzle of lies but piping hot," he answered grimly.

"What do you mean? There aren't islands?"

"Oh there may be—I doubt we'll ever see them. Or if we do, that we'll leave them."

"Aziz has read the journal. He thinks it might be true about the islands, but he says there's nothing in it about gold."

"Of course that's what he says, snug in the back with West and the doctor. Your friend Aziz knows more than he's telling— why would he come if not for money?"

"To discover something new. To explore."

Reinhold snorted derisively.

"Men like West don't head out into the Arctic to explore without a damn good reason. West knows something is there and I'll bet Aziz knows as well. Otherwise West would have just sent us up on our own and see what we found. And if not us, then another rotting hulk and another pack of cheap fools to man it. He needs us to get him up there because he isn't sure where the islands are. Once he knows and doesn't need us, he'll dump us the first chance he can and take the treasure for himself. Of course he promised the moon. Act happy and watch your step."

He laughed shortly and moved off to the foredeck.

I pushed away from the men in my mind as I imagined another set of the same conferences belowdecks, each set of men coiling against the others like pools of stagnant water breeding larval eggs beneath dark and impenetrable surfaces.

*eight*

The morning watch brought clear, cold skies and dazzling
sun; the days were returning to a recognizable shape now—
light, then darkness, then light again. The bile of last night
seemed to fade and men worked with enthusiasm and vigor. We
scoured the deck, cleaned the lines, mended sails. Shanties were
flung out in clouds of steam. The wind carried a spray of fine crystals through the sunlight. All the lines carried a tracery of ice—
delicate diamonds that melted under our hands. Though it was
late summer, the days had in them the quickening of spring, and
that same promise—of flooding, fruiting life welling up in secret
channels, that tension of holding back and that building.

The water we moved through began to fill again with ice—
pure white and searing blue in the sun. The icebergs were fresher
than the icebergs to the south, great knives of ice, and bulky
mountains freshly carved. There was little of the arching grace of
the eroded ice, none of the pitted gray shapes of melt; in its place
was a sharpness, an austerity of line and plane, a landscape of
fractured glass.

We stopped frequently for more tests from the doctor—for a sounding lead, or a chain of colored bottles to be released, or hunks of ice harvested from this iceberg or that one; sometimes he had us climbing up to gather meltwater from their secret pools. The doctor brought out a massive spool of copper wire with a weighted bucket tied to the end for more precise measurement of greater depths and for bringing up some small sample of the bottom. This we hauled down to the ice several times a day, and waited while it whined down to the bottom, then hauled it back up and watched the doctor coo over the gray-brown muck as if it were a nest of baby birds. The tests yielded numbers and readings, vague noddings from the doctor but no explanations of what we might be discovering. The doctor seemed never to sleep; I saw him an equal amount as I rotated through my watches, peering at his gauges and making calculations in his books.

I recall one night in particular—it was punishingly cold and I was huddled in the deckhouse with Reinhold and Pago when the doctor emerged from belowdecks and rushed muttering past us. His coat clinked with vials and his arms were spilling over with torn scraps of paper. He marched out on deck and sat in the lee of the mast. The night was very dark, so I could catch only a glimpse of him now and then as moonlight flashed off glass. He was on his knees, hunched, with the bottles in a circle before him; even in the darkness I could see his back shuddering, his breath skipping out in ragged clouds. A ghastly yellow light flared in front of him. He had piled the paper inside the circle of bottles and was pouring the contents of one flask on it. It burned with a bright, even chemical light, first yellowish-green, now syrupy yellow. It lined every fissure of his face and tipped every edge of his clothing in its unnatural, jaundiced light. His lips were pulled back tightly as he squinted into the paper and he seemed to be speaking rapidly to himself. He waved his hands over the glowing core of paper and it flared red. He reared back, then leaned over it again, his beard nearly touching it. The phosphorescent light was smokeless and perfectly steady, like a tiny star brought into being on the deck of the ship. It had the coldness and distance of a star too, but its steadiness offered no comfort, spoke instead of unnatural manipulation, of light that was not light though it was not darkness. Over it, Architeuthis grinned, his long, even teeth catching the glow, his head nodding rapidly. The glow extinguished suddenly and the doctor rose and shuffled past us to the hatch.

West was seen on deck less often during this time, but took to playing his Pianola in the long twilight; the creaking of the ship in the Arctic silence grew into moaning, resolved into melody, and died off into the blue-black darkness.

We steered from east to west to east again, never sighting land, or anything besides ice and more ice. On the fifth of September we finally sighted land to the west, and made for it. We pulled out of the pack and into a sheltered bay, open to the southeast, about three miles across. The bay was filled with pancake ice—plates of ice four or five feet in diameter, upturned at the edges, like a crowded field of lily pads. The land was low—icy, snow-capped hills with black rock protruding. A few forlorn clumps of grass poked out along the edge of the shore at the head of a gravelly beach. I went ashore with Dr. Architeuthis, the captain, and some others. While the doctor gathered samples, the captain had us gather the grass, which he hoped to use as both insulation and—boiled into a vile paste by Hunt—protection against the onset of scurvy. Reinhold and I moved inshore, tearing at the clumps between the frozen rocks.

"Hey, what's this? Kane," he called out, "come have a look at this."

He was standing in front of a set of symmetrical circles of stone about six feet across. In the center of two were blackened traces of fire. We called the doctor, who pored over them.

"Tent circles," he said. "The rocks were used to hold down the edges of a skin, probably caribou." He rooted around in the center of one, pulling out shreds of a skin.

"Is it recent?" asked Griffin. "Perhaps the Eskimo could help direct us."

"I doubt it," replied Dr. Architeuthis, "but it's impossible to tell from this. Nothing rots in the cold—could be ten years old, could be a thousand. I estimate it's at least that old, probably, given that there are no tribes in this area now, and no memories of them from the eastern tribes."

It was unfathomable—they looked a year or two old; you could easily imagine a man lying out the rocks, setting a fire on the small platform, gathering his family around in the cold. That these tent circles could simply be sitting out, for a thousand years, unregenerate in the march of days and the wash of seasons—it was repugnant, unnatural.

The others remained rooting around and then returned to the gathering of samples. I wandered down along the bay, pulling at the low tufts of grass. Beating my arms about me, I trudged until the rest of the party were specks in the distance. I counted steps from one clump to the next, counted stalks in each clump, and sang snatches of songs under my breath as I worked.

So counting and so singing I moved out onto the southern arm of the bay; here the wind had swept the rocks clean and there were only traces of ice between the rocks. The pancake ice glittered in the evening sun and the *Narthex* sat placidly at anchor. I sat, now singing, now whistling, and watched the tiny men scramble over the shore. The cool air was soothing, and gradually I calmed; gradually my heart ceased its skittering and resolved to a steady pad. I spread my armload of grass behind me and reclined on the rocks, let the sun whisper brightly over me.

The crack of a rifle brought me to. Shadows stretched now over the bay and the wind blew colder. I saw a boat's worth of men making their way through the pancake ice. I grabbed up the grass and hastened back. By the time I reached them, the beach was dark and the sky purpling with the push of night.

"Had a nice nap, did you, Kane?" said Hume shrilly. "Left the others to do your work?"

"I moved down the beach. Sir." I dumped my armload into the boat. He moved up beside me.

"You're a lazy bastard and insolent to boot, and if my stew weren't waiting on board I'd flog you right here." He gave the order to shove off.

We pushed out of the bay in the morning before a stiff breeze and light snow. Whatever Dr. Architeuthis had gleaned from our stop did not change our course.

As I had now seen the map and knew our destination, Dr. Architeuthis began to teach me more about what we were measuring and how to measure. He taught me first the observation through a sextant, and then the layers of math that refined and honed it, until I could determine the boat's location with precision.

During a lull, we went ashore and he showed me how to survey this unknown coastline, sighting from point to point and sending crossing arcs back to build a picture of the land. Farther up the coast, he sent me ashore with Pago to map a set of bays and points on my own. It was cold and long work, my hands freezing and the pencil seeming unable to mark the paper, but the anonymous land took shape under me, became bounded and known. As we moved on, that small pocket of the known floated in my mind, my mooring point in the whole of this boundless desolation.

The doctor brought me into the lab also and showed me the

work under way there. He brought me first to the terrariums along the windows. Inside the steamed glass, I could see a dense knot of vines hanging in the center, tendrils winding around each other and spiraling out in all directions.

"Lovely, isn't it?" said Dr. Architeuthis. "I call it the ouroborus vine. It is able to withstand very low temperatures and long periods of dormancy. When it grows, it is capable of growing very aggressively on a small supply of nutrients. The vines support each other out to a certain distance; then they collapse, strangle each other, and the nutrients are returned to the core plant. That way it can spread if there is fertile ground around it, and feed on itself if not."

He led me to another corner, where a pot of dark brown liquid bubbled into a condenser.

"This, I hope, will carry us through in the far north. Meat is simply the stored energy of the sun, concentrated first in plants and then in the flesh of animals. By concentrating further the vital essence of a range of foods, and combining them into a singular form, I hope to capture both the inherent energy available in them and the whole spectrum of necessary nutrients. Much of what we eat is composed of excess water or useless bulk. Here," he offered, handing me a bowl of brown paste that was bubbling slowly on a burner. I took a small spoonful—it was vile, tasting of chemicals in reaction, bitter and metallic. The doctor laughed.

"Taste is, for now, a secondary consideration."

The remainder of the lab contained instruments related to finding our way. He had arrays set up for testing ice and water samples, for monitoring the effects of pressure and the yields of various gases in combination. He showed me sketch maps of the underside of icebergs, built up from soundings and currents and saline variations, building a void up from the pieces of data. He showed me the centrifuge and theodolite, the hydrometer, and their uses, as well as the scientific processes to follow—the observation, the collection of data, the recording of anomalies and exceptions, the vigilance around the position and deployment of instruments, the precise intervals of measure.

On deck, he taught me to identify the great range of birds that passed over us in long streams—phalaropes and kittiwakes, brants and fulmars, eiders, old-squaws, and scoters.

It was marvelous to begin to understand the rivers of air in their courses, and the rivers of sweet water flowing through the salt. Once I traced a warm water current with great precision for over 120 miles, tracking it within the shadowy bounds of the ocean flow, discovering for myself through the gauges when it turned and rose, when it tumbled into pools, when finally it spent itself out into the broad reach of a channel. Dr. Architeuthis showed me the same in the liquid earth—rivers of rock flowing out from the center and along the surface; he showed me the arc of the Sandwich Islands, the wake of a river of rock erupting from beneath the huge and shifting plates of land.

Despite my new proficiency and position as acolyte, I was still forbidden a further look at the map. I was never allowed in the laboratory without him present, and never permitted to come near the wall that held the map.

And so a week passed, and two weeks. By now we knew our way, how to find the leads that Griffin saw, to plant the ice anchor for a warp, to brace for ramming. We moved efficiently through our paces and our ugly, awkward *Narthex* fairly danced along. The murmured traces of our meeting seeped out on night watches and in hurried snatches in our bunks—equal parts of hopeful greed and anxious dread—and dispersed.

The cold, clear air and the blaze of sun seemed to purge us of our poisons—eyes became clear and muscles lean and strong. Faces took on sharp lines and bodies stood straighter. There was no illness among us, no colds or fevers, no injuries. We awoke each day with greater vigor, more enthusiasm, bursting with strength, like waves rising and gathering. We flew to our tasks, to our meals, took reluctantly to our bunks. Despite our odd clothes we were warm even in the coldest weather. Only Preston took on a peculiar waxy paleness.

The dogs, too, changed with the shift north. They crackled with energy, snapping and snarling, whining for no reason. When we moored near large floes, Reinhold brought them to the ice and harnessed them to sledges. Once they had resolved their wrangling, they flew with easy grace. At night they slept now in tight individual balls instead of loose clumps, as if each were drawing up into his individual self, to be measured individually by the cold and darkness.

The sour greed of the meeting flushed out in our sweat, and hope built again the dream of days—Reinhold dreamt of rabbits, and I? I saw that new and fresh world, emerging from the slow march of numbers that I produced for Dr. Architeuthis. I could not see a life beyond that first step, onto that untrammeled land, but it made no difference—over me I saw great torrents of air bounding over each other, and the unrestrained earth pulsing out her treasures into bright water.

I had a growing certainty that the march of these days, that my encounter with the captain and my choice to sail were not random occurrences, but the steps of a path that my heart had driven me toward—whatever it was, a reward for my sufferings, suited to them, earned by them. It was indistinct and glorious—beyond my capacity to imagine, yet exactly suited to me, and myself worthy of it at the limits of my potential—and so I suppose it was in its own way.

I continued to be driven toward it—I noticed in myself a greater appetite and phenomenal energy. I felt as if I should never have to sleep, as if I were bursting with strength—for once I felt the equal to my heart. My mind, too, was seized by a tremendous thirst. I felt that I could understand all the world if I could but pass it before my eyes—and in me no hint of creeping loss; rather the steady, impossible hope that every day I could wake to such energy, such easy absorption, and not crumble again into indolence and confusion. Each step of my passage fell into its place as a necessary part of my progress—my heart, its ceaseless clamor, had driven me here to make me strong enough to hold it, and now, in this realm of crystal and light, was ushering me into a new world, a stronger, purer, better world that I was to share with these new men. And ahead of me unfolded—it is a grand word but suited for grand days—my destiny.

The ice thickened daily, and the sun grew more reluctant to rise with the morning; the load of ice on the lines grew thicker as we rose, and it returned through the day. We had several days of steady storm and snow, but the *Narthex* slipped up on the floes like a lady into a carriage, and we waited restlessly for the weather to break. Even belowdecks, Griffin found tasks to keep us busy— shifting cargo, piling coal, patching leaks. Much of our time was spent in preparing the ship for the day—not long distant—when the ice would cease to open for us and we would have to over- winter. The captain planned to have a space in the hold left open, which we affectionately dubbed the Ballroom, for our exercise. We unpacked lanterns and lamps for reading a library of books Grif- fin had included, and even a small printing press that we set up. Adney declared himself editor in chief and began an epic poem in limericks to carry us through the winter. Griffin also produced a great heap of scrap furs, which we took and stitched onto our patchwork clothes.

On the evening of September 17, the clouds fell away and treated us to a spectacular sunset: the clouds arranged themselves in layers, starting just above the horizon, and as the sun fell, it caught each one in turn, blazing red-gold, while the ones above retreated into purple and indigo and the ones beneath turned from gray to silver to radiant orange. The water was black and the ice shades of amber and blue. The sun dropped below the last layer of clouds and shone out as bright as day over the ice for a moment, then flickered into crimson and elegantly slipped beneath the horizon.

The next morning the captain summoned us to the deck.

"Boys, we've gone off soundings now—that may mean we're in the channel that leads to the islands, and it may not. With the thickening ice we can't move the way we ought, so we're splitting into three teams for testing: Dr. Architeuthis, Creely, Preston, and Kane to the east; myself, Hume, Pago, and Adney to the west. Reinhold will head north with Ash and the dogs. You'll march out two weeks, taking samples as directed by the doctor, then return to the ship, and we'll turn her nose into winter harbor. Clean the decks, pack your boats, and be off."

We packed the smaller iceboats—they were around eight feet long and fit four men very comfortably within their high gunnels. We lowered into the water quickly and moved slightly north of east. Hunt and Aziz gave us a hearty cheer from the deck as we wended away.

The weather was pleasantly cold—about ten degrees—and the skies low and overcast, with a wind pushing down steadily from the north. I was pleased to be free of Hume, whose sour face had hung over me as I scrubbed and loaded. We made fair progress, only dragging the boat twice over broad floes and rowing steadily the rest of the time. After the herky-jerky pace of the *Narthex*, it was a pleasure to move so steadily; Creely started a shanty and we all pulled in time. On deck my energy had built to restlessness, and I was happy to have the oar to strain against, to feel the pull of my back and arms, the rush of blood in my veins. Here was the work I had sought; the soft rush of my oar and the surge of water past the gunnel gave me the impression of tremendous speed, of shooting ahead, dancing through the ice with the clumsy *Narthex* far in our wake. The fragile sides of the boat skimmed through light brash into channel after channel; the mass of obstinate ice seemed unable to thwart us now, unable to snatch us as we passed, and I taunted the yards under my breath as we passed them. Dr. Architeuthis steered us away from distant icebergs, and the associated morass of pressure ridges and debris fields. When our way was blocked, we slid up on the ice edge, strapped ourselves into the rue raddies—a torso harness rigged by Ash before we parted—and pulled the boat to new water. The iceboats had runners built into the bottom and, despite their sheathing, moved well over the snow.

After five hours we stopped on a floe for a pot of tea and I could barely swallow mine before I was chafing to leave again. As the afternoon wore on, the wind shifted around to the east and blew directly on our backs. This slowed us somewhat, but we still made excellent progress. By eight, when we stopped to camp on a floe, the doctor estimated that we had made sixteen miles.

The tent was tiny. The doctor explained that the less space there was for our bodies to heat, the warmer we would be. We could only cram in when it was time for sleep and then only head to foot to head. Creely and Preston crowded in and hunched over the stove, while I remained outside to help the doctor with his experiments. They passed out our hoosh, and the doctor sent me, despite my protestations, back into the tent to rest. The stove had made the tent wonderfully warm and dim, and gradually the warmth of our stomachs spread to our heads and we started to drowse.

Once we extinguished the stove, however, I began to feel the

damp cold of my bag; my right side was against the outside wall
of the tent and I felt the seep of cold air penetrate my layers of
clothes. It was impossible to move enough to get warm again. We
think of cold as numbing, but it does not. It crawls and prods and
pricks and stabs; it envelops us in discomfort but does not then release us into numbness. So I squirmed and shook and panted, trying to find some warmer pocket of my bag that would distract me
long enough to sleep. My muscles ached from the long day of
pulling, and the cold made them throb; twice my leg shot straight
out and locked in a cramp and I cried out despite myself. Beside
me, a lazy drone arose from Creely's bag as he snored steadily. Late
in the night, the doctor came in, his feet pushing out into my face.
The cold settled on my head and commenced pounding dully. I
could as well have marched through the night for all the rest my
sleeping brought.

I was grateful to hear the doctor's voice announce that it was
time to break camp. Creely pulled himself from his bag, yawned,
and stretched most infuriatingly, then slid out, pulling his boots
on as he did so. I looked over at Preston and could tell he had slept
as poorly as I—his eyes were bleary, his face pale and tinged with
blue amid the waxy yellow.

"I'll make breakfast if you like," I volunteered.

"I'll make breakfast," he snapped. Then he added: "If you
don't move, we can put the stove on your bag and you can
stay in."

I was more than happy to do this, and as my bag was frozen
solid on the outside, I had no trouble staying still for the stove.
Soon the tent was roasting. I sat deep in my bag, warm for the first
time in many hours, and sipped my hoosh. Preston doled out the
others', then sat back smiling.

"I was beginning to think I'd never be warm again," he said.

"Tonight Creely's on the outside," I said. "Both sides."

He chuckled and shook his head.

We were interrupted by the brisk voice of the doctor.

"Time to move."

We dragged ourselves from our bags, pulled on our boots, and headed out into the cold. The wind was blowing steadily, still from the east, and drifting snow had nearly buried the boat. Creely and Preston dug it out, and I loaded it and lashed our gear down. The doctor stood with an anemometer in one hand and he was spinning a thermometer around his head on a length of twine with the other.

"Only way to get an accurate reading," he explained.

Our bags were heavy with moisture from our bodies and stiff with cold. The tent, at least, came down easily. We shoved our gear under the thwarts and lashed it in place, then struggled into our harnesses and headed for the water. Off we pulled, strong and steady, and sang through the rising wind. We chilled quickly when the doctor made us stop for samples, but heated up again comfortably as soon as we were under way. A day, two, through the brashy channels angling north, and then west again, stopping to draw ice, water, and air samples, and making excellent progress. Creely tried to set up a trolling line off the back for a while, but nothing bit. We settled easily into the nighttime routine even as our outer bags steadily froze stiff in the evenings.

The rowing was difficult and the wind slid through our thin coats. My muscles were still stiff from the week's work and nights out in the tent, and it took me longer each morning to warm up. Snow began to fall steadily and the wind began to blow in strong gusts. By the end of the first week, we continued to make good progress, though we were now hauling more than half the time—sometimes across ridged plains and sometimes sliding over sharp hummocks. The days were brief and gray, and the low sky sat dully over us.

Visibility was much poorer with the snow. The ice we moved into was thicker and less even, a development that fascinated the doctor to no end, indicating that it was older ice, and likely remained through several seasons, perhaps many years at a time. We stood freezing as he drilled and scraped and measured, stomping our feet to stay warm. Preston cooked while we huddled in the lee of the boat. The howl of the wind made talking difficult, so we huddled miserably in the silence. Dr. Architeuthis, like Reinhold, seemed not to feel the cold. He stood in the wind and looked out with an air of mild curiosity, as if he were looking for an acquaintance at the train station.

The ice got steadily worse. We had to find our way through high pressure ridges, or haul the boat over them—a delicate operation with only four men. The boat upset frequently and we had to reload it with numb fingers.

After a backbreaking day, the doctor estimated that we had made only four miles east, though we had traveled two or three times that distance in our meandering. We had covered over a hundred miles east in ten days—good time through the ice, but as it got worse, we slowed to a crawl. Now we were pulling the boat up twenty-foot hanging cliffs over ridges that ran miles in both directions, or fighting through packed fragments too thick to row in but unable to bear our weight. We were forced to move obliquely, sometimes leaving the boat as we rigged a pulley to draw it up and then down, or extending the raddies out to firm ice on either side and then struggling to pull it forward. The steady cold slowed us also; rising in the darkness, it took us longer and longer to pack the boat. By the end of our two weeks out, we moved into a broad plain of firm ice with only windblown ridges to slide the boat over. When we had burst free from the hummocks, the doctor pushed us to haul late into the night for as long as the conditions held.

When we set up camp, we all crowded into the tiny tent as

soon as it was up. By staying very still, with the stove balanced precariously on my legs, we cooked the hoosh through numbed fingers without setting ourselves on fire—though I cannot say that it seemed an entirely unwelcome prospect. With the stove roaring, feeling soon returned to our limbs—stinging at first, then throbbing pain, then a fierce itching that, because of our balancing act, we had to endure unscratching.

After dinner, we left the stove burning for a while. The tent was close and very damp and indescribably warm and pleasant. Turning our bodies to the side, Preston and I managed to light a candle in the hollow between us and its feeble light cheered us.

It went out abruptly when the doctor came crashing in to check us for frostbite, and examined our faces and fingers with a lantern. Once he was satisfied, and settled into his own bag, we lit the candle again; Preston and I lay simply watching the flicker of the flame between us. Creely, impervious to the cold, was soon snoring evenly. I watched Preston's eyes droop and close, his head falling forward slightly. I shifted my eyes to the dance of the flame and watched the rivulets of wax run down on my gloves.

I awoke from dreamless sleep to the face of Dr. Architeuthis, smiling at the opening of the tent.

"We're splitting in teams, marching out for the morning, collecting samples, and back for dinner. Creely and I northeast, Kane and Preston southeast. We'll keep the tent up here, save us some time. Now let's get moving."

We headed off into the starlit morning, and there was little to complain about. Free of the boat at last, I felt like I could walk forever; Preston and I moved briskly over the ice as the low ridges caught the light from our lanterns. The sun blazed up in the east, dazzling us as we moved. At first the light was sharp, and bit like the cold, but as it rose it suffused through the low clouds and the light evened out.

The wind had quieted and it was not so cold, but the problem was not cold. It was light. The sky was overcast and the light was bright and grew perfectly even—there were no shadows and the ice had no edges. As we marched, we found that we could not tell whether the ice rose or fell before us. I would reach out with my foot and stub it on an invisible rise; two steps later, I would pitch on my face in a depression I could not see. We tried using an oar like a blind man's stick and tapping, but even that did little good. It would strike ice, and we still could not judge our steps.

After an hour of falling steadily, and of cracking toes, barking shins, and bruising hands, I was furious and frustrated. The drift snow filled my coat and melted, getting clammy and heavy on the inside and freezing on the outside.

Preston did nothing to improve my mood. He plodded along, grunting as he fell. He said nothing, offered nothing, and so we trudged in silence. We found a few narrow leads, nearly stumbling into them because we misjudged their distance and size. You had to touch them with your hand before you could be convinced that they were not several hundred yards off. I tried all sorts of tricks—squinting, blinking, throwing a glove a few steps ahead, then walking to retrieve it. They did little good. We blundered ahead, falling into each other or crashing into the ice; I gashed my hand on a sharp piece of ice and was relieved to see the dark red drops in the snow.

My disorientation was compounded when I pulled out the compass to check our bearing. The needle wavered lazily from east to west without fixing itself. I shook it, but it continued to wave, like a drunken metronome. I showed it to Preston.

"Is it frozen?" I asked.

"It's the magnetic pole," he answered. "We are close. The compass is useless."

"Useless?" I said. "It can't be." I shook it vigorously and

slapped at the surface. I warmed it against my skin and shook it again, but it continued to wobble.

"Piece of junk," I muttered. "Now how do we know where to go?"

"This way," said Preston and began to march away.

I followed, but remained preoccupied with the treachery of the compass. It seemed so basic and essential a fact: the compass points north. North! It doesn't wander, lie, equivocate. *North!* I wanted to shout at it. *You bastard, point north!* It was complicit in this whole maddening mess, this whole absurd joke of the ice— first we cannot see, and now our compass does not work. I would rather have the cold.

I strained out into the whiteness, looking for water, a rock, anything with an edge or line—mountains, valleys, a pile of stone, anything. I became convinced that we were wandering in a circle.

It is well known, I reasoned, in the desert or at sea, in a landscape without landmarks, men inevitably move in a circle. It is our peculiar inertia to circle unless jostled free. We are subtle betrayers even of ourselves to thus return to find our way and so become more lost—as I had determined that we were. I began scouring the featureless snow for signs of our footsteps but could not see even my own as we made them.

Preston was marching ahead as if we were on a thoroughfare. Fool, I thought. Idiot. He doesn't even suspect we are moving in a circle. He is trampling our tracks.

I determined that we were circling in a clockwise direction, as we had naturally inclined away from the other parties as we moved, and so circled back to the south. We had only to go left to find our tracks. Once these were discovered, we could find our true direction and move off to the east. I moved to the left as I walked, straying diagonally away from Preston and peering into the featureless whiteness for some evidence of our passage. We should have dropped crumbs, I thought, or coal—the next time, coal for sure. I pressed some blood from the gash in my hand to form a spot in the snow. Preston plodded ahead on his errant way without taking notice of me. I resolved to overtake him and confront him with my conclusions before we wasted more time.

"Preston!" I shouted through my layers. "Preston! Hold up a minute!" I ran forward, falling twice on my face before I reached him and grabbed his shoulder.

"Preston, I think we're circling, and we need to move to the left to return to our track."

He looked at me, eyes narrow and weary from squinting.

"We're moving southeast," he said.

"No," I said, "we've started to circle, I'm almost sure of it." I explained my theory about moving away from the others.

He shook his head and started walking again.

"Wait," I said, grabbing his arm, "we should just head left a little—a half mile or so. Then we'll see our tracks and can reorient. There are no signs—no sun, no compass. We can't even see the damn ice. Just going does us no good at all."

He looked at me for a long moment, then kicked at the ridge of snow we had just crossed.

"See the drift? The sastrugi—the ridges—run east to west. If we keep moving across it, we're moving to the southeast. So shut your mouth and close your eyes, and maybe you'll find everything a little easier."

He turned and marched off. I stomped sullenly behind him, punching my arms stiffly to try to keep my coat from freezing. How did he know the drift hadn't been in another direction? I couldn't see it anyway. The wind could have shifted. There could be a big mountain a hundred yards away that bends the wind, or forces the sastrugi into strange directions. The lack of magnetism could affect the snowdrift—maybe the snow adhered differently.

He didn't know. I stomped and stomped, but as I calmed, I noticed that the snow, though invisible, did seem to follow the same pattern: low, even snow about two or three inches deep, then thicker drift up to a foot, then a hard ridge, bare at the top, then the low snow again. The distances between ridges varied some, and the depth of the snow in the troughs, but the essential pattern remained the same. I shuffled my feet through the snow until I felt the edge of the sastrugi rising under it, stepped up, then shuffled down the other side.

I still stumbled, to be sure, still stubbed my toes and wrenched my ankles, but order gradually settled back over that empty whiteness—drift, ridge, valley, drift, ridge, valley. I tried to resolve it into a rhythm, drawing out each stage until I reached the next one, but the distances between the hardened lines of the ridges were too variable. I tried closing my eyes and navigating by feel, but I still tripped. Even with my eyes closed, they burned white; my head was starting to ache.

Preston finally stopped.

"We're here," he said, dropping his pack.

I dropped mine beside it and flopped down in the snow.

"No sense in getting cold," he said. "Let's get the samples and head back."

He started chipping away at the ice by his feet. I struggled to my feet and started to do the same. The racket of axes on the ice was a welcome change from the silent marching. We had been instructed to try to get down to the water, if possible, test the temperature, and bring back samples from the ice at one-foot intervals. We got down about four feet when Preston waved to me to stop. I thought we had simply gone down enough and began to gather samples.

"No sense in digging here all day, eh?" I said cheerily. I had pushed several chunks into a bag when I realized he was on his knees beside the hole. His body was racked with coughing. I moved up beside him.

"Preston? Preston, are you all right?"

He hacked and his body shook. He coughed again and the snow in front of him turned a violent red.

"Oh God," I said. I pounded him on the back. He coughed a few more times, rasped, and was silent. He rolled onto his back and struggled to catch his breath. I stared at the steaming red blot in the snow. After a day of only white, it seemed impossibly, hugely red; my own small spots of blood like nothing. He sat breathing shallowly as he recovered.

"An infection," he said, wheezing. "Got it in the tropics ten years ago."

"But the cold can't be very good for it."

"Dr. Architeuthis says it's my only chance—keeps it from growing worse, he says. If I go south, my lungs fill right up. I have to keep moving north. First it was outside of the tropics, then forty degrees north, then fifty. Driving me into exile bit by bit. Right off the top."

"Is there a cure?"

"Doctor says in the archipelago, there might be something in those plants, about the lack of sunlight. I don't know. But I don't have much choice. Become an Eskimo."

He laughed harshly and coughed again.

"That's why you went before."

He nodded.

"What did you find then?" I asked.

He grimaced and coughed more before replying.

"Ice," he said finally. "We found ice."

I stared at his blood in the snow. It looked almost black now, like a hole leading downward out of this world of white.

"Let's finish here," said Preston after a moment, hauling up his pack. "We have a long march ahead of us."

We dug out our samples and moved off. As we stumbled back, the wind picked up and the light faded. Fortunately, the wind was at our backs now, and seemed to bear us along. The lessening light was a relief also; though we could see no better, it did reduce the glare somewhat. Preston led and I tried to keep up. My feet were numb and my head started pounding fiercely. I have never been so happy as I was when we crested a rise and saw the light of camp glowing in the distance. I ran the last hundred yards and collapsed gratefully into the tent, nearly upsetting the stove, where Creely had a lovely hoosh simmering.

*nine*

I lay there and ate contentedly while I listened to what the other two had found: ice and snow. The doctor stumbled into a lead at one point and Creely had been forced to fish him out—"and no fancy lectures this time, just some old-fashioned cursing." By the end of the day, Creely had had trouble with his eyes—even now they were watering profusely. Dr. Architeuthis had finally forced him to cover them and roped the two men together—"We waltzed all the way back," he told us, laughing. We fell silent and listened to the hissing of the kerosene. Tonight, it was my turn to be in the middle, and I lay with the stove on my stomach, watching the flame dance in the peak of the tent. Our clothes were all sodden, as was the thin silk of the tent, and we were well tangled before we all struggled into bed. Despite our fatigue, we managed a laugh, then said our good-nights.

In the close air of the tent, I waited for Creely's snoring to swell; he was restless and kept elbowing me.

In the middle of the night he cried out; there was a rustling in the tent and a lantern flared. The doctor sat over him as he moaned softly.

"My head—I feel like someone's pounding spikes into it."

The doctor pulled open his eyes and put some drops in them. "Snow blindness. These drops should help you get to sleep."

I looked over at Creely in the lantern light; viscid drops rolled down his face like clear resin.

The sun had not yet risen by the time we had secured all of the samples as well as our frozen bags, but the sky was golden gray and orange, and the stars retreating. The boat was completely buried so Preston and I began to shovel it out. The doctor bound Creely's eyes as Preston packed gear and stowed the tents. Our harnesses were frozen solid, and it took twenty minutes of beating them against the side of the boat to loosen them enough to slide into them. At first Creely pulled along with us, but he fell so often that finally the doctor ordered that he walk alongside.

We moved off the ice plain and back into the hummocks again. The loose snow stuck onto the bottom of the boat, adding weight and resistance with every step. The sun rose over a blowing, drifty wind; luckily the clouds kept the glare from getting too bad, and we could see where we were going. I felt awful for Creely, crying out as he pitched forward onto his knees. He was forced to stand by as we fought the boat over hummocks, dancing from one foot to the other, and shouting encouragement from beneath his blindfold. Occasionally he would gamely start a shanty, keeping it up as he stumbled and sprang up with new emphasis, shouting out the words with forced gaiety.

We slogged in the harnesses, praying for open leads. We found one that was so thick with brash ice that it was as easy to pull as row. As soon as we pulled the boat out, more ice accumulated on the bottom and we had to stop to knock it loose. We spotted another lead in the distance, but as we drew closer found that it was not open water, but simply fresh, black ice. Still, it provided a more level surface, and gave us a good pull before it disappeared in the hummocks.

When the doctor called the halt, the sky was darkening and the wind picking up. He said we'd be lucky if we made five miles, but added optimistically that a night of wind might open some leads for us. We pitched and made our hoosh and sat watching the stove flame for long into the night. Creely and I sat in silence as the wind came up, and listened to the snap and flutter of the tent. In the morning, the doctor went out on his own, then came back in.

"Sit tight, we can't move in this weather. A day in the tent may clear up your eyes as well, Mr. Creely." He ducked back outside and was gone for several hours.

We fired up the stove and sat in comfort as it blazed. Creely told some stories about the Far East, the ports of Formosa, and Preston about Brazil, where he had been trading for two years before he shipped with Griffin, and for a few meager hours we all had the chance to forget where we were.

After a time, the doctor appeared and ordered our stove out—if we were stuck for a few days, we needed the fuel. Reluctantly we doused, and tried our candles, but they wouldn't stay lit. So we each pulled down into the very ends of our bags and pulled the tops shut over us. We passed long hours in the silence and dark before the doctor ordered us to make our dinner. Creely looked better—his eyes squinting but not oozing. Preston looked weary. Still, a little hoosh and we all cheered up. We sang what songs we knew, and some we sang twice. The doctor returned and we doused the stove again, and retreated again into silence.

Outside, the wind hummed through the guy ropes, and the walls of the tent shuddered. As the snow fell, the sound of the storm grew muffled, as if we were being draped in blankets and drifting to sleep; the temperature rose and the inside of the tent became very comfortable. I listened to the delicate brush of the snow between gusts and drowsed.

In the morning the wind had resumed and the snow was still falling. The visibility was poor, but Dr. Architeuthis felt it prudent to push on anyway. The snow had drifted high in the lee of the tents and the boat was entirely buried. It took us two hours of hard work to get everything unearthed, packed, and stowed. The wind became maddeningly indeterminate—now blowing fiercely, now dropping off into a breeze. We struggled into our harnesses and pushed off. The snow was very soft and deep—over our knees at first—and we were able to slide the boat along at a reasonable clip. Gusts of wind struck it and threw us off balance, or we stumbled on the uneven footing. After three hours of steady hauling, we came to heavily hummocked ice. The doctor called a halt to take some sightings and determined that we were drifting south, and it was therefore necessary to shift northwest in order to intersect with the *Narthex*. The ice in that direction was heavily hummocked, so the doctor decided that we would make better time by carrying the boat and relaying. The doctor threaded our harnesses through eyes that Ash had built into the gunnels. Thus we were able to run the harnesses from our shoulders—Preston and I in the front and the doctor on his own in the rear—and pick the boat up entirely.

We first unloaded the boat quickly and marched off. We actually didn't have much to carry, and so we sped along. After a half mile, we depoted our gear and returned to the boat. Emptied of our gear, the boat was easier to manage, though still not light. Gusts caught it several times and sent us sprawling, but on the whole we made excellent time.

The process of relaying gave the illusion of great progress as we were always moving quickly, and I do believe we made better time. We camped, having marched close to twenty-five miles in order to make eight miles of progress. Creely's eyes improved, and he was able to join us in the harnesses; Dr. Architeuthis carved some snow goggles for him from part of the boat's seat. Another day of relaying brought us no leads, just the weight of the boat through the high hummocks and fragmented ice. Another day and another and another, breaking our backs for precious miles.

On the eighteenth night, the temperature dropped well below zero and the wind picked up. In the morning, Dr. Architeuthis reluctantly ordered us to stay in our tent, but forbade the lighting of the stove, to conserve fuel. I decided to go out, and spent the day with him in the wind and fading light trying to read gauges, and to break through the hummocks to get more and deeper samples of the ice. Most of the instruments had not been designed for the Arctic in September—they were too small for our clumsy fingers and impossible to read in the fading light. Still, the doctor recorded everything he could with great care, and gathered up countless samples into the endless stream of stopper bottles he produced from his pack.

We leaned into the wind and made our way back to the tent again. After dinner, we made a hollow with our bodies and lit the candle, huddling over it for warmth and comfort.

"From tomorrow, regardless of the weather, we will need to stay on the march," said the doctor. "Otherwise we may lose the boat in the drift of the pack." He doused the candle and we pulled back into our bags and tried not to think about the cold.

When Dr. Architeuthis roused us again, it was still dark and the wind was still howling.

"A quick breakfast and let's be off."

We made weak tea and dipped our pemmican in it to warm it, then dragged ourselves outside. It was bitterly cold and the wind burned and battered. We began relaying again, and made fair progress until we began the second run with the boat. We were marching through shallow drifts between exposed ridges of ice when a gust caught us from behind and lifted the stern of the boat into the air. I was in the bow with Creely and he stumbled just as the boat pitched upward. He fell heavily onto the ice and the boat dropped on him with a sickening crack. We pulled the boat off him quickly; he lay on his back groaning softly.

Dr. Architeuthis examined him, then turned to us.

"He's broken some ribs, and there may be some internal bleeding. He won't be able to march."

There was a moment of awful silence as we looked at him lying there.

"Right, then. We'll have to leave the boat for now. We'll carry him in shifts. Have to come back for the boat once we get to the *Narthex*."

Preston and I made a quick sling from our harnesses and the doctor worked Creely into his bag. The bag, like the boat, had loops to run the harnesses through that let us easily hoist Creely onto our shoulders. His head lolled as we marched and he cried out whenever we jarred him; when the wind dropped, I could hear him gasping as he tried to breathe. The wind rose again until we could barely keep our feet. I did not dare to ask how we knew what direction we were going in. We crawled into our tent hours later and struggled to lay Creely gently in the middle. We managed to balance the stove on his frozen form and get it going. Preston tried to feed Creely some hoosh but could not get him to come around. Even after an hour of roaring stove and two cups of tea, we were only starting to warm.

The air was clearer in the morning and not as cold; we were able to make good progress. In the afternoon, we found water again—when Architeuthis nearly tumbled into an open lead. Water was an encouraging sign, but it added another hazard to our progress. Without the boat, we had to find our way around the leads, or wait for the edges to close to make our way over them. Creely still had not fully recovered consciousness, though he did not seem to be worsening. The weather was, for the first time, co-operative—mild air, little wind, but cold enough to keep the ice solid. We used floes to ferry ourselves over some of the smaller leads. We went as quickly as we dared, working west and north over the shifting ice.

The occasional lead gave way to frequent leads, and then to a welter of smaller floes rolling in a swell. Dr. Architeuthis called a halt, and we fought to erect the tent. We were in the middle of a floe about fifty feet across. An icy spray flew up as our floe knocked into its companions and coated our gear with rime. At last we got our tent up, and Creely inside and us into our bags. Given Creely's injuries, there was no space for the doctor to wriggle into his bag, so he sat near the doorway and draped himself with it.

I put the cooker over Creely's legs and managed to light it on my first try.

"The turn of luck," I said, as I threw the pemmican in. The tent heated up rapidly and feeling returned to our hands and faces. The cooker flame flickered with the gusting wind, but stayed lit. The familiar wet heat returned, and the welcome smell of meat simmering. Preston pulled Creely's head into his lap and tried to feed him some hoosh again. At first Creely rolled his head away from it and shook spasmodically, but Preston brought it back again and again to his lips until finally he drank. The shaking stopped and he relaxed into sleep. Weary muscles sagged and my head drooped on my neck.

The tent shuddered as we crashed into other floes and the tent wall sagged under the weight of the water; the wind rose in pitch to a whistling whine, then dropped to a throaty roar. I would not have imagined I could sleep, but sleep I did, until Preston wrenched me awake.

"The tent," he shouted. "I think it's going."

Before he had finished, the tent walls plunged inward, then

shot outward; the tear of silk was lost in the shriek of the wind as the tent walls shredded into ribbons. I wriggled out of my bag and threw our cooker and the oil into it. The doctor pushed Creely's head into his bag, and held it shut. Around us, waves were breaking over the edge of our tiny island. Preston and the doctor scrambled out and looked in dismay at the remains of our tent.

"We have to move," shouted the doctor. "Head for firmer ice and make a forced march to the ship. Pack up."

We shouldered our packs and hoisted Creely in his bag. The doctor roped us all up and we started out. The floes around us were no bigger than ours and some were much smaller. The spray coated them and froze in the wind, so they were all slippery. By heading back the way we had come—I think—we found larger floes and firmer ice, though no respite from the wind. Then we swung off to the west, trying to stay in the thicker ice. I don't know how Dr. Architeuthis decided which way to go; I imagine he was gathering data on the march, but perhaps he just slogged and hoped.

Creely seemed mercifully insensible as we staggered along. I was exhausted and the others were no better. I could feel, through the rope, the tug or slack of each misstep, of each pause, each slowing. The rope communicated the full misery of each to the others, and yet dragged each ahead, drawing strength from the whole. Even the doctor, who strode ahead (and often wet his feet in hidden leads as a consequence), showed signs of wavering. The storm gave no sign of abating.

The doctor finally called a halt. We set Creely in the snow and sat heavily.

"We will eat on the march; we need the food to keep moving." He handed us each a biscuit and some pemmican. I tore greedily at mine, before it could slip from my numb fingers. Then the pemmican was gone quickly and I stood a moment looking mournfully at the biscuit, and on we went.

The doctor tried a shanty and abandoned it, skipped and slowed, pounded me on the back when I started to waver. I beat my hands against my sides to keep the blood moving through them, and beat my arms against my sides, and beat my hands against my head.

We stayed awake by the continued articulation of words—curses and prayers at first, each man lost in his own roaring world; then histories and singsongy rhymes, exhortations to keep on trailing into whimsical opinion. I closed my eyes to concentrate, to gather my thoughts, build myself a thought I could carry through this time—but I could not, as they scattered in the roaring as I sunk to my knees, or stumbled, as I looked at my hand, which I could see but not feel. I could not hear the others—could not hear myself—and still I kept on in fancied conversations, answering questions firmly, my head nodding. Then a stagger ahead—establishing a ground instantly forgotten—and then a pause to marshal again, and so a fresh assertion, fresh push, and loss upon loss.

After an age, Architeuthis's head appeared. He handed me another hunk of pemmican and moved off again into the darkness.

The storm blew out and a weak day dawned. I had hoped to see the ship in the distance, but there was only ice. We had a double portion of pemmican at noon, heated in the lee of a bag, to keep up our strength. Creely stirred for the hoosh and managed to feed himself. We gathered our packs again and slung him up between us. Our packs had a little oil left, some pemmican; the bulk of the weight was our sleeping bags—which grew heavier day by day—and the ice samples we had collected.

The doctor estimated we were still at least twenty-five miles from the ship, though we were making good time with the mild weather and without the boat to weigh us down. It lasted another day, then two, and the ice held; the doctor spent noon peering through his telescope for the ship, but saw nothing.

As the light faded in the middle of the afternoon, we were confronted with a broad lead, running north-south and angling over us to the east, a half mile wide and trailing off into the distance at both ends. It was filled with a soupy mix of crystals and seawater, nearly solid in places but open in others. I cooked under a heap of bags as the doctor looked for the ship and Preston scouted to the south for a way across.

The doctor did not see the ship, but he did see another storm brewing in the southwest, black clouds standing out even against the looming night. Preston returned to report that there was no way across to the south. We had been lucky since the tent was destroyed—but that luck was ending.

"We have few alternatives," said the doctor. "I do not believe we can survive the storm camped in the open, though we might on the march, if we can continue to move. We must get across the lead and push north before the storm pushes us further away from the ship. We could try to cut free a floe and ferry across, but the sea ice is freezing rapidly and is likely already too solid to move through. We must wait for the lead to freeze and then cross and head north as quickly as we can."

Sea ice, as it starts to freeze, is not like freshwater ice; the salt makes it spongy and springy as it freezes, instead of brittle; as we moved onto it, I could feel it give underfoot, and could feel the reverberations of the others; if I stood still on it, I could feel the waters creeping up my boots. It was now completely dark, and the first of the storm winds were rising. We sat huddled together, the doctor going out at intervals to test the ice. We ate cold pemmican and watched the stars disappear in the south.

"We must go now," said Dr. Architeuthis finally. "Spread out so that we have a hundred yards between us. I will carry Creely. When you hear my signal, run. Try to slide your feet rather than raising and lowering them, but move quickly. Even if the ice starts to give, you may be able to make it across."

"What happens if it isn't frozen in the middle? Or if we fall through?"

Preston had already shouldered his pack and moved off into the darkness. The doctor looked at me, not unkindly, and said: "Keep running. Try to slide."

I made my way down along the lead and waited. Off in the distance, the doctor shouted: *"Now!"*

I took off, and I could feel the ice buckling underfoot, wobbling and pitching, and a splash of salt against my coat. I looked down at my feet, which I could barely see, and thought about sliding them; saw one disappear, and then a pause, and the other popped up. I closed my eyes and yelled and forgot about sliding, but just ran as fast as I could. I tripped violently and fell forward onto the snow—the snow! I was across! I shouted and laughed and heard first Preston and then the doctor answer.

"Come on," shouted Dr. Architeuthis. "We must get north before the storm hits."

We clapped each other on the back, harnessed up, and moved off quickly, invigorated at conquering the lead, and feeling that we must surely reach the ship now. I wonder in the long history of exploration how many hidden triumphs lie buried with unsuccessful expeditions—how many men congratulated each other and thought, Surely now, we would not have come through that if we had not been meant to live.

The wind came up behind us, billowing and then roaring steadily, and fresh snow began to fall. Fresh snow was a good sign because it meant the temperature would not get so terribly cold.

When we paused, I looked over at Preston; his face was a dead white and his eyes were fish-empty. He tugged often on the harness as he stumbled and wavered against it like a kite on the end of a long line. The doctor called a halt again after some hours on the march. We huddled together to hear him.

"We cannot go further tonight. We shall make a snow hut here to get out of the wind and then two will go ahead to find the ship. The other will remain to care for Creely and wait out the storm under the bags. I, for one, will go ahead. Who else can go on?"

Preston righted his rolling head and announced that he too could go, but the doctor shook his head. I looked miserably at him, and raised my hand. We cut a low ridge of snow blocks to the south. Then we sliced open my bag and the doctor's and laid them over the men, anchoring the bottom edge in the ice. Preston fired the cooker and gave us a quick cup of cocoa. We stood for a moment with our heads and hands poking under the bags, then put down our cups and said our good-byes.

Outside, we roped up and moved off into the darkness. In the hours of suffering that followed I have only sensation to guide me. Dull thumpings at great distance as I fell and struck my knee, my hand, my face—the tremendous effort of lifting a foot once, and then again—the detached observation that we must be moving very slowly—the sickening bend of black sea ice under my weight—the tugging of the rope at my waist—a surge as my senses rushed back and I found myself trudging still, still in darkness, still cold.

I have no memory of reaching the ship, though obviously we did. I was told that I had violent strabismus as I came aboard, my eyes rolling like marbles in my sockets, and that Architeuthis had been essentially dragging me along. I slept for more than ten hours—and had to be restrained in my bunk because I kept rising and walking in circles. I am told that I raved for hours before settling into sleep; I was fed and slept again. The doctor slept an hour, ate, and went back out in the storm with Reinhold and Pago to bring back the others. By the time they found the bags, the storm had lifted and the temperature had fallen. They put Creely on a small sledge and hauled him back. They did not bother to look for the boat in the jostle of the pack. Preston was able to make it back under his own power, though he slept the same raving sleep that I had. When we awoke, we were both weak, but coherent. My eyes still wandered some, but otherwise we were ourselves again. We gorged and slept and gorged again, calling to Hunt from our bunks for more food.

One of my hands blistered badly from the frost, and I was weak for several days. Aziz emerged from the boiler room to nurse me himself; he made me special teas from packets he kept hidden in his loose sleeves. He said little, and did not converse with the other crewmen, but was always there when I awoke, silently proffering a steaming mug of tea or a weak hoosh. Even when I awoke in the middle of the night, he would be sitting nearby, and smile and offer up a mug. As I recovered my strength, he retreated below and I could not prevail upon him to reascend.

Creely was insensible for two days, but slowly recovered. Only the doctor seemed to have escaped unharmed. The captain took a turn at nursing each of us in his stiff way, but he took a special interest in Creely, as he had been so badly hurt. Creely stayed in bed a few days, but soon dragged himself out and was back on the watch before I was. I was standing in the deckhouse with Griffin on my first day back and I saw him look out at Creely and shake his head in wonder.

"You couldn't kill that man with an axe," he said softly.

The other expeditions had had very different experiences. Reinhold and Ash had had good weather to the north, and had gone over 120 miles. The dogs had performed beautifully. They returned to the ship with all of their supplies and a full set of samples.

As I was recovering, Adney perched on my bunk to tell me about their foray.

"On our ninth day, we were still moving through mostly open

water between large floes when the captain spotted walrus in the distance. We made for them as quickly as we could, but they had disappeared by the time we got close. We spent several minutes nosing around looking for them, with Hume telling us what a set of lazy grandmothers we are, when suddenly there was a terrific crash and the bottom of the boat starts to splinter. This walrus pops up beside the boat, his eyes all glazed over. He hooks his tusks over the gunnel, lets out this tremendous bellow, and tears a chunk out of the side of our boat, oak siding and all. The king had been stand-ing, of course, and he catapulted into the water. He hadn't even wet his ears when he started squalling like a baby—he's a natural tenor—and thrashing around. We being a little busy with the boat, which was a little busy sinking, didn't get right to him. Instead we rowed over to a floe and unloaded our gear before we lost it. If you could have heard him—cursing blue and screaming about the wal-rus attacking. He thrashes over toward us and Pago reaches into the water, pulls him out like a herring, and tosses him onto the floe. As soon as he gets his breath back, he starts working his way around letting each of us have it. I was hoping Pago'd throw him back.

"So there he is on the ice, when the walrus comes back—not just swims up lazily, but bursts out of the water and lands on the floe bellowing and charging at us. Pago's got the rifle out and he starts firing, but the walrus doesn't even slow down. Four, five, six shots before he rears up, and two more before he stops. My-self, I was rooting for the walrus.

"Anyhow, Pago drops him about four feet away from us and there is Hume curled up in a ball and blubbering—I mean tears rolling down his face. It was too much."

He pulled out a dirty yellow tusk, which was longer than my arm and wickedly curved. Its surface was scored with long, deep grooves.

"Nasty piece of work," I said.

"How he got to be an officer is a mystery to us all."

"Was it rabid?" I asked.

"Griffin said there are rogue walruses that develop a taste for meat and they'll go after anything—other walrus, seal, fish, men, even a polar bear if they can catch one in the water. I'll never forget his face over the side of the gunnel—pure rage. He was trying to tear the boat apart.

"So we took our samples and turned back. Without the boat, it took us fourteen days to get back—floe hopping and paddling mostly. Fortunately, Hume's dunking didn't stall him for long—spent the afternoon polishing his poor burnished trumpet and went right on blowing. Closer to the ship the ice thickened and the going was pretty easy."

I recounted for him the whiteout, Preston's illness, Creely's accident, and the sprint over the lead. His eyes grew large as I described the destruction of the tent and the march back. When I finished, he clapped me on the back.

"Kane, you are a certified Arctic explorer of the first rank. I wish I had been along."

"It wasn't especially heroic," I said drowsily, "just one foot and the next and trying not to think about how much your feet hurt."

"That's all it is," he said grandly.

I was dropping off to sleep again when Reinhold burst in.

"Hume—he's dead!" he said excitedly.

"What?" said Adney. "How?"

"Don't know—he just keeled over on the watch. He was dead by the time I reached him."

"What did the doc say?"

"He doesn't know—nobody knows anything. Nobody knows anything."

*t e n*

Hume had appeared perfectly normal during the days back from the trip—grousing around the deck as usual. He showed no symptoms prior to his collapse and no clues afterward—just a pale, shrunken body swaddled in a patchwork of dark furs. Captain Griffin came forward to wrap him in sailcloth and gently close his eyes. He lay under the flat gray of a twilit afternoon sky on a deck that appeared, if anything, excessively ordinary and undistinguished. Even the dogs were listless. Still, an excited chatter broke out among us as we speculated. Griffin silenced us with a wave of his hand.

"Leave him his dignity at least, that you may have some yourselves when you come to die," he said gruffly. "Pago, help me wrap him. Sew the end shut with some pig iron in it, and I'll get my Bible for a service. No sense in keeping him waiting."

As they wrapped Hume in his coarse cerements, I slipped below to tell Aziz what had happened. I had been down for only a minute when I heard the door of the doctor's cabin slam shut. Aziz and I piled up some cases, and I clambered up and put my ear to the ceiling. From through the boards I could hear the shrill voice of the captain shouting.

"An outrage! It is an outrage! What did you intend exactly? To burn him up in pieces and measure the heat?"

"Captain, I do not understand," answered the smooth voice of the doctor. "We must know why he died. Surely a simple autopsy is not—"

"We do not *need* to know. We know he is dead—that is enough—we do not need to butcher him. His body could not take the shock of the sea; he was never especially hardy for a sailor. Suppress your ghoulish curiosity, sir, and let us bury him in his sailor's grave."

"Honestly, Captain, you confound me—it is common sense when a healthy man dies for no reason and with no warning to attempt to plumb the cause, if for no other reason than the safety of the other men."

"The other men are perfectly safe. Now return the body so that we may have a service."

"A simple autopsy will be the matter of a day. He has plenty of time. Have your dinner, Captain, and I will return him to you ready for your ceremony."

"You will not. Your autopsy would reveal nothing. It is not worth the harm to his dignity to let you cut him into pieces and weigh and measure him for nothing."

The doctor snorted.

"It is not for nothing—I will discover if he had a sickness that perhaps the others may already have or if our food is tainted or there is poison in the water."

"You will find nothing," the captain answered. "Men die when they are finished living, when the world ushers them out or drives them forth. You are trying to solve things that are mysteries, that are beyond our comprehension."

"This is basic science, Captain, not the blood and the body—perhaps it is lead poisoning or gas. It is vital for us to know."

"You are working at puzzles—fit the pieces together in the right way, rearrange them, and you will find their patterns, and so the puzzle is solved. But mysteries remain despite your puzzling, your cutting and chopping and prodding and measuring. You cannot solve them, because they are not composed of pieces that you can break down and rearrange. I have seen many men die and suffered the useless butchering of ignorant doctors who wanted to poke and prod to satisfy their own interests."

"This is fine to hear from old women and frightened priests, Captain, but surely it is not the argument of an intelligent man offered in the light of day! Are not your mysteries simply larger and larger puzzles? And as we uncover new pieces, will they not fit together like the parts of a map, until a region is fully mapped?"

"We have seen the accuracy of your map by now, I hope!"

"But now we know what we did not—because our maps are not accurate does not mean that mapping is useless. On the contrary, it means that we must be that much more vigilant in our mapmaking, surer of our observations, our measurements, our calculations—that we may finally have a map that is true."

"I have known many men like you—dividers, cutters, labelers, locusts all. For all your work, can you answer the most simple question: why does this blood continue to course through my hand? Blood there in my hand and in the hand of every man since time itself began, and tell me sir, can you explain it? It does not take the body of Christ to exceed you."

"We will be no more frightened of ghosts and monsters. Would you have us ignore what we see? What we can prove and replicate and have others verify? You are medieval. It is preposterous. Should we huddle in darkness when we are capable of creating light?"

"There are lights that are worse than the darkness—the light you stuff into dead bodies as you carve them into pieces for your pleasure, seek to know yourself in dead things."

I could hear the doctor scoff.

"That's the trouble with you mystics—you slide into vagueness and hide as soon as you are cornered and called to account. You throw up your hands and mutter portentous nonsense."

"I would tear out my eyes if it would help me to see more of God."

There was a long silence, then the captain began again quietly.

"There are many words with truth in them—perhaps you can feel the truth of them even if you cannot bring yourself to believe them or trust in them. It is a poor measure of truth that you must be able to cut it open on your table."

"I had a feeling of indigestion last night; I feel tired today— or perhaps it is the first sign of the mystical wholeness of the universe—yes, and I shall abandon science and wear a hairshirt and cover my face with ashes—no, wait—it is indigestion." The doctor laughed harshly.

"I will not permit the butchery of my men at your hands, sir," said Captain Griffin stiffly. "I will not."

"You will let them die from a cause I can discover and perhaps prevent?"

"You will discover nothing; you may find this or that which does not fit into your limited model—may look and impose your judgment in ignorance. You do not know why men die. You see only the wake of death passing, and call yourself capable of building the ship."

"You are in the employ of Mr. West, are you not? They are his men, and so we shall put it to him. If he wants to safeguard their health, I will proceed. If he wants to hold hands in the dark and chant, I will not stand in his—or your—way."

There was silence for a moment, then shuffling feet and the sound of the door closing. Aziz and I ran into the boiler room to try to hear their conversation with West. I scrambled onto the top of the coal heaped in the bin. It kept shifting beneath me and I could hear only snatches of what was said:

"Widely held standard medical practice—his morbid preoccupations—danger to the crew—ill-used in death—defenseless against the encroachments of—you yourself, sir, could be the next . . ."

Their voices rose and fell and rose again; the captain's was shrill and insistent, the doctor's righteous and calm. Finally they ceased to speak and a long silence followed; I managed to wedge myself atop the edge of the scuttle. West's voice was quiet but clear.

"Dr. Architeuthis, proceed. Captain, you will have your service after the autopsy is finished."

"Cross this line, and the world slips again into chaos," said Griffin, so softly that I could hardly hear him.

"I shall thank you, sir, to return to the management of the ship and keep your philosophizing to yourself," said West, his voice rising.

"Cut him, cut him," replied the captain. "Of such truths each to itself must be the oracle."

"Perhaps, sir, you are overtired," said West evenly. "I encourage some rest, that you might recover yourself."

The door creaked and shut again; footsteps passed down the corridor. I waited a few moments and then made my way up to the deck. As I opened the hatch, the doctor's door opened.

"Ah, there you are, Kane. I need your assistance."

I came into the lab. Hume's body was stretched out naked on the white marble table. The doctor descended over him with a scalpel, and Hume's sluggish blue-black blood ran to the edge of the slab, pooling, and draining down the channel at the edge of the table and disappearing into the drainpipe. I saw Hume's sour face, and in it the sad and sour face of a child recoiling; I saw him twitch as the scalpel pierced the skin of his chest, the skin pulled back like the doors of a secret tabernacle to reveal his flesh white and his organs black beneath it. Using a hacksaw, the doctor removed the front of the rib cage and excavated the upper chest and neck, dug down into the crotch. One by one he cut free the organs and placed them carefully aside, pendulous liver and rubbery yellow intestines, shriveled lungs and the blackened calculus that was his poor heart. Other, smaller organs followed, unrecognizable handfuls of gland and connective tissue, a kidney; the doctor turned from the table, from Hume's still-sour face and the great empty cavity of his body, to a row of glass jars arranged by size, with labels on their lids; he dropped each piece in and sealed the jar. In his precise hand he wrote *Hume* and the date, and handed it to me to place on the shelf. Using a bucket of seawater, the doctor rinsed the cavity free of blood and rinsed clean his slab. He took a large hooked needle and heavy thread and sewed Hume's chest shut with rough strokes, pulling it until the flesh bulged on either side of the stitches. Then he took a small cloth and carefully washed his face and had me help get his shirt back on. Hume's flesh was damp and spongy, and it left a smell on my clothes for many days afterward.

"Well, Doctor?"

"I don't see anything here thus far. But I'll perform some tests on the tissues." We slid Hume into the sack and lugged him back to the deck.

Dinner that evening was a somber affair. We ate without pleasure and gathered on the deck by the mainmast. The doctor and Pago laid out the shrouded body at the railing while the captain read into the faint twilight. He finished and Hume's body was

hoisted as we sang a hymn. A small splash announced its departure. We bowed our heads a moment and returned to our work.

That night, I stared at the bunk over me, seeing in its lumps
and hollows the absent shape of his life—Hume pulling on his
shirt, or stooping to shine his boots and laying them carefully
aside.

I thought of the pinched displeasure of his face, the shrill
whine of his voice, felt myself recoil from him even in death as if
he had passed to me some germ that would breed in my blood,
banked up by my heart, that would lay waste to vital muscles
within me and leave me exhaling from myself his stench of rot, in-
terred in the same small and desolate world that had held him.

I clutched after sleep as my heart pumped bile up into my
throat, and I tried to spread my mind like oil over the sad and
shivering creature that was my soul. From the blasted landscape
of the ice to the barren cavity of Hume, I saw only emptinesses,
blank spaces unfilled and unfillable; inside me, I felt the queasy
turning of my own guts and the squalid thump of my heart.

*eleven*

Five bleak days passed. We made the motions of preparing to sail, but did not move. The captain kept us busy—repairing lines, checking sails, stowing the gear from our treks. At the completion of each task, we would wait, poised, for the order to weigh anchor, but it did not come. After a pause, Griffin would bellow another order from the deckhouse—rerig, restow, scrape clean the anchor chain, clear ice from the rigging that we had cleared a scarce hour before. The Narthex swung on her chains, as if anxious to be off herself, her nose swinging east, then west of north, like a great horse tossing her head with slow impatience, her sides knocking into the ice to keep it off. Smoke rose from the stack as Aziz fired the boiler, and we could hear the chuffing of the engine, then a whirring groan as it died away.

With the time to notice, I was struck by the suddenly falling temperature—it was now steadily fifteen or twenty degrees below zero—a sharper blade of cold than that we had had steadily prodding us. We could only stand a few minutes out in it without getting frostbitten. Shivering on the deck awaiting orders, I found us more often in the darkness than in the light, and the days, when they came, much shorter and strengthless; this searing land of light was flickering and fading; after hours of gray warning, the sun broke weakly over the horizon at ten, and disappeared at two. Around the ship, lumpy ridges of ice cast achromatic shadows; the whistling call of a skua echoed over the ice occasionally, but we saw no walrus or seals; lures idly cast overboard dragged through greasy slush and caught nothing. The dogs paced for no reason, turning in tight circles, starting fights and abandoning them, leaving their food to weaker dogs.

Adney and Reinhold started shanties, but without work to drive them, they died away in the silence; with no wind to animate us, and no ice to battle, a kind of lethargy settled over us, a low fatigue exacerbated by the freezing temperatures; stubborn lanyards pulled back as we pulled; obdurate sails would not shake free their frost. Every action called for more effort than seemed its due, and returned less than it promised. It was not simply the death of Hume that dispirited us—if anything it occasioned some glee, albeit muted—but the lack of results for all of our efforts, the lack of discernible progress, for the hint of reward. West's promises seemed not simply evasive but mendacious and the strength of our backs revealed it. The doctor moved through us like a wraith, not responding to questions or greetings; waved us aside or shouldered past us, muttering and scribbling. He no longer called on me to help him, spending most of his time in the laboratory. No announcement was made about the cause of Hume's death.

At twilit noon on the fifth day, Griffin ordered us at last to weigh anchor. We moved off under steam to the northwest. Even that little motion seemed to revive us; the shuddering of the ice under our bows, the whisper of breeze in our face, the sliding past of gray floes quickened our hands, sent our blood coursing again,

created in us the hope that, at least, we might leave this gray dead-
ness behind; as we pushed away our lethargy, even the miles of ice
beckoned again.

Most of our work was done in darkness or in moonlight now.
Griffin dispatched Reinhold and Adney to scout the route ahead.
They returned and led by lantern, marching over the ice if the
lead was narrow, or steering in an iceboat if it was broad. We
moved out of the floes and into more open water. Several heralded
it as a sign that we were nearing the approach to the volcanic archipelago, and stayed past their watches, looking for the glow of
magma in the water. Men strained after blurry shapes, looking for
any oddity, any novelty hidden in the craggy ice.

We soon returned to heavier ice. The scouting became useless;
there was little open water—even the few leads we did find were
quickly frozen over. We ground ahead where we could find passage, and battered where we could not. The silver moonlight was
unhelpful at best, and treacherous at worst; its black shadows
could hide soft, young ice or solid floes. At first we advanced cautiously, dropping men to the ice to scout before we attempted to
plow ahead. But the doctor got impatient with our progress and
demanded that West order Griffin to go ahead without scouting.

In response, Griffin threw the ship headlong at the shadows,
his jaw set as she squealed against the ice or shuddered and shook
and slid back. The doctor also demanded that the dynamite be
used; Ash stood ready to slip to the ice to blast us ahead, descending again and again to set charges. The deck was showered
with chunks of ice and water, the screw roared to life, and we
bludgeoned on.

The ice, for its part, did not yield easily. Open leads disappeared into dead-end canyons of ice; small floes remained wedged
beneath our bows despite battering and blasting; even the young
ice on occasion would not give way and we were forced to batter

our way back to our last point of turning. The ice grew thicker as we advanced; icebergs were more numerous, and the floe ice was more than twenty feet thick in some places, rising in great ridges about us. As we moved through these dark canyons, we seemed to shrink—first a ship of dwarfs, and then of mites, sheer walls of ice towering one hundred feet and more over us. The sun, when it reached us, was waning, like a heart slowing, a red ember glowering on the horizon as if retreating in bitter recrimination.

Without the light, the ice lost much of its majesty; its thousand colors disappeared into gray and black, a dead land without rot, without decay, the currents of its life arrested. Our curiosity was suffused with dread in the darkness, and we moved ahead with trepidation, casting glances over our shoulders, watching the water, our minds casting out for some trace of life from that reptilian monotony. We hung lanterns from the rigging, and scouted when we could, but there was often not even room to launch the boats in the narrow corridors.

On the twenty-eighth, we broke out into a sort of valley between masses of ice, and there caught our final glimpse of the sun. It hung, pale lemon, in gray clouds, then turned fiery orange as it fell, spreading red and orange across the horizon, a cold and distant apocalypse. Then it too faltered and fell into darkness; we were left with a string of lanterns and the distant and tiny stars.

In the last of the light, Adney saw, out over the ice, a small and oddly shaped spot of faint color—brown against the silver of the ice. We dropped into the boat and found, resting on a level floe, a log, with traces of roots—much battered to be sure, but clearly there. This caused tremendous excitement—we hauled it back and threw it up on deck. The doctor pored over it, cutting free samples and digging into the pith.

It was a tropical hardwood, of a type unknown in North America, though similar to some east Asian tropical varieties. It appeared from his examinations to be a tree in the traditional sense, relying on sunlight to grow, as opposed to some new phylum that used geothermal energy. Still, a tropical hardwood in the middle of the Canadian Arctic! No one slept that night.

The doctor paced the deck in the erratic light of the lanterns, calling out for this route or that one, snorting dismissively about the possibility of the ice to stay fast before us. He carried charts in his hand, and paused to make notes on them occasionally; he took soundings when we stopped and maintained his careful record of salinity, air and water temperatures, wind speed and direction. He seemed preternaturally calm, as if full sunlight still shone down on him, and the way stood revealed. We followed the path of one large iceberg for several miles into a battlement of icebergs. The temperatures fell into the minus thirties; even the mighty berg had ground to a stop and we halted behind it.

Around the ship, the ice rose like jagged, broken teeth; sharp lines silvered in the moonlight and deep crevasses stretched beneath them. We spoke in hushed voices and moved quietly over the deck, as if to avoid drawing notice to ourselves—with one exception. Reinhold seemed to take delight in the echoing canyons of ice; he bellowed and sang and guffawed defiantly. His voice boomed over the ice and penetrated into every corner of the ship. We spent two days jostling among the icebergs, and they ceased to move, though shallow channels of water still opened between them, kept free by the small but frequent shifting of the icebergs.

We would have made preparations to spend the winter there, but there was no level surface on which to descend. We had prepared the Ballroom, and the captain made some modifications to our routine—such as heating cannonballs in the boiler and dispensing them to our cabins to keep us warm, and shifting the watches from four hours to two so that we didn't suffer the frost for as long.

Watch was still an interminable affair—spent hopping around

the deckhouse or trying to avoid provoking the dogs. The dogs revealed vile tempers; there was none of the peaceful lounging of Newfoundland. They permitted only Reinhold to touch them and snarled at anyone else who drew near. Otherwise, the routine of the ship remained the same—Griffin inventing pointless tasks in endless scheduled repetition and badgering us to do them. The doctor refused to let us prepare to overwinter because he remained convinced that we were very close, and that the ice would open again for us, and so we must be ready to move. He pointed to the open water.

"In this temperature, in the absence of light, it is impossible," he told us, "without some other source of heat. We are close."

His certitude was echoed among the men, several of whom carved off chunks of the log for themselves and pressed to push ahead, if not in the *Narthex,* then in the boats. We remained in this state of nervous readiness for three days, then four.

On the fifth day, I was awakened by a terrible groaning and squealing. I rushed to the deck to see the eastern wall of the channel looming even closer over the deck. The mainmast spars poked into the wall of the iceberg.

"The iceberg in front of us is twisting, and it's pulling that ice with it," Adney said. "The channel sides are too sheer for us to slide up. We've got nowhere to go."

We watched from the deck as the spar bent, buckled, and finally splintered against the wall of ice. From below, we could hear the metal sides of the *Narthex* protesting as the ice advanced.

"I've been marking off the progress of the iceberg over the rail for the last few days," Adney said, showing a set of notches in the rail. Some were already obscured under the advancing ice.

"Well, that looks promising," I said, and he laughed.

"It's a mirage," he said. "We'll sail right through it tomorrow. Wait and see."

"I wonder if this expedition has gotten further than the previous one did."

"Don't know," said Adney. "I wasn't along."

"Why'd you come along on this? You weren't in prison, were you?"

"No," he said, laughing. "Prison might have been better. Why'd I sign on?" He looked off into the darkness. "You can't believe how easy it is for a girl to get pregnant. And then there's the world on its ear and me not even finished with college."

"You just left?"

"I would've been pretty useless there. Not quite ready to strap on the green eyeshade. My father gave her some money."

"Did you love her?"

"Christ, Kane, I didn't even know her. The body's got its own things it wants to get done, and we'd do better to stay out of the way. Doesn't have much to do with what we want or think or choose."

"So how'd you end up on this trip?"

"Much the same as you, I expect," he said, looking me in the eye. "Out of alternatives when the choice came. Or are you Saint Brendan in the flesh, come back to find your Isles of the Blessed?"

"Not much money in that, I think."

"I don't know—it was supposedly the gateway to heaven. You might be able to sell tickets." He laughed brightly.

The deck lurched and the sides began squealing again. The captain rushed from the deckhouse and ordered us to prepare the whaleboats to abandon ship if necessary. Around the ship the ice, too, groaned and roared; high-pitched whistling came from down the canyon, and booming cracks faded into low creaking. The ice, which had seemed dead for so long, was waking into a pack of beasts that began to circle the ship, prodded and played with it. We threw our supplies into two boats, but with the ice almost to

the davits, there was no way to lower them. We hauled the remaining iceboat to the stern, along with our supplies; then we
stood on deck and waited.

After an interminable hour of groaning, the ice stopped moving. Silence settled again, which was even more disturbing than
the noise. Creely called up from the hold that we were taking on
water, and we moved to man the pumps. Four of us fell on the
handles and started to heave, but they would not budge. In the
days since we had used them last, they had frozen solid. Griffin
divided us into two groups—one passing buckets up by hand, the
other working with Hunt to heat pans of oil on the stove to drench
the pumps and perhaps unfreeze them. I was on the bucket line.
Our hands, swaddled in their sets of mittens and numb already,
could not control the buckets; we were lucky if half a bucketful
made it over the side. Reinhold stood at the hatch of the hold passing buckets up, and he was rapidly soaked. His genial cursing
kept us all moving, set us into a sort of rhythm, and the buckets
began to move faster.

Creely called up that the water was still rising. Griffin ordered
the oilers into our line.

With their help, the buckets moved faster, but more numb
hands meant more spilling, and I doubt if we actually got much
water out. Ash continued to work at the pumps, hammering at
them, using a torch to heat one section, then another. Creely called
up again that we were losing ground. We began to heave the buckets frantically, nearly losing one over the side.

"Stand back!" groused Ash, and poured kerosene over the entire pump mechanism and set it afire. We moved in, though some
parts of the pump were still burning, and now the handles moved
stiffly. We pumped furiously and they began to slide more easily.
After a minute or so of pumping, however, no water had come out
of the pipes.

"Damn," said Ash. "Blocked." He raced to his workshop and emerged with a long piece of rubber tubing, which he attached to the kerosene can. He shoved the other end down the pump pipe and lifted the can over his head. He waited as the kerosene drained into the pumps, then dropped the can, lit a rag, and stuffed it down the pump. Flames came roaring out.

"Just fire the ship," said Pago. "That'll take care of it."

Water trickled out at first, then chunks of ice, and finally a reassuring roar. We cheered and began to sing as water gushed over the side. Our breath hung over us in great clouds, and icicles formed on our beards and coats. After half an hour with both pumps and buckets, Creely called up that the water was retreating, and we cheered. Two hours further, and Griffin ordered the buckets stopped. Ash joined Creely below to try to find the leaks and patch them.

The pump work was not bad—drier than buckets and not too strenuous. Once the initial danger had passed, we slowed our rhythm to an easy swing; Reinhold changed the fast-paced pump shanty to the slow story of Tom O'Grady's search for love, which was equal parts melancholic love story and catalogue of exotic venereal disease. While we were singing, Creely clambered up from the hold. He was soaked, and his eyes were empty.

"What ho, Mr. Creely?" called out Adney. "Is our bath ready?"

Creely smiled weakly and stumbled down the fore hatch, his boots cracking as they froze.

We pumped another hour, until four others replaced us. Belowdecks, Hunt had a stew simmering, and tea and fresh biscuits. He was a remarkable man in his way.

Griffin came in while we were eating.

"Four hours on and four for sleep," he said. "Two on the

pumps and two below helping Ash and Creely caulk. Sleep in your clothes."

We finished our dinner somberly and retired to our bunks to sleep in our soggy, stiff clothes. The ice, which had remained quiet while we worked, began to crack and screech again, though more distantly.

The summons to work came one black minute later, and we staggered back on deck. Adney and Preston took the pumps and Reinhold and I went below. Ash had rigged a harness for himself, which held him facedown out of the water. He pulled himself along the wall like a spider and reached down to block the leaks he could see. Creely stood knee-deep and felt beneath the surface for other cracks. Reinhold held the lines that controlled Ash's height and direction. I tore sailcloth into strips to stuff into the cracks. They used spikes to drive the strips of cloth into the cracks and hoped for them to freeze solid before the pressure pushed them out. We couldn't use the tar in the cold water—it wouldn't set. Ash said the doctor was working on a cement that would work under these conditions, but he didn't hope for much.

They worked furiously, and the pumps kept the water from gaining, but the leaks seemed to multiply as they worked. Creely moved from the worst leak to the next worst, skipping from corner to corner; Ash worked fastidiously, covering one square foot of the wall before moving on to the next. With his harness, he could work steadily, pausing only to warm his hands on cannonballs that Aziz brought up from the boilers. Creely could tolerate only about ten minutes in the water before he had to stop, remove his boots, and beat life into his feet again. His hands, which he kept bare, were white to the elbow, and he could not hold the cannonballs by himself. Still, after only a few minutes' pause, he would stomp back into his boots and wade back into the water.

He could not keep from cringing as the frigid water flooded over the top of his wellies, but he set his jaw and returned to the wall.

We finished our shift below and moved up to the pumps. Creely's face stuck with me as we worked, and I tried to pump harder as I thought of him.

"Poor Creely," I said, to spur us on. "He should get a break from the water."

"Wouldn't take it if we offered," said Reinhold, "not after Griffin's ordered him. He'd jump into hell first."

We pumped harder still, the creaking of the pump echoing off the sheer walls that rose around us.

"We should abandon," I said, "rather than waste ourselves trying to keep afloat."

"We'll float free yet," answered Reinhold. "Besides, where would we go? We're better off here than in a whaleboat. She's a stout little gargoyle."

At the end of two interminable hours, Preston and Pago stumbled up in relief. Hunt met us in our quarters with cocoa and more biscuits and we dropped into our bunks.

We battled the water for three days. Ash rigged a makeshift stove in the hold, which made their work more comfortable, though the water was still freezing. The leaks seemed to multiply as they worked, and no sooner was one section of the hold blocked when another would begin to leak. The ship groaned and squeaked under pressure from the ice, but it did not give. Under the foredeck in our quarters, where the pressure was the worst, the force of the ice pressed droplets of sap from the wood like slow wine from grapes. We awoke from dreamless sleeps to the sound of wood splintering somewhere, of cracks like gunshots, but still the *Narthex* did not yield.

In the afternoon of the third day (Griffin insisted the hours be called, though there was now no change in the darkness—except perhaps the faintest graying of the black at noon), the regular groaning and grinding resumed, and we could hear the metal sheeting squeal under the water. With immense slowness, the deck began heeling to starboard and tilting forward. The dogs whined and scrambled over each other to keep their place. Adney shouted down the hatch to rouse the men and we gathered by the deckhouse as the entire ship rose and canted. Ten degrees, then fifteen. At twenty, Griffin ordered us to lower the boats. Creely stumbled on numbed feet and clung to Reinhold to keep from falling. At about twenty degrees, the heeling stopped and the ice fell silent once more. We stood at the ropes, waiting to drop into the channel, waiting to hear the crack that signaled the end of the *Narthex,* but it did not come.

Gradually we relaxed and moved out to inspect the ship. Adney called up from the hold.

"The water's draining out the bottom; the hold's almost dry."

We gave a ragged cheer. Ash ordered a pot of tar and set about mounting the stove to burn level. Creely staggered below and took his first real rest since the leaking began. Pago and Reinhold manned the pump and we cheered as we heard the sucking sound that meant the end of the water.

We coated the walls and floor of the hold with strips of sail-cloth and bound them with the tar. Ash expressed some doubt about whether they would hold, but it was the best we could do. Then he rigged an insulating jacket for the pump, fed by a kettle, which kept it from freezing and needed only to be stoked. The ship's routine returned to some semblance of normal, albeit at a funhouse slant.

The only lasting change was Creely's condition. His fingers blistered from the frost and chafing brought on by the prolonged exposure to seawater until they looked like overripe bananas, the skin peeling off in strips. His feet swelled also, though he told no one about them; the doctor discovered them when he tried to help him with his boots and found that he had to cut them off. Creely's feet were puckered from the dampness and greenish white in color, with black patches where the skin had died. Three of his toes came off in his socks. Despite constant and careful ministrations from Dr. Architeuthis, Creely's skin peeled away in long sheets reaching almost to his knee. True to form, he insisted that his injuries were not so debilitating, and had to be restrained from rising to take his watch.

The doctor dismissed me from my work with him, preferring to make the endless rounds himself, and remaining below for long periods in the laboratory. We saw little of West also during this time, except when we were called to the boats. We heard only the Pianola moaning up through the deck.

The pressure on the bow continued to be very worrisome. We would bolt upright in our bunks at the sound of a rivet firing out of its socket like a bullet; the planks in the hold bent and twisted, and even the mighty king post, which divided our portion of the ship from the officers', seemed to be warping. Ash did what he could to repair the damage that we could find, but often we were unable to trace the sound of splintering to a beam or board, or to find a missing rivet where we had heard them shooting out for hours. Even those places we could find to repair, we were often unable to; frozen beams that are oozing sap do not readily take new screws. We added braces where we could until the entire hold was a maze of crisscrossing trusses and stanchions.

The wailing of the *Narthex* under pressure was a trial for us all; each new set of sounds, we felt, was surely death throes. The unceasing noise of the ice abraded all our nerves and kept us from sleep despite our exhaustion. We filed silently past each other with the ghastly faces of insomniacs, and lay in dreading silence in our bunks as the *Narthex* was slowly dismembered around us.

The temperature for the end of November and the start of December fell to an extraordinary mean of minus forty-nine degrees. Outside of a heated cabin, it struck like a sledgehammer. Our breath crackled in the air like firecrackers as it froze. Any brush of bare skin against metal was agonizing. The wind, when it rose, sought out every chink in our patchwork clothing, separated every seam, tugged and tore at our gloves and hats. Inside the cabin, the stove, when fully stoked, kept the air above freezing if you lay close; against the walls, ice formed rapidly from our breathing and soon grew to be several inches thick. There was no respite from it. Even those who lay close to the stove found themselves first drenched as the frost on the outer layers of their clothing melted; then it refroze. Given the choice between sodden and chilled or dry and frozen, some opted for the latter, believing that the frost had insulating qualities that kept them warmer.

Griffin kept us working at a tremendous pace; in addition to the repairs, he had us mending the rigging, though there was no way we were sailing for months, and building shelters on the deck for the dogs. He had planned, when the time came for us to overwinter, to bury the ship in the snow and thus to insulate it. In our present circumstances, we had no snow and no safe harbor, so he kept us ready to sail. We arose every morning to clear the decks and rigging of ice, then cleared them again before lunch, and again before dinner. He drove us like cattle to our tasks, refusing to hear our complaints or excuse us from our duties; he brooked no criticism, heard no reason. It was as if he believed that our suffering could push the ice away, could keep us afloat, and so the more it squeezed, the more he drove us.

Under the lash of Griffin's tongue and the nervous exhaustion brought on by the noise of the ship and the looming walls of ice, we began to bicker. I retreated for the calm of Aziz's boiler room when I could, if only to avoid the others and share a cup of tea.

On deck, men blamed others for imaginary offenses, criticized their work or their sloth, quarreled about their food, their bunks, the sound of their footsteps, the irregularity of their breathing.

It is in each to trace out the history from origin and circumstance, the buffetings of fate and choice, the blindnesses and visions that brought us separately together in that dark and freezing ship. For some, like Creely, it was the next step in a pattern of years of hardship; for others, myself, blind mischance, a leap gone awry, the reaching after a dream that was mired in ice and darkness. With an abler head, I would have noticed that these men, like me, had no clothing, had accumulated no wealth; that, though older, they had no firmer footing in the world than I, wrapped in the same patchwork of scraps, prey to the same mix of unrevealed mystery and vague hopes in the plotting of strangers—I should have judged them criminals or incompetents, fools, ill, insane, a little of each.

Men divided themselves into camps and used every moment to complain about the members of the others. Pago, Ash, and Preston made up one; Reinhold, Adney, and Hunt another. I spent what time I could down in the hold with Aziz. He was not allowed to fire the boilers, but he had a small stove and his cabin was less cold than the others.

No songs rolled up in fogs as we worked, no hands joined in without being ordered to do so. With Hume dead and Creely down, Griffin strove to be everywhere at once, castigated each in every moment. Each group drifted within different sets of expectations and assumptions, anchored only by the incessant demands of the captain. If we did not despise each other so fiercely, we would surely have mutinied.

At the same time, the extraordinary strength that had come in the light began to fade; where we had been lean, we became gaunt; where vigorous, listless; paralyzed as we were by the ice, our sense of our great capabilities withered until it was all we could muster, with a blast of venomous cursing from Griffin, to straggle from our beds.

My body shrank within my clothes until I had to lash them on with ropes. Old wounds returned to me now, old scars opened, old bruises and sprains received at half-remembered times came welling up, marked my skin, and suppurated, a dream history of all of my scarrings and woundings, all my weaknesses, as if my body were composed of poisons that traced out ghostly tunnels in what remained of my healthy flesh, undermining what little strength I had. My heart, its demonic strength banked by these poisonous floods, pushed them forth into my extremities; my fingers blistered and burst with pus; my skin turned blue and black where it was not a cadaverous white; it was as thin as paper; my gums bled, and my teeth sat loosely in their sockets. My stomach, formerly so pleased with my food, roiled and rioted, and my bowels ran.

We were then a population of loss—lost to each other, to our work, to our purpose. The questions that had compelled us thus far—what was to come, what glory, what destiny, what wonder, what money even?—these dropped away, and we were left with a ceaseless round of small hungers and melancholic lusts. The food did not satisfy, yet we demanded more, begrudged it of our companions—our enemies—ate our fill, and hoarded the rest to eat without satisfaction later. Sleep, too, did not bring rest but dreams of small irritations—we dreamt even of cold—yet Griffin had to pull us forcefully from our bunks. We measured our lives in raisins, in the uneven lumps of biscuits, strings of fat, scraps of fur; in our lethargy, we had only the energy to covet and loathe. We rose mechanically to our duties, to black walls of ice and frigid, squally snows. Pago and Creely complained of pain in their joints and crushing headaches; we suspected them of malingering.

Biting into a biscuit at dinner, Adney pulled free a tooth in a gush of blood. He reported to Dr. Architeuthis, who diagnosed scurvy in all three and ordered us on scurvy rations: stew of scurvy grass and plates of sauerkraut, lime juice, and raw potatoes. Such was the state of our spirits that some believed—myself in that number—that none of them were actually sick, but had contrived the entire spectacle, first the joint pain and headaches, then the hoax of the tooth, in order to deprive us of our hoosh and cocoa. With each spoonful of soggy sauerkraut and the bitter grass stew, each gnaw of potato, we grew to detest them more and more—if it was not intentional, then they were weak, and making the rest of us suffer for it. We had sunk so low that we did not hope for change but merely endured, merely rose to face each day. We had months to wait in the darkness before the sun returned.

# twelve

I awoke, panicked, and cast about me for a mooring. Alien piles and boxes surrounded me, distorted by the weak light of a lantern. My heart raced and I cried out as I jerked my head up. I looked blankly at a tiny room, and the hunched form of a man, his face turned grinning to me. My nose stung with the metallic smell of burned coal; I clutched a thin blanket. But then the seep of cold, deep cold, asserted itself in me, brought me back to myself, to my senses, to the ship and the ice and our lost mooring in it.

Aziz leaned toward me, a smile playing over his lips.

"We're here," he said, "unfortunately." He handed me a cup of steaming tea and resettled against a pile of bags, drawing them up around himself for warmth. He watched my face with amusement as I found my way back. The sharp sweet bite of tea cleared my head and I smiled ruefully.

"Slept well?" he asked.

I nodded. "A little too well, I guess. Forgot I was here."

He turned to me intently, still smiling. "It is odd to think that we have ended up here together," he said, "locked in this dank, freezing ship a thousand miles from anywhere. Each of us, each step to another."

"How did you end up here?" I asked. "You've never told me."

"This place is as good as any other," he said.

"Other than the freezing cold, the starvation rations, and the distinct possibility we'll all die."

He laughed.

"Honestly. Did you stumble into it like I did? How did you come to translate the journal?"

He looked off into the lantern for a while, and when he turned back to me his eyes were bright and eager.

"I was born in a small village, high in a mountain range at the edge of a vast black desert. The people of the village, my people (though I shudder to think of them as such) had lived in this village for generations. Long before I was born, we had lived in the valley below, on fertile land by a river. But we were pushed out by another people, up the mountain and into the black sands of the desert. The valley people regarded us as animals, and saw it as their duty to purge the land of us. They began by taking from us, stealing, and daring us to respond; then they threatened us, and finally they simply herded us like animals up into this wasteland and forced us to scrabble out our living among the rocks and sand. They retreated to the valley and destroyed the passage up. They told their children that we were beast men, demons, that we had been spawned by the desert, that we would kidnap them and devour them in our desert caves if they ever left the valley.

"Life was extremely difficult for us, because little would grow in the thin, dry soil of the mountains; the wind howled out from the desert and stripped our fields of what little we had cultivated. Plants baked and shriveled without bearing fruit under the heat of the desert sun. The few animals we brought with us did not survive—cows tumbled off the cliffs or wandered into the desert;

horses went mad in the blinding sandstorms; both gradually weakened on the sparse forage, gave no milk, did no work, and finally starved to death. Our chickens, searching for food, filled themselves with gravel and eventually suffocated, their full gullets choking off their throats. We were forced to range very far along the ridge of the mountains to find mountain goats, and to subsist on foul stews made from lichen and moss.

"The desert was especially malicious. Its wells would rise up only to disappear, or turn foul overnight no matter how carefully we tended them. We spent days on end searching for new water, digging huge pits in hopes of finding some. Water was hoarded and guarded jealously.

"The black sand of the desert seeped in everywhere, under doors and through windows, into water and food, ears, noses, mouths; it invaded our bodies, flooded and filled us. The grind of sand in our teeth and its arid taste became, to us, as the air. The grimness of our lives brought forth an answering grimness in us: we became petty and violent, savage, greedy, thoughtless, bitter—poor thieves of nothing.

"After a while the traders ceased to come because we had nothing to trade and the route in was very dangerous; our tools became broken and makeshift. Metal became scarce and we resorted to bone and wood. Starvation moved through us, withering a face, swelling a belly, drawing away a child, a neighbor, a family blown into dust.

"We passed a dark time before we learned to find the wells as they shifted, and to drink the brackish water, to catch and milk the goats, and to cultivate what frail plants we could. We scraped the lichen to make the foul stews, and so we learned to cling to life on the plateau.

"One day strangers came into the village along an unknown route. We met them with fear, revulsion, and greed, and I am sure, but for the weakness of our men, we would have killed them on the spot. They treated us with kindness—gave us chickens to eat, a luxury which we had all but forgotten. The strangers waited and watched in silence until we had eaten all of their chickens, and every person in the village was drowsing over their full stomachs. They explained that they worked for the circus and that they were looking for children to join them. They spoke about the beauty and excitement of the circus, of the spectacle of lights and music, the cheering of the crowds. They talked about always traveling, always seeing new towns and cities, new wonders, always being admired and treated like royalty. They described huge banquets thrown in their honor, of fantastical, succulent dishes brought on silver trays. They did not need to tempt us with wealth—for us, food was sufficient, and they knew it. We were bewildered at first; we had forgotten that there was a life in the valleys, that there was a world that was not the desert and the shifting wells, the black sand, and the bone tools. We listened to the stories of the circus men, dazzled, and rushed to offer our children. The men selected five and vanished into the mountains.

"In two years time they returned full of stories about our children's success, about the lives of extravagance and splendor they led, about visiting with kings and princes. They said that our children had responded so well to the training that they had achieved great renown. Their parents swelled with pride, and others rushed to offer their children to the circus men. The parents of the original group begged the men to bring the children back with them the next time so that they could see for themselves, and hear the stories from their lips. The traders promised not for that year, but for the following year, as the circus would be touring in the north then, and they could come without missing too much.

"And so the traders returned with three of the children on horseback. The villagers rushed to greet them, but recoiled in horror. The children had become terribly deformed: one had both eyes on one side of his head and the mouth on the other; another had no jaw and a long, flickering tongue; the third had no arms, but could bend his legs as if they were rubber and use his toes with marvelous dexterity. The traders had done their work well; the children were not merely mutilated but changed more profoundly, more horribly, for you could see in their deformities the awful persistence of the body to adapt, to be distorted and still to grow, to press into the world despite its wounding weight, despite its confinements, its scarrings.

"The children waited silently on their horses while the men spoke to their horrified parents. They seemed otherwise strong and healthy, and undisturbed by the alterations in their bodies. These were still their children, the circus men said insistently, externally different but internally the same, the same children they had loved and allowed to leave.

"The circus had given the children a chance to see the world, to live a life that none of them had ever dreamed of. There had been a cost, but had it been so much? Ask the children, they said, and see if you have chosen wrongly.

"Gradually the parents crept forward again, reached out tentatively, looked into the bright eyes of their children. After long quiet moments, they burst into tears and embraced their changeling children, and the children burst into tears.

"There was a huge celebration that night and the whole village watched as the children performed. The snake-tongued boy told hypnotic stories in a croaking lisp and danced a sinuous dance to music played by the armless boy through a horn held with his feet. The third boy told fortunes and sang songs, his voice bubbling up impossibly pure from his tangled throat.

"Afterward they sat with their parents; they told about painful operations and brutal training, about sickening drugs and painful clamps and harnesses they had had to wear. But now it was not so bad, they said blithely, and told stories about all that they had seen, the palaces and broad sweeping rivers, the bright colors and lights of the city. They presented their parents with bright banners, shiny tools, and fat chickens.

"Throughout the night, the parents of the circus children sat in a tight half circle near the fire; they looked at their children and at each other furtively as they wrestled with themselves. They forced smiles to their faces and looked out over the laughing faces of the other villagers, watching for approbation or mockery; they looked down at their own shabby clothes and broken bone tools, swallowing their shame and their horror. As the evening passed into night, so too did some of their reservations; with the flush of the traders' wine, the father of the snake-tongued boy hoisted him on his shoulders and paraded him around the fire. Those whose children had not returned were taken aside by the traders, plied with rugs and jewels. The mothers, wailing, retreated to their tents. The fathers cursed the traders, took the goods, and followed their wives.

"The caravan stayed for three days and performed every night; they slaughtered their livestock and roasted it over a roaring fire of wood they had carried in, and everyone ate mightily. The smell of roasting meat even brought out the parents of the lost children. For the village, having subsisted on lichen and stringy goat meat for so long, it was as a dream, a deliverance into paradise. When they left, the entire village turned out to see them off, waving the bright banners they had been given and shouting and crying. The children cried as they left and promised to return as soon as they could.

"In their wake, we sang their songs and told their stories for many weeks; their banners faded on the doors of their parents' tents. The parents were treated with an odd sort of deference.

They were clearly different from the other villagers, but whether that difference was a mark of shame or honor was not clear. They kept mostly to themselves, and spoke to others only about the prospect of the traders' return.

"As the traders returned year after year, however, and more parents offered their children, this ostracized group became an elite. What began as a quiet shame was pushed resolutely away; it devolved into professed ignorance and then to actual ignorance. They saw only the distinction, only the peculiar talent of their children to be warped—they held it and cherished it, clutched at it.

"The traders began to leave behind some harnesses and straps so that parents could begin training the children very early when their bones were the most malleable. They brought metal helmets in odd shapes that left children with heads that bent and canted to one side or came to sharp points, or straps that slowly pulled their faces to one side or drew their heads down into their bodies. The traders offered advice on how to break their arms and legs and splint them so that they would heal with bends in the middle. Slowly the villagers' understanding of themselves became poisoned by the vision of their own specialness; they discussed the mutilation of children with the ease and distance of businessmen. Like farmers, they delved into the endless variants of drugs, methods, and tricks, of diets and times of year, of techniques for mother and child, concerned only with success, only with innovating, making new, better, and not seeing or acknowledging that better meant simply more horrible and more terrifying.

"The traders offered drugs for the women to take when they were pregnant so that their babies might be born with an especially hideous deformity—'a gift' they called it—an extra arm or leg, withered and shriveled, a gargantuan head, or an extra eye or nose, sometimes even an extra head. Often these children were born dead or very weak, but those that survived were hugely successful, showering great wealth and distinction on their parents.

"The traders did not take every child, and at first it was pitiful to see those rejected children—those whose parents had not been able to bear to listen to them cry and had taken their helmets off or loosened their straps, so that their faces had been pulled and stretched and not settled back; or had failed to heal their breaks properly and left them with stunted, flapping limbs; or those whose imaginations lacked the ambitious horror of their neighbors and simply failed to disfigure their child distinctively. All of the pathetic and pitiful faces of failure—born of greed and bad luck and weaknesses of mind and will and heart—were held up as a reminder not of the horror of the practice, but of the consequences of halfhearted pursuits. The parents of these children were reviled, and their example spurred other parents to more ruthless and brutal ends. There was fierce competition among the families to have their children selected; many added extra clamps or straps, contorted their children into fantastical shapes and piled rocks on them, broke and rebroke their limbs in hope of making them great. Many women died from the traders' drugs, their monstrous offspring dying with them. Some of their husbands beat their heads with rocks and staggered bloodied through the village. Our tents were gradually filled with strange, half-uttered forms, dream fragments not wholly dreamed and so caught, and lost. At night the peaks echoed with the screams and cries of children and of mothers and the howling of madmen and the wind.

"Among all the horrible, created children, the limbless or extra-limbed or woven and fused, the milk white and hairless, the claw-footed, the bloated, the impossibly tall and thin, the scaly or hairy, the children with their heads embedded in their chests who rolled about like balls, the children so supple they seemed made of tongues—of all these, the rope eaters were the most prized.

"When they were very young, their parents would feed them a tiny but indigestible thread, and leave the end of the thread hanging out of their mouths. This thread would slowly pass though them, causing great suffering and bleeding. Often they got terrible infections and would swell with rot. But slowly the body would get used to the thread, as it does to everything, and the child would grow strong again. Then the parents would fasten a thicker thread to the first and begin to feed this to their child. Again the children would sicken, would bleed, would crawl on the floor clutching their throats and stomachs. The traders gave many drugs to soothe the pains, but nothing seemed to work; the children screamed and cried without ceasing, waking to cry again. If they survived, their parents would fasten a thicker and thicker thread, until they passed a rope through themselves, holding it in the side of their mouths and wrapping it about their waists.

"Some could not bear it and cut the rope, and pulled it out of themselves, screaming as they tore their insides; sometimes one would hope to ease the burning for a time and not keep his rope moving. The acid of the stomach would eat through the rope eventually and flood the channels that the rope had made and burn them out from the inside. Slowly, inexorably, the rope would come out, often pulling their entrails with it. The rope was a choice that could not be revoked, once begun, and it was often fed to infants with the milk of their mothers. The few who managed to clear their bodies of it were driven mad by the pain; they lived in the desert, trailing the filthy end from their mouths. The few who managed to survive and endure its constant motion became prized members of the circus.

"It is hard to explain what made the rope eaters so compelling.

Given the horrors I have described, it may seem strange that these were the most terrible. It is a horror that must be witnessed to be understood. Those children who were extremely deformed produced in one a flash of horror that soon subsided and could be forgotten easily. The attraction of the rope eaters was more insidious. A part of their appeal lay in the possibilities of the body to change—to witness the pain of a body rebuilding itself at the same rate it is being destroyed.

"But their true horror lay in the unmasking of our own internal mysteries; if the rope could pass through unchanged, it rendered, somehow, the whole of the body simply a tunnel and the whole of life a mechanical process. The rope made it clear what a pitiful thing our bodies are and what a mundane process life—for through it we could see ourselves wretched, distorted, compromised.

"People passed the rope eaters at first, anxious to see the more spectacular of the freaks, but they returned and returned again, unable to ignore them. They looked on you with eyes that knew the pain of years of suffering, and that look would drop into you like a pebble, raising barely a ripple. But it would rebound through you, building until you were washed with waves of dread. It struck you like the death of a dear friend—for that is what it was—the death of that special, magical vision of yourself that was not this grim machinery of eating and excreting. Their peculiar horror was slow to catch, but catching, spread, contaminating those who had seen them for months afterwards, and returned, like fever, even years later, never leaving them entirely free to dream themselves.

"My father was a rope eater who retired to the village. It was never really clear why he had returned; perhaps something in its harsh landscape answered some harsh and brutal aspect in himself. Perhaps it was the only place he could go. His life with the circus had made him wealthy, and his tent was filled with valuables—gold, rare spices, and beautiful rugs.

"I had many brothers and sisters, but none lived. At first my father ordered my mother to take the traders' drugs in massive quantities in hopes of producing a spectacular showpiece, but my mother did not have the constitution to sustain them.

"After several such failures, he allowed her to stop taking the drugs and she gave birth to healthy twin boys. My father began their training immediately, strapping the first into a metal helmet of his own cruel devising and feeding the second the thread that ran through his own days. He kept both on his bed, their wailing mingling with his groans and bellows. I suppose there was a sort of love in it, a closeness brought by suffering and expressed only through suffering. But in the end it was overmastered by his greed; he tightened the helmet of the first too vigorously and burst his tender skull; he pulled the second's thread incessantly, trying to hurry it along. Finally he pulled too hard, tearing my brother's fragile insides. He bled to death, staining my father's cushions with his own red-brown dye.

"I was born not long after and my mother resolved to keep me hidden; she delivered me to an old woman who lived out in the desert and told my father I had been born dead. My father raged and cursed and drank himself unconscious. And so I was allowed to grow up without the straps and harnesses, without the rope, the training, the drugs. I had only my hand to recommend me.

"The problems of the village to find water and food were compounded in the open desert, especially when the storms came and we were suffocated by the sand. We had to move constantly, rising early and walking through the heat of the day to reach water. The desert was relentless and inconstant; we froze at night, huddling with our animals, drawing thin blankets over us, struggling to keep our flame lit in the drafty tent; then the searing sun would rise. The sands became so hot that frayed cloth could burst into flame by brushing against it, and we would have to hide out until the sun abated. The sands shifted with tidal sweep, laying bare rock ledges and the foundations of ancient cities, bones, and brackish wells, then shrouding them again. Sandstorms struck like an army of snakes, rising from the dunes themselves, coiling about your knees and legs and tearing the breath from your throat. They would vanish in a moment, leaving you blinking and coughing in bright sun, revealing to you a changed world, as if you had been transported to a different and unfamiliar corner of the desert. And that sun would recommence its pounding.

"My mother came to visit when she could, to bring me presents and to shower me with kisses. She could not come often, as we were usually far from the village. But the old woman was kind to me, and I learned to love the desert in its moods, the sweep of the dunes and the roll of clouds and sand at sunset when the sky ran red, the restless moan of the wind coming from endlessly far away, and the vast and empty silence of nights when nothing lived for miles and miles but us, and the darkness pressed around our fire.

"I was discovered by the spies of my father. I had not doubted that he would discover me eventually, but I had supposed I was safe since I was past the age when he could disfigure me profitably or feed me the thread; with my mere hand, I was a curiosity and no more. I did not know my father.

"Something took hold in his brain—whether it had its roots in resentment of my freedom, or vengeance, or profit, I never learned. He arrived on a blazing afternoon, when the sun had beaten every last trace of life back into the ground, had beaten down even the wind, one of those desert afternoons when one had no choice but to submit to the sun, to lie still and wait for the darkness. I was mending a corner of the tent idly, moving as little as possible. I lay on my back and held the fabric over me, tracing the rip with my fingers; the old woman lay behind me sleeping. I heard a shuffle outside and the rasp of breath. I looked out and saw my father staggering into camp. He was grotesquely fat, bloated with a lifetime of poisons; he was swathed in brilliant fabrics, his head and neck draped in the whitest white and his body in red and orange; his eyes burned out from the depths of his face; he was like a herald of the beating sun itself, sent to drive us down into the sand.

"In one foul hand he clutched a length of rope that wound around his neck and disappeared into his mouth. In the other he had the gleaming curve of a scimitar that he leaned on as he stumbled. He looked off in the distance as he approached, staggered, paused glaring. He reached the center of our camp and turned his eyes to me; I froze, as an animal, and waited. He looked at me with uncomprehending fierceness and fury, not as if I was the focus of his anger, but as if he were the blaze of the sun itself, concentrated into this core; his great bulk seeming to spark and crack, full of fire descending like the roll of a colossal boulder over me. His stained mouth gaped, roaring for breath; his yellow teeth clenched around the rope that hung from the distended corner of his lips.

"Then his eyes went out, as abruptly as snuffing a candle, as if he had simply drained into the sand. He began to move jerkily like a puppet. I could see his eyes seeing, full of horror at himself. His arm began to swing mechanically, scraping through the sand as he moved towards me stiffly, empty, blank and dead and destroying.

"So I fled, abandoning the old woman and the camp, down into the village and out along the traders' route. I left the desert, the press of heat and chasing sun, the black sand, crashing into the rocks, tumbling and rising again. I must have missed the road, for I found myself on smaller and smaller trails, mere goat tracks, then finally just scrambling over bare rocks. The mountains grew steeper and more treacherous as I advanced, and a few times I clutched the face of the rock, advancing only because I was afraid to retreat.

"Even by desert standards there was little to eat. I had seen no goats and no streams, and so had to content myself with grasses and lichens. The nights were very cold, like the desert, and I slept huddled into cracks for warmth. I moved on as soon as there was light. I could still feel the colossal weight of my father looming like storm clouds and I awoke several times crying out, expecting to find him standing over me.

"The land into which I moved was extremely desolate—loose rocks tumbled down steep cliffs into rocky, dry valleys. Stunted bushes straggled up from dusty gray soil; I saw no birds, no animals, no hints of men. I descended whenever I could, half running when I reached the valley floors, and finding beyond them another range of cliffs, another barren plain. Compared to the magnificent barrenness of the desert, this land was merely empty. I thought for a time that I had reached the end of the world, that the world did not end in a great cliff yawning out over nothing, but like this, desolation stretching out into infinity, a land of rock where life had not reached.

"One evening, I found myself clambering down a long rocky face when I happened onto a tiny trail. It was no more than worn spots in the stone, but even that stood out in the endless gray through which I had been moving. I hurried along it until I lost it in the darkness.

"In the morning, I resumed following the trail; it soon widened and, as the ridge gave way to a valley, joined a cart track. I was both eager and fearful, for I had known only the old woman and my mother. I hid out in the day and moved at night, skirting the villages. I stole from gardens and farmhouses and drank from plentiful streams. After the arid desolation of the highlands, and a lifetime in the desert, the valley was a paradise replete with treasures.

"The villages gave way to a vast plain, and at the end of it, straddling a muddy and indolent river, was a huge city. I made my way to it and was amazed—hordes of men crawling over men like ants; the din of a thousand tiny storms breaking around me; faces hard from shouting, greedy, idiotic, drooling. In dark corners men muttered to themselves and from balconies shouted and chattered; women with tattooed faces marched in swarms of children like gnats; circles of boys sat chanting verses in unison, their eyes shut tight, their voices droning into the crowd. I passed through markets with great piles of meat heaped up under clouds of buzzing flies, carts groaning under the weight of vegetables and fruits, the clawlike hands of beggars, blankets heaped with the dull gilt of trinkets and beads. I saw a man in a cage filled with rats outside a temple; his face was rapturous as they tore at his flesh.

"I had a hard time at first—men were shocked and repulsed by my hand, but I soon learned to hide it, and to speak with the faces and tongues of men. After the bright extremes of the desert, the city offered so many shadowy refuges.

"I began by begging and eating garbage, which had enough food for armies in it; eventually I found work with a jewelry maker. I had been drawn to his window as I begged and he had seen me and invited me in. His works were marvels, exquisite but not gaudy, like the golden tracery of a single breath which I could hold trembling in my hand. He also made fine watches and ingenious mechanical birds that sang with the silent spinning of tiny gears. I was particularly useful to him because of my hand—with it I could do things that even he could not.

"And yet, for all my dexterity, I could not equal him; I made watches of tremendous complexity and fine balance, but in the end their distinction was merely complexity and not grace—they were always soldered and screwed and heavy. He laughed at my grasping—'Three hands,' he said, 'three hands are still not enough for you!'" Aziz held up for me a marvelous silver teacup, woven with a silver filigree, that slid with odd balance into his twinned hand, turning it over in the light to reveal the shapes of birds and of fruit woven in layers and animated by the movement of the tea within it.

"I passed a happy time in his shop, enjoying my imperfect progress and my sense that I was involved in a great endeavor—the making real of delicate and magnificent creatures that needed the gift of my dexterity to nurture. We lived comfortably in the clutter of his shop, surrounded by the flutter and lilt of his birds and the fantastical grace of his jewelry.

"But that beauty bred destructive hungers in jealous men, and thieves burst into our shop and killed him, and used his torch to melt down his golden breaths into blobs of gold—a reverse alchemy, taking his work and transforming it with their crude touch into the mere, as to lead as his woven grace had been to their only gold.

"I fled again, to the docks, and hid myself in the hold of a ship, squeezing between two bulkheads and holding my breath. I heard their footsteps in the hold and their feral calls, panting and snuffling. They moved on finally and I was left to console myself in the darkness. The ship sailed in the night and I remained hidden, stealing from the stores what I needed and scurrying back into the shadows like a rat.

"When we were several weeks out of port, a cabin boy discovered me. The sailors, children ever, were terrified of me and some wanted to throw me overboard. Others argued that I was the devil's and that my murder would draw his wrath. My fate was settled when their engineer sickened and died. Though they suspected me of having been responsible, they were too frightened to accuse me directly. And now they needed someone with my mechanical knowledge. They locked me in the engine room and sealed the door with chants and charms and left me to work. And so I became a sailor, however grudgingly, and have been one ever since.

"I hoped to find at sea an expansiveness that would free me, that might grant me some peace from the grasping of men that had twice sent me fleeing, but I did not. The seas are vast, but crushing also; they trap as surely as the city or the desert ever had. I settled for a place no better or worse than other places—unpleasant enough to remain uncoveted, and so keep me somewhat free from the exiling envy of men; I have clung to this small hollow, trying to keep from getting dragged into the fray of the world. I am not proud of having retreated into hiding, but have found safety here at least, in the darkness and damp quiet, a space out from the world, which is a strife and a clashing.

"West discovered me after his translator died during a trip to Zanzibar—he grabbed me as I passed in the market and ordered me to assist him. He has found me both useful and discreet since then, and I, some odd measure of refuge."

He paused, gazing into his tea, his face lost.

I could think of nothing to say and so said nothing. It is so seldom that a man is laid bare before you, lays himself bare, that I could but gape in wonder. And as quickly as he had opened himself, he closed again, rising to tend the lamp. The room seemed to rush with cold air and to fill with distance. My tea was cold in my hands.

*thirteen*

On the fourteenth of December I stood shivering in the deck-house, my hands cupped around a cannonball. Griffin had forbidden the use of the deckhouse stove, to conserve fuel. He stood with his hands on the wheel, as if we might drop free at any instant. He clung to the wheel as a drowning man might throttle his savior, refusing even to venture onto the deck or to survey his instruments. Preston huddled by the pump, stoking its small heater. The rest of the crew was below in the Ballroom, shifting stores. Outside, a steady wind was blowing, carrying a fine, almost gritty snow.

"Kane, how's the barometer?"

"Steady, sir," I replied.

He had been preoccupied with the barometer all morning, calling out for a reading every few minutes. I was starting to become exasperated, as it had not moved a fraction of an inch since yesterday.

"Are you sure, Kane?"

"Twenty-nine-point-nine-oh inches. It hasn't budged all morning, sir. Would you care for a look yourself?"

"There is no call for insolence," he said sharply, and left the wheel to examine the barometer himself. He fussed over it for a moment, clutching it in his hands to clear away the frost. Then he brought his face very close to it, holding his breath.

"Well, sir?"

"I believe, Kane, it has frozen in this damn cold. Check with the doctor. He has another one in his cabin."

I went below to the officers' quarters and knocked on the doctor's door. I heard a grunt and entered. I noticed immediately that his cabin was absolutely frigid. Delicate fingers of frost reached up from the floor and extended down from the ceiling; the bottles were covered with a lacy webwork so fine that it looked like cobwebs. The doctor was making notations on his chart with the help of a magnifying glass. He had some sort of leather apparatus over his face that covered his mouth and nose completely. It was covered with icicles that hung down over his chest like a beard.

"Captain Griffin, sir, wants to know what your barometer is reading. It seems that ours has frozen—"

I was not able to finish—the doctor had dropped his glass with a crash and clamped his hand over my mouth. He threw me roughly back out the door and slammed it shut behind him. He mumbled something to me, his eyes very fierce, but I could not understand it from behind his mask. As soon as he dropped me, I began to remonstrate, but he cut me off with a wave of his hand. He pulled off the cumbersome apparatus and shook it in my face.

"Do not breathe in the laboratory!" he shouted. "You will ruin everything."

"But I just—"

"You just nothing—you just came in and began blabbing without thinking, and your wet breath coats the walls, and then what? Did you think? Then the map is useless, then we are lost, then the islands slip away from us forever. What do you think this is for"—he held up the ice-covered mask—"you idiot?"

"Be that as it may, sir," I said tersely, "the captain would like to know what your barometer reads. Ours has frozen."

He turned without speaking and, taking a deep breath, went back into his cabin. When he returned, his face was somber.

"If it can be trusted," he said, "it is 28.78, and falling. I will bring it up to the deckhouse, if you can keep it warm."

"I'll light the stove, sir," I said and returned to the deck.

The captain had resumed his post at the wheel, and kept his eyes fixed on the wall of ice in front of him as I stoked the stove. He did not acknowledge the news that the barometer was falling, nor did he acknowledge Architeuthis when he brought the barometer and mounted it beside the stove.

"It is Dutch," he said, as if it were diamond, "so you must kept the heat even. Uneven heating will disrupt the expansion of the metals and it will become useless. I suspect that is what has ruined yours. Stand here"—he pointed—"and rotate it slowly until the room temperature is above freezing. Then it will be all right on its own."

He shook some of the ice from his peculiar mask and retreated to his cabin. I opened the stove up fully and turned the barometer idly in my hands.

"Well?" asked the captain finally.

"Twenty-eight-point-seven-six, sir, and .06 in the last hour. Can't make much difference to the icebergs really, can it?"

As if in answer, a shudder passed through the ship.

"Maybe the storm will open the ice and let us closer," I said miserably.

The small deckhouse heated rapidly and I was able to put the barometer down. The warmth of the stove felt wonderful on my numb fingers. Outside, the temperature rose slightly, to about thirty below; the wind remained steady and the snow continued to fall. My watch was relieved, but I remained in the deckhouse with the captain, watching the barometer. The captain ordered the deck prepared for a blow, but there was little to do. Everything had already been stowed, or was lashed tightly and frozen, so that we would have been hard pressed to unlash it. We moved the dogs into the Ballroom.

At noon, the barometer read 28.5, and was continuing to fall. The ice remained quiet for several hours, as if crouching down before the storm, then began to rumble like thunder. By this time, we had all gathered in the deckhouse and stood entranced, staring out into the swirling washes of snow. Adney had left one storm lantern suspended from the bowsprit; we could see it swinging with a disarming gentleness. Our waiting silence was broken only by Reinhold's voice calling out the readings every half hour—28.32, 28.28, 28.24, 28.19 . . . Pockets of snow moved idly over the deck before dispersing; lines draped as the wind died. It was an awful feeling to watch the barometer and know that we should be in the midst of a howling gale, and yet look out on such a peaceful, pastoral silence.

Adney went out to check the anemometer.

"Only force four," he said. "We should be flying kites."

There was nervous laughter that subsided again into silence. Hunt and Aziz joined us, and then the doctor, all in silence. We stood packed-in tight, straining, barely breathing, looking out over the deck, poor Christians waiting for our great white lion to be released.

"Twenty-eight-point-one-four," called Reinhold.

"Twenty-eight-point-one-oh."

The storm struck with sudden violence, screaming over the deckhouse, snapping cables as it descended. The light on the bowsprit was snuffed, and a wall of white crashed up against the deckhouse window. Wind forced snow into every crack and crevice, and the boards of the roof rattled. Roaring filled my ears as from the thousand throats of a thousand madmen, then a single throat, impossibly loud, impossibly steady. Nothing could maintain that intensity. From the back of the room, I heard Reinhold's shout faintly:

"Twenty-eight flat."

Wind backed down the stovepipe and snuffed our fire in one blast. We stood dumb as statues and stared; it felt as if the whole atmosphere had been stripped away in a moment and the tearing pace of the naked earth through space itself were audible; I felt we should be mashed flat, crushed beneath it, that we should submit, only submit. I reached out to the wall and felt the timber straining under my hand. It seemed impossible that the ship did not simply explode, shiver into splinters and disperse in the wind. The vastness of the ice was lost in the storm; the power of the wind pressed us into the deckhouse cabin and threatened at every moment to compress us further.

From far away, I heard the sound of wood splintering. The wind seemed to abate for a moment, and with a tremendous crash, the mainmast fell through the roof, shattering the deckhouse and pinning Pago beneath it. The wind scattered embers from the stove across the deck that flared into dozens of small fires.

The mast had fallen over the hatch to the officers' quarters and imbedded itself in the deck. I was caught in a tangle of ropes and could not see to free myself. Beside me, Reinhold and Adney were straining to shift the mast off Pago's legs. The doctor leaned in to help them and they succeeded in lifting it while Pago slid backward. Reinhold snatched him up and they struggled down to the fore hatch while Griffin and Adney put out the fires. I pulled out my knife and with numbing fingers started to cut myself free. I tried to stand against the wind to see what ropes still held me, but I was knocked flat. Finally pulling free, I crawled over the deck to the fore hatch and clambered down.

Everyone gathered in the passageway to the Ballroom, talking excitedly. I could hear Pago groaning and, beyond them, the whining of the dogs. Creely succeeded in lighting a lantern, allowing us to start to sort ourselves out. Hunt headed to the galley, followed by several of the men, to boil water for the doctor.

In the swinging yellow light of the lantern, I could not tell whether the dark patches at Pago's waist were blood or merely water; when the doctor's hands came away darkened, I knew. A trickle flowed down from beneath Pago and pooled against the wall; it sent the agitated dogs into a frenzy. They growled and barked; several leapt at the wall of boxes across the doorway and snapped at the doctor's back. With the ship angled so far forward, they threatened to come tumbling down into the cabin.

"Kane! Get them back in the hold!" yelled the doctor.

Captain Griffin lit another lantern and brandished it as I moved up beside him. I found a coil of rope on the floor, which I used like a club to beat them back. The floor was slippery with blood by this time, and I had a difficult time keeping my footing. Three dogs stood abreast in the passageway, snapping and lunging forward.

"Get back there, you bastards," I heard the captain mutter.

While he held them back, I set the rope on fire with the other lantern and swung this at them. Now they began to retreat, their fur singeing where the rope caught it. Finally they slipped back into the chaos of dogs and we managed to pull the door shut. From behind the door, a massive free-for-all started, a fury of dogs joining the fury of the storm.

Pago had ceased to groan, though he was still conscious, looking almost idly down at the doctor fiddling with his stomach. Griffin moved up beside them.

"Well?" he demanded.

"His pelvis has been crushed—entrails, as you can see, are emerging. And he's losing blood."

Griffin looked worriedly at Pago, who smiled wanly in return.

"Least I'm warm, Captain, at least I'm warm."

"Can we shift him into the men's quarters?" asked Griffin.

"With all due respect, Captain, there isn't a point."

"Of course there is a point, Doctor Architeuthis," hissed Griffin. "Let the man rest a little easier, instead of lying in this hallway." He avoided Pago's eye, as, I suppose, we all did. We lifted him as carefully as we could by his sodden clothes; Griffin shouted ahead and the door to the men's quarters was opened for us. We placed Pago on a bunk next to the stove, which was blazing. He settled back and smiled.

"Oh, that's nice, Captain, yes. Very nice."

We stood in helpless silence as the wind mounted, dogs howled, wood and ice squealed and cracked. Pago's eyes closed, looking out at the flicker of the stove; his lips moved, barely more than a trembling, last words lost in the roar of wind. Now his head rocked gently, as if he were singing a lullaby; his eyelids wavered and drooped again. We stood in silence by.

We were roused by Griffin, who moved us around the bed and began the Lord's Prayer, shouting to be heard over the storm. He pulled the blanket over Pago's head; I should have liked to feel sad, but the noise of the storm intruded on my thoughts—it was insistent, invasive, unrelenting. We moved back from the body; Adney and Preston began to swab up the blood in the corridor, but there was little point. It had already begun to freeze.

Hunt arrived from the galley with a steaming pot of tea and passed out mugs. I hunkered down next to Adney, hoping his lightness could somehow cheer me. I could think of nothing to say and so sipped my tea intently.

It is something to watch a man die, especially a close companion. One would think that an experience so common in a man's life would let us bound it, understand it on our own, or that we could turn to books somehow, or to some store of wisdom that might let us move past without miring us in it—it should have the stench of commonality to it. We should be numb to it—not numb to the loss of our friend, but numb to the blind fact of death itself. And yet we were all confounded.

"Will," I said to Adney, "what do you think for the storm? Will it last?"

"I imagine so," he said evenly. "Our trusty Dutch barometer is most likely below twenty-seven if it wasn't smashed by the mast."

"Still, though, we're safe here in the ice, don't you reckon? Icebergs keep their own company, don't they? I mean, the mast is gone, to be sure, but the ice is solid—like rock. We could as well be in a cave during the storm. And the fire's quite nice, wouldn't you say? Yes, like a cave, and a nice fire and maybe we'll have beef stew. And biscuits. That'll hold us till this blows over. Don't you think? Like stone." I heard myself speaking and could not quite manage to stop.

"These are big icebergs here, very big. Deep enough, they may even be lodged on the bottom. We're wrapped up tight here, like Christmas candies. Nice and tight like Christmas candies.

"What do you think, Will? Another few hours and then we'll be back to normal? Or will it open the ice for us? I think we're tight as Christmas candies, don't you think? Besides, she'll hold, the old *Narthex*, she'll hold, won't she?" I managed at last to clamp my mouth shut and look over to him.

"Well," he said, "I hope so."

"Yes, but—well," I replied, "it's a lot of strain to be sure, but these icebergs won't get pushed around easily." I turned to Preston, who sat beside me.

"Beef and biscuits, don't you reckon, Preston?"

He regarded me without hostility or amusement.

"How many of these big icebergs do you think there are loose around here, Kane?"

"A lot, I think. Hundreds, thousands probably."

"Say an even hundred. And those not very big, only about one hundred feet high apiece."

"Yes, so? I'm afraid I don't follow."

"Think of each as a sail, one hundred feet high, and maybe three times that underwater, each driven before a wind of hurricane strength. A hundred sails or a thousand. It's a damn armada."

That shut me. I sucked at my tea, trying to keep from shivering, trying not to hear the wind, the grinding roar of ice on ice, the groaning of timbers, trying not to see a thousand sails bearing down. I did not have long to feel sorry for myself.

Without warning, the whole ship canted toward the bow. The floor rose up and we tumbled into the cabin wall, with several dogs tumbling down the corridor on top of us. A great brawling mixture of man and dog roiled along the front of the cabin as the ship continued to tilt. The stove spilled out and coals began to smolder on our bunks. Creely shrieked as his hair caught fire—a dog howled piteously—a boot struck my chest as I scrabbled to right myself. Just as I regained my feet, the ship jerked again and dropped with an explosive splash nose first into the water. Cracks formed immediately and water began pouring in; some of the small fires were doused but pieces of flaming debris still floated, catching on fur and hair.

Reinhold led the climb out of the cabin, pulling himself up the corridor and anchoring there to help the others. Griffin, then Preston, then others, one by one, scrambled up the corridor and out on to the deck. The dogs in the cabin scratched at me as I tried to get out of the water, searching for purchase, then entreating for help.

The dogs in the hold clawed over each other to escape it, only to fall skidding into the stove. Reinhold grabbed a few as they passed and heaved them onto the deck, but could do nothing for the others. Over his shoulder, I could make out dimly the black bulk of the king post. It is hard to imagine that any sound could lift itself above that cacophony, but one did. From the heart of the ship came a shuddering groan so loud and so long that we rushed as a body back into the hold. The groaning built, as if the entire ship were crying out for release. As I watched, a crooked seam appeared on the face of the king post, a licking tongue of lightning. With a booming crack, the massive king post split, edges driving past each other; the floor warped beneath me and the walls jumped inward; then with a groaning sigh, the ship settled and was still.

I pulled myself up the companionway with Reinhold close behind me. Loose lines whipped in a scouring wind. Men straggled to the rear of the ship, while one group hacked at the mast, trying to free the hatch to the officers' quarters. I moved aft, helping the other group lower an iceboat toward the water. There was not enough space between the hull and the ice to lower it completely, so we rested it about halfway down. Ash and Preston lowered themselves on ropes to work it around the stern and into the small patch of water there. The bow of the ship was caught under the extending ridge of the iceberg in front of us; the bowsprit was already underwater and the planking of the foredeck was buckling. The whaleboats had been crushed against the bow. That left a small dinghy that hung off the stern.

Ash and Preston succeeded in working the iceboat to the water. Adney dropped over the port side and wedged himself between the ship and the ice. From there, he tossed the bundles we lowered down to Preston and Ash. Reinhold and some others worked to free the dinghy, whose lines had become tangled, then frozen solid.

Behind me, the rest of the crew had chopped through the mast and cleared the hatch. The doctor, Griffin, and Hunt disappeared below. Any hopes we might have had that the walls of the icebergs would shelter us from the wind were foolish ones; the gusts seemed to be concentrated by the narrow corridors, stripping off hats and gloves, yanking lines from our hands, and knocking us off our feet.

The doctor reappeared first, clutching a long roll of parchment and several bags slung over his shoulders. He moved directly to the gunnel, shouting for me to assist him; he cradled his possessions carefully and lowered himself down on top of Preston, then clambered into the dinghy.

Griffin and Hunt struggled up through the hatch with West swaying between them. Reinhold and I finally got the dinghy loose by swinging it over to port, where Preston could guide it into the water. He leaped in and Ash took his place in the crevice. Using the port davit and a harness, we lowered first West, then Creely down out to the boats. One by one, men mounted the side and slid down. Hunt mounted the rail to descend, but slipped and, letting out a baffled cry, shot past Reinhold and vanished into the water.

Reinhold jumped down to try to find him, but he did not surface. We passed down a boat hook that he used to prod around; Preston brought the dinghy over and poked underwater also, but there was no sign of him. The ship began to pitch forward again, nearly casting Aziz down under the bow. I descended, then Reinhold and Griffin. Ash moved into the boat and Aziz passed the last of the emergency supplies down. Griffin moved into the stern of the boat, holding on to the halyard firmly for Aziz to descend. Balanced on the thwart of the iceboat, I could barely see his head through the gusting snow. Griffin pulled the line taut and yelled for him to come ahead.

From far above, his voice reached us thinly, like a bird's in the roar: "I will stay."

"Don't be a fool," shouted Griffin. "The ship will be driven under in a manner of minutes."

"The boats are overfilled as it is. I will make my own way."

Griffin turned to us.

"Kane, Adney, get him—"

West cut him off with a wave of his hand.

"Let him stay."

"I will not. We cannot leave a man to his death in the middle of a storm."

"He does not wish to come. We should be thankful for his sacrifice. Now we must move, sir!"

Griffin stood gripping the rope with both hands. It hummed in the blasts of wind and the small iceboat lurched underneath us.

"Pull away," shouted West, "before we capsize." Adney and Reinhold prodded the ice walls with their oars. Griffin, glaring, refused to let go of the halyard; he leaned overboard, his feet hooked underneath a thwart.

"Restrain him," ordered West. Ash and the doctor moved forward and pried Griffin's hands from the rope. He struggled against them, but they bore him down to the center of the boat.

"You cannot!" shrieked the captain.

"Hunt is dead already," said West. "We can do nothing for Aziz. Now we must move." West nodded to Reinhold and Adney. As if by some prearranged signal, Aziz cut the halyard and it fell in a heap onto Griffin's chest.

Captain Griffin bellowed and twisted, but Ash and the doctor held him fast. Over us, the *Narthex* heaved again and lurched down into the water. The wave that rolled off the hull nearly capsized the dinghy and we were forced to pull away. I turned away from Griffin and tried to paddle.

I saw Aziz waving through the gouts of snow and I saw some ease in it—it was not the shaky blessing of a suicide, but the confident wave of a man with other things in his mind, and I had the distinct sense that it was not we casting off from him, but he from us.

I watched him as he disappeared, and looked with sadness at the naked, obscene rudder of the *Narthex* flapping ineffectually in the wind, her stern lifted to the sky in a final desperate gesture of submission.

With all of us and the supplies crowded into the iceboat, there was not enough room to row. Creely lay over the middle of the thwarts, struggling to sit up from time to time, protesting our refusal to let him help; Ash and the doctor continued to wrestle with Griffin. The rest of us crowded on the gunnels. We managed to get the oars out and into some semblance of use. I paddled awkwardly, Adney poled off the floes, West worked the tiller fiercely. We were so low that we shipped water with every wave, and they came at us from all sides. Once Griffin stopped struggling, Dr. Architeuthis baled when he could—it soon amounted to shoving the water out when the boat dipped low. The wind blew frozen spray into our faces, and the effect was like slivers of glass shot from a gun.

The men in the dinghy had an easier time as they were not so heavily loaded; their boat was so small, however, that each wave knocked them in a new direction until they were plucked from it by another. Fortunately there was no room between the icebergs for us to become separated. Ash threw a line to Preston so they could pull themselves forward as we made progress.

We poked down the lead, spending more of our energy on remaining upright than on moving. Behind us, I could hear the mournful whimpering of a group of dogs who had somehow worked their way down near the water. Reinhold called back from the dinghy, but there was no room on either craft. They pawed the edge of the floe and looked anxiously after us. They soon disappeared in the gusting snow.

Our channel widened slightly as we made our way along, and soon we were all able to paddle, after a fashion. We managed to keep from sinking, and found narrow leads between the icebergs. We worked ourselves into one gap and found shelter from the wind, then the ice creaked and shifted and we had to move again to avoid being crushed; we emerged into a wider lead and fell back into the teeth of the wind. Channel led to channel but none improved on the last. Waves built in one channel and came shooting at us broadside in another; they bounced off the ice and did battle with their former companions, met new foes, made new alliances, and turned on us, contorted by the wind; growlers— smaller hunks of ice—prowled the corridors, driven by hidden tides and currents, and set upon our hull ferociously. I paddled blindly, with no impulse to steer, no thought to guide, just pulled and pulled, not hoping even to escape but purely fleeing, though I could as easily have been pulling us into greater danger—I would have passed through the gates of the City of Woes without pausing, abandoned hope, entered, fled circle on circle till I found myself again in ice and storm. We were fortunate not to be separated from the dinghy.

We slipped out from the mass of icebergs into a lower plain of pack ice. Here we had no protection from the wind, which built over a vast distance and tried to force us back among the icebergs. I would have returned gladly, but the order came from Griffin to keep paddling ahead. We were leaking badly by this time and he was searching for a place for us to land. The pack ice had an astonishing swell running northeast through it—even large floes were borne up by it. We struggled to move across the swell, beating back jostling chunks and pausing before gaps in the lead until it passed, then paddling ahead frantically.

West brought us at last to a low ramp that led up onto a floe of considerable size. Small waves were breaking on the ramp, and pieces of ice smashed against it and shattered. We slid forward on one such wave; Adney, Ash, and I leaped out and tried to drag the boat fully onto the slope. There was no purchase, and the boat was heavily laden. It was all we could do to prevent it from sliding back into the water. With each wave, another man joined us in the slope until only Griffin and Creely remained. Ash cut some footholds for us and finally we managed to drag the iceboat and the dinghy clear of the water.

We flipped the boats over, propping the dinghy on top of the iceboat's gunnel. Ash dug a tarp from the emergency bundle and spread it over both boats. We lashed it down and packed the edges with snow, then crawled inside. Dr. Architeuthis used one of the bags to block off the opening at the end of the boats; we crouched on the inner edge of the gunnels to keep the boats from shifting in wind. Creely was laid on some furs in the center; West huddled at the far end underneath the peak. The wind and snow still blasted through, but we were out of the worst of it.

Adney dug out a stove and fired it; Reinhold found a lantern. There was barely enough room to shift my weight without elbowing someone, or accidentally kicking Creely. Griffin refused to come in, but instead went back to the ice edge and paced back and forth in the driving wind, calling out into the corridors of ice for Hunt and Aziz. Inside, we were all hunched unnaturally under the curve of the boat hulls—but it was far better than being in the water. The stove threw off an intense heat, and insulated by the other bodies as much as anything, our clothes began to thaw, then steam. I noticed for the first time that I had lost my gloves somewhere. My fingers were bleach white and stiff. My feet had been soaked, but gradually warmed and began itching and then aching.

Adney soon had cocoa ready. Pairs of men hunched over shared mugs and traded sips.

The doctor clambered from man to man examining hands, faces, and feet. Almost everyone had a touch of frostbite—some were worse than others. Ash had taken it on the nose and ears; Adney in the heel; Preston and I in the fingers. My hands looked terrible, but feeling did return as I beat them on my thighs. Only Reinhold escaped untouched, despite his bare head and tattered gloves.

We sat in silence as we sipped, listening to the faint voice of Griffin, the thrumming of the canvas overhead, and the blasting of the wind. Every now and then the bass rumble of the ice welled up. The cocoa finished, Adney set to making a hoosh. Men muttered to themselves, or stared blankly at the flame.

After a time, Reinhold went outside. When he returned, he was half carrying Griffin, who was coated with snow and had big hunks of ice on his pants legs. He collapsed in the corner of the shelter without eating anything. Around him we sat in silence.

From beneath the roar of the wind, I heard Reinhold's voice barely audible:

*Oh, ye Dead! Oh, ye Dead! whom we know by the light you give*
*From your cold gleaming eyes, though you move like men who live,*
*Why leave you thus your graves,*
*In far off fields and waves,*
*Where the worm and the sea-bird only know your bed,*
*To haunt this spot where all*
*Those eyes that wept your fall,*
*And the hearts that wail'd you, like your own, lie dead?*

Men leaned closer to hear him, like blind insects toward the light. He continued, his voice slow and sad:

*It is true, it is true, we are shadows cold and wan;*
*It is true, it is true, all the friends we loved are gone.*


From each side of him, men glared angrily at him. He pressed on, his voice building with defiance until he spat the words:

*But still thus even in death,*
*So sweet the living breath*
*Of the fields and the flowers in our youth we wander'd o'er,*
*That ere, condemn'd, we go*
*To freeze 'mid Hecla's snow,*
*We would taste it a while, and think we live once more!*


He began the second verse again, now shouting at the storm and shaking his fist. One by one we joined him, yelling out the words. He began again, chanting more than singing, and we joined, swaying our bodies in time, and then again, lapsing into the melody, and again fiercely, and softly, moaning through it, and heartily, and beseechingly, and again and again, crying out against the storm, against the ice, for Pago, for Aziz, for poor Hunt, for the dogs, for our poor selves. We sang on through our thin hoosh, through howl of wind, through endless, interminable, measureless ages, rousing again as we lagged, drifting into sleep and waking to join in, until finally we sang—hoarsely rasped—against the silence. I crawled past sleeping bodies, past the still, stiff form of the captain, and peered out from under the frozen canvas; from between black clouds, diamond white stars appeared fixed and unyielding while around them danced the gauzy wisps of the northern lights.

*fourteen*

When I awoke, I had an aggrieved sense that it was my due to rest until the sun returned, to sleep, to eat my fill. Instead we were pricked from sleep by the cold and roused from our lethargy by Griffin. He lit the lantern and Adney fired the stove. Soon the low, close air filled with the smell of tea. Architeuthis and Ash clambered out, letting in a blast of frigid air that nearly doused the stove and set off a brushfire of genial cursing. Despite the stove, a viscous, heavy cold had settled over us, pressing us beneath it and sliding into any gap or crease that we bared; when I sat up, it seemed to flood into my clothes, and I shuddered.

A night's cramped breathing had already coated the underside of the boat with ice; drifting snow and frost sparkled from our clothing. Griffin barked orders, as if nothing unusual had passed the night before, and I strained to bring my mind to bear on him, but could not; his voice was like the shrilling of a locust. Tea was passed and it began to cut through my drowsing brain. We finished and passed back our mugs, waiting expectantly for the hoosh to follow.

"No hoosh," said Griffin, his voice finally resolving into words. "We need to start our rationing. One hoosh a day, and tea the rest."

"But why not have it in the morning?" I asked plaintively. "We need it to work all day."

"You've had tea. The hunger will keep you working. Hoosh at midday. Now let's get moving."

Grumbling, we gathered our gear and crawled out into the cold. Creely and West remained inside. Architeuthis and Ash returned as we stowed the gear and prepared to dismantle our shelter.

"Not so fast, boys," said Ash.

Dr. Architeuthis approached the captain.

"Lots of ice movement during the storm," he said. "It's difficult to see where we came from, but the whole pack is in motion. It's likely that the ship's sunk but we should see if we can find Aziz or the dogs, or salvage something more from the wreckage. We can send some men to scout if you think it wise, but I believe we'd do better to insulate the boats as best we can. The entire pack will freeze solid soon enough and we'll be able to walk to find the ship if she's still up—and we still need to."

"I see," said Griffin. "Any sign of land?"

"None that we saw, but the islands can't be more than about fifty miles to the north—"

Griffin waved him away.

"Captain, the Barrier is just to the north. It is certainly our best hope from here. You can't think that we'll go back south. We'll never make it. The map clearly indicates—"

"The map has sunk our ship, sir; it has killed four of our men. It has deposited us on the ice in insufficient boats with less than three weeks of rations and fuel. I would suggest that the map has done enough for us already. We will move east onto firmer pack and out of these icebergs, and south from there to Lancaster Sound." He glared at Dr. Architeuthis.

"But why south?" asked Adney. "If we are as close as the doctor says, why not continue north? We could be two days' march from the islands—warm air, food—and instead we're heading back into the ice. Even if we make the sound, it will be months until the whalers return."

"We don't even know if the islands are real," burst out Reinhold. "That crazy beetle hunter's book—he probably made the whole damn thing up. We don't even know if he went."

"What if he did?" said Adney. "What if it's right there—right over those ridges? Then we freeze to death or starve on broth when we could have saved ourselves. And besides, it's not just the book—you saw the log for yourselves—how did that get there? The doctor's got proof it's there anyway—don't you, Doctor?"

Dr. Architeuthis sat smiling by the entrance. Without speaking, he reached into his bag and pulled out the map. He unrolled it carefully over Creely's stomach. Adney lit a candle from the stove and held it high. The map looked black in the candlelight. The lines from the wall of the cabin had been traced and retraced until they looked like black gouges; I saw flashes of tiny figures—they might have been numbers—laid over each other in insectivorous clumps like angry wasps; these were crossed by slashing lines with antipodal lines cutting them. Architeuthis pointed into the maze of lines.

"Here you can see the sharp drop in salinity—a sign of the meltwater from the volcanic vents. We found the log here"—he pointed—"and lost the boat here. The heat indices do not rise, because at this distance the water temperature is held down by the increase in iceberg mass created by the glaciers Strabo mentioned. Based on the mass of the icebergs and the patterns of their fracture, the glacial Barrier must be here"—he pointed again—"which means that we were only about fifty miles at best and around seventy or seventy-five at worst from the strait."

Men began shouting, Adney and Reinhold above all, and jabbing at the map. Creely called for his skeet rifle and ordered the dogs released, then rolled over, and the map fell off into Griffin's lap.

"The map is rubbish," Griffin said. "Sending men north with our supplies is a death sentence for those who remain, and suicide for those who go—all for a place that exists only in the math of the good doctor. We are not so far from Lancaster Sound—perhaps two hundred miles. With some good hunting and prudent rationing, we can make it. Though we've missed the whalers, there are Eskimo there who can help us. We'll overwinter and then be picked up in the spring."

"The only chance for the weak is to favor the strong," said the doctor. "We will not all make a two-hundred-mile journey; we would be fortunate if any of us made it—and there is no more guarantee that we would find the Eskimo, or that they would be disposed to help us. We can make the fifty miles north in four days with good conditions. Look at the map—we are so very close." The doctor pointed; it certainly looked awfully close.

West looked at the map and pursed his lips.

"We are here?" He pointed.

"Yes," the doctor replied, "more or less. If we got even thirty miles north, the air would be warmer and it is likely that we would find better hunting and fishing in the warmer waters."

"And if we make it," said West, "how do we return to the south?"

"We'll have wood—we can build a larger boat, and get supplies. We'll overwinter, and then sail back to Lancaster Sound on the pack."

"And this," West asked, pointing again to a spot just to our east, "is this land also?"

"Possibly," replied Dr. Architeuthis, "though it is likely to be indistinguishable from the ice at this time of year."

West stared at the map for a long time, and then up at Griffin for a moment.

"Once we complete our searches here, we will head for the land to the east, all of us," West said. "It looks like about thirty miles. There we will establish a base for hunting and fishing. If we are able to secure game from the land or the sea, we will send a small group north with supplies while the others hunt and gather their strength. If we do not reach the islands, those who wish to continue north may do so, and those who do not, may go south."

"And if there is no game?" asked Reinhold.

"Then we will take such measurements as will determine whether we are in the channel to the strait, and if there is clear evidence of the islands, we will send a team north to find them. If not, we will move south along the edge of the land. There is likely to be smooth ice there and we will make better time than over the pack."

"Did you order some smooth ice along the coast for us?" asked Reinhold.

"The water along the coast is shallower; the icebergs become grounded there and hold off the worst of the pack. The water along the shore stays clear longer, and when it does freeze, it is smoother than the open pack. In addition, the animals tend to stay closer to the shore, so the likelihood we'll find food is higher," answered West evenly. "The shore ice forms a sort of Eskimo highway along the coast of Greenland; it should function the same way here."

Reinhold whistled softly. We were all relieved to hear West present such a sensible plan. It was the first time I had been hopeful since abandoning the ship. I even managed some sleep that night and woke up feeling nearly alive in the morning.

We circled back through the mountainous bergs, camped at the edge on the flat floes, and ventured in again with the dinghy to look for Aziz or the ship, or the dogs, or floating supplies. Some bleary nights, I imagined the plump face of Hunt poking through the tarp with a steaming vat of beef stew, his nervous face beaming. We found some decking and four tins of oil washed up on the ledge of an iceberg. Once I thought I heard the dogs barking in the distance, but it could have easily been the ice.

After four days of looking, we packed up and moved off onto the pack ice again. Over us, a half-moon offered a dim white light that did us little good in the ridged shadows. The pack was absolutely silent but for the echoing scrapes of our oars and muttered oaths. As we moved, our breath hung behind us in great clouds, as if it would remain there for a thousand years, as if nothing alive had passed in the thousand before us. We made our way down such channels as would take us—Griffin calling out when we had a choice, which was seldom. He seemed to avoid portages when he could, often steering in roundabout routes to avoid putting us back on the ice. In a few situations, we had no options; we dragged up, laid Creely carefully to the side, and hauled the loaded boat out. With both crews on the lines, the boats moved fairly easily, though they were in constant danger of toppling on the uneven surface of the ice. Dr. Architeuthis steered the dinghy in silence, content for now to let Griffin lead.

The work, far from warming me, seemed only to awaken me from my numbness to feel the cold again. I feared for my hands, which I had bound tightly; the dark kept me from knowing what was water, what pus, and what blood. The others pulled in silence beside me, faces set, shoulders hunched to keep off the sharp and pouring cold. Creely began to call out—first for an oar, then a line, then a harness for the dogs. He thumped my shoulder and laughed out loud, his head bobbing on his shoulders. His voice swung from a gay laugh to a perplexed mutter and he lapsed into silence. After a moment he began again in a singsongy voice. When we pulled out onto a floe again, the captain nodded to the doctor, who took Creely's head in his hands. He took a pulse and, with the help of a lantern, looked at his eyes. Creely jerked his head away from the lantern, then turned to squint at it. Architeuthis shrugged to Griffin, his face expressionless; Griffin called us to hoist away.

And so we trudged on. The moon dropped and shadows rose. Creely's voice rang out, stilled. We moved from slushy water to tracts of more solid ice, where we relayed the boats a half mile at a time. Reinhold and Architeuthis rigged a harness that ran across their shoulders that let them carry Creely and still pull the boats—that way we did not leave him when we relayed. We saw no flick or flutter of life, no splash of seals or jumping fish, no cry of bird or huff of bear, no click or hum of insect. Any moment we paused, the silence settled like the cold, poured over and stifled us; the crump of our boots seemed pitifully muted, and the rasp of our breathing amplified. My old and hated heart thumped on with just enough force to let me know it would not be releasing me soon. Such a time passed as I know not—the stars too seemed frozen in their places. I looked at them and thought of the great patience of ancient astronomers to map them, to see shapes in their disparate points—animals, gods, histories—to see them wheeling, careening, tumbling overhead. They stood over me, refusing to resolve into shapes, into bears or dragons, compelling the darkness rather than diminishing it; stood, obdurate, reminding me only of the distance that lay to light and to heat.

We did stop finally, on a floe like the others, heaved the boats up, and covered them with a tarpaulin. Ash chipped free hunks of drifted snow that we piled on the sides. Adney spread the bags inside as best he could before we passed Creely in, then we followed one by one. Ash came in last and pulled the tarp tight over the opening.

We sat in silence as my mind churned for what to say—what to say that would not pain—how not to cry out. Beside me Reinhold began to sing again, softly, without defiance, and so did Adney and I and the rest, and in that song a wave of relief passed from us, of quiet gratitude. With the stove roaring, even Griffin joined his squeaky tenor softly to ours.

Adney lowered four strips of pemmican into the water as it began to boil, and a handful of potato shavings. The smell made me ravenous. He spooned it into mugs and passed them to us. I shared with Preston. He took a sip and passed it. I had a warm swallow with the memory of a potato in it and my mug was empty; I passed it forlornly back. Griffin made cocoa. I started to gulp it, then held off, and passed it to Preston. He sipped twice, then licked the edge of the mug. It was just enough to make me hungrier. As soon as the last cocoa was served, Griffin doused the stove. We rerigged and pulled off across the ice.

After an interminable time, Griffin called the halt and we assembled the shelter. Adney lit the stove and made tea. Now I was more careful, drawing out my share into three sips and pausing between each. In the cold, the hot tea tasted of nothing. The stove was doused and we sat in silence and stillness. From the end of the shelter, a roaring snort announced that Reinhold, at least, had fallen asleep.

The next march was as the last, except that we saw no water. The ice was badly hummocked and we were often forced to pull the boats off one peak from the top of the next one, with two or three standing below to try to keep the boats from falling and getting wedged in. Creely felt impossibly heavy, but bore the knocking and tumbling remarkably well when he was lucid; much of the time he remained mercifully insensible.

When we emerged after sleep, we found the wind was blowing steadily from the north and the outside of the boats was nearly drifted up. We struggled to get loaded in the wind, but once we started we fairly flew along. The wind was freezing—it felt like a lash driving us east. When we made camp again I was exhausted and shivering and the others were as bad as I. There was no singing.

"Good progress, boys," said Griffin, over the hoosh. "We must be nearly there."

I plotted the taking of my meal as I marched—first to the cocoa as some small chunks might still be floating undissolved, and second to the hoosh for sinking meat.

That night my scheme was successful—I had a bite of stringy meat in the bottom of the cup that I sucked delicately. When the cocoa came, I pushed the meat with my tongue between my upper lip and my gum and held it there while I sipped. Then I pulled it back down and rolled it around biting on it and prodding it, swallowing it finally with great regret as I drew hostile stares from around me. We had another sing that night after dinner, running through some shanties and some psalms and retiring not so cold as the night before.

The weather was steady, around thirty below, but the wind was light and the ice was not badly broken, so the hauling was not too bad. We spent that night planning the hunting and fishing parties. Lacking any real skills, I was put to helping make some nets for fish. Adney and Ash would hunt inland with one rifle. Preston and I would fish; the doctor and Reinhold were going to hunt along the ice for seal, using spear and line rigs and our other rifle. I could hardly sleep for drooling.

At noon of the next day, West saw a ridge of hummocky ice and the low rise of land in the distance beyond it through his telescope. We whooped and shouted and our voices echoed across the ice. We reached the rough ice sometimes in the undifferentiated evening—I could tell only because my stomach was screaming out for my tea. Griffin called a halt and looked through the scope. The land was not far—we could all see it clearly—but the ice was heavily hummocked and several icebergs were locked in close together.

"Come on, Captain," called Reinhold. "It's not far—let's press on and make a proper camp on the shore."

"Very well," said Griffin. "Let's heave-ho, men. It's not far now."

In point of fact it was far, and difficult. The icebergs jammed into high ridges, and drifting snow had covered some loose piles of splintered ice that gave way under us as we scrambled over. When we reached the shore ice it was just as West had predicted: a quarter mile of smooth ice leading up to a rocky landfall. And we were hanging almost thirty feet over it on a pressure ridge pushed out in front of an iceberg. Ash had to take apart the raddies and rig a harness for the boat to lower it down. It was a treacherous climb, but we made it finally, and then fairly ran across the ice to the shore.

It was exhilarating to be on the land again after months on the ship and ice. We shouted and sang as we brought up the boats and set up camp. We were on a low gravelly beach, with a ridge of low hills rising behind it; we pitched the boats behind a row of rocks for protection from the wind; Griffin ordered a double portion of pemmican for all of us. We all sang heartily, and slept bundled tightly, our stomachs feeling marvelously full.

In the morning, the hunting parties were dispatched. Preston and I pulled apart a section of rope. He wove a small net from the pieces and a section torn from his own undershirt, while I dug out our fishing hooks and line. We headed out into the darkness, moved south along the shoreline. We hacked holes in the ice and Preston mounted the net while I lowered the hook with a small piece of pemmican skewered on it. Preston explored south down the shore and I raised and lowered and raised and lowered the bait. I thought sluggishly about what the fish might be think-ing—jerking the line to attract attention in some imitation of piscine distress. I thought about drawing it tauntingly, seduc-tively, arrogantly through the water, provoking the fish into bit-ing. I thought about simply eating the pemmican myself and to hell with fishing.

With no reaction from the fish, I moored the line to the ice with a spike and followed Preston. The shoreline consisted of a long, low, gravelly beach with some boulders marking the rise into low hills. Even the fine gravel had frozen into a solid mass like concrete. We went about a mile down, discovered nothing of merit, and made our way back up. My line held nothing, though the pemmican was still on it. Preston's net also held nothing. He moved a little farther offshore and hacked another hole in the ice. He lowered the net, anchored it, and headed off, inland this time.

Our day of fishing and meandering yielded nothing, and the others' the same; no game or any signs of it inland, and no seals or bears on the ice. The doctor argued that he was required to spend his time gathering measurements rather than hunting, and West agreed. Adney and Ash hunted inland, Reinhold and the captain out on the ice, and West himself would remain to care for Creely, who seemed neither better nor worse.

Another day, two, seven, and the land yielded nothing. Griffin cut our rations in half again—the same meals, but less put into the hoosh and the cocoa. The doctor added the contents of small vials to each hoosh, measuring out thick drops, and then carefully stop-pering each again. It was vile, but at least it tasted of something. Beyond the standard pemmican and water, men devised all sorts of creative touches, given their limited store of ingredients. Some added a pinch of tobacco, some even blackened stones; some car-ried a scrap of potato peels or a dab of grease; Reinhold used a "soup bone," a fragment of shoe leather that he added to every cup, then carefully removed, wrapped, and stored for the next. Others swore by a scrap of glove or coat, the remains of a tattered page, or a sliver of wood from our log, for luck as much as flavor. There were fierce debates about exactly when to add the pemmican; some favored early, as the snow was melting, because it "blended the flavors more"; others argued that that process washed out the flavor of the meat, and that the pemmican should be added only when the water was warm, "to keep the taste from boiling away."

One evening during our medical examinations, Reinhold told the doctor to look at Griffin's foot, which had been troubling him. Griffin dismissed it, and glared at Reinhold, but eventually showed his foot to the doctor. Returning over the steep hummocks one day, Griffin had fallen and wrenched it. The ankle had swollen up considerably, and there was an open but bloodless white gash running along the arch. The doctor bound it up and suggested that Griffin remain off the foot until it healed.

Preston and I were the first to catch something. After dozens of holes, Preston pulled up a set of tiny shrimp in his net. There were fifteen of them, and they were each less than an inch long, but they still seemed miraculous. A cheer went up that evening as they were ceremoniously added to our water. Even on my finely tuned palate, they tasted of nothing, and crunching through the shells put me in mind of eating a mouthful of toenails. They scratched going in and scratched going out, but the doctor insisted on making us eat them, shells and all.

Our meager rations soon began to tell on all of us. It was difficult to rouse, difficult to concentrate. Preston and I set the nets and lines and retreated to the boats. Ash spent some days tightening up the hut and rigging a doorway that helped to keep the inside warmer. Then he refused to go outside again, remaining huddled in his bags. If he was handed a full cup, he drained it, angering all of us. Preston remained his silent and uncomplaining self, but began staggering badly while out on the ice and nearly lost our net. Griffin relegated him to quarters, and cut rations again. I caught nothing on the lines, but the net yielded a few shrimp every few days. Creely got steadily weaker, yet somehow hung on; he lay in front of us all the time, so we could not help but notice as he shrank and withered. He awoke us all several times by bellowing out in the night—more in anger than in pain—and he slept on without waking.

It was impossible not to think of meat. I thought of roasts most often, and steak with butter on them, and salt in big flaky hunks; I thought of corn on the cob, bursting sugar corn that stuck in your teeth. I checked my teeth with my tongue, bit my tongue in anger, and tasted the brick-dusty poverty of my own blood. I thought of cakes also, of hot doughnuts glazed with sugar and rich chocolates—not the bitter, dark chocolates but the sweet, buttery milk chocolates—and eggs hard-boiled, deviled with mayonnaise, of plates of hash and ketchup and runny eggs, of mopping them up with toast, and glazed hams as big as my head, covered by pineapple and cloves, and drinking the fat from the pan and juice from the pineapple, and dark hunks of brown sugar and cloves. I thought of legs of lamb and mint jelly, and sprigs of real mint, and turkey bursting with stuffing and surrounded by roast potatoes, and pork chops double thick and smoked, and handfuls of bacon and spicy sausages that spit water as you bit into them. And I saw the sad and worried face of Hunt over a basket of rolls.

Several of us lost teeth, and our gums swelled until they were like old, crumbling rubber. Eating the shrimp became very painful and some elected to suck on them, then swallow them whole, rather than lacerate their mouths further. We ceased to use the lanterns entirely and spent hours huddled in the darkness waiting for the flash of the stove. Griffin rationed the oil carefully, and the snow in the pot was now barely melted when we were passed our cups and the stove extinguished.

The doctor took advantage of the spare minutes when the stove was fired to examine each of us on alternating evenings. He prodded our gums and looked at our pupils and the color of our throats. It was during one such examination that he determined Creely's feet had to come off. I had been seated nearer the entrance—now built up into a nice tunnel by Ash—and so had not seen them. But I was called to lean down over his chest while the others held his arms and legs. We waited while Adney fired the lantern, and listened miserably as the doctor sharpened his knife and saw as best he could on a rock. He cut free the boots and cut through layers of socks. They progressed from gray to black to blacker. He drew up the pants legs. Creely's feet were more than dead, they were badly rotten; both feet were entirely black—not blue-black like a bruise, but coal black, as if they bore no relation to flesh whatsoever; streaks of black like a clutch of shadows covered his lower leg and extended up beyond his knee, blending at the top with his fish white flesh. Dr. Architeuthis looked grimly at Griffin and then West. I suppose there was some mercy in that we could not smell the rot so strongly in the cold. Reinhold and Adney held his legs.

We did not even have a drink to offer him; he chomped on a piece of oar until he bit through it. Soon after that, he passed out while the doctor sawed. Blood soaked the floor of the hut, and froze underneath us, sealing our bags together. At last the doctor sat back and laid down his tools. He heated the pot to searing and held it against the stumps; the metallic stench of burned blood filled the air. There was no sound from Creely. Dr. Architeuthis bound up the stumps delicately and fell back against the thwarts. The lantern was extinguished and time passed.

In the morning, the doctor was in good spirits again. Creely had survived the night, though he had not regained consciousness. The doctor spooned some tea into Creely's mouth and felt his pulse.

"What is the chance for his weakness to yield to other disease?" asked West.

"Even if he can recover from the amputations, he is unlikely to survive. He is, however, perfectly safe from disease. That is one of the benefits of the Arctic. There is no disease here."

"What do you mean, we can't get sick?" asked Reinhold. "We *are* sick, all of us already."

"What you feel is your body consuming itself," said the doctor. "It is a peculiar genius of your body to preserve itself despite you, and in the most remarkable ways. Your debility is caused entirely by gaps in the things your body needs—fuel most of all, but other elements vital to the smooth functioning of your systems. It is deficiency you are feeling, not the presence of disease. You have likely never been so free from disease in your lives. Preston, for instance, has ceased to cough. Do you see?"

And so he had.

This was not a comforting thought, however, and it shifted my attention back to my own body, and to my cannibal heart. Never had it seemed so clearly evil, so clearly my enemy, prolonging itself as it fed on me like some wasp breeding a larval horde in its host. My own health had been steady—I was exhausted all the time, and weak, but I could rise from my bed every morning, for the nothing that was worth. I had taken to eating the strip of pemmican I was given to fish with, until eventually it was withheld. I caught nothing, though the nets continued their steady, if limited, production. There was no game.

The doctor continued his measurements and agitated for a trip north, but even West felt we lacked the resources. He himself was not strong enough to go, and he would not part with the necessary supplies to let the doctor go.

One black morning, Adney leaned forward over the stove.

"Morning, boys. Merry Christmas."

Griffin lit one of the candles and ordered the remaining two biscuits be added to the morning pot. He read a psalm and let the stove burn as we sat in silence together.

Adney raised his mug. "Tomorrow better than today," he said, and smiled.

We drained our cups and moved out into the cold.

*fifteen*

That afternoon, I returned from empty nets to huddle in my coat. Creely mumbled softly—half conscious but not lucid. We jumped as a loud crash shook the boat and the roof shuddered over us. Outside, Reinhold roared: "Come on out, ladies, Santa's here!"

We stumbled into the weak moonlight and saw that he had gotten a seal, our first. We shouted in disbelief and laughed and clapped him on the back. Even West came out for a look. It was good size, almost seventy pounds, and a sleek black with mottled gray around its flippers. Reinhold fired his rifle into the air to bring back the other hunters.

"He was sleeping up on the ice; I practically kicked him in the head," he said. "Couldn't get my gloves off to fire the rifle—had to bash him to death with the rifle butt."

I shouted with joy—the others danced around me singing and jumping. West clapped him on the shoulders. We brought out the pot and Reinhold butchered the seal with extravagant care. We gathered all of the blood in mugs and passed them around. It was still warm and tasted salty and fishy and delicious. We got two full mugs each, enough to make me feel gorged.

Reinhold stripped the skin and separated out a thick layer of blubber, then cut the dark meat into strips and piled the organs in a small heap. He cut off and separated the bones and piled them up on the side. He wrapped them all in a square of cloth and presented it with elaborate ceremony to Griffin.

"Well done, Reinhold, well done," said the captain. "I think this rates an extra Christmas hoosh."

We piled back into the hut and gathered around the stove. Adney fired it and threw some of the seal meat into it, then added a little of the blood and some of the bones. We sat in the soft orange glow of the stove as the smell of the hoosh flooded us. Griffin let it actually melt and warm, and the hut became warm. He read some psalms and a blessing and we dug in. After weeks of tepid water, the hoosh was syrupy in my mouth, and the meat swollen and sweet.

With a dozy moment to sit back, I thought of Aziz, making tea on his small stove, and wondered if he held on, somewhere in the cold and darkness, scrabbling out his days in the hold of the ship; or if the *Narthex* had been driven under the ice and if, after a moment of terror, he was peaceful now, and carried along in a current I had traced out months ago, before we had descended into the chaotic ice.

Ash fashioned a blubber lamp, balancing a wick in a pot lid; it felt unnatural to be able to see finally. We were filthy and grubby, our faces gaunt but greasy from the hoosh; our patchwork clothes had disintegrated into gray rags.

But with our bellies full and the hut warm, we settled back happily and had a sing. The doctor used the light to examine each of us, clambering over Creely, who was singing his own, unrelated song. We all had some scurvy, and some frostbite, but nothing too serious. Then he pushed us back and began to examine Creely.

His stumps were black under the bandages, but seemed to be no worse than they were before. He finished with the legs and began to unwind the cloth around his hands. Several of the fingers stuck to the fabric and separated from the hand; they were like black twigs. He looked over to West.

"We shouldn't even—," began the doctor.

"Save what you can," said West.

"There's no chance to save anything, Mr. West," said the doctor. "We're just putting him in pain. There is no logic in it. And no mercy," he added.

"Do your best for him, Doctor," replied West.

The doctor set his jaw and balanced the lamp on the thwarts. Reinhold and Adney leaned over onto Creely's arms and Reinhold began talking soothingly to him.

The knife was not sharp, and even the dead flesh was obdurate. Creely began by screaming, then raving, and gradually was silent, as the doctor moved from knife to saw. The hut filled with the awful, muted smell of rot, and blood flooded onto the rocks. At last the doctor sat back, wiped off the knife and the saw, seared and bound the stumps tightly in the remains of the gloves, then pulled the bag back on. Creely's head lolled back and we sat in silence. The lamp was extinguished.

He cried out in the night, jerking upright and beating his stumps on the thwarts until Reinhold and Adney wrestled him back down again. He raved again, and was still. In the morning, the captain ordered another hoosh for all of us from the seal meat. Reinhold was able to get a few sips into Creely, though he did not wake. Griffin ordered us about our tasks again: Adney and Reinhold out to hunt; I to the nets. Preston had regained the strength to go with me now, and it was nice to have even his silent company.

West and Griffin remained behind with Ash, who dug out space for the meat at the far end of the hut and piled up the boats with snow to provide more insulation.

The weather was cold but not brutal, and the wind was light. Over us, the stars echoed the ice; the moon, now full, sat high up, silvering the blue ice and casting shadows into the darkness. The nets were empty and the line empty. I baited the hook and threw it back in. Once we had finished resetting the nets, Preston began to wander up the shore ice to the north, and I followed. We reached camp and kept going; there was no sound or light from inside the hut, and no one moved on the shore.

The ice was smooth and even; the wind had polished the center clear. We marched quickly along, the sense of progress itself giving us an energy to go faster and farther; the horror of the hut pushed us off, our clothes stained with the blood of Creely, the silent ice a balm.

The moon, I noticed, did not pass across the sky, but hung over us like judgment. Preston shuffled ahead, not looking back, but aware of me behind him. In the low but steady light, the shore ice shone clear and we went north through a long curving bay, around a headland, past a low set of cliffs, then across a broad lane like a river; then passing under the eaves of icebergs, we pushed up almost to the shore. We saw no flicker of life as we passed along, no rustle out on the endless expanse of the pack, no tumble of gravel or flutter of grass. Even the wind had fallen to nothing.

Then, ahead of us on the ice, we saw a dark figure moving toward us with great rapidity. There was a metallic scrape that echoed across the ice. It was Dr. Architeuthis; he glided up to us, his face flushed.

"Skates," he answered to our looks. "Primitive to be sure, but very effective. Ash made them for me from the braces on the dinghy."

We stood for a moment in the quiet. With our momentum stalled, I suddenly felt very tired.

"How far north have you gotten, Doctor?" asked Preston. "Have you seen the Barrier?"

"I have been almost twenty miles north on two occasions," answered the doctor. "I was hoping tonight with the moon to be able to see it and gauge the distance accurately, or perhaps at least to see the fog of the vents, but I did not. It is so close—we are practically there."

"Did you find any more wood? Or animals?"

"I have been focused on measuring, and certainly the variance in salinity is highly promising. We must take a portion of the meat while we have it and push north before our strength has left us entirely. We will have ample time and resource to recover from there. We will laugh to think we stayed in that freezing hut so long."

"Yes," agreed Preston. "The ice is so easy to travel on; we should make fifty miles in two or three days."

"You must help me," said the doctor. "West is the key. He will not authorize an expedition unless he is able to go himself. If he assents, the captain will not stop us." He turned and scratched off down the channel.

"Come on, Kane," said Preston. He too turned and headed after the doctor.

By the time we reached the hut I was stumbling and exhausted. The light from the entrance shone almost cheerily, and I could smell the hoosh as I approached. Inside, everyone was chattering. Creely was sitting up, a cup of hoosh balanced in his lap. Griffin was spooning it into his mouth with great care.

I took my place and Adney handed me a steaming mug with two thick strips of seal meat in it. I took a draught of the broth and caught one of the strips in my teeth, then passed the mug to Preston. He eyed me evenly over the edge of the mug as he sipped.

I glanced down at West, who was gulping greedily at his meat, his small eyes peering into the mug, looking for whatever last little bits might be due him.

Creely's face was wan, but he managed to smile weakly as he sipped the hoosh. He was balanced somewhat awkwardly, leaning against Griffin as he tried to hold himself upright. His arms were crossed around the mug in his lap, and what remained of his legs stuck rigidly out into his bag.

"Douse the stove," ordered Griffin. "And today's the last of the oil. We're on blubber from here, with a small reserve for emergencies. Mr. Ash, see to the lamp."

Ash took down the blubber lamp and began fashioning a pot lid into a deeper reservoir. He mounted a bracket on top so we could begin cooking over a blubber flame from now on. The blubber stove was extremely smoky and the light was dimmer and more yellow, but it worked well enough.

I had imagined that the hunger would end at some point, that I would get drifty and dizzy and no longer care about food, but I cared deeply, and incessantly—I cared about nothing else, even being warm.

The next day, the nets held a few shrimp, but a surprise waited on the end of my line. When I was able to chip it loose from the ice, it tugged back sharply, nearly jerking the line from my hands. I wrapped the line quickly around my arm and began backing away from the hole. The line jerked and tugged, biting into my sleeve. I gave a final tug and a small Arctic char flopped on the ice. I was thrilled—our first fish! It was small—surprisingly so, given the weight on the line—but it was food. I moved it carefully back from the hole and broke its neck on the ice before pulling the hook free. Preston came over smiling. He cut open the fish's abdomen, wrapped the intestine around the hook, and threw it back in. We looked together at the fish sitting on the ice, and then at each other.

"It's all or nothing," he said, "We can't have caught half a fish."

"It's small in any case," I said, "and besides, we need our strength to keep fishing."

We squatted down on the ice and Preston cut the fish into chunks. We each got two handfuls of the clear flesh, sucking it off the bones; he ate the liver, I the heart; an eye each, chunks of the rubbery stomach. He scraped the skin over his teeth, and gnawed at the edges beneath the scales. It had only a faint taste of oil in the flesh; the rest just tasted like the cold; but it did fill me nicely, and I could feel my stomach burning pleasantly as I disgested. We made our way back to the hunt after brushing each other clear of scales and bones.

We had not been the only lucky ones. Reinhold had shot another seal, this one smaller than the first, but still a banquet. By the time we returned they had butchered it and made up a blood hoosh with chunks of seal fat floating in it. The blubber stove burned brightly—Ash had figured out how to make it both bright and hot and divert the smoke it produced into a funnel-like chimney. We had so much meat now that it crowded the south end of the hut, and pushed us up against the entrance. The shrimp were added to the heap, and Griffin increased rations to two hooshes a day. We felt like kings. I did my best to forget about the fish—we all had enough now in any case. It was of no consequence.

That evening we sat long in the light, watching the wick burst with light. West pulled himself to the center of the hut, his back against the heap of meat.

"You have all been most patient," he began. "It has taken us a long time to pull ourselves away from the danger of immediate starvation. Now we must turn to survival. We have enough meat to survive to the return of the sun. Animals will arrive again in numbers the closer we get to that time, so our hunting and fishing should be more productive. In the meantime, we have the resources for a group to push north for the islands. If we are successful in reaching them, we can return for the others. We will build our strength in the warmth and then push back to the south to meet the whalers.

"If we do not find them, we can return, hunt heavily to prepare for our journey, and push south then. In either case, we will be moving by the middle of March, before the ice breaks up. We will not need to rely on our boats then, and should be able to reach known shores over the ice, riding the pack south if need be."

He looked around at us to see if there was any dissent.

"Good," he said, rubbing his hands over the light. "The doctor, Kane, Reinhold, and I will make up the expeditionary party. Preston and Adney will remain to supply the camp with food, Captain Griffin and Ash to maintain the camp and care for Creely. We are nearly free of our grim prison."

We gave a rousing cheer, and we clapped each other on the backs.

"We will spend tomorrow in preparations and depart the following day; if any of you have gear or supplies of use, please pass them over. We will need every advantage if we are to make it there and back."

We shuffled and knocked as we sorted ourselves. Adney pressed his nearly whole gloves and a fur-lined hat on me, and took my own ragged set in exchange. Preston gave me his clasp knife, his initials graven into the handle. The others did the same awkward dance, Adney and Reinhold debating lightly the lack of merit of their two rifles. Ash fabricated a second blubber stove and showed the doctor how to use it efficiently.

The following day Ash crafted crude skates for us, with wide platforms of wood above to act as snowshoes if we came into softer snow. The doctor and Preston made a small sledge from the oars and wood from the dinghy. We had a full three hooshes that day and spent the hours before sleep packing the sledge tightly with heaps of meat and the best four of the bags—we possessed little else of value—and wrapping it in a portion of the tarp stripped from the outside of the hut.

We had a sing that night, Creely conducting merrily with his stumps, his beard shining with fat from the hoosh. I felt drunk from the food and the excitement of actually moving, of having the chance to leave. I could see the spring, and the light returning to find us whole and triumphant, hailing and astonishing the arrogant whalers.

We pushed off to cheers and shouts in the morning, our skates rasping on the ice. The weather was promising—only around ten below zero, and a light wind at our backs. The sledge was not heavily laden, and Ash had rigged two harnesses so that we could take turns pulling it.

We made good time over the ice, the sledge jerking along behind us. By noon, when we stopped for tea, we had gone four or five miles—a different world already. We pushed off again quickly as the wind rose. The weather held through the afternoon, and we sped north along the shore ice, weaving in and out of the coastline as a three-quarter moon rose overhead.

We made our camp by propping the sledge on its end against a boulder and draping the tarp over one side. On the other, we cut blocks of hard snow and packed the gaps. When we had finished, we had a hut of our own as warm and tight as the one we had left. With the stove blazing and our own mugs of hoosh, we settled contentedly into our bags.

The next day the weather was colder and the wind stronger, but it was still at our backs. We elected to skip the noon tea as it was too time-consuming to pitch the hut in the cold, and marched on into the afternoon. The coastline wound ahead, low and gravelly, the rocks black and the ice silver. That evening, the doctor estimated that we had covered nearly twenty miles—great progress for men in our condition. Reinhold and I had a sing to ourselves as West huddled smiling in his bag.

We were roused in the morning by the wind. The doctor came in under the tarp in a great rush of it.

"Looks like we'll have to sit tight today," he said. "But not to worry, we've made excellent progress, and we have plenty of meat to sustain us. We can rest today and prepare for tomorrow." West looked evenly at us, as if measuring us, then retreated into his bag.

We sat and listened to the wind buffeting the tarp, remarkably cozy in our bags, with the blubber lamp burning extravagantly. The storm blew itself out the following afternoon and we pushed off again. As we got back in the swing of the travel, I began to notice how much slower West was than the rest of us. He was uncomplaining, but he lagged consistently behind, and the doctor gamely slowed his pace and called for halts to let him catch his breath. He made a show of gathering samples and consulting the charts as West puffed up behind.

Still, it felt wonderful to be moving again, and the rich food was beginning to reinvigorate me. Reinhold and I skated off during the breaks to explore the edge of the heavy ice in case there were seals. We moved so quickly on the skates without the boats that it was difficult to resist just going and going to feel the ice glide underneath my feet. The storm had drifted the snow in long dunes out behind the rocks like silver shadows from a moon low in the southern sky, pointing us north again. The lane was open before us, the ice smooth, and our skates left a glittering trail of sparks behind us.

"We'll not go too far," grunted Reinhold happily. "Drop the sledge and have a bit of a hunt—see if we can't make real pigs of ourselves."

We pulled away steadily with the sledge for three hours, long after we'd lost West and the doctor behind us. The shoreline bowed and sank into the sea; offshore, the pack was low and uneven, with a few icebergs poking out in the moonlight. The cold air was blazingly clear, but the light sat softly on the ice and made distances hard to judge. Reinhold kept an eye on the pack, looking for promising spots to hunt. We came into the center of a broad bay and Reinhold turned out toward the sea. He slipped out of the raddies, took the rifle from the sledge, and motioned for me to follow him. He wrenched off his skates and began sliding forward. I took off my own and followed. At the edge of the shore ice, the hummocks were sharp and heavily jumbled, but only four or five feet high.

Reinhold crouched low and began to creep along, setting his feet down with great delicacy and sweeping his head from side to side. I did the same, though I had no idea what we were looking for. After a time he stopped, unslung his rifle, and lowered himself to the ice. He motioned for me to do the same and pointed to the featureless ice in front of us. I lay down and squinted at the ice, looking for the dark blob of a seal. Reinhold inched forward on his elbows, then lay listening and holding his breath. After a pause he moved forward again. I did the same, but when I snapped off the tip of a small wind ridge, he looked sharply at me in annoyance; so I simply lay still and watched.

He moved ahead of me about thirty feet, and then lay still again, drawing the rifle up beside him. He inched around until he was facing me. Still I saw nothing in the low hummocks. We waited; nothing moved, there was no sound, there was no interruption in the low ridges of the ice. If I had not been cold, I would certainly have fallen asleep. As it was, I struggled not to move, though tremors started in my legs. Reinhold drew the rifle up at last, and pointed it directly at the ridge in front of him. The rifle cracked and he sprang forward, bashing dementedly at the ice. I came up beside him as he lay the rifle aside and began jumping on the ridge of ice with both feet. To my surprise, it split, and he kicked to open a hole in it.

Inside was a low dome, only about eighteen inches high, sitting above a dark pool of open water less than two feet in diameter. Reinhold fell on his stomach and plunged his arm into the water, thrashing it around under the ice.

"Damn," he muttered, "damn bastard better not have . . . *Ha ha!*"

He roared with pleasure and reared back, hauling out a huge seal through the hole and slapping it down on the ice. He had a jury-rigged hook in his hand that he'd caught under the seal's jaw. A stream of blood pulsed out onto the ice and sent small bursts of steam into the air like breaths.

"But how did you know it was there?" I asked.

"They keep a hole open through the winter out here so that they can breathe. You need to get out past the thick ice near the shore. Small hummocks are best—the space between the floes. They bob up to keep it open as the ice around it freezes—sometimes they have to gnaw at it to keep the air space."

"But it wasn't open. How did you spot it?"

"The tops freeze over eventually, but they are a little higher than the regular ridges, and end up round at the bottoms, but sharp on the top like the others. You can see from the shape which direction they come up to breathe." He pointed at the dome, which was slightly oval.

"The top of the oval's where the head comes up when he breathes, and also where the ice is the thinnest. The water splashes down and the other end get thicker and thicker, so it's hard to shoot through, and even to break through."

"How did you figure it out?"

"The doctor got the basic idea for it from the Eskimo. So he sent me out with some nice sharp principles for seal hunting. I spent a long time out on the ice just looking around and listening. Finally one time I heard a scratching under the ice—a seal working his hole a little bigger, gnawing away at it like a squirrel. So I shot into the ice at the noise. I hacked down to the hole and there he was. Sometimes they sink when you shoot, so you have to be quick about it."

"Master Gooka," I said, "esteemed perfesser of Eskimology."

He laughed, and hauled the seal up onto his shoulders.

"Come on," he said. "See if the ladies are caught up."

The doctor and West had not reached the sledge by the time we returned. We turned the sledge on its side and built up the hut. Reinhold did the butchering while I fired up the stove, and in a few minutes we had chunks of meat simmering in the seal blood. After we had eaten, we kept the stove burning and watched the greasy smoke curl up and disappear out the ventilation hole.

"What do you suppose has happened to your man Aziz?" asked Reinhold. "Do you think he got off the ship before it went down? Made it to the islands?"

"I hope so," I replied. "Somehow I don't think the islands were what he was after."

"What else is up here? Was there something in the journals West didn't mention?"

"If there was, Aziz never told me anything about it."

"Maybe he'll be basking on the beach with old Strabo when we get there." Reinhold held his wrists together and gave a waggling double wave.

"Do you still think we're going to find the islands?" I asked.

"No. I don't know. I think we'll find something, but I doubt it's what we've been promised."

"So why go at all? Shouldn't we be pushing south?"

"Not really our place to say, is it? At least not yet."

"But when will it be? The way we are going, we'll all starve to death before we get a chance to decide for ourselves."

"Rest easy, Saint Brendan. I'm getting seals pretty steadily now, so we won't starve. Keep your strength up and bide your time. We'll make it back one way or another."

"What about Creely? And Captain Griffin? They'll never make it."

"I spent a winter out once before, up in Spitsbergen. We were whaling until too late in the season and got caught by the pack. We had to overwinter at the whaling camp. Even with plenty of blubber and meat, it was a long, cold winter. To pass the time, we bet on toes—whose would fall off when, in what order. There's only so much you can control, and best to have a sense of humor about the rest. I won," he said chuckling.

"You like freezing to death at the ends of the earth?"

He laughed again. "Better than being in prison," he said. "Or brawling for money in the carnivals. I won there also, by the way."

"You've been in some rough places."

"Best not to let me steer," he said. "Bad luck seems to land in my path."

I was silent for a moment.

"So we just leave them behind?"

"You do your best for them but at a certain point you've done all you can and you need to move on to save yourself. We have the chance to help each other through this, as many as we can—and it will not be all."

The hut was warm and close, and the flame on the blubber lamp swirled and danced. We sat in silence mostly, ate when we were hungry, and listened to the wind scrape across the ice.

Finally from outside the shelter we heard the crunch of footsteps. First West, then the doctor crawled into the hut. West collapsed on the floor and fell asleep immediately, without removing his clothes or getting into his bag. Reinhold gave Dr. Architeuthis a mug of hoosh and we wrestled West into his bag.

"Well," asked Reinhold, when we were settled again, "how much further do you think?"

"Twenty or thirty miles," replied the doctor. "The land is starting to steepen along the channel; we should reach low mountains tomorrow. I've been a little surprised that we haven't seen more young icebergs here, but I suspect that when the pack forms, the bay where the two glaciers sit traps most of them and melts them there, and then sends sheets out to the south. Keep your eyes open for driftwood that has come down the channel, either cast onto the shore or embedded in the ice."

"Can't wait to warm my toes," said Reinhold. "And you"—he elbowed me—"I'll need a fan boy to keep my brow dry."

"Yes sir, Master Gooka," I replied. "I am your humble servant."

"I'll consider you for the position," he said. "I've got very high standards. Best to practice up."

It was snowing hard in the morning, but it was not cold, and the wind was light. West sat blinking in his bag. He seemed recovered after three mugs of hoosh, and urged us to get moving. We broke down the shelter and strapped the seal onto the sledge. West spent some time fumbling with his skates as Reinhold and I rigged up and started to shove off.

"Stay closer," said the doctor sharply. "In the snow there is more chance for us to be separated, especially if the ice is smoother the closer we get to the glacier."

We waited patiently as the doctor helped West to his feet and we moved off. The snow swept slowly out of the darkness, and the whispering as it settled onto the ice created a sensation of gentle intimacy, as if we were headed down a padded corridor to see a beloved but convalescent relative. The snow hid the shoreline and the edge of the uneven ice, leaving our small circle scraping along the soft darkness.

West did not call us to stop. He merely slowed down, then stopped and sat down on the edge of the sledge. He made no apology of any kind, nor did he offer up when he would be ready to continue. He sat, and we waited, and eventually he rose again and we could continue. In the morning he could go an hour before resting. By the middle of the afternoon he was stopping every fifteen minutes, and needing five minutes of rest each time. Reinhold leaned impatiently into the harness as we stood waiting. Around midafternoon in the timeless darkness, the doctor called a halt and said we were camping. The wind was coming up, and the snow was starting to drift heavily—better to wait for it to clear.

I had no objection to an early halt and a big dinner; we were so close now that we could afford to take our time. We pitched camp and made a hoosh, hacking out big chunks of meat from the seal. The wind continued to rise, and keened over us; tongues of snow drifted in through seams in the sledge, and the stove light jumped and wavered. We sat in silence, Reinhold tending the stove from time to time, and drifting in and out of snorting sleep.

After a look from West, the doctor pulled out the hoosh pot again and prepared a second dinner. Reinhold and I made no objections and filled pot, mugs, mouths, bellies, and drifted into sleep. We awoke to find that we were buried deeply under the drifting snow, and it took quite a lot of work to dig ourselves free. The shore ice was largely covered by the drifts, with small patches of ice showing in the center of the channel. Over our shelter, nearly two feet of snow had drifted up, and it was still snowing.

Reinhold and I began to dig out when the doctor stopped us.

"We'll stay today, until the snow stops; we've got plenty of food and a windproof shelter. The more we eat, the less we carry. This will blow out by the afternoon."

Reinhold grumbled a little, but we packed the walls back up and returned to our bags. West had cocooned himself inside his, and showed his head only to get his hoosh. We had been eating so much and so well lately that my bowels were a mess—noisy and uncertain, and completely unproductive—but it didn't prevent me from enjoying another hoosh at noon, and two more in the evening. Even my heart purred greasily along through the enforced rest.

The storm took another full day to blow itself out. We kept a tunnel open so we wouldn't have a hard time leaving at the end, but it took us two hours to dig out the sledge finally. Our bags, which had gotten damp in the shelter, froze quickly as we folded them onto the sledge. Outside, the shore ice had been transformed into a maze of sweeping drifts, exaggerating the sweep of the shoreline and obliterating the low hummocks in the distance.

Ash's skates worked as well on the snow as they had on the ice. We were able to march over the drifts without sinking in deeply, and the skate blades gave us traction when we pushed down to the ice itself. After two days in the tent, I was ready to pull, and the doctor did not object as we moved ahead rapidly. It was too dark to see much of the land along the shore. I pictured towering mountains looming over us, and the spitting glaciers in the distance. The snow evened out as we pulled, and the sledge moved quickly over the snow. After three hours of steady pulling, we headed into the shore and set up the shelter for lunch. We fired the smoky stove and made up a thick hoosh.

There was still no sign of the doctor and West, so we ate our own hoosh, doused the stove, and went back to look for them. We found them more than a mile behind us; the doctor was half carrying West, who glared angrily at us. The doctor looked cold and worn.

"Up we go, sir," said Reinhold cheerily, as he slid his head under West's arm and lifted him off the doctor.

"Shelter's just down the ice, and the stove's all set up for lunch. A little hoosh in you and you'll be feeling like new."

We marched back up to the shelter and prepared a hoosh for the doctor and West. West fell asleep immediately, and the doctor followed soon after. Reinhold fidgeted for a while, then headed back outside.

"I'm going to head inland a bit, see what the land is like—if we're in mountains yet. Maybe I'll find some of the doctor's fruit trees."

He dropped the flap and I heard his footsteps crunch away. I pulled my bag up around me and leaned back against the snow wall. The wind had dropped outside and silence settled over us. The stove did not sputter and the doctor and West did not stir. I closed my eyes, but the jerk-jerk-jerk of my chest kept me awake, making a crunch as it tapped my head against the snow. I couldn't believe that my body wouldn't avail itself of the chance to rest, but so it was—managing barely to survive his labors, the stubborn mule expects exhaustion, and regards anything else with uncomfortable suspicion. I listened to my heart for some pattern behind the brute muscling of blood, the secret for which its punishing had been preparing me. It slowed, then skipped and slowed again, my brain glancing dully off it. I opened my eyes and found the doctor awake and staring intently at me.

"Reinhold?" he said sharply.

"Inland, sir," I replied. "A little antsy, and wanted to see if we were in the mountains yet. Been out about an hour or two, I guess. Are you feeling better?"

"Much, thank you, Kane," he replied. "West slowed down less than an hour after we started, and I carried him along most of the day."

"How much farther do you think, sir?"

"Within ten or fifteen miles, I am sure of it. But the traveling is likely to get more difficult very soon. The mountains leading in will be steep, and we may not be able to continue across the ice."

"All due respect, sir, but how'll he manage? Should we rest a few more days with him and then push on? Or leave him with a good load of food, and find our way in, then come back and bring him over?"

"We can't do that, I'm afraid," said the doctor, "though it would be sensible. He'll want to be along with us, even if it is difficult. I think we're better off to cache the meat and bring him on the sledge. I know it'll be hard, but it's not a great distance now."

"Would it make sense to scout from here as a base? Find a route over the mountains and the glaciers without our gear?"

"One more solid day's march, and we can set up a base camp, and scout from there. It should bring us to the bay of the glaciers, and we can make our way inland from there."

"Will there still be mirages in the darkness?"

The doctor gave me a condescending smile.

"Mirages are creatures of the light—light reflected by air of different temperatures. It is possible that the even, strong moonlight could create some kind of mirage, but it is unlikely to be the sort of wholesale disguise that Dr. Strabo experienced."

"Another hoosh, Doctor."

I jumped as I heard West's command issue sharply from within his bag. Dr. Architeuthis put on the pot, added some blubber to the wick, and some snow and meat to the pot. West sat fully enclosed within his bag, peering out at us suspiciously.

"Reinhold?" he demanded.

"Scouting inland to gauge an approach to the mountains," answered the doctor.

"No more side trips," he said, pointedly ignoring me and speaking directly to the doctor. "No hunting, or running off, no meandering about. Forward only, and only as a group." He settled back into the darkness. The doctor said nothing.

West's mug disappeared into his bag and there was an interlude of greedy mastication, then he thrust his mug out again and the doctor refilled it patiently. West ate a third mug and then cocooned himself completely into his bag. Outside I heard the crunch of Reinhold's feet; soon after his voice boomed into the tent.

"White glove and chocolate time, ladies? Or have we started the pinochle?"

I smiled broadly. The doctor merely leaned forward as Reinhold sat heavily on his bag and stirred the hoosh pot.

"Well?"

"I went about two miles inland, sir, due east, then angled north for about a mile, then back here."

"And?"

"Low hills all the way, and nothing but snow and ice. No incline to the north as far as I could see, but the snow came in before I got too far—that's when I headed back. The light was pretty good up to that point, however. If there are mountains, they are liable to be north quite a ways still."

"If they are volcanic, it is likely that they rise quite sharply, as they will have arisen recently. What was the snow like?"

"White, as usual, sir. Thick flakes as you'd expect with the temperature above zero. And quite a bit to come, by the looks of it."

The doctor continued his questioning for quite some time, with West emerging from his bag to listen more closely. None of it seemed to yield any new information of significance, though this did not seem to discourage the doctor. We finished the hoosh, doused the stove, and slept.

In the morning the wind was up, and the snow blowing heavily, but the doctor decided we should push ahead in any case. First we dug a hole out of the tent space to hold the extra meat, and then built a considerable cairn on top of it from blocks of snow. We took about a week of seal meat, and stashed the rest. West remained inside his bag the entire time, and indeed did not come out even as we were dismantling the hut and loading the sledge. Reinhold looked quizzically at me, but said nothing. We heaved West's bag onto the sledge as gently as we could, and strapped him down. We bound our own frozen bags onto the back, slipped into the harness, and pushed off.

The thick snow dragged on the sledge, and the harness bit into my shoulders, but the work did keep us warm. The wind buffeted us from the west and north, nearly knocking me into the sledge a few times; the drifts built up quickly, and we were soon forced to haul the sledge with our hands in order to guide it up and down without jarring West too badly. Marching in the wind and snow is never pleasant; adding the darkness and the newly laden sledge made it distasteful. We had been marching for about two hours, making perhaps a mile or two, when West wriggled his head free from the bag.

"Enough, you fools!" he shouted over the wind. "Make camp and wait for the storm to blow out." He disgorged himself from the bag and stood stamping his feet as we rigged up the shelter. As soon as the tarp was over the sledge, he threw his bag inside, and we built up the snow walls on the outside. The doctor went in and fired the stove. When we came in, there was a hoosh ready for us. West again ate several portions, and retreated into his bag. Reinhold and I ate in silence. After he had finished, and trimmed the stove down, the doctor announced that he was going to run some tests while we waited out the storm; he pulled out of his bag and began to put on his heavy mitts.

West shot out of his bag.

"You will remain in the tent," he said evenly.

"I must run some tests," said the doctor, "gauge our distance and direction; make sure that we are still closing in on the glaciers."

"We are, and you know that we are. There is no further need of testing."

"We could, by following the eastern shore exclusively, have been turned to the east into a smaller bay or channel. A few quick tests will—"

"We go together or not at all. You seek the discovery for yourself. I have brought you all here, paid for everything. You will not leave me behind now. There is no further need of testing."

"We have only limited—," began the doctor.

"There is no need," said West. "Now I suggest you rest, as you will need all of your strength."

The doctor removed his mitts and returned to his bag. After a time, he consoled himself by experimenting with the ice at the floor of the tent—scraping it up into a small vial, adding to it, shaking the vial, and examining the results. He brought out Strabo's book and pored over it again in the dim light.

From that point forward, West ceased to speak entirely; he had long ago stopped talking to Reinhold and me; now he did not speak to, or look at, the doctor. Communication became a set of grunts and stares. As he stirred, he expected to be fed until he stopped putting out his mug. If he kicked the stove, he expected it to be lit. The storm blew on for long hours, for a day, then two. Reinhold went out periodically to dig a passage clear and to clear the snow from on top of the tent. We went out only to relieve ourselves. Every time any of us left our bags, West emerged from his and sat stiffly alert, listening to make sure we did not go far. The doctor spoke little, whether from anger or shame or preoccupation, I could not tell. He passed the time by endlessly recalculating numbers from his notes and comparing them to the journal. He muttered to himself and nodded and added new annotations to his notes.

Six hooshes later—roughly on the afternoon of the second day—the wind abated and the temperature plunged. Even deep inside our cave of ice, now sealed by the frozen condensation of our breath, we could feel the air harden and grow brittle, and hear the wind begin to scrape. West came out from his bag and poked his head outside.

"Come," he yelled in to us, "the wind is down. We'll put in a full march now and see if we can't reach the glaciers."

We scrambled up and threw the remaining rations and supplies into our packs. We pulled our frozen bags out the tunnel and began to hack at the drifts that had built up around the sledge.

"Come on, come on!" shouted West. "We cannot stay here in the cold."

The temperature had dropped from a relatively comfortable twenty below zero to what had to be near fifty below. Even straining hard to free the sledge, I could not manage to get warm. My gloves froze, as did the sleeves of my coat, until I was just clubbing at the wall of snow with thick paddles of arms.

"The doctor and I will begin marching. You follow in short order. We must be off."

West and the doctor moved off as Reinhold and I worked the sledge free. We had to be careful for the tarp, which was brittle and stiff, and anchored deeply under the drifts. Finally we got the sledge out, and piled the packs and bags on top, and then bent the tarp roughly over the heap. We lashed it down as best we could and began to haul.

The days of inactivity had not helped to prepare us for the cold. The difference between a "moderate" twenty below and our current forty or fifty below was an order of magnitude: I did not even begin to feel my feet as we marched, despite angling my toes down and pounding them into the snow in an effort to get the blood into them. The wind sought out not just the gaps and seams, but wherever the fabric of my woebegone clothes had worn thin, and pulled the feeling from my limbs. First my arms, bound in the raddies, and then my legs went entirely numb, and moved of their own volition. My face burned and stung underneath my swaddling; I would find myself continually choking behind the mask of ice I had built up and I had to smash it off on my shoulder.

Reinhold did not try to speak over the wind, but I heard him huffing out songs in the gaps, and could see brightness in his eyes from beneath his layers. We had gone barely a mile when we stumbled over the doctor and West. They had burrowed into the snow, with the doctor laying over West like a blanket.

We pulled West onto the sledge and covered him again with the stiff bags. Then we pulled off into the blowing snow. Eventually the wind swung around behind us, and though we were still very cold, we made good progress. Finally the doctor called a halt again and we began to make camp.

Rebuilding the shelter in the wind with our stiff limbs was impossible—we turned the sledge on edge and cut the lashings free along one side, and then pulled it over us. We were swiftly buried by the drifting snow. Huddled in the darkness, I felt utterly without choices—no sense to move, no energy, exhausted from the cold, deafened by the wind, locked in an unsteady band of white amid the empty black. Back at the camp, prodded by the experiments of the doctor, I had wondered what sat in the black that I could not see—microscopic creatures, energies without form like spirits, his rivers of air and earth. But here beneath the tarp, the world was emptied even of its horrors, of malice, intent, energy—simply was, and was not, life, and so was removing us from it. How many empty miles of ice and snow are possible? How many empty hours since light and dark had shaped chaos into time? It was not entropic, but static; growth was the aberration, and this the equilibrium. I made no action to resist or join, but lay in darkness waiting, persisting without hope.

## sixteen

Ahoosh cheered us considerably, and we regained the energy to build a proper hut. The softening wind lulled us again to sleep. I awoke to the doctor jostling me roughly.

"Come on, come on," he said excitedly. "Get your gear and come out. We've reached the Barrier."

I scrambled out of my bag and out of the tent. There, about five miles away, but clearly visible above the blowing snow, I could see a massive glacier, perhaps two hundred feet high, that stretched off in the darkness to the east and west.

I hooted with joy, and Reinhold did a dance in the snow beside me, clapping me on the back and swinging my shoulders back and forth.

"Where's West? Is he coming out?"

"Mr. West is not doing so well," said the doctor. "He's still unconscious. We'll remain camped here so he can rest. Reinhold, you'll hunt along the Barrier edge and tend to Mr. West. Kane and I will explore the face and see if we can find a way up or through."

"Couldn't we find the edge and come up on the side, sir?" I

asked. "Or will we find the mirage as we get closer and be able to hike in?"

"We'll have to see when we get close enough, Kane. It doesn't look like we've come at it the same way as Strabo, though it is difficult to tell from this distance. I doubt that the mirage could persist in the winter. I think it most likely that we will either find a slope up and be able to climb to the top, then hike into the islands, or more likely, that we will be able to make our way through the underside, where seams of heated rock will have melted passages that lead us out into the archipelago." I tried to imagine a black garden, warm and fragrant and lightless, great tropical fronds reaching over us, and rustling movements in the darkness.

"Come, Kane," said the doctor abruptly, "let's have a hoosh and be off."

We ate enormously, packed light bags, and left, Reinhold bellowing out three hearty cheers. We reached the Barrier easily enough—the ice was fairly even, and without a sledge or harness I felt fast and strong. The face of the Barrier was deeply fractured, with fissures running the two hundred feet down the face and disappearing beneath the ice. At the base of the glacier were low heaps of debris, fragments that had calved in the fall and been frozen in. Beyond this foot, the top of the glacier bent out over us, as if pushed from the top, rather than flowing along the bottom. Spears of ice protruded out like breached battlements.

"You see that." The doctor pointed. "The rocks must be melting the base of the glacier away even as the top advances, causing it to tumble over itself."

The pitch of the top did not show us any easy place to climb. The ice itself was not like sea ice or like freshwater ice; it was densely plastic and difficult to chip away. It came off in a spray of pellets rather than shattering into sharp chunks. The doctor examined the face of it carefully, breaking off pieces, tasting them, turning them over in his hands.

We moved back and forth along the face, advancing into a few cracks, but never getting farther than a dozen yards or so before the crack closed or was filled by rubble. We turned to the west and moved along quickly now, the doctor poking his head in and out, rapping on the fissured walls in various places, then hurrying ahead to the next. A mile on, then two; the face of the glacier was remarkably consistent, not winding into bays and hollows, but forcing itself out in one uninterrupted mass. The moon rose and lit the fractured ice with blue and silver. Suddenly the doctor called out and ran ahead. In the distance loomed a vast semicircular opening cut out in the bottom of the glacier. It was more than one hundred yards across and reached up forty or fifty feet. The doctor stood in the entrance and bellowed, his arms stretched out over him in triumph.

The walls of the opening were perfectly smooth as though polished and new; they had no cracks or fissures running through them, and the floor was smooth and black. It was like wandering into a cathedral that had been built overnight in all of its geometric perfection; it pulled my breath up out of me.

"Come come," called the doctor. He had pulled a lantern out of his bag and lit it. I gasped.

"I've had it in reserve," he said, "for exactly this purpose." After the dim yellow of the blubber lamp, the oil burned bright white, and the light burst out like a tiny sun. The doctor moved back into the tunnel, the light not even reaching to the sides.

"It's a meltwater river, created by the heat of the rocks. In the summer it must reach to fill the entire channel. Imagine, Kane—it must explode out of the glacier like the Nile in flood." He was racing along now and I struggled to keep up, breaking into a run now and then. He was swerving from side to side to make sure we stayed in the main channel. In places, the smooth walls were scored by long, thick streaks that wound over and through each other like calligraphy done in a giant hand.

"Rocks, in the turbulence," he said. "Look at the size of them!"

The meltwater tunnel ran on and on, straight back into the glacier, without dipping or curving, without cleft or declivity; occasionally we would see an opening high up in the wall where a tributary poured in from above. On and on we went, a mile, two, more, deeper and deeper. Finally it began to bend and dip, sending us sliding down a smooth slope. As we had been walking, I felt increasingly warm. I took it as a part of being out of the wind, and of our increased pace, but as we descended, the air felt warmer than it had felt in months.

"Is it—," I began.

"Warmer? Absolutely. It is close to zero now and has been warming steadily as we descend."

"Will we come to the water? Or onto land?" I imagined a vast underground lake lined by grottoes filled with blue light reflected up off the water, waves lapping gently at the shore.

"We may," admitted the doctor, "but we should advance carefully. There must be a basin of meltwater at the head of the river. It must be below the level of the river and rise in the spring as ice melts from above and below. The basin fills until it overflows. Or perhaps the lava has its own season and rises in a slow tide of some kind, raising the levels of the meltwater. In either case, the ice is likely to slope down into the basin, and we would not want to slide down into the water."

We paused while he roped us together. The tunnel had narrowed now, and our lantern touched the walls on either side and showed the ceiling flickering above us. We had been walking for about fourteen hours altogether when the doctor called a halt finally. We ate some chunks of raw blubber and sucked some chips of ice, then moved off again.

The tunnel began to narrow and split off at last, several channels of different sizes heading up and off to the sides. Dr. Architeuthis took a few paces down each, and peered ahead with the lantern to find the main channel. On several occasions we had to go quite far down side channels before returning to the main channel. Some of the branches connected back to each other in flowing panes, what sailors called "eyes of God" in the icebergs, and some of the smaller channels opened to show large chambers beyond. The doctor hacked small markings in the walls with his knife when we moved out from one channel to the next. The noise echoed harshly in the cavernous darkness. The air was warm enough now that I shed my jacket and marched along in sweater and shirt, and even so I was sweating. Still the walls showed no signs of melting, and there was no running water anywhere.

Eventually the channels resolved back into a single channel, this one perhaps ten feet high and twenty feet across. It sloped steadily downward into the very heart of the glacier. The roof angled down also, and developed smooth ridges, like the shallows of a gentle sea. We stooped, and then crawled, the sides closing in as well as the top. We were now miles below the surface of the Barrier. For the first time I began to feel the weight of the ice above us.

"We'll eat again here, and then make our way forward," said the doctor. He opened the top of the lantern and inverted the cap, then filled it with ice chips and some blubber. It was a small hoosh, but as our first warm food in almost two days, it tasted succulent.

"What is the temperature, Doctor?"

"It is close to twenty degrees above zero," he said. "Much warmer, and we'll have to swim." He grinned. "We must be nearly to the basin," he continued. "I believe it will open on the other side into a tunnel similar to this one, leading into the archipelago."

"Should we bring Reinhold and West into the glacier, sir? So West can recover in the heat?"

"We'll find the way first, and then bring them on through. There may still be some rough sledging ahead and West is in no condition to manage it. They'll come along soon enough. Reinhold has likely filled the tent with seal meat and they are gorging them-selves on it as we speak."

After the hoosh, I was feeling dozy. The air felt pleasantly warm. My legs and feet were aching from the prolonged march but it was wonderful to feel warm again. I could feel also mount-ing in my chest the dim echoes of the excitement I had felt on the *Narthex* as I first learned to read the instruments—that a fresh world was close, and due us; that our efforts had earned it and we were close to our deliverance. The doctor propped the lantern on his coat and tied it so that it would slide along the floor between us. The floor was ridged now also, and as we crawled forward my hands and knees slid and pitched. Soon we were inching forward on our bellies, sliding up and down between the ridges. We were both panting heavily. Finally the doctor paused, his head turned sideways and wedged between the ridges. I dropped my ex-hausted head to the ice, happy for the break. He worked his way free and inched back down to me.

"Kane," he said, "you are small enough to fit through—you must go on ahead and see how far it is to the basin. Once we re-turn with Reinhold, we can open the tunnel, but it would take us too long now. You go on ahead and report back the distance. I will wait here and run some tests on the ice."

"Are you sure it opens out?" I asked. "That it doesn't just end?"

"Think of the tunnel," he said, "the mass of it, the speed of the rocks. That mass comes from somewhere; it doesn't just ooze out of the ice. And the temperature—we must be close."

Obediently I went forward, twisting my head and shifting my hips to work between the ridges. I counted my lurches forward to keep some sense of the distance. Behind me the doctor shouted encouragement as he hacked at the floor with his knife. I dragged the lantern behind me on the rope. Gradually I left him behind, hearing only the echoes of his knife on the ice. In the jostling, the lantern went out and I was left in the darkness. I slid my hands forward, expecting at any moment for the world to drop away; the passage narrowed and narrowed again. My coat got wedged in and I panicked for a moment, then backed out to free myself. I could not turn around, so I wriggled backward until the chipping grew louder. There I found space to turn around and made my way back. The chipping stopped and all I could hear was the doctor's breathing echoing under the ice.

"Doctor," I called. "I've gone as far up as I can. My coat got stuck into the ice. I think the condensation is making it stick."

"Then take it off." The doctor's voice was suddenly up very close to mine, his face only a few feet away.

"Leave the lantern and your gear. You will move faster in any case, and the heat from your body may help you get through."

I wriggled out of my jacket and out of my sweater. Underneath my bare skin, the ice was cool and impossibly smooth. It did not stick to my skin, nor soften or melt when I pressed on it. I dragged the lantern around and pushed it over to the doctor. He sparked it into light, and the light leapt off into the distance.

"Good boy, Kane. You are very nearly there. You are on the

verge of doing something absolutely tremendous. You must get through. Force your way."

I turned and pressed on with renewed energy, sliding easily over the ice without my jacket to restrain me. The plastic ice did not yield, but it did not hold me either. I slid ahead into the crevice and left the light of the lantern and Dr. Architeuthis panting behind me. His soft, insistent voice carried up to me even at a great distance, prodding and begging and exhorting me to strive onward, its pant and hiss bearing me up and on.

The undulant ice seemed to give way in the darkness before me, and on and on I went. The heat inside the glacier did not seem to be radiating from anywhere, but rather inherent in the glacier itself, as if I were inside some great beast, and I felt like I had become an equal part of it, not distinct but separated, and finding my way down to where it was I belonged. The passage continued to close until there was no gap between my head and the smooth edge of the ice, and still I went forward, rippling down into darkness effortlessly.

I awoke to the pound of blood in my ears, my body locked firmly into the ice. My reverie of progress had ended and I had been released to where I was: miles below the ice, in a thin shirt, in total darkness, without even the space to lift my head. I could feel the ice pressing in on all sides of me and I cried out in panic first, and then horror. The ice that I had felt opening I now felt closing, the fluid mountains rolling forward onto me, and I thrashed, though only within the loose confines of my own skin, and screamed and passed into unconsciousness again.

part three

Go Still

*seventeen*

The sharp jerk of my leg brought me back to my senses. At first I thought the doctor had somehow made his way up to me, but it was my mere heart again, drawing me back from what would be rest—for dying then would have been not only easy but pleasant. But the blood pulsed and ran in my leg, jabbed and yanked me back. Now I was very cold, and the ice was still un-melted beneath me, though it had yielded enough to let me move backward again. The slope was steeper than I had imagined and it was difficult to find purchase on; I angled first to the right and then to the left, and got stuck against one side or the other. My jaw, ankle, knee caught and twisted, bent and banged as I worked up and back, resting from time to time, and trying to turn around. The panic surged up in me in waves, paralyzing me as I pushed up against the mass of the glacier, straining to create the space for my own small pocket of heat. For once the cadence of my heart beat-ing back against the ice fortified me, its endless revolt no longer aimed at me but become my ally and pushing back weakly but re-lentlessly, impossibly, drawing me back into the wider, more open area of the passage and finally bringing the soft glow of the lantern into view.

"Yes? Yes?" shouted Dr. Architeuthis as soon as he heard me. "You have found passage? We are there?"

I scuttled the last yards into the low opening he had made and slumped against the wall.

"There is no way through," I said. "The passage narrowed until I became trapped and was only able to extricate myself with great difficulty."

"And did you throw a chunk of ice on ahead? To see if the basin was near? To see what lay ahead of you?"

"My arms were stuck beside me, my head wedged at an angle. There was no room to throw anything."

"But ahead of you, was there heat? Light? Signs of any kind? Could you hear the flow of water?"

"Nothing, there was nothing."

"Yes, well," he said. "Perhaps if you could have had the heat of your body melt you through. We can return with some supplies—perhaps Reinhold has killed a seal—and with a few good feedings and perhaps a layer of grease on your skin, naked perhaps you may get further." At this, my panic surged back.

"It is not a matter of ten feet more, or a hundred," I said. "The glacier closes off into nothing. There is no space for man to pass through."

"It is *always* a matter of ten feet more," he said fiercely. "Yours or another's with more will than you, with more courage, more discipline; nothing is given, only wrested, and either you have the strength or you lack it."

The wick of the lantern burned between us with perfect unwavering stillness, throwing out in silence a sphere that bent and distorted as it ran over the furrowed ice.

"And what if you get there, you make it, and burst out into

the islands, and you are so broken and weak, broken and not made whole, that you cannot make your way back?" I asked.

"Then you will have something inside you, irrevocable and ir-reducible; you will have wrenched the whole world ahead, de-flected it from its circling descent, and brought it forward. In generations of men, one man may. You."

His voice was swallowed in the immense darkness and did not echo back.

"We shall make our way back out," he said. "Regroup, resup-ply. With fresh meat from Reinhold, we can come back, dig deeper." I said nothing, and we made the long trek back.

Reinhold had no fresh meat for us. When West came to, he was delirious, and Reinhold had been forced to strap him into his bag. He cackled with laughter when he saw us enter, and began cursing at me.

"Kane, how does it feel to be weak? Do you enjoy weakness and insufficiency? You miserable bastard. Eh? I'd be there now without you to hold me back. Thought I was doing you a favor bringing you along, dragging your bloated carcass behind me." He subsided into mumbling, and the doctor sedated him.

"Me and the gentleman have just been exchanging recipes for pot roast," said Reinhold. "Port, I told him. Nutmeg, says he, and he had a bit of distemper, so I restrained him."

"Any lucidity at all?" asked the doctor.

"None, sir. Been awake as you saw him for the last ten hours or so. Wouldn't eat the hoosh—said I'd poisoned it."

"We'll have to force march him back down to the cache if he's to have any chance."

"Does he, sir?" I asked.

"He just needs proper nutrition and some rest, Kane. A week or two of fresh meat and he'd be ready to head out again. We'll leave in an hour, double march back to the cairn, and build a more

substantial shelter. A week of the seal meat should have us looking differently. If West has recovered sufficiently we can return
here and make another try."

We beat each other into our stiff harnesses and moved off.
Over us, the sky was no longer its flat black but shot through to
the south with soft shafts of purple like the rain-slick bark of a
tree where a bud will burst through. I looked over to the doctor.

"It's coming," he said, smiling. "A few more weeks." We put
our heads down and moved off. The sledge moved easily over the
hard-packed snow and I was thankful to be free of the glacier.
Hoosh at midday huddled under the tarp, and we were off again.
West did not wake.

We made fair time; shapes of ice and drift loomed up with an
odd but comforting familiarity like seeing the face of an old acquaintance in a crowd in a foreign city. It had taken us three days
with the storms to get to the Barrier, but it had been only eight or
nine miles. We reached the bay, though we could not see the cairn
in the darkness; we took two hours to make a solid camp, bank-
ing up the walls and building a small entrance tunnel with a block
of ice to keep out the wind. Reinhold carved the ventilation hole
to the south, and then packed the entire outside with loose snow.
The doctor lit the stove and made a thin hoosh with the remains
of our rations. West revived enough to be fed some teaspoonfuls
of hoosh, but vomited them up again and went back to sleep. The
doctor brought out the lantern again to examine Reinhold and
myself; satisfied that we were sound, he doused the lantern and
we watched the soft light of the stove as we digested in silence.

I came to with a snap of the tarp and a painful stabbing in my
head. I strained to open my eyes, but they were distant and
leaden; I heard a tread like footsteps, the march of soldiers, and
felt, within my dumb trunk, my heart, without the sense to yield;
from my great distance, it seemed like a curiosity, then an affront,

and on and on it beat, and gradually I felt pain return and drag me back, first a stinging in my shoulders and face, and then a burning across my back and stomach, like a jet of acid. At my elbows and knees it paused, then continued—a fierce itching, and shooting pains that made me cry out.

There was no response from the others; the stale air stank and smothered. I croaked and struck out with my legs spastically, trying to rouse someone, but there was no stir. My head jabbed again sharply as if I had been struck with a hammer, and then struck again. I struggled to sit up, wavered, and fell back, throwing my arms out helplessly. They hit against the edge of the tarp and I dragged myself upright with it, pulling it out from under the edge of the snow wall in the process.

My clothes had frozen into blocks, and I beat myself against them. I dug my heels down and threw my head against the wall of the sledge behind me. Eventually I managed to work it loose and knock it backward, bringing the roof tumbling down on me. The outside air was crisp and fresh and I gulped it in. In the moonlight I could see what I had suspected—that West had worked free of his straps, crawled over to the ventilation hole, and blocked it with his glove. Densely packed into the tent, we had nearly suffocated in the storm. He lay curled beneath it, a grisly smile playing over his skeletal face.

I knocked the stove free from the sledge and rigged it roughly in front of me. Twenty minutes of wrestling, and a match held, and then the wick caught, and the thick yellow light spread under the tarp. I wedged the doctor's pack onto the top edge of the sledge, creating enough space for the stove to burn freely and let the fresh air in.

Reinhold came to first, shaking himself like a big dog, and then smiling to see the flame. Next the doctor sat up, unseeing at first, like a somnambulist, staring at me with an angry blankness and down at the flame and back at me. In one pass his eyes cleared and he looked simultaneously relieved and exhausted.

I explained what had happened and he made his way over to West. West's exposed hand was black and curled as if it had been burned in a fire. When the doctor raised West's head from the floor of the hut, he revealed a torn flap in West's cheek, open from beneath his nose back to the base of his jaw, still hooked on to the edge of the sledge runner. The bloodless skin looked like paper, the gums black over black teeth. Once the hut had warmed and the air cleared, we helped the doctor wrestle him out of his bag. His limbs were loose, and there was no substance to him, no mass of padding, like an armful of kindling. The doctor cut free his boots. West's toes came off into his socks, and his feet were fully black, with streaks of black reaching above his knees. We worked him into one of the bags and propped him between us, close to the stove. We pushed close to the stove. Reinhold made his way out of the tent to find the cache, and fired his rifle to signal to us when he found it.

With the heat, pain arrived, and receded, and we ate, and ate again.

"We must move again while we have the strength," the doctor proclaimed.

"We do not have the strength," I said. "We need to recover ourselves." I looked over at Reinhold.

"West cannot recover out in this cold, and we will follow," replied the doctor. "Our bodies are consuming themselves—sacrificing our fingers and toes, then hands and feet, trying to keep our hearts and heads functioning. They are cunning beasts that hoard the heat and leave our weaker parts to fend for themselves. We must get him, and ourselves, back to the camp before we are run to ground. We must push on as soon as we possibly can."

Of our march I have few memories. One, that is easiest and so preoccupied me to the exclusion of others, was this: I began to go blind. You would think it would be easier to go blind gradually, light fading, edges softening, until the world retreats into blurred darkness—after all, the world was largely dark in any case, lit only by the stab of the stars and the slow wallow of the wick in blubber. But for me I think it would have been easier to have been struck blind, as they say, cast into darkness and left to find my way. As it was, in the final twilight days I had my sight to stew on, and dim outlines to keep me lost.

There was then uncertain space—objects rising up where none should be, and disappearing—and me, lost, battered prey. The mug resting by my leg, and with numb fingers seeking, but failing to find. The others were patient with me, but there was little to be done. Once you have had sight, you cannot lose that idea of space, but your rough fingers cannot shape what you find—it remains overlong, unfamiliar, undefined, chaotic—and your unreliable mind finds always the agency of malice behind it and not its own inability to imagine what you cannot see. In the last dark days when even the stove was a vague spot, I was still making my space in the same way, placing and ordering objects and fighting with my memory to translate through them. It took two days on the march for the memory of light and space to die out and to be truly in darkness.

I pulled like a mute beast with all the strength I had in me—bearing up even Reinhold as we made our way south. But the mind is itself and not what we think it, and it reaches out with unimaginable hands into that chaos and finds a shaped order that your eyes cannot hold—like the inside of your mouth that you have never seen except in reflections, but that your tongue knows perfectly with a knowing that is not spaced but still ordered—and I came to understand something of the darkness in itself, not as a mere boundary to the light.

Mercifully, the weather was even and not so punishingly cold. West began to rave again, when we could hear him, bellowing out and singing and cursing at us.

"And in these days," he called out, "shall men seek death, and shall not find it; and shall desire to die and death shall flee from them." I do not know if he was cursing us then, or exhorting us. I am sure I lost my senses also, across the miles of ice, my legs pounding dully after my dull heart, and me insensible above it.

In the darkness, I thought foot on foot of being here, of destiny that had somehow twisted beneath me into fate, and of my own self and its weak and ineffectual desires; of desiring greatly a gift that I had not the grace to be offered, and of sitting in the rigging beneath an impossible blue, of a stack of arms and legs, of the doctor and my coarse hand on the delicate knob of the sextant with the sea heaving beneath me.

The key, of course, is finding a fixed point from which to measure. Then it becomes easy, though it is not simple; oddly enough, it is exactly the opposite. Once you finish calculating the variables for the imperfections of the lens, for the flaws of the mirror, the distortions of the light, for the uneven effects of the cold on different metals, of light, of atmosphere, of the bend of the very earth beneath you, once you have dug through the books and run over the tables and charts, you are buried in great complexity, but that fundamental point of measurement has not changed.

And then the journey begins, you begin to move, the land passes beneath you, and the wavering line in the mirror dims and fades. You plod on, measuring yourself by your own steps, the lengths of your body, your heavy foot, confident in the weight of your numbers, wrapped and blind in them, carried on by your original energy, however compromised and deformed, however distorted and deceived it has become. There is something comforting in the complexity, in the tracing out, some weight in the columns of numbers and figures, the footnoted charts and weighted years of annotated tables, as if the very complexity somehow sharpens your eye and hones your powers of observation, as if it fixes that point more clearly and focuses it before you, and holds your foot to it as you march in the cold and darkness.

But what a terrible deception lies in this, this comforting obscurity of calculation, because it lets you deceive yourself (and oh how willingly you are led) into believing that this easy complexity can stand in for vision, that the ordered march of numbers can pull you forward, can somehow change the one hard cold fact that remains after you recognize the bouncing, shifting treachery of the light and the ignorant hopefulness of your science: that it is only the determination of that fixed point and your uncertain eye upon it that matters.

March on march until we heard shouting in the distance and Reinhold called out to the hut, the echo sounding familiar to me. We all called out and stumbled forward, yanking the sledge behind us. In the distance I heard bellowing, and the roar of an animal. I felt Reinhold and the doctor jerk free from the harness and felt the harness drop away. They cried out and cried out again; many voices were shouting; and there was the crash of splintering wood and the rough thump of flesh on stone, then the crack of a rifle. I dragged after them, stumbling up onto the beach, anchored by the sledge.

I struggled to be free of my harness, but could not. I yanked hard on the sledge again, eventually upsetting it and wedging into the rocks just down the beach from the boats. Their voices were buzzing now, and low. From the black inside of the camp, I could hear a low moaning.

# eighteen

hat is it?" I called out. "What's happened?"

A hand came to my elbow and cut me free.

"A bear," a voice—Adney's—said. "Reinhold is badly wounded, as is Preston. The captain and Creely are both uninjured, but it made off with our meat, such as it was. We're lucky you came when you did. Is West still alive?"

"If he is, then just barely," I replied. "I've lost my sight. We have some seal on the sledge."

Adney moved off. After a time, hands pulled me up, and the harness was cut free. I was led up under the boats, where Griffin called to me:

"Kane, good to see you, boy. Come on in. They're just mending the roof with your sledge, then we'll have a small fire and get you warmed. Ash," he called out, "we'll pull under the boat with the tarp anchored to the south, and break up the dinghy."

"What happened, sir?"

"Bear broke in the end by jumping on the keel of the dinghy. Preston was underneath and got knocked out. Our rifle was trapped beneath him. Adney jumped up and tried to drive it off, but it ignored him. Ash and I pulled Creely back and tried to restart the lamp while it gorged on our stores. Finally Ash got the torch lit and was trying to drive it off when you arrived. Reinhold leapt onto its back, but it threw him off. The doctor finally managed to get some shots off—it didn't appear hurt, but it has left us alone, and dragged off our seal with it."

"And Reinhold, sir? How is he?"

"He's had a bad knock, but he's made of iron. He'll be all right."

We unpacked the slege and settled into our new, smaller quarters, Griffin issuing sharp orders, though taking care not to overtax any of us. He did not ask about our trek, for which I was grateful.

A fire was started and the wind subsided as the cracks around the hut were sealed. We had a weak hoosh, and I slept.

When I awoke the hut was cold again. Adney was clambering over me, back from a fruitless hunt.

"I can see the coming of the light," he said. "Just faintly in the sky, a long way off, but it is there."

A weak cheer went up across the hut.

"It should break the horizon in about two weeks," said the doctor.

"We need to start south by then, if we can," said Captain Griffin, "if we want the ice to hold. I don't imagine we'll make better than five or six miles a day."

"We should wait for the ice to break up," said the doctor. "We can rely on the boat and drift out with the pack. You cannot march on your foot yourself; we can let the ice do much of the work for us."

"The boat won't hold us all. We can't drift out into the sound and have it melt beneath us."

"We can ride the ice and use the boat to ferry us to shore when the need arises; hunting and fishing should both improve as the light comes back—we'll be able to build up our stores again, and regain some strength. We may even have another chance to go north—the Barrier is only forty miles away."

No one responded to this invitation.

With the hut restored, and Reinhold, West, and the others tended, the doctor and Griffin went through the stores remaining. With the addition of our seal, we had two weeks of fuel and half rations for us all. The captain did not ask about our journey and Dr. Architeuthis did not offer. Instead they focused on the care of the men, hunting parties, the state of the ice and currents of the water. The doctor took the rifle and went with Adney to look for seals. Inside the hut, West mumbled and shook, but did not wake. For the others, I could not tell if they were asleep or awake—even the jovial snore of Reinhold was silent. The hunters returned eventually in silence and made the hoosh. Dr. Architeuthis examined each of us in turn.

"Will my sight return, Doctor?" I asked.

"It should," he replied. "Perhaps a week. There is nothing I can see as the cause—some time to rest and steady meals in the hut. Our Atlas must not weaken." He rubbed my shoulder with an awkward affection.

West came to for the hoosh and he was lucid. First he demanded a full accounting of the stores, and then of the men, and then of the weather and ice, and then demanded a second, full hoosh made. Adney took the rifle again and left, and Dr. Architeuthis silently began to melt ice and shake his droplets in. Adney returned with a fox he had shot approaching the ridge. It was no more than a bag of gristly bones, but it added weight to our meal. None of us could trust our teeth to the bones except Ash, who cracked them with vigor and scraped the marrow into the pot.

Adney went out again and stayed out, except for meals, and to minister to Reinhold. He brought in an occasional fox, and shot some birds—the first we'd seen in months—but no seal; he lacked Reinhold's skill at finding the holes and saw them only in the distance. The doctor brought shrimp in from the nets. We soon used up our seal meat and moved to cold hooshes made from whatever grace the day had granted us. Reinhold began to sit up weakly, and his raspy breathing filled the tent.

My sight returned slowly, and it brought me back into a world of ghosts. With the blubber gone and the lantern out, we resorted to candles. The broken bones of foxes were added and then removed from each pot, in hope that some gluey trace of nutrition might pass from them to us. Ash tried to dry the shrimp shells and burn them, but could not get them to light. Adney managed to scrape handfuls of lichen from the rock that yielded weak and smoky fires.

Each of the men had lost so much weight that their bones angled sharply through the blackened skin of their faces. Their joints were so swollen that you could see the binding in their clothes, and the voids in between. Pools of blood seemed to sit open on their faces, and yellow eyes sat deep in black sockets; behind cracked lips solitary teeth sat in translucent gums. Aside from the hunters, most of the men sat upright, hands in their laps, staring blankly ahead. They drank hoosh when it was handed to them, but made no other efforts to stir themselves, took no notice of the day passing, like a tribe of lost revenants awaiting the return of their necromancer. Only West, glaring from inside his bag, gave any sign of volition.

One evening, Dr. Architeuthis built a stronger fire with wood from the dinghy to make a proper hot hoosh and do a more thorough medical exam. The fire roared up and the hut became delightfully warm. The doctor began with West, who refused to let the doctor examine him.

"At least let me see your frozen hand," said the doctor. "Perhaps we can save the arm."

"My hand?" said West. "And what is to be done about it? No medicines, no instruments. Can your eyes heal it? You only want to butcher me. You can't wait for it. Why not eat the others first, eh? Creely first? Why is it me?"

"If the rot worsens without stopping it, you'll die," said the doctor.

"And that would make things easy for you wouldn't it? Except then I'd be frozen and harder to eat—better to keep me soft and warm, eh?"

"We will restrain you if we must, Mr. West, but I need to look at it, for your own safety." He glanced over to Ash, who rose onto his haunches.

"Oh by all means bring over your bone breaker, Doctor. I'll not go lightly. Come, come, Creely first, or Kane."

"No one is eating anyone, Mr. West. As the sun returns there is more than enough to feed us. I need to conduct my examination now." He moved forward and Ash moved up behind him.

"Keep your distance. I'll give you a look, butcher." He pulled his hand from within his bag and held it out to the fire. It was curled into a gnarled crook, black and twisted and shriveled all the way to his elbow. The elbow was grotesquely swollen and yellow, with trails of pus edging down the black forearm.

"Right as rain," he yelled. "Now look somewhere else for your gobbets."

"Let me see," said the doctor, putting out his hands.

"Nor stop me nor turn me nor drive me forth," shouted West, "as if the staff should lift up itself, as if it were not wood." Then he appeared to calm down, and a broken smile bent his face.

"If it's to be, than I am first," said West. "Mine first for me."

And glaring directly at the doctor, he put his gnarled thumb into his mouth and snapped it off. The doctor and Ash leapt forward but it was too late—West cracked and crunched the black thumb with relish, bits leaking out through the open flap in his cheek. He laughed shrilly.

"Ha! Can your feeble sailors do this? I am twice the man."

He bit down on his fore and index fingers, tearing free long strips of his black skin down his forearm.

"Make yourself useful, butcher, and sew up my cheek. I'm losing all the juices."

Dr. Architeuthis sedated West with a vial from his pocket, and pulled the remains of West's hand from between his clenched jaws. He and Ash laid him back in front of the fire and slid him out of his bag. His legs were pale sticks, streaks of black extending up into his thighs. They cleaned up as best they could, tamping gently on large areas of open sores and bruising stretching down his haunches to the black rising up. His ribs were yellow, purple, and black, with their own mosaic of sores and rot. Again they cleaned gently, bound up his wounds, and then strapped him firmly into his bag.

"Well, then," said Dr. Architeuthis mordantly, "who's next?"

The others of us had the usual sores and nips of frostbite, and some rot. Reinhold grunted with pain as the doctor felt his ribs and back, and sank into sleep as soon as his examination was finished. The doctor clipped off Ash's fingertips and the tips of his ears as if he were clipping his nails. Ash cauterized them on a glowing coal, barking more with irritation than with pain. I had developed a cough, and with it a mild fever, but the doctor did not seem to be worried about it.

"I thought you said I couldn't get sick," I said.

"You can't," he said, trying to smile a little.

"So where did my fever come from? Was it something I ate?"

"What you have not eaten, I think, is the trouble. It is most likely a focal infection," he said, "rooted somewhere in your body—frequently the teeth or throat, but perhaps within an internal organ, often the liver. You carried it up here with you, most probably you have had it for many years, and it has waited for your present weakness to reveal itself. Now you are weak and it becomes stronger. But with some fresh food you will recover yourself. Atlas will not fail."

Fresh food was not forthcoming, though some storms brought back the sun, and warmer weather with it. Adney rolled back the canvas roof and we turned our faces feebly to the sun. The doctor was tireless—preparing all the food, examining us daily, caring for us with the most careful ministrations.

West's song, when it came, was Italian. He rumbled out the vibrato, the skin dancing on his cheek, before slumping into silence and death. I lacked the strength to dig, but could hear Griffin and Adney pounding at the gravel with a thwart from the dinghy—a sound that seemed to have been there always, irregular, discordant, bitter.

The days passed in gaps for me now—long dark silences, and then a blaze of light, and the ice foot off in the distance. The doctor and Griffin arguing about leaving. My teeth chattering themselves loose and scattering into my mouth. The doctor's face over mine tense and worried. Bright red spots on a field of white. And then another hacking cough and a wrenching in my stomach. Teeth again jumbled in my mouth—a mouth full of teeth.

It came clearly to me that I was dying; that dying was not a momentary severing, but a set of small steps of decline and submission. I sat dully and watched the others sitting for hour after hour. Of course the hours that sped now were the hours I cherish, the stained, sick hours, dark and bloody hours after the bright hours I had spent cursing, not like these, black and gray and dark and now, in my last days, shot with scarlet at last, these days. This day.

Today. I could not bring myself to think of today as the last. This could not be the last, though I knew it was not far. Today. The closeness left me license to search without shame for the light in these days, but the end was not so close that I did not need to search. I could not bring my face to bear on the bloodstained handkerchief, could not listen to the cough as it worsened, and tried to (and could) think of my companions, of us working, sailing through the bright and fractured ice, of Aziz passing me a cup of hot tea and leaning back to tell me a story.

Starting with a flicker in my throat, but once caught, tearing, I coughed into my sleeve, the cuff already spotted and stained with blood dried to a reddish brown like the breast of a robin.

I took comfort that there was on the other side of the world one man who answered me in opposite—who balanced my pain with his joy and my hardship with his ease, my red for his green, in each of my flaws and failures and weaknesses his own virtues and triumphs and strengths. I saw him, languid days unrolling before him, heaped plates leaping up to rest gently beneath his fingers, fruit bursting whole from the ground, wine draining from grapes; before him new lands heaved up from the sea, trees whole upon them, shaking off the deep like energetic dogs from a pond. A straight and smooth row of bright teeth cracking into an apple.

I awoke shuddering and shaking in the darkness, Griffin's arm over my shoulder, gently supporting me, his voice soft in my ear. My head rolled back, thumping hard against the boat, and my eyes lost their focus. Then the blaze of light from under my eyelids, which were torn somehow, and the light was burning in. A sharp pain in my face, and the delightful cool of rocks as the light fell. I retched soup into my lap and turned to the doctor, my head pounding and my neck too weak to support it—a great weakness, my flesh falling from my bones and skin tearing from its own weight; before me the angry faces of strangers. Fever cleanses and leaves one sober, chastened, humble. Fever passes, but I felt now the return of fevers rising in waves, fevers recurrent, native, and abiding.

My fever broke finally, and the days took on their relentless march again, neither slower nor faster, the only shift the wobbly sun that staggered up and fell back for a few hours each day.

*nineteen*

The sun had brought storms with it, and we were often confined to the hut. When the sky cleared, we dragged ourselves out, blinking like cave creatures at the bright new world around us. Inside the hut, I spent my time by Reinhold.

His mind struggled fiercely in these days to drive his limbs through the pain. His forehead would crease with concentration as he dragged himself from his bed to the entrance of the hut, hanging his head and panting, then pressing on again. Unlike Creely, who had the blessing of incoherence, he was fully aware of his debilitation. His eyes glared out like beacons from within his bag. Each failure to rise brought a mounting fury; his will pushed out into his body, trying to force it into motion, and his body collapsed under the onslaught. He would lie facedown on the floor, grinding his teeth and growling, and then heave himself forward until he reached the end of the hut, and then turn and come back. In all it was about fifteen feet each way, and it took him nearly an hour. Finally he would collapse into his bag, exhausted and enraged, and lie facing the wall, the rage rising from his back in waves like heat.

Despite the pleading of the doctor, he refused to stay in his bag; when they bound him in, he threw himself over and inched like a worm, groaning with the pain. When they restored him to his place, I moved beside him.

"Slow down there, Magellan. You won't make it around the Horn today."

He managed a weak smile and leaned over to whisper in my ear. "It's open eyes that see, my friend."

"What?"

"The ice is breaking up and we'll need to be ready to go when it does, not dragging around here."

"So the captain said. But we haven't the food or fuel or rest to be marching. We wouldn't get a mile."

"We get plenty of food; that's not the problem."

I laughed despite myself. "Warm water and lichen with a dash of roasted leather?"

"It's the what and not how much."

"What do you mean?"

"The doctor's planning another trip north. By himself this time."

"He doesn't have the supplies. He might make it back to the Barrier, but not over it, or through. Even he doesn't have the strength for that."

"He'd need to be a lot stronger."

"Yes."

"Lots of heavy, hot meals to build him back up again."

"Exactly. Not just fox bones and shrimp."

Reinhold watched my face, as if I were a small child watching him do a card trick, earnestly trying to find the coin that had disappeared. "And where will that come from?" he asked.

"Well, if the hunting improves with the weather, I guess that would be a start, if he convinces the captain to try again. I can't imagine Griffin would risk it."

"He won't. And the hunting won't get better."

"It won't?"

He shook his head. "Why does the doctor need to hunt when he's got all that he needs?"

I looked at him blankly.

"Look at us," he hissed, "penned in like cattle and chewing on our cuds. He's just got to put some meat on us and we're ripe."

"But we'll get strong again if we eat."

Reinhold began to look exasperated with me. "Look," he said, "we've been here all winter and not one of us has died. Not one— winter journeys, man hauling over the ice, months of darkness and cold. Not one. And now, just as the sun comes back, we start dying. Game is returning, yet there is nothing to eat. We get fevers, which he has explained that we cannot get. We go mad. Except for him, and he is getting stronger every day, did you notice? The only one among us."

"I'm getting better, and Adney and Ash are still strong."

"You're too dumb to stay sick, even for your own good," he said, laughing, and then bit it off as the doctor came back into the hut. Reinhold shook his head at me and sat back, pretending to sleep. When the doctor approached, he groaned heavily and rolled his head back.

"Reinhold?" said the doctor, shaking his foot, "are you feeling better?" He did not respond, but lay limply, his head angled unnaturally to the side.

"Kane? Has he come round?"

"No sir, sleeping gently until just now."

"I see," said the doctor. "Please get me if he comes around, will you?" He made his way back out and Reinhold rolled over to me.

"See what I mean?" he whispered.

"No."

"He's preparing all the food now and giving us all a little something special—lets us eat but stay weak. Ash is his prize pony—strong and healthy, but no will to act. Adney eats on the hunt. One for the camp, one for himself. I'd do the same. He'll be a problem. For the rest of us, he's just waiting to knock us off so he can pack up and be on his way. But Creely and the captain, stubborn old bastards, aren't keeping to his schedule."

"But how long has he been at it? Since we came back from the Barrier?"

"Hume," said Reinhold decisively. "Healthy men don't just die. Why do you think he wanted to do the autopsy? And then no word about it afterwards. He was doing a trial run, see how his specially designed food worked. Then West on the trip up. He was hoping to cache him at the base of the Barrier, for the trip back. He's got it all marked out in his book."

Adney and the doctor came back inside to prepare the midday meal and Reinhold lolled his head back, but winked at me, as if this were all a great game. When the doctor put a mug to Reinhold's lips, he pushed his tongue up and out and let the hoosh run down over his face. I took my mug and stared into it, and then over at Reinhold's prone form. I raised it to my face to smell it and he jerked and cried out, knocking it from my grasp, then grunted and shook and pretended to lapse back into unconsciousness.

"Kane!" said the doctor sharply. "You clumsy . . . I'm afraid there is no more."

Reinhold, his eyes shut, nodded triumphantly.

We did not have a chance to speak again until the following morning; I elected to eat, and I watched the doctor carefully, but could see nothing amiss in his preparation of the food. When he headed out to hunt, Reinhold wriggled over to me again.

In hushed tones, he unrolled the whole of the doctor's plans—times, places, symptoms. He explained the course of the doctor's peculiar posion, of how, with slight variations for our constitutions, it functioned in exactly the same way for each of us—where it had started to take hold and the signs of its progression through our systems, of the alterations the doctor had been forced to make following the bear attacks ("Me out and Adney in"). He explained that he had read through the doctor's book while we were at the Barrier, had seen the annotated charts, with the correct tunnel clearly marked ("He hoped to cache you there for the next time through"); he had also seen the schedule of dosages and dates, and they were coming to an end.

"Easter Sunday," he said. "You can't say the man doesn't have a sense of humor."

I began to see the doctor as I had never seen him, in all his cunning and baseness and patient evil; I could see that what I had taken for pride and a desire for glory was in fact a cold and brutal greed.

"What do we do? Will we have to kill him?"

"Not yet," said Reinhold. "Hold yourself in. Don't eat his food. Gather your strength. We'll have our reckoning."

"Who knows? Anyone?"

"No one. Maybe Ash, the others, nothing. The shock'd kill them now in any case."

The next days were filled with terror. I watched the doctor constantly, waiting to see him betray himself. I stayed with Reinhold when the doctor did his inspections, and I poured my hoosh onto the ground from my lap, holding back only what small fragments of meat there were.

I volunteered to mind the nets, and the doctor cautiously agreed. I barely had the strength to walk, and was forced to stop frequently to gather my breath as the ground swam around me. Once the net was too full, and I could not pull it onto the ice, but was forced to dump out half the catch before I could haul it out. I ate handfuls of the shrimp raw, looking around quickly to make sure I was alone. The shells cut my crumbling gums badly, but it was good to have something in my stomach.

Every time I returned, I crept in as silently as I could, expecting to see Architeuthis hunched over Creely or the captain, strangling them with quiet satisfaction. The doctor, for his part, refused to reveal himself. He lingered over breakfast, speculating idly about temperatures and the state of the ice; he spent an hour talking to the insensible Creely. As he approached the captain, I descended, watching every twitch of his long fingers, each flick of his canine teeth. He seemed not to notice me hovering by him, as he listened, his face grave with false concern, to the captain's heartbeat and breathing.

My heart rose in terror as I saw his long fingers encircle Griffin's white neck, and his thumbs slid over the windpipe. He's toying with me, I thought, showing me how easily he could kill the captain. I thought he might even have had the barest smile playing about his lips. He rolled Griffin's head back and forth in his hands and set it gently back down on the bag.

"I don't know what is keeping you alive, Master Griffin," he said lightly, "but we'll all pray it keeps up."

After dinner that night, Reinhold urged me to stay up, to watch the doctor, as Easter was now only two weeks away and he would be getting anxious to carry out his slaughter—wholesale if need be. I tried to remain awake, but could not. I had so little physical volition in any case, I could make few demands. I lay in my bag, listening to the doctor's breathing, which was tauntingly loud, and to the stiff beat of my heart. My sleep came with a violent suddenness, a black blow that felled me until late in the morning. I awoke choking and spitting, trying to clear my mouth of anything that may have been placed there during the night. I was ashamed of having fallen asleep, and could feel the rebuke of Reinhold's glare all morning.

That day was the same routine—the same lengthy examinations by the doctor, the same unacknowledged dance of threat and counterthreat, the same stagger to the catch, and furtive shrimp eating. In the night, the same fight to stay awake—this time stabbing my hand on an exposed nail head; the same dreamless sleep struck me, and I awoke to the same guilty dread, the same feel of poisons in my mouth.

Dr. Architeuthis took notice of my fatigue and my strange behavior, and tried to minister to me. He made a great show of examining me, running his fingers over my head and neck with awful slowness, and listening with satisfaction to my heart.

"It is his secret pride," whispered Reinhold to me that night, "that he can get to you. If you die, he shall win; the others cannot feed themselves. Could you hear him gloating as he examined you? He knows he is close and he is beginning to slaver. You must be strong."

Reinhold, for his part, was possessed of a new and seemingly limitless manic energy. He ate none of the hooshes, though I fed him shrimp when I could. He had ceased to pretend to sleep and instead sat at the end of the hut glaring out at everyone as the candle was extinguished. In the dark cold that marked the end of sleep, he would be sitting there still, like a granite statue at the gates of a pagan temple. I became increasingly exhausted as I tried to gather the shrimp and dodge the doctor. In order to avoid examinations, I put on great shows of health and good cheer, volunteering for extra duties to put him off and frustrate him, goaded by Reinhold at the end of the hut. That night Reinhold shook me out of my sleep, from blackness into blackness—I thought for a moment that my blindness had returned.

"Kane, blast you, wake up!" Reinhold took my head in his meaty hand and pressed my ear to his mouth.

"It's nearly time, and the doctor has stepped up his efforts. He is cleverer than I thought—he's been mixing it with spirits and leaking it in through the wall of the boat. I tore up my undershirt and stuffed it into the cracks to blunt it, but it is still getting through—the stench is terrible." I could smell nothing.

"We have three days to stockpile the shrimp; make a cache on the ridge; I will get a rifle. In the meantime, watch your step!"

I slept again, but did not rest; I woke more exhausted and more wretched than the night before. A storm had blown up in the early hours of the morning, so we were all confined to the hut. Without even my sorry shrimp I was starving, and the smell of the hoosh was strong and rich—surely old fox bones could not do so much to water. I sat with my mug in my lap and thought of guzzling it, but did not. I turned to Reinhold and was shocked to see him glaring at me. He leaned over and spat a single word in my face: "Traitor!"

His eyes were wide in their sockets and blazing; they were empty of any recognition of me, of any thought, of any process at all—he saw an odious insect before him. His head turned at an unnatural angle, and he pressed forward. I dropped my cup and fell backward over Creely, who lay still in the middle.

"What do you mean? I have done nothing."

"Reinhold!" said Adney sharply. "What's wrong?"

"What, puppet? Time to cast me out?"

"Reinhold!" said the doctor. "Please, calm down."

Griffin reached out now to restrain him, and Reinhold struck him with sudden violence, using a large sharp stone he had hidden in his sleeve. He rose up with a roar, tearing off the roof of the hut and bringing the wind howling in. Glaring down at us, he swung the rock back and forth. In his other hand, he produced a long spike.

"I will remain," he bellowed, "here, at the side of my companions. I. I am not lost." He spun the spike in his hand with deliberate slowness, and brought it to rest over his palm, point down over the gunnel.

"Here," he said with emphasis, and drove the spike down into his hand with great force. A gush of blood spattered my face.

"Reinhold, for God's sake, please," said Adney and lunged forward. Reinhold struck him backhanded with the rock and sent him crashing into the tarp.

Turning back to his hand, blood oozing now from around the spike, he looked softly at it, as if it were a small animal he had nursed but could not save. He raised the rock and in three strokes drove it fully home. Then he turned back to us; he ground his teeth, and his body shook with ragged gasps. Over us, the wind rose, keening, and he rose, up over his pinned hand, a great beast, wailing. He turned his fury to the boat, hammering blows upon it, cursing, mumbling; he thrashed it free from its mooring in the ice and scattered our supplies. We huddled numbly in our bags as the wind lashed us. Reinhold heaved the boat up the beach away from us, though it must have weighed more than five hundred pounds. He screamed and bellowed, and tore at his clothes.

I watched him as long as I could bear it, long after I became numb, after I had ceased to feel the lash of wind and the burn of my freezing skin. I began to feel that sweet drowsiness that I had heard in so many sailor's stories, as if I were swaying in a hammock filled with down, weightless at last and adrift. I awoke to the jerk of my head against the ice, stirred by the merciless stomp of my heart, called to witness as my friend destroyed himself.

Ash and Adney pulled the tarp over us, and the doctor moved

to help Griffin; we huddled together, listening hour after hour as Reinhold's great strength spent itself, dissipated, and renewed against the wind. Storm rose and wind, and the scrape and cry grew fainter, and still my obdurate heart held me up and the black blow would not descend. The storm blew out and he scrabbled on, wrenching the boat over the rocks, falling and rising, indomitable. Ash and Adney emerged and pried him loose from his mooring, gathered him up, and swaddled him in blankets. He had torn away his coat and shirt and his great chest heaved still. They laid him gently among us.

Preston coughed roughly and groaned, and then Reinhold began to sing in his rumbling bass. It was a shanty, and his voice landed softly on the pulses, as if he were still hauling rope. His voice was wavering, but clear; it rose at the final chorus and passed into silence. I felt tears spilling down my face and the weight of my hands hanging limply in my lap; I heard Adney's voice low and fierce and angry and finally doleful.

"Don't," he said. "Don't. Don't."

In the morning, Adney and I cleaned and dressed Reinhold's body in shirt and coat, Adney taking the time to straighten the tufted clumps of hair over his brow and pull up his collar smartly. I buffed his boots gently with my gloves. Adney hauled in the bag we had ruined on our trip north and cut free the liner. We wrapped him inside and Adney sewed it shut with careful strokes. The doctor, Adney, Ash, and I carried him on our shoulders to the low gravel ridge above the camp. Adney sank to his knees and began to hammer and pry. I took my place beside him. Rock by rock we beat our way down into the frozen gravel. I used my hands and then loose rocks to work the stones free. The wind rose around us, and the rocks slowly gave way. We made a hole, such as it was, and laid Reinhold in it. I stood back and Adney piled rocks high over him, adding, at the top, a red scrap of his shirt.

Griffin, his head bandaged, limped up to the ridge, followed by the doctor and Ash bearing Creely between them. Griffin spoke softly into the soft wind.

His voice faded, and Adney's swelled in a hymn and we joined in, even Creely, bobbing his head to keep the time. I imagined that on a small and distant lane, in a plain and peeling white spire, my lone grief struck a lone bell, and that one unruly tongue flung out broad its grief. That sound spread wordlessly, passed from man to man, and then from bell to bell—a wave of bells, like candles lit from candles, that rolled across the land.

*twenty*

The doctor and the captain began a low debate about the arrival of Easter. Captain Griffin thought it essential to have a small service and celebration, while the doctor felt that the condition of the men was so slight that any deviation was likely to prove fatal—that they were now as vulnerable to good news as bad.

A mug was set before me and I drank. I could not navigate between treachery and survival—if I was to be poisoned, so be it, so I could slide into easefulness, so pass, so end. But my strength returned with the attentions of the doctor. Adney had some small luck on the hunt: a fox, shrimp, our first goose, pale char. We had finished the candles, so we ate the meat raw and quickly, before it froze. We passed the days in silence, wraiths; only Creely jittered and mumbled. I was able to resume fishing, though I relied on a length of thwart to support me.

On Maundy Thursday, the captain ordered a fire from the remaining wood so that he could have water to wash our feet. The doctor protested the extravagance, but relented. It made me uneasy, as I did not share the captain's faith, but it seemed to give him such peace and calm that I did not deny him. My feet emerged at a great distance from me, yellow-white and angular, and he passed over them with a gentle wash of water, his head low in the quiet night. My hands before me in my lap were covered with cuts—dozens of them, open and not healing, nicked and battered, my hands like stone that has sat in the teeth of the wind for many years. And yet there was along the back of my hand a single vein, pulsing and alive, carrying with it the small and secret voice that spoke ineluctably of life.

The gray morning brought warm air with it, damp and earthy, as if the whole world were not ice; the pack did not move—indeed lay silent, suspicious—but as I moved across it to the nets, I could feel the rush of currents far below. Another gray morning, but then the sun blazed up and the sky showered down blue, and the ice seemed to tense, as if it were preparing to heave off the pack and cast up fresh continents of fruit. The nets were full and the lines wriggled with fish.

As I returned, I saw the doctor up on the ridge. I made my way to the shore and was about to call out our good fortune, but paused. He was kneeling over the piled stones, oddly animated in his devotions. From his hand there was the brilliant flash of polished steel in the sun—a blade, and the doctor, his hands bloody, chewing.

I rushed into the hut and dropped my load. I took the net and my bag; I filled my pockets with shrimp and I fled.

South I ran, along the shore, not looking behind, not daring to pause, resting only by leaning on the thwart and off again, repulsed and horrified, through the night and the next day, grabbing handfuls of raw shrimp and snow that burned like acid, crashing down onto the gravel and heaving up again. I scraped lichen from the rocks and cut blocks of snow to form a tunnel with a small hollow at the top for a fire. I looked for a place to batter a hole into the ice, but it was too thick. So I crawled in and lit my small fire close to my face and slept.

And on like this I went, sometimes finding lichen to eat, sometimes a spot to lower the line, sometimes a shelter, and sometimes huddled in my bag waiting for the dark hours to pass. I became better at making the shelters and, with a small blaze of debris, could get warm for an evening before pushing on.

Five days brought me to the bottom of the land; the low hills curved away to the east, and before me stretched the pack. I built a more substantial shelter on the shore to take the time to gather some fuel and fish. Wind kept the headland clear, and in the lee of the shore, open to the sun, there was a miniature forest of shrubs and dwarf trees, like a hidden world, just emerging from the snow. Digging out the hollow for my shelter, I dislodged a stone; behind it sat a small cluster of hibernating bees, small enough to sit in the palm of my hand. Even as I held it, the bees remained stuck tight to each other, and the ball gave off a low blush of heat. They were bitter and weightless, like a mouthful of air.

I found a shoal offshore, where the ice had split among the rocks and I could dig my way down to the water. I gave myself two days to rest and fish, and then move along. I kept my mind away from my companions, from the dark and ghoulish hut. Even as I imagined the outline of the camp in the distance, my heart began to race and I struggled not to flee across the ice in that moment. Only the steady work of gathering the lichens and fishing, which exhausted me into rapid sleep, let me stay on the shore—that shore that still felt tied to the repugnance I had seen, that I could still see, of strips of flesh sliding between teeth and tearing.

By the afternoon of the second day I had two fish, and a substantial heap of material for fuel. I resolved to be off at first light, but the wind rose and the temperature dropped and I huddled miserably in my hut, bobbing with eagerness to get away. I kept my small fire burning and listened to the scrape and moan of the wind and fought to think of nothing.

Then a sound came from out of the storm of immediate and substantial form, and then a gust that nearly extinguished my fire, and into my shelter pushed the wolfish face of Dr. Architeuthis.

*twenty-one*

He brushed aside my small fire and produced a lamp and a strip of blubber to feed it. Soon the fire was blazing, and a hoosh being made with thick cubes of dark seal meat. The doctor kept his eyes on the pot.

"Adney got a seal. Leads are opening to the north."

Hunger—which had been my companion, and weak and dim as I was weak and dim—now reared, and I craved the taste of meat again, and the heat of the hoosh. My mouth flooded.

"What was your plan, Kane? We thought you'd fallen through, but when I saw that your bag was gone I figured you had decided to take your chances on the ice."

He took a full mug of hoosh and handed me the pot. I singed my fingers on the sides as I gulped it greedily while avoiding his steady gaze. When he spoke again, his voice had a pleased resolve in it.

"From here, we can go south and east over the pack; the ice should be moving within a week, so we have some time to prepare. If we can work our way over Jones Sound to the west, we will be released into Baffin Bay and the whalers will pick us up. It is less than two hundred miles, and with the two of us strong, we should have no trouble making it if the weather holds."

And so he settled back against his bag to sleep. He made no mention of his own actions, of the men we had abandoned to their deaths, of the whole complex of duty and obligation and mercy—only forward. His pack was neatly filled behind him with useful items, and his hood recently mended. His bag had been scraped clean of moisture and rested lightly on the gravel. I sat in that dimness, the light crawling over his face, and I feared him and loathed him and was horrified by him, and by myself and the horror of the days that had brought us here.

Now I can say of that moment that I feared for my life, that I was unbalanced by hatred, by hunger and cold and a thousand deprivations, that I sat over him as he slept and was without a choice in my actions, that I was justified, excused, that other men would have done the same as I. And to be sure those things brought me to the edge, those cleared the way for me to act as I did, but the truth is different—that it was not justice, though some justice was done by it, and not righteousness, though I could take that mantle on; I felt within me, hovering, a choice of light and darkness, and chose, and embraced and relished in that moment the dark root I had within me, and I raised up the thwart and struck him in the head, and again and again until my hands were covered in his blood and he, at last, was dead.

Out into the storm I passed, taking in my appetite his food and gear and my own supplies, out over the ice, which in the storm was rolling and cracking under me. I ran to exhaustion and ate rawly from my pack, and huddled in my bag to sleep. Over me the wind keened and the snow pelted at me in the gusts. Even as the storm died, the pack was now in motion around me, floes crashing into floes, sending up cascades of water, swirling as I stood on them, bearing me out to sea. I jumped from floe to floe and used the thwart to vault over the gaps, and to pull floes closer to me. I spent three days on the ice, spinning, descending, in motion if I was conscious, insensible now to the cold and wet, only moving.

In a gray dawn, I saw shoreline to the south, and against it a jagged black shape, indistinct in the light, but made up of created shapes and angles. I rushed forward not daring to hope—it was the ship! My heart sang in me and I shouted and laughed and ran now, heedless of my stumbling and bruising on legs stiff and dead. I leapt from floe to floe, sliding here and there into the water, and scrambling up again.

It was much as we had left it—no more split nor sunk— driven forward with her stern in the same gesture of submission to the ice, and partially submerged. The mainmast lay still over the shattered roof of the deckhouse, and the foremast jabbed out at the ice. The rigging was shredded and ice draped, the wispy remnants of shrouds still carrying their wreaths of frost. Even thus trapped, thus stripped and broken, the ship retained its dark strength, not haughty but resilient.

I called out from the ice and beat the hull with my hands. I scrambled up the banked snow at the bow and onto the deck. The fore hatch was submerged beneath the ice. I climbed up the fallen mast to the splinters of the deckhouse. The hatch had been cleared of debris and kept clear of the drifting snow. I pulled open the hatch and the gray light slunk a few feet inside. A pile of ash from the deckhouse stove was swept neatly into the corner. The interior silence was as an ancient tomb's, not only lost itself, but in the lost city of a lost land, and holding within itself a forgotten king of a forgotten people; there was no rustle of hidden life, no hint of link to the world I inhabited, to my lost present. Lashing open the hatch, I entered as a thief or boy—hardly daring to breathe, curious, ashamed, audacious.

The cabins were untouched and unlived in; there was no fine wash of dust, no hint of decay, no smell of rot, no spiderwebbed corners. I recalled the nightmarish haste of our departure, the rush of terror in the storm, the suffering of Pago, the crack of ice and the bellowing confusion of the men, the sickening rush to beat down the dogs and escape. It bore no relation to this silent, dreadful room: there was no rush of life and fear here, but the silence and stillness of death held through these months, through a thousand years, unregenerate and unrenewed. In the gray light, Hume's quarters looked wretched and naked, the light dwelling on patch and hole, on the worn, the broken, the insufficient and incomplete.

I gathered some pages from a book, made a cone of canvas, and struck my flint into it. A weak and smoky flame straggled to life; it flared briefly as each page caught, then subsided again. I filled my pockets with pages, and scraps of the pitch-soaked canvas, and headed into the laboratory. Its walls were crowded with the doctor's instruments and racks of glass tubes and bottles, all labeled with his precise handwriting. A few of the bottles had shattered when their contents froze, but the contents stood still, holding the shape of the bottle over the halo of broken glass. Against the windows, the terrariums had shattered and the ouroborus vines lay wrestling in a baleful heap, tendrils already climbing again toward the light. In the center stood his marble slab, pure white and smooth, with its low channel running around the edge to the drain in the corner. It was all clean and precise in the wavering light; much, I imagined, shuddering, as he would have hoped to find it.

The next cabin was the captain's, which I had never seen; I

glanced inside to see if Aziz had perhaps installed himself there as the new master of the ship. The captain's few belongings remained neatly placed. A pile of clothes on the bed was frayed and mended, but neat and clean for all of their hard service. An extra set of boots stood at the foot of the bunk, deeply pitted and scraped, but polished. There was little else—he was a man unencumbered by frivolities, simple as faith itself.

The final cabin was West's, which I had also never entered. I paused at the doorway, half expecting his mad face to come shrieking out. The cabin was surprisingly empty, almost ascetic. A bare table and chair, a bare and comfortless bed, and a tiny chest. The Pianola, tormentor of our storm-struck nights, stood next to the bed. I saw then West's face again, contorted with hatred and anger, a carnivore, with the tendons of his thumb trailing from his mouth.

I turned again and stumbled aft. I was surprised to find the hatch open but ladderless. I hung over the edge and swung the torch around. Below me I could see empty sacks and a loose pile of broken things—tools and fittings stripped to their last splinter of wood. Scraps of the books sat neatly in the corner beside the fire bow of Aziz and a pile of shavings in a blackened circle; next to it was a pile of kindling in the bottom of the coal scuttle and a tattered pile of bedding. I called out eagerly, but there was no response. A series of bent nails pounded into the aft wall led up from the pile of shavings—the remains of the ladder still embedded in the wall. Clutching my smoldering torch, I clambered painfully down on the nails and dropped to the floor.

A closer inspection of the boiler room revealed nothing new—no remains of food or animals, no clothing, no trace of where he was or might have gone. I refilled my torch with canvas and pages and turned to the door into the hold.

It pushed open easily, and the light leapt up in the darkness.

The hold was huge and empty, the torch barely reaching the walls and leaving the ceiling hidden. I clung to the wall and stared out into that minotaur darkness; it seemed fluid and palpable, not empty as the cabins had been, dancing away from my torch as a page flared and flowing forward as it died. Edging ahead, I kept my hand on the wall to keep my balance; the bottom of the hull was covered by ice, so I had to move carefully. As I moved, my fingers kept catching on the wood. I was not getting splinters, but my rough fingertips would hook as I tried to glide them over the surface. Given the pitch polish of the English oak, I was surprised by the roughness.

I leaned to the wall to examine it and was shocked to see it scarred and pitted over every inch of its surface. I threw a handful of pages into my torch and held it right next to my face. As I stared, it resolved into minute and intricate patterns. It was a script, tiny and densely layered; each line was less than an inch high and the lines were piled over on top of one another, up into the darkness and down into the ice. It flowed and shrank, advanced, wove. My eye was sucked into it and compelled to follow it as it leapt and danced and dove. I could not read it, and yet it seized me, turned me to it, burned itself into me. Each letter, each line pulled me on, leading me forward, deeper into it, a story incomprehensible and infinite, fierce and sad and despondent, beautiful and terrible, a final reckoning that demanded and compelled, etched in that granite wood. Eyes upward and fixed, I tripped over something lodged in the ice and my torch scattered into sparks. I pulled another page from my pocket and gathered the sparks to me; the torch sagged, then glowed to life again.

Before me lay the body of Aziz half frozen in the ice. He was on his side, facing me, and his body was curled into a ball. His three hands were gathered into his chest, holding his silver teacup; they led one to the next, forming an even circle beneath his chin. His face was soft and peaceful, with none of the demonic gauntness of ours, like a sleeping child's, coppery in the red light, and cleansed, as if he had pulled forth all the poisonous bile in his soul and poured it out onto the walls.

I crawled to him and placed my hand on his shoulder; it was impossibly thin and frail, like a bird's. By keeping my eyes fixed on his face, on his peacefulness, I could keep my eyes from his terrible work, the pull of darkness against the light. I stood, holding my eyes on him, and fled the room. Outside the hold, I threw my torch up through the hatch and climbed after it, ran down the corridor and out into the dusking afternoon.

I sat on the deck panting, trying to still my heart and slow my breathing. Aziz's revelation—whether blessing or curse, I knew not—filled me with dread and awe. He had unleashed something of the darkness in that hold; he had battled with it and left behind not spoils but carnage. Yet there was a terrible triumph in it, and in his face, though sunken and frozen, the peace of conquest, torn free from the slow slide of the rope that had driven him here. There was no hint that he had found the islands, or even that he had sought them. I could not imagine his wresting—blind, freezing, alone in this wasteland, calmly setting his fires and etching careful line after careful line into the wood of the hull. I shrank from my own thoughts; I had my own dark, blind, mad hours, each of us our own hours, our own wrestling, to be faced in darkness, in blindness, in solitude—our revelations incommunicable and only our suffering in common. I thought of his story—of hiding for years in the holds of ships—his prison transformed into the means of his release, the four walls of his new freedom and the end to his quiet and solitary seeking.

I thought back to happier days, to resting in his quarters by the boiler, to the taste of tea, and his quiet stories with the gentle roll of the ship beneath them. Even my heart fell into gentle murmuring, as if offering its own memorial to those faraway hours. I thought of him now, frozen, faced with his terrible work in the hold. I could not leave him there, peaceful though he seemed, to wreck and decay, to be scavenged. I had to free him somehow, mark his passing. My first impulse was to chip him free and carry him south. But whatever he had been—guide, wellspring, font, beacon—he was no longer; whatever power he had unleashed in his revelation, it was solitary; it was of this time and this awful place, frozen in it, as he was, and rooted, his alone the triumph.

I thought of killing myself, but I could not face again the dank and freezing air of the ship. What remained was no shelter, no haven or comfort, nor even a tomb or sepulchre—no, it was a corpse, grotesque, naked, bloodless.

And yet I did not merely flee, as I had so often in the past, did not turn my face and look for a new world that might be free of a consideration of him, an empty world as yet unstained by my error and weakness. I ascended again to the deck and went into the laboratory; even there I could feel the tug of his writing like the undertow from a distant storm, pulling the tide back from the shore. Gathering the books and remaining canvas into a pile, I made a small fire on top of the twisted ball of vines. Slowly I added whatever free wood remained—the bunks, whatever pieces of the Pianola I could wrest free. The blaze grew rapidly. The dark leaves of the vines were slow to catch, stubbornly resisting the lick of the flames, but then they caught too and burned fiercely bright. I retreated from the cabins to the deck and finally to the ice below.

I stood near the whispering flames, smoke burning my eyes, feeling the blast of heat on my face. It was the first heat—real heat—I had felt in many months. I sucked it into me, reveled in it, held my hands out to it in worshipful silence until I could feel the pounding ache of blood returning to benumbed fingers, the terrible itch of flooding life in me.

As the fire engulfed the hull and mast, the ice began to crack and hiss in protest; tendrils of white steam rose and twined with the black smoke. The heat was terrific. I retreated to a nearby boulder, itself warm from the flames. My blood ran freely to my frostbitten hands and feet, ran freely through them in agonizing pulses out of my frozen sores, leaking from my boots and staining the stone beneath me. These pains subsided, however, and the blistering heat faded to gentle waves, like the caress of bathwater. I stretched out on the warm rocks, turning my face to the dancing flames, and drifted into sleep.

## twenty-two

I awoke to the stab of my heart pulling me again into the dim morning. My clothes and boots were stiff with frozen blood. The return of heat had brought with it the return of hunger; my stomach, long silent, began to churn again. I raised myself and beat my arms against my shoulders. I clambered down to the ice to see what remained of the ship. There was a blackened circle with new ice formed in the center. It was as if it had blasted into heaven as I slept.

I tried to marshal myself to simple survival, that last and most animal of purposes, but even that passed from me. I resolved I had but one path remaining: to find a place suitable for dying. I had passed away from the world of heat to this desolation, where light and darkness have only just been, and imperfectly, divided—water swirled into continents of ice and sliding back into water and up into snow. Yet I felt that it was not here but elsewhere that I was to finish my days, for no other reason than that my merciless heart had refused to cease in my last hour of warmth and comfort. So I plodded onward over the rocks and into the low, flat coastal plains. The land was boggy but still stiff with the frost. The frozen earth jabbed back underfoot, making me stumble from the unexpected texture of it. I scraped together small fires as the evening fell, and huddled under drifts of snow. You want for your heart to break and it doesn't, for your body to fail and it doesn't—for the world to end, but, remorseless world without end, the punishing sun arises and winds begin again to blow.

Far away at the edge of a range of hills, the sun glowed below the horizon; above it, the clouds rose in layers, a fierce orange fading to an angry red, a softer purple, then gray, and finally blue-black. Here the land was stunted and scroggy, low shrubs amid the rocks, the ground mossy and soft under my feet. The hills rose in low brown waves, rippling back from the water, hills giving way to broad valleys marked by bumps like boils, filled with murky water. I slept where I fell, cradled in the mosses, and rose as the sun rose. Beneath me bloomed the flowers of the spring, breasting through the snow, and pulling the land from white to brown and green. Slow rivers of meltwater formed and the frost boils became shallow lakes that stretched for corrugated blue miles. The hills rose in gravelly ridges over the tundra, each marking its own horizon until another, farther, rose in the distance.

As I climbed one, I passed jagged windrows of feathers running across the hills, like foam from ancient seas or the fall of angels.

I came down onto a vast plain that emitted the low and rustling roar of a thousand tiny forms in motion. A white bird rose, beating heavily at the air, and then another, a cloud of them, a wave across the plain to the horizon, heaved up and billowed around me in a shower of white feathers as if the earth itself were lifting into heaven. They hung swirling in the air over me and sank back to earth and rose again, like echoes fading. On the ground around me were dozens of nests filled with gray-brown eggs that burned with heat. I fell to my knees and ate eagerly. The birds danced squalling out of reach, but using the rope as a flail, I was able to knock them down, white feathers in my black and bloody hands. I envied them their placid grace in flight, until I knew the tumult of hungers that it cost, till I felt the frantic beating of their hearts.

I was a pilgrim in the end, not chasing miracles, splinters, fragments of bone, but compelled, unreleased, called to witness, and then returned again to my own sunken and sordid self, chasing a spark into the earth, back from the ice and darkness, the drive of men that became the lonely tramp of a man, of a deep night in cold and darkness, and the awakening into a brilliant and endless day, washed in blood and consecrated in a cascade of feathers. Our islands and their treasures flood past in the torrent of our days: we can alight like birds for a moment of panting rest before our hungers drive us out. And so I live on with small hungers in the heavy weight of my body, created and creating, going, for all my days, still.

# Acknowledgments

With much appreciation to the following:

For my many rescues and for encouraging the persistence of my follies: my family, Ed and Perdita, Tad, Dan, Karen and all of the Sallicks, Melanie, Nina de Gramont, and Dennis Kennedy.

For the space and time to finish: the fine people of the Vermont Studio Center and the Sabot family.

For his enthusiasm, support, and energy: my agent, Peter Steinberg.

For his care and thought: my editor, Gerry Howard.

My thanks to you all—this would not have happened without you.